THE SECOND

THANKSGIVING

A Novel of Plymouth 1623

By

Douglas Lloyd McIntosh

If my people, which are called by my name, shall humble themselves, and pray, and seek my face, and turn from their wicked ways; then will I hear from heaven, and will forgive their sin, and will heal their land.

Second Chronicles 7: 14 (KJV)

All Biblical quotations in the 1623 story are taken from the Geneva Bible of 1560, the English version used by the Pilgrim settlers at Plymouth.

In memory of my grandparents

Homer H. Higginbotham

Cecile Aliff Higginbotham

They saw the Hand of God in history because they lived it.

TABLE OF CONTENTS

PROLOGUE

Wade Jordan at the White House, October 1863

Wade Jordan had no idea the extent to which he set hearts aflutter among the young ladies of the more prestigious social set in the capital city of Washington. The impression he made came naturally—and certainly without any conscious intent. The towering young man himself neither noticed, cared about, nor indeed had the slightest clue regarding the ardent emotions and romantic rumors that swirled around his imperturbable but vaguely brooding presence as he drifted from one highfalutin parlor or dining room to the next. In part he remained unaware, blissfully or otherwise, because he flat did not want to be here in the first place, impelled by politeness and his duty to attend pretentious dinners and tea parties night after tedious night.

He could not wait to leave, to start the long ride back in the general direction of the Mississippi, which now flowed unvexed to the sea, as the President of the United States had recently put it with his usual poetic eloquence.

No thanks to Wade, however. He had been trapped here in the east, caught up in an entirely different affray when Vicksburg finally fell, and now he yearned only to rejoin his army unit in the west, the nearest thing he had to a family at this point in his life, after his elderly grandparents had been murdered by pro-slavery guerillas back in Kansas.

Perhaps Wade also underestimated his impact on the young ladies because he knew he looked about sixteen years old. He appeared about sixteen, that is, except for the daunting fact that he stood six and a half feet tall without boots and had to duck when he passed through a lot of the fancier doors in Washington, hopefully remembering as well to remove the slouchy blue riding hat characteristic of the westerners. Within those doors he rarely could make himself meet the eyes of the young ladies, whereas out west he could stare down anything from a large hostile drunk to a mean dog.

The young ladies found his shyness rather becoming, especially in contrast to many of the other proud young officers in attendance at virtually all social functions, and it was really too bad, the young ladies told one another, that Lieutenant Jordan was "only a boy."

This was usually said dismissively after a flirting expedition by some particular young lady had failed as decisively as Pickett's Charge, though only at the cost of pride rather than human life. Lieutenant Jordan remained merely impervious to the flirting, not openly and brutally resistant, as he had been on Cemetery Ridge against General Pickett and his brave but doomed men.

In fact Wade was quite a bit older than he looked, having turned twenty-three back in July, the same week as Gettysburg, where after falling in with a former college professor turned Maine colonel named Joshua Chamberlain, he had not only shot down his share of Pickett's men on the third day of fighting but had almost been killed himself on the second day in the ferocious hand-to-hand combat on Little Round Top, where he would have surely died except for the courageous action of a boy from Vermont who got killed in his place.

On July Fourth, after the three day battle finally ended, Wade had sought out that boy's body and paid practically everything he had in his pocket to have Private David Conrad shipped home to his parents for burial in the church yard of a little Vermont village.

Wade should not have been in that battle at all. He should have been out west with his hero, General U.S. Grant, taking possession of Vicksburg, as happened on that same historic Independence Day, making it an occasion to celebrate not one but two crucial victories for the Union forces. It was the General himself who had sent Wade east, though, and how Wade had managed to wind up in the middle of that big Pennsylvania fight took a lot of explaining whenever somebody brought the matter up, which was often.

When people did bring it up, Wade never would tell the whole story, just that he was on a mysterious mission for the General, which was true as far as it went. He never mentioned that he had been initially sent off to escort a beautiful young plantation girl, Arabella Guider, supposedly a Union sympathizer, to the safety of the Federal lines back in Tennessee and on to Washington carrying supposedly vital intelligence.

Nor did he relate how the blue-eyed Miss Guider had played his naive emotions like a fiddle so that he could not bring himself to shoot her when she turned out to be a Confederate spy, when she caused the other men in the escort to be captured and forced Wade to kill three Johnny Rebs with his pistol and then make a wild fifty-mile ride with the screaming Arabella bound hand and foot and thrown across the front of his saddle like a trussed turkey.

Naturally, as soon as they encountered Federal pickets in Tennessee, Wade was the one placed under arrest, and before he could make anyone believe his implausible story, the slender and charming young woman, as milky-white and harmless-looking as the Dove of Peace, had only to bat her eyes—the bluest Wade had ever beheld—to seduce the camp commandant, at least metaphorically. After a delightful dinner in the officers' tent, efficiently draining these fine gentlemen of every particle of useful information, she easily made her escape, no doubt heading for Richmond with her pretty head chock-full of priceless intelligence.

The red-faced commandant almost groveled with embarrassment and apology once everything got straightened out, but by then the damage was done. Under additional orders from Grant to speak to people in the War Department, Wade had pursued Arabella east, but he never did catch her, though that was ultimately how he wound up intersecting the Army of the Potomac in Pennsylvania just when some of Bobby Lee's boys showed up in Gettysburg on an expedition to steal a consignment of shoes from a Yankee factory and inadvertently started the big fight.

Maybe someday the whole sad tale of his Mississippi misadventure could be told, but for now Wade felt too humiliated to admit the half of it. If he ever encountered Arabella again he didn't know for sure which he would do, shoot her or kiss her, but at least the unfortunate encounter with a conniving Southern belle made him that much more impervious to the Washington flirts, who could not hold a candle to the Real Thing.

Wade's own claim to fame, and the reason for all those uncomfortable invitations that he had been explicitly ordered to attend, was that he was as far as anyone had been able to determine the only Union soldier who had fought in both the Battle of Shiloh and the Battle of Gettysburg. Not only fought in two of the bloodiest battles—more American soldiers had been killed in each than had been lost in all of America's wars combined up until the outbreak of the rebellion—but performed distinctly heroic actions in both.

After joining up for the army in 1861 Wade had been promoted to lieutenant in the field on the first day of Shiloh, April 6, 1862, after the real, West Point-trained officer had been shot dead in the initial volley of Johnston's early morning attack, along with all the sergeants, leaving a lowly corporal to rally the troops, thereby preventing one more catastrophe in a day of Union catastrophes.

His colonel would have been happier if Wade had only been made a sergeant, a single step-up promotion more in line with custom, but it was General William T. Sherman himself who elevated his rank, and Grant had backed it up when he heard the story, so there wasn't anything Colonel Raney, an incompetent political appointment, could do except seethe and regard Wade as an enemy.

Officers who did not know what they were doing always seemed to think they would look better if they had underlings more incompetent than themselves, whereas a real soldier like Grant knew the opposite was true. Jealousy of a subordinate's ability was the sure mark of a fool, but before Sherman or Grant could get around to ridding themselves of Raney in a manner that would not offend his political backers, some good old Southern boy did the job for them with a long-barreled squirrel rifle.

After Shiloh was the point at which Wade's boyish appearance first became an issue. He had tried to grow a set of chin whiskers and mustache, to match the fashion of the day along with the rest of the officer corps, but it only worked as a source of mirth behind his back. His men claimed he did not need to shave every day, though they said it affectionately and not to his face. His youthful looks had caused serious errors of judgment in the ranks, and over the last two and a half years men in both armies had paid a serious price for underestimating him. Those in blue had paid with bruises, black eyes, and broken teeth. Those in gray had paid with their lives.

Now Wade felt more self-conscious than ever, the only clean shaven officer in the entire District of Columbia, as far as he could see. By now he probably could grow whiskers if he tried again, but he had been through enough that he no longer had anything to prove and refused to become a slave of fashion. He mostly dreamed of rejoining his men in the west, and as a son of the frontier he particularly chaffed at those dull social occasions, with the china teacups and multiple pieces of silverware that he wasn't always certain how to use without watching somebody else go first.

It bothered him to watch all the fine ladies and preening gentlemen displaying their refinement while men were dying scant miles away to protect them. By this point he could tolerate being here only by trying to do what Grant wanted, which was find out what was going on in War Department procurement and see if he could make any more friends for the westerners, who tended to be neglected in favor of the Potomac boys.

It always pleased Wade to think about his hero, that calm, rumpled, cigar-smoking and utterly decisive little man who made such a contrast with most of the pompous and dithering peacocks who passed for generals here in the east, though President Lincoln had finally gotten rid of the odious chief peacock, General George B. McClellan. Old Abe had shucked off the little bantam rooster once before and then brought him back, but this time everybody said he was definitely gone for good, though the Little Napoleon himself was probably waiting for the call to return once again to save the North's bacon.

In contrast to the medals, silk scarves, epaulets, and other glittering finery customarily worn by the dinner party generals, Grant always wore a wrinkled private's uniform and had to be pointed out to folks who had never seen him before. One time a drummer boy had asked Lieutenant Jordan why the General always went about so modestly, and an old sergeant standing by had pointed out that some of them Confederate boys could shoot pretty good, so why offer them such a tempting target?

That was all very true, as Colonel Raney would soon find out, but Wade just thought the General, like himself, simply did not crave

calling attention to his own person. Grant was willing to do the job—
and perhaps do it better than anybody else in all history—but he shied
away from putting himself up as anything fancy.

* * *

Right now Wade was cooling his heels in a waiting room outside
the office of the Secretary of War, and he was quite surprised nobody
had asked his opinion of General Grant yet. As soon as people found
out he came from the west, the question arose fast and often, usually
several times a day. Wade wanted to tell them the General was a
military genius—despite Wade's rough frontier habits he had read
enough books to know what the term meant. The only modern general
he had heard tell of that held a candle to Grant, as far as Wade was
concerned, was an old Britisher named Wellington, the man who had
rolled up the real Napoleon's armies all across Portugal, Spain, and
France, and finally dethroned the little emperor himself in a Belgian
killing field called Waterloo.

Wade usually contented himself with a more modest assessment
in keeping with the bashfulness of the subject. He customarily wound
up trying to tell an anecdote or two about General Grant to make his
point, but a lot of these easterners quickly proved impatient with
western-style storytelling. He understood the President had the same
problem.

"Lieutenant Jordan?"

Snapping out of his reverie, Wade stood and turned in one fluid
motion to look down at the little man addressing him. He was a
lieutenant too, with the unmistakable ramrod look of West Point and
the confident air of general staff. He had had no trouble growing
black mustaches and a long goatee, all of them waxed to a point. He
was undoubtedly a great hit with the ladies and knew it.

"I am Edmund Crispus, of the secretary's staff."

"Good to meet you, sir." Wade had a feeling nobody called him "Eddie."

They shook hands. Crispus was apparently one of those fellers who made every handshake with a stranger a test of bone-crushing strength, but nobody had ever yet won one of those contests with Wade. His big hands were too calloused from using an axe and every other kind of tool, including firearms, since he was a little child. Despite his size, people always seemed to expect the rest of him to be as soft as his face.

He chose not to destroy the little man but merely hold his own. Crispus turned slightly red and quickly disengaged.

They were joined by another young lieutenant Wade already knew, Frank Milberry, sporting a little grin suggesting he fully understood what had just taken place.

"The secretary will join us in a moment," Crispus said.

"That's fine, sir."

"He'll be riding in an open carriage, but I thought we might ride alongside, we junior officers. Do you have your horse today? We can always provide you with one."

"My own is tethered downstairs, Lieutenant."

This seemed to surprise Crispus and disappoint him. In truth the only reason Ranger was tethered downstairs, no doubt intimidating all the other horses, was that Wade's landlady, a kindly Christian woman who reminded Wade of his grandmother, had taken pity on the big lieutenant and rented him a tiny attic room, the only accommodation she had left to offer and possibly the only unoccupied room in the entire city, as near as he could judge. As soon as she heard about today's planned event, Mrs. Simmons recommended that Wade bring his horse, and once again her knowledge of Washington customs had proved invaluable. Still, Wade found it strange they were going to mount up at all, since all they needed to do was walk across

Seventeenth Street. The War Department and the White House stood that close to each other on Pennsylvania Avenue.

"Didn't you notice that fine big black?" Milberry said. "The ungelded one?"

"No, I can't say I did," Crispus said, lifting an eyebrow as he regarded Wade anew. "Have you no concern that the beast might catch scent of a likely mare at a moment of crisis?"

Wade blushed. "None, Lieutenant."

In the humiliating wake of the Arabella madness, Wade had more confidence in Ranger's self-mastery than his own.

"There's quite a tale in his acquisition," Milberry said. "Why don't you tell him, Jordan?"

"I'm sure Mister Crispus has more important things to think about."

"No, no, I'm all ears."

"There's not much to tell, really."

"Oh come now, Jordan," Milberry said.

"I got the horse the next night after Shiloh, when General Grant confirmed my commission. He looked me up and down and said now I was an officer I had to have a horse, and I'd need one that could carry me without breaking down. He picked Ranger out himself, and a finer horse I've never seen. The General is quite a judge of horseflesh."

"General Grant's riding is a legend at the Academy," Milberry said.

"Yes, sir!" Wade said. "He's had two horses shot out right out from under him. At the battle of Belmont he rode a big horse right up a narrow gang plank into a river boat, and if he hadn't done it he would have been taken or killed by the enemy!"

"So you were promoted from the ranks?" Crispus said, oh so innocently, earning a dirty look from Milberry.

"Yes, Mister Crispus. I haven't had the advantage of you boys that went to the Academy. When that Shiloh fight started, I was just a corporal." Wade refrained from making any contrary remarks about West Point though he had observed a powerful lot of foolishness on the part of some who had gone there. General Grant, after all, was a West Pointer, as were most of the best enemy commanders, including Bobby Lee, so the place couldn't be entirely worthless. Milberry seemed an all right sort as well, friendly and anxious for Wade to feel right at home.

The open windows of the anteroom provided little relief from the unseasonable October heat. Over the din of incessant street noise, Wade's Indian Scout ears detected some kind of bustle moving in their direction from behind the great oak doors that separated the waiting seekers, amongst whom Wade reluctantly had to count himself, and those on the inside who could deliver the favors sought.

The doors to the inner sanctum were opened and flung aside by a colonel, no less, who quickly sidestepped in time to avoid being trampled by the Secretary of War himself, whom Wade would surely have recognized by the force of his presence if he had not already seen his etched portrait in the newspapers.

Edwin M. Stanton was a dapper little man who radiated power, but he stopped in his tracks the moment he beheld Wade standing inadvertently in his path. He peered upward, gazing at the young giant through thick little glasses that rode high on his nose, causing Wade to wonder if he had worn out his eyes reading thick law books by candlelight. The eyes were close together and would have resembled bunny eyes if they weren't so intense and dangerous. A fierce double-pointed beard projected downward from Stanton's chin. He was clearly not a man to cross, and here was Wade standing in his lane.

Startled, Wade realized he had automatically brought himself to attention. Instead of scurrying aside, therefore, he saluted. After all he was supposed to go along on this afternoon's little jaunt.

Milberry hastened to make the introduction.

"Ah, the young hero!" Stanton said.

Wade blushed his deepest shade of crimson but broke the salute to take the outstretched hand. The bustling former attorney clearly gathered from the red-faced glow how much he had embarrassed the young lieutenant and took immediate steps to put the overgrown boy at ease.

"I understand you're a friend of Grant's."

"Sir, I would hardly describe myself as a friend of the General's, sir," Wade managed to stammer out, "but we *are* acquainted."

Stanton found this funny, so naturally Milberry and Crispus laughed too, though Wade couldn't understand the humor.

"I hear that you have been accomplishing some miracles of supply on behalf of your acquaintance," the Secretary of War said.

"Oh, no, sir, thank you, but I don't deserve any special credit. It's kind of like getting an old mule to finally make up his mind it's a good idea to start moving. I just prod a little bit here and there, trying to ask the right person the right question."

"I hear you're so good at asking your questions, perhaps you should attain higher rank as a commissary officer."

Wade blanched, horrified to hear his worst nightmare falling out of the secretary's mouth. "No, sir, I doubt that would be a good idea at all."

"Your mentor was an officer of commissary, back in the Mexican War."

"Yes, sir, but General Grant also led men in battle. This is a bigger war, Mister Secretary. Your soldiers need to stick to what they do best. I think I'm better suited for killing Rebs."

All the surrounding officers and some of the waiting lobbyists looked stunned at the young man's effrontery, but Stanton only nodded. "I hear you're credibly proficient at that too, young man. Well, we shall see. For now," he checked the gold watch from his vest pocket, "we'd better get moving to see the President."

* * *

When Wade had finally reached Washington City back in August, he found the place an overheated muggy swamp of mud and mosquitoes, a place so foul and oppressive in summer that its native predators, the members of congress, did their best to get out of town if they possibly could. Now the unpredictable weather was putting on a late burst of Indian Summer heat before the arrival of cold autumn and worse winter.

Once outside Wade began to understand why it was such a major operation to cross the street to the Presidential Palace, the old name for what most plain folk now simply referred to as the White House. For one thing Stanton climbed into a carriage full of frilly-looking civilians, mostly ladies, to whom Wade and the other young officers were not introduced. From the War Department to the door of the mansion would be a long way for a bunch of these eastern women to trot, even if they didn't have to worry about being run over in the street. In carrying out General Grant's instructions, Wade usually went places early and stayed late. This was his first direct experience of the clouds of dust churned up by wheel and hoof as thousands of people scurried through the mid-workday streets of the wartime capital. Whether by foot, horseback, wagon or buggy, the whole crazed mob apparently needed to be getting wherever they were going a whole lot faster than they were. This became abundantly clear to the tune of the maximum amount of hollering and profanity.

Crispus and Milberry took it upon themselves to clear a path. They and their mounts proved surprisingly effective at the task, moving the secretary's carriage out onto the street at the rear of the War Department, then around the corner onto Pennsylvania Avenue. Since they had obviously carried out this duty many times before, Wade rode on the opposite side of the carriage to let them do it.

They were crawling forward when a furious man, absolutely drunk, stepped out into their path and started screaming at the people in the carriage. Crispus and Milberry had ridden ahead to start preparing for the turn across traffic into the White House grounds. Wade was deciding how to react when Ranger, as stubborn and aggressive as any ferocious dog, blew a disapproving snort and charged the man. The furious eye and charging bulk of the big black horse were enough to send the drunkard skeedaddling back to the boardwalk, where he fled north. Wade quickly reined the beast in before he could turn and run the man down. If he hadn't, Wade knew Ranger would have gone after him all the way into the lobby of the Willard Hotel.

Afraid to check on any reaction in the carriage, he surreptitiously gave the big warhorse an approving pat on the neck.

With little time to spare, they finally made the turn. As they tied up their horses with all the others, Wade realized with a start that he was a bit less impressed than he would have been before seeing some of the plantation mansions he had passed on the march under Grant. Some of those places looked far more imposing in size and elegance than this big house, an appalling fact in light of the human misery propping them up. Wade's grandparents had prayed and worked against the evil of chattel slavery for most of their lives, both of them sheltering runaway slaves and his grandfather speaking out fearlessly against the institution in the worst days of Bloody Kansas.

One aspect of the White House had shaken him the first time he saw it. There were no fence, no gate, no troops encamped, no guards in plain sight except a couple of pickets, no obvious protection of any sort. Anybody at all could walk right up and knock on the front door. For all Wade knew old Abe would answer it himself.

Didn't anybody know there was a war going on? Dangerous Confederate cavalry units operated scarcely twenty miles away, sometimes less.

Wade himself was considerably less worried about cavalry, as far as the safety of the president was concerned, than he was about Confederate secret agents, having had recent experience along those lines himself. He had no doubt the blue-eyed Miss Guider could easily sail right into the president's parlor with a Derringer concealed in her hand muff.

If he had a chance to speak to Mr. Lincoln, he hoped he would have the nerve to tell him he needed more protection. As noble and Christian as Bobby Lee and old dead Stonewall had been known to act upon the appropriate occasion, especially in the magnanimity of victory, there were other Rebels prepared to forego all gentlemanly obligations and fight dirty.

All thoughts of telling anybody anything flew right out of his head, however, as soon as they walked inside. Wade found himself as caught up by an overwhelming sense of awe and history as any other mortal.

Trailing along with the other lieutenants, Wade followed as Mr. Stanton and his guests strolled into a very large room on the eastern side of the mansion. Wade thought it must be a ballroom though he had never seen either a ball or a ballroom, only read about them. A lot of furniture would have to be pulled aside, though, to make room for a dance. There were enough couches and chairs and tables in this room alone to furnish three-dozen houses back where Wade came from, and a single sofa probably cost more than any frontier cabin.

Well, at least they had a president whose character had been formed in one of those rough cabins, not lazing his life away on a soft settee.

For all its size the room was quite crowded, abuzz with the proprieties of urbane conversation. By this time in his life, after years as a successful railroad lawyer, Mr. Lincoln was probably more comfortable with this fancy pants crowd than Wade ever hoped to be, so he tried to make himself inconspicuous, which was hard given he was a lot taller and twice as wide in the shoulders and chest as any other man in the room.

Quickly growing bored with listening to the Secretary of War play politician, Wade caught some women giving him the eye from behind their fans, so he busied himself trying to figure out which door the president was going to come in.

A little writing table with a sturdy chair had been set up incongruously in the middle of the big room, and he figured that was where the signing was going to take place. The chattering and gossiping crowd had gathered round the spot as if magnetized.

Then he noticed that many of the ladies seemed to be swarming a side area some distance from the presidential desk. Curious, he drifted over in that direction.

At the center of this ring of attention stood a formidable-looking old lady with white hair, and the other women treated her with the same kind of awed respect soldiers held for a successful general. Though obviously highly refined, the old lady was not shy about using her voice, and Wade could hear her words easily. A young woman dragged her civilian husband forward for a handshake, then said something too low to be heard over the murmur of the crowd.

"Thank you my dear," the old lady said, "there's no end to what women can accomplish with faith in God and a decent education."

The young woman's older husband, an obvious political type, looked a bit pickle-pussed at this, more so when the wife blurted out, "My daughter says she wants to be a lawyer, like her father!" This time it was loud enough to hear.

"Good for her," the old lady said. "Nothing would be better for our rights than a few good lady attorneys."

"Next you'll be wanting the vote," the politician said, rather sourly Wade thought.

"Not I," the old lady shot back. "Women don't necessarily need the vote to exercise our powers, sir. Just our freedom."

"Right now, madam, we happen to be fighting a war to free the slaves."

"Which is why women in their thousands have volunteered to nurse our wounded in the hospitals, Senator. The ladies are fighting this war too. For the slaves surely, but we also fight another war for ourselves as well. We have been ever since the Garden of Eden."

The politician seized his wife and beat a hasty retreat as the old woman turned to shake more outstretched hands.

Though wearing a mantle of years that would put her at least in her mid-seventies, the lady stood straight and self-assured. From knowing and loving his own grandmother, Wade recognized the type. He liked her at once.

"Who's that, Frank?" Wade said as Milberry slid up to his side, punch glass in hand.

"You'd already know if you were married, my friend."

"Oh?"

"That is none other than Sarah Josepha Hale, the editor of *Godey's Lady's Book*, a magazine read by every woman in America who can pound her poor husband out of the subscription money."

"Looks like a tough old hide."

"Oh, indeed, Wade. A tireless campaigner for women's education and property rights."

"And that's not all she's campaigned for," Edwin Stanton said grumpily, surprising the young men by joining them. "She's the main force behind this ninnies' convention."

The secretary of war was looking askance as a number of small children crept forward through the thicket of grownups to find a place at the head of the crowd. A number of people had obviously thought highly enough of this occasion to bring their kids, as well as their spouses, but on Stanton's part Wade recognized the tone of a busy man who would rather be back at work than standing witness to a signing ceremony.

Before Stanton could bellyache anymore, the nearest pair of doors opened, and the President of the United States entered.

His entry quieted the place to near silence, and Wade knew as it happened that seeing Abraham Lincoln in the flesh was the most exciting moment of his life. This was mostly a callous Washington crowd, though, and the only ones who seemed to share Wade's feelings equally were those awestruck children.

Lincoln looked the crowd over for a moment, then ambled through the flock of ladies to greet their heroine.

"You are Mrs. Hale, of course."

"Yes, Mr. President." She curtseyed as she gave him her hand.

"This is a day of triumph for you, dear lady."

"I fear you give me too much credit, sir," she said, but Wade could tell she was mighty pleased.

"Nay," Lincoln said, low enough that the full room failed to hear, "if we could find some generals who possessed the tenth part of your perseverance, this struggle would soon be over."

Standing nearby, Wade could think of one General who fit the bill, and he'd be willing to bet Lincoln was already ruminating along those lines himself or soon would be.

Mrs. Hale allowed the president to lead her to a comfortable chair near the signing table where a young man, no doubt one of the president's two secretaries, was laying out pen, ink and a formal-looking document.

Once the young man was finished, Lincoln moved over and stood behind the desk and chair. His kindly eyes sought out the children, not just the bold ones out front but also those shyly peeping from behind the legs of their parents.

"You children don't have to hang back. Why don't you step forward so I can have a look at you? I promise I don't bite."

As the rest of the children came out from hiding, Wade doubted if any of the boys was the president's own Tad. Washington gossips whispered that the boy lay in the grip of some mysterious illness physicians had not been able to diagnose. The first lady was not in evidence either. According to rumor she continued to mourn their third son, Willie, who had died the previous year, mourn him to the point of extremity and madness some said, an accusation which infuriated Wade as much as his landlady. So what if the expectations placed upon a president's wife supposedly required a rigid and unnatural decorum as thousands were dying in battle? The death of a child would be a terrible blow to any mother.

"I always think it a good thing to see children in the halls of state," Lincoln was saying, looking around at the crowd. "They remind us that we are fighting this terrible war for the sake of future generations and not merely the ephemeral politics of the current hour. Just this last summer, following upon campaigns of weary and bitter struggle by our valiant soldiers, our arms have been rewarded with victory, both at Gettysburg in Pennsylvania and in the west, at Vicksburg."

The listeners broke into applause, which Lincoln raised his hand to quell, his sadness seeming to resonate the terrible human cost that rendered those victories almost unbearable. As a soldier, Wade found himself deeply moved by the gesture, by the man's mournful countenance, reflecting a tenderness and tragic sense that cloaked and humanized the steely determination within.

"For these and all the blessings of life our hearts should be lifted in grateful thanksgiving to a beneficent Providence, and thus it is appropriate that we gather here today as I sign this proclamation," Lincoln indicated the document on the table, "making the last Thursday in November a national Day of Thanksgiving, to be celebrated from this day forward with prayer and feasting all across our great land. Hitherto, the celebration of Thanksgiving Day has been a local holiday, primarily in our New England states such as Massachusetts, where the tradition began. I have invited Mrs. Sarah Josepha Hale here to witness this signing, for no one has fought longer and harder than she to make Thanksgiving a national observance for all Americans."

Lincoln looked down and caught the eye of a little girl. "Do you know of Mrs. Hale, young lady?"

"Yes, sir!" the little girl said emphatically.

"And what do you know of her?"

"She wrote 'Mary Had a Little Lamb!'"

Mrs. Hale laughed along with everyone else, but it was a friendly laugh, and the little girl looked as pleased as the President.

"Indeed she did! But in addition to nursery rhymes, Mrs. Hale is both an educator and the foremost editor of ladies' magazines in our country."

Wade could sense that this high praise rubbed a number of the watching politicians the wrong way, another violation of gentility by this Midwestern clodhopper who had beaten them all to the presidency. As many had brought their wives, however, who were clearly enthralled at the President's words, the path of domestic peace lay in keeping any anti-female resentment to oneself.

"We honor her today," Lincoln went on, "for her nearly forty year campaign for Thanksgiving Day, to make it national, and I am thankful it is my hand that shall proclaim it so."

Lincoln sat down at the little table, slipped on a pair of spectacles from his pocket, picked up the document and began to read aloud.

"By the President of the United States of America. A Proclamation.

"The year that is drawing towards its close, has been filled with the blessings of fruitful fields and healthful skies. To these bounties, which are so constantly enjoyed that we are prone to forget the source from which they come, others have been added, which are of so extraordinary a nature, that they cannot fail to penetrate and soften even the heart which is habitually insensible to the ever watchful providence of Almighty God.

"In the midst of a civil war of unequaled magnitude and severity, which has sometimes seemed to foreign States to invite and to provoke their aggression, peace has been preserved with all nations, order has been maintained, the laws have been respected and obeyed, and harmony has prevailed everywhere except in the theatre of military conflict, while that theatre has been greatly contracted by the advancing armies and navies of the Union.

"Needful diversions of wealth and of strength from the fields of peaceful industry to the national defense, have not arrested the plough, the shuttle or the ship; the axe has enlarged the borders of our settlements, and the mines, as well of iron and coal as of the precious metals, have yielded even more abundantly than heretofore. Population has steadily increased, notwithstanding the waste that has been made in the camp, the siege and the battlefield; and the country, rejoicing in the consciousness of augmented strength and vigor, is permitted to expect continuance of years with large increase of freedom. No human counsel hath devised nor hath any mortal hand worked out these great things. They are the gracious gifts of the Most High God, who, while dealing with us in anger for our sins, hath nevertheless remembered mercy.

"It has seemed to me fit and proper that they should be solemnly, reverently and gratefully acknowledged as with one heart and one voice by the whole American People. I do therefore invite my fellow citizens in every part of the United States, and also those who are at sea and those who are sojourning in foreign lands, to set apart and observe the last Thursday of November next, as a day of Thanksgiving and Praise to our beneficent Father who dwelleth in the Heavens.

"And I recommend to them that while offering up the ascriptions justly due to Him for such singular deliverances and blessings, they do also, with humble penitence for our national perverseness and disobedience, commend to His tender care all those who have become widows, orphans, mourners or sufferers in the lamentable civil strife in which we are unavoidably engaged, and fervently implore the interposition of the Almighty Hand to heal the wounds of the nation and to restore it as soon as may be consistent with the Divine purposes to the full enjoyment of peace, harmony, tranquility and union.

"In testimony whereof, I have hereunto set my hand and caused the Seal of the United States to be affixed. Done at the City of Washington, this Third day of October, in the year of our Lord one thousand eight hundred and sixty-three, and of the Independence of the United States the Eighty-eighth."

Lincoln picked up the pen, dipped ink and signed. Applause, led by a deliriously happy Mrs. Hale, once more filled the room, this time without remonstrance from the President.

Lincoln made himself comfortable in his chair, evoking a kind of familiar homeliness that made Wade ache for the simpler comportment of the frontier.

"We may hope the day is not far off when our brothers and sisters in the South will join us at the Thanksgiving table." Pocketing his spectacles again, the President looked around at the children. "Do you children know the story of our Pilgrim fathers?"

All the little heads nodded up and down enthusiastically.

"When did the *Mayflower* land and where?" Lincoln said. "Who can tell me?"

Many hands shot up, and Lincoln pointed out one little boy.

"1620. At Plymouth," the boy said.

"Quite right. And when did they have their first Thanksgiving in Plymouth, when they celebrated with their Indian friends?" He selected another little boy.

"Their first harvest, sir, in 1621."

"Very good. Perhaps we should address a question to one of our grownup friends." He looked around as everyone who had been out of school for many years shifted uncomfortably, some trying to avoid the President's eye, which seemed to amuse him. "If the first Thanksgiving was in 1621, when was the second? Mr. Stanton, perhaps you would care to take a crack at that one, sir."

Wade immediately suspected some lawyerly trick was afoot, a friendly jibe between one-time professional rivals.

Stanton probably suspected it too, for he stammered slightly before falling into the trap. "The second Thanksgiving? Why, the next year, I suppose... 1622."

"Our distinguished Secretary of War has given the answer that most people would venture, but unfortunately there was no Thanksgiving in 1622. Is that not so, Mrs. Hale?"

"Indeed not, Mr. President," the lady replied without hesitation. "The harvest was very poor that year. The Pilgrims barely had enough food to survive the coming winter. They had very little to celebrate in 1622."

The point was made, Wade realized, that the little woman the male politicians scorned knew her history better than one of the most brilliant and highly educated men in America. The President did not grind the barb in, however, but stretched back in what Wade recognized as Western storytelling posture.

"No, the second Thanksgiving was not until 1623, and there's quite a story in that." Lincoln looked over the children again. "I wonder, is there a boy here, eleven years of age?"

Another young fellow shyly lifted his hand. Wade remembered Willie Lincoln had been eleven when he died.

"Come closer, son." Lincoln placed a tender hand on the boy's shoulder. "There was also an eleven year old boy at Plymouth in 1623. He and his family were among those who stood alone in that wilderness at the edge of an untamed continent. This boy, his mother and father, his little brother and sisters can serve as a powerful example to us today. Their faith and courage played a mighty role in how the second Thanksgiving came about, or that it came about at all. There's a bit of a yarn in that, and for once it's all true."

Wade had seen and heard enough superb storytellers in his life to know that he and all the other listeners were about to receive something special, especially if the busiest man in the world wanted to take a bit of his precious time to tell them a tale. The drawling, high-pitched Midwestern voice already held them fast before Lincoln really got going.

People crowded forward, as politely as possible, in order to see and hear better, and not for the first time in his life Wade was glad for his commanding height. He could look over all the intervening heads and see the children settling in for a listen, some of them sitting right down on the presidential carpet.

"We've got a lot of wrong ideas about the old Pilgrim fathers," Lincoln said, as Mrs. Hale glowed. "We have all seen etchings and paintings that have them dressed completely in black, with buckles on their hats. I never did know what those buckles were supposed to be for, at least until I got to Washington, when I found out a man's head could expand faster than his waist line.

"The truth is, it was the Puritans who thought the Lord had a grudge against colorful clothes, and they didn't come along until a few years later. The Pilgrims were not Puritans, exactly. If we could see the Pilgrims, whether dressed up in their finery or in their everyday duds, they'd look like regular Elizabethans, the kind of colorful peacocks we see strutting around the stage when we go to the theater to see one of Mr. Shakespeare's plays.

"It's important to know their story, these Pilgrims, for you children especially, because everything that America is today or hopes to be in the future got going back there in Plymouth Plantation. But there's one thing we should remember above all."

The President looked around at his audience, briefly meeting Wade's eyes and those of many others before moving on. For Wade the intensity of the President's glance had the power of a mule kick right in his innards.

The silence deepened before Lincoln spoke again.

"You must know and remember this," he said. "Our nation began with a miracle."

CHAPTER 1

Plymouth Plantation, March 1623

The day rose bright and hot for so early in the year, and the skeletons were soon out working in the fields, clearing more land.

The Bone Men had an unseemly appetite for cleared land, a source of amusement for the Wampanoag, who often crept close to watch their baffling customs and other strange behavior from the edges of the great surrounding forest. As soon as the fish began to run, the People would be planting corn themselves, of course, and every village had its own field, sufficient to grow crops enough to feed its inhabitants through the cold moons of bad hunting, plus a little more for trade.

These puzzling white newcomers pushed on, however, removing rocks and stumps and living trees from an ever-widening swath of land far out of proportion to their paltry numbers. They used the felled trees to build a peculiar wooden wall completely surrounding their tiny village with its large, odd huts also constructed out of trees, though with roofs of thatch just like those of the People. The idle gossip of women and children had long since concluded the Bone Men prepared land because they expected more of their kind, soon to arrive as these had, aboard gigantic canoes from across the Great Water.

If so, the effort would prove laughably futile, for the already existing fields had failed to produce a sufficient harvest the previous autumn, and the English had barely survived the snows to disgrace the land now as nothing more impressive than this tiny, weary, slow-walking tribe of blanched skeletons. They kept moving though, chewing away at the forest, in spite of exhaustion and the lack of meat on their bones. Most of their womenfolk had died the first harsh winter. The Wampanoag women claimed the Bone Men ate so poorly for lack of experienced hands to do the cooking, in the same manner the absence of those who knew how to sew left the Englishmen's deteriorating clothing to hang about their skinny bodies like rags. The warriors scoffed that the whites simply had no more skill at farming than at hunting or fishing. Did not a war party or band of hunters manage to keep itself fed without the aid of women? The Bone Men starved for no other reason than their own strangeness and stupidity.

* * *

Though only eleven, John Cooke already knew how to wield an ax. He was swinging a little hatchet now, trimming the branches off a log as his father moved on with a full-sized ax to bring down the next tree.

Francis Cooke spat on his hands, measured the trunk with his eye, studied the angle of fall that he wanted, and began to sink the blade repeatedly at the proper point. He used long fluid swings more appropriate to a man who had been working in the forest all his life than to a lean forty-year-old who had labored at nothing but combing wool until he and John sailed on the *Mayflower*.

John lopped off the last of the branches and stopped for a moment to watch his father. Since they were alone, this was a good time to steal a moment's rest without risking a rebuke from one of the more sour of the older men, the ones who seemed to expect children to work more diligently than the complainers themselves. The cool shadows of the trees felt good in contrast to the sun's anvil out in the fields, where other scattered men and boys labored in the unaccustomed heat.

John admired his father's skill, but as he watched he was thinking of another, whose face he had trouble forming in his memory, though he saw her frequently in dreams, where he always identified her without the slightest doubt or hesitation.

"Father, can we truly believe it? Is mother's ship at sea by now?"

Francis stopped to wipe his brow. "God willing, half way across! And with your sisters and little brother too."

"Do you think we'll recognize each other, after all this time?"

"Recognize or not," his father said, "by the Lord's grace, this family has been split asunder for the last time. Once we're together again, we stay together."

John loved to hear this kind of cheery talk, quite cheerful indeed by Plymouth standards. It sent his spirit soaring beyond the struggle of their daily drudgery. After more than two years on this harsh shore, so many of the other men had given up to despair, which was probably why Francis usually reserved his more buoyant affirmations for just the two of them, to avoid harsh contradiction and downright opposition.

You would think, his father observed, that men wanted cheering up, encouragement, a lifting of their hearts, but some only wallowed in their own misery. The complacent ranks of the gloomy were not necessarily restricted to the ungodly either. Indeed, certain brethren distrusted hope itself as somehow sinful, it seemed, as if craving improvement in their circumstances cast an insult in the face of God for His ordering of the world. These same types credited the Almighty with the authorship of every setback, accident, illness or death, often without acknowledging that the Lord might ever do something good for a change.

"It's absurd," Francis often said in private, pointing John to the Old Testament book of Job. "If God is the maker of all our misfortunes, what is the enemy of our souls up to all this time?"

Before John could ask more questions, hoping to prod his father into talking about his plans and visions for the future, always a source of encouragement and downright enjoyment, they were interrupted by a cry from the fields.

"Brother Cooke! Come help us, you and the boy! We have struck a rock here that is too big for us!"

John looked back in disgust at the interruption, but Francis spoke before he could complain. "Come, John. Let us go help those fellows."

"But what about our own work?"

"Come, come. Time may be we shall need their help."

John doubted that but held his tongue. They walked out into the direct sunlight.

"Look at that stone," John said in disgust. "'Tis a puny thing for such a fuss."

"Could you move it by yourself then?"

"I'm not full grown yet. They could move it if they put their backs into it."

"Could they now?"

"Yes!"

"Well, perhaps they could, my son, but since they say they need us, let us do it willingly, pleasing God rather than ourselves."

"Yes, Father."

"Good lad."

John lowered his voice as they approached the others, standing around the half-buried stone looking flummoxed. "When do you think Mother will be here?"

"Let us pray soon—right soon." Francis put his hand on his son's shoulder and peered up at the sky. "It is not quite spring yet, but the weather is mild. Our days have been good and getting better. Mayhap the weather is fair upon the ocean as well."

CHAPTER 2

Mountainous Seas

Out in the vastness of the Atlantic, the great tempest roared out of the north and bore down upon the tiny ship *Anne* with more rage and power than its most experienced sailors had ever witnessed and survived.

The ship's master stood lashed to the quarterdeck, steering with the whip staff, a long sturdy pole on a pivot that controlled the rudder. Trusting no one else with the fate of the *Anne*, including his two experienced helmsmen, he piloted on with nothing to look forward to but more hours of unremitting struggle. One miscalculation, one misjudgment in a moment of exhaustion, would send them all to the bottom, the master and his sailors, along with all those praying fools packed in the filthy stinking hold below deck.

In the long hours of battle between man and storm, begun long before the dawn, the master had no compassion to spare for his passengers. He fought for his own survival and that of loyal men who had sailed with him for years. The best of these braved the deck along with their master, ready to spring to the rigging as the wind required.

At present the *Anne* carried only a small triangle of jib forward and a scarcely larger square of mizzen staysail at the stern. Using every ounce of experience and skill, the captain kept the ship upright by playing the rudder alternately with and against the wind pressure on these pathetically small sheets of canvas. Periodically the storm tore away one or the other, and the sailors clambered up to hang a replacement at terrible risk to their lives in the howling blow and plunging seas. So far the wind had not managed to tear both sails away simultaneously, a possibility the master shuddered to contemplate. In that event he might be able to avoid being capsized for a few moments if he were very, very lucky, while the sailors strove for love of life to hang new canvas before he lost control. Better for it not to happen.

Glancing upward to check the wind direction, he knew it was daytime, but a day as dark as night here in the heart of the storm.

The waves bulged to the size of mountains. Shaking in the gale, the little ship slowly climbed to the pinnacle of each roller, then plunged with a stomach-churning slide down the other side. The master scarcely knew which was more frightening, the moment at the crest when a flash of lightning illuminated the terrible distance they were about to drop, or the shuddering impact at the bottom of the trough, where the next approaching swell stood higher than the masts, taller than the loftiest spires of Europe.

Yet he had to watch these fearsome sights, to keep the rudder headed into the wind and catch each monstrous wave at the angle that would keep them afloat.

The passengers below were lucky—blessed—if they only knew, not being able to see. Putting all thought of them aside, the ship's master somehow found the stamina and sheer determination to battle on.

* * *

Hester Cooke held five-year-old Jacob in her arms, and miraculously the little boy had somehow been able to fall sleep. Her daughters, nine-year-old Jane and Little Hester, one year younger, clung to their mother on either side. She had wedged herself and the children into a little cranny between a beam and a bulkhead, near the spot where they all slept together on the deck of the hold, since Hester feared to place the little ones in hammocks, the grossly uncomfortable sleeping accommodation favored by the crew and most of the other passengers. Many had toppled out of a hammock over the course of innumerable uncomfortable nights, and Hester preferred to protect her own children from such a fall at the price of sleeping on wet boards.

Now the water stood inches deep, not rising higher only because the brethren and the sailors spelled one another desperately on the pumps. How the men remained upright at all formed an unanswerable mystery for Hester. She pitied their aching arms and backs but had her own hands full with the children.

The ship had been following the same sickening pattern for hours. First the deck would slant upwards, groaning in its very timbers with protest, whilst anything that hadn't been roped down went rolling and sliding toward the stern. Then the ship seemed to pause for a moment, as if weightless, before plunging forward. The bow suddenly dived down, slanting the deck in the opposite direction. Finally the ship would level out all too briefly before beginning to tilt upwards again. The unending process devastated its human victims with nausea, terror and hopelessness. They felt caught in a trap they would never escape.

The moans and sobs of men and women and the crying of children could barely compete with the fearsome shriek of the tempest.

Hester felt a persistent tug on her left arm and looked down to find Little Hester looking up at her with tearstained face. She bent down to bring her ear close.

"Mother, do you think God has forgotten us?" the little girl said.

"Forgotten us? No, never!" Hester spoke excellent English, though with a strong French accent that certain persons of more judgmental leanings in the congregation looked down upon. Her manner of speaking had always been a source of pleasure for her husband, who found the accent charming, and that was all that counted for Hester. She rejoiced, however, that all the children spoke proper English, like their father.

Jane moved her head close as well. "How can we know?"

"Do you remember that place in the Psalms we have spoken of?" The girls undoubtedly remembered, but it would do them good to hear the comforting words again, as it would for Hester to recite them. "'They that go down to the sea in ships, and occupy by the great waters... They see the works of the Lord, and his wonders in the deep...'"

They braced themselves anew as the deck suddenly reversed direction and plunged forward. People screamed as if it hadn't happened a hundred times before.

Hester went right on with her reciting. "'For he commandeth, and raiseth the stormy wind.'" She paused to look at each worried little face in turn. "It is all God's wind, children, all God's waves, so let us be very brave."

The girls did not appear convinced.

"'They mount up to heaven...'"

As if to illustrate the point, the deck tilted toward the rear as the ship once again began to climb upward.

"'...and descend to the deep, so that their soul melteth for trouble. They are tossed to and fro, and stagger like a drunken man, and all their cunning is gone. Then they cry unto the Lord in their trouble, and he bringeth them out of their distress...'"

"But, Mother," Jane said, "We have been crying out to the Lord for hours, we and everybody on this boat."

"God's promises do not provide us with a duration of time. Sometimes God's people must endure lengthily before we see His promises fulfilled."

"But why?"

"Ah, Jane, we could only find out in Heaven, and when we are there we shall probably be too happy to ask."

"Tell us the promise," Little Hester said.

"'He turneth the storm to calm, so that the waves thereof are still. When they are quieted, they are glad. So He bringeth them unto the haven, where they would be.'" The last line bore repeating. "'So He bringeth them unto the haven, where they would be!' Let us say it together for ourselves. For us."

The girls and Hester claimed the promise in unison. "He bringeth *us* unto the haven, where *we* would be!"

Outside the great storm went howling on.

CHAPTER 3

A Fugitive from the Forest

The land had begun to dry as the last remaining snow from mid-February melted off, soon leaving the ground sufficiently dried out but not too much so for a good safe burning.

Francis was working with John and some other boys stacking wood around a number of obstinate stumps too large to be pulled out of the ground by brute force, at least for hungry men without the aid of chains and oxen. They were nearly ready to light the first fire when Francis saw his son's face burst into a grin.

Turning to look, Francis was not surprised to see Philip Delano approaching. The young Frenchman had a cheering effect on everyone, young and old, male and female alike. He was one of Plymouth's tiny company of Huguenots, originally a derisive term their Catholic enemies imposed on the *réformés*, French Protestants who had joined themselves to their English brethren in the Dutch city of Leyden, where the refugees had arrived after fleeing persecution in France. His actual name was Philippe de la Noye, but he felt no resentment toward his new friends and their need to Anglicize his surname into something more comfortable for stiff English tongues. He would happily bequeath Delano to his descendants, provided he ever had any.

Not yet thirty, Delano bore himself like an aristocrat. Though he loved to amuse listeners with highly selective anecdotes about his past, he remained secretive about his birth, his family background, the exact reasons for his flight from France, which might well conceal considerably more interesting factors than religious persecution alone. Francis suspected Philip's faith in Christ and commitment to the theological ideas of his countryman of the previous century, John Calvin, had somehow blossomed as the unexpected culmination to a wild youth attended by a long train of scandal.

Whatever had occurred, Francis was content to leave the matter in the past, as God did, without condemnation or embarrassing questions. This ready acceptance and aversion to gossip on the former wool comber's part helped explain why Delano had always considered Francis his closest and most reliable friend among the congregation.

All the single men of Plymouth had been parceled out among the family houses, and Delano lived with the Cookes, a source of envy for John's friends, who never tired of the Frenchman's vitality, charm and unfailing good humor. Only when they were alone did Francis see Philip fall into despair as deep as any of the other men, but that was a face the younger man felt a duty to conceal from all accept his closest brother in the Lord. In private Francis had occasion to build up his housemate as much as Delano encouraged everyone else in public.

Though he could hold no official position yet in governance or church because he had so far never married, Delano exuded some mysterious quality of leadership that caused others to take their cues from him. Perhaps sensing this gift within himself, he remained buoyant both by natural personality and by force of will, urging all who would listen to maintain their courage, for God and their own hard work would conquer every problem—eventually.

"Hello, young fellows," Delano boomed in his gorgeous voice. "Monsieur Cooke told me you possess a talent for destruction, and seeing the hopeless state of these miserable stumps, I can well believe it. If the forest knew what was good for it, the trees would pick up their skirts and run away in the night. This woods, she cannot stand against you!"

By now everyone passably understood Delano's accent, though Francis started well ahead because of Hester.

After a jaunty wave at the grinning boys, Philip took Francis by the arm and led him aside, murmuring in a low voice, "Francis, how good are your eyes today?"

Something in his tone made Francis worry. "My attention has been on our work."

"As I suspected. Then you did not notice anything amiss some moments ago?"

"Nothing."

By now John had drawn close enough to overhear.

"John," Delano said, "I think I must speak to Captain Standish. I do not think your father has the making of a soldier at all. He is not what we call an observant man."

Francis became impatient. "Philip, what did you see, for all love?"

"A party of savages watching us, from those trees yonder." Delano almost imperceptibly tipped his head northward.

"Probably some friends of Hobomok," Francis said.

"No one has seen Hobomok for three days. And these were not dressed as the local savages attire themselves, not that I am any judge of their finery."

Francis let his eyes roam the edge of the forest. "Where exactly?"

"I consider it both impolite and militarily inappropriate to point."

"Just point, Philip. They could be anywhere."

Delano stared at a fixed spot. "Follow my gaze. A pointing finger might provoke them."

Suddenly at that precise position in the tree line a white man burst out of the woods and came running toward them, waving his arms frantically. The man wore rags so grievous he made the men of Plymouth look courtly by comparison. His face and the body under the ragged clothing showed evidence of extensive cuts and bruises. The fire builders noticed him by now, as did other workers in the field. His wild-looking eyes fixed on Francis and Delano, the loping man suddenly collapsed, toppling forward onto the ground.

Francis and Delano took off running to render assistance. John started along, but his father yelled, "John, run and get Captain Standish!"

The boy whipped around and dashed for the stockade.

Francis and Philip quickly covered the intervening space and knelt down beside the fallen, who looked weaker and scrawnier than from a distance. They turned him over, and Francis braced the man up into a sitting position. The fellow looked from one to the other, as if too hopeless and desperate to believe his own senses.

"Ye are Plymouth men?" He spoke with a strong Scots burr.

"Aye," Francis said, "the fort lies yonder."

"Thank God... I made it."

"You are one of Thomas Weston's men?"

Francis referred to the headman for an outpost of traders roughly thirty miles north of Plymouth, outside the territory of the Wampanoag tribe. In general Weston and his followers considered the older and larger settlement a menagerie of sanctimonious Bible pounders, and the Plymouth folk regarded the traders as ungodly servants of Satan. The two groups had nothing to do with one another by unspoken, longstanding and quite mutual consent.

"Aye, from the trading post at Wessagusset."

"Who are you, sir?" Delano said.

"My name is... David Thompson."

A couple of the other Plymouth men were approaching by now, along with a number of wide-eyed boys. Delano shouted, "You boys, stay back. You brothers, bring water!"

Without questioning why both of them were needed to bring water, the two men turned and hurried back in the other direction.

Francis and Delano bent down closer Thompson.

"You came from Wessagusset by yourself?" Francis said.

The Scotsman nodded wearily. "Did the entire distance on me feet, I did, walkin' when I weren't able to run... Took me over two days and two nights... This be the third day." A well-fed man, which Thompson certainly was not, should have been able to make it in a day.

Delano whistled. "There is trouble with the Indians?"

This was the obvious explanation, and Francis appreciated the Frenchman's customary directness. The very possibility explained why he had acted to keep others away.

Thompson shook his head. "Not yet, but it's a bloomin'. That's why I come. They was on me trail most o' the way... lost them a few hours ago, somehow... war party o' the Massachusett. Bloody savages!" Suddenly he seemed to remember the other men's reputed sensibilities. "Oh, begging your pardon, gentlemen."

Francis and Philip were looking at each other, however, and had no anxiety to spare for profane language.

Francis turned back to Thompson. "Say no more, sir, if you please, for now. We had best take you to Governor Bradford and Captain Standish."

"Can you move, my friend?" Delano said.

"Aye, laddie, just give me a hand up."

Just then the two other men arrived with a pail of cool spring water. One draught from the dipper refreshed Thompson to some extent. Francis and Delano hauled him to his feet and took his arms around their shoulders. They started for the stockade, fending off every curious look and question with determined silence.

CHAPTER 4

Rumor of War

The five men climbed to the ramparts of the recently completed fortress that dominated Fort Hill, the westernmost and highest point within New Plymouth, in order to confer well away from prying ears. The wooden stockade walls began here atop the hill, running east and downhill from the fort almost as far as the shore of what the settlers called Plymouth Harbor, a little inlet projecting southward from the larger Plymouth Bay. These high walls formed a long diamond-shaped bulwark encompassing two parallel lines of houses. Town Street ran between the twin rows of houses, alongside the tiny brook trickling down from the hilltop spring inside the fort. Captain Standish often declared the presence of fresh drinkable water the citadel's greatest defensive advantage, surpassing its elevation. At the bottom of the hill, beyond the lower gate, which closed the eastern end of the elongated defensive rhombus, the water of the harbor lapped far more gently than the tumultuous Atlantic out beyond the distant narrow strip of protective land known by its shape as the Cape Cod fishhook, another geographical godsend that spared Plymouth Beach and the settlement's own harbor shoreline the worst ravages of surf and storm.

From the parapet of the fort a man could see everything, and at least one sentry stood duty at all times, two at night, always with a lighted match, actually a fuse of slow-burning rope, ready to fire off either the sentinel's own musket or one of the six small cannon pointed out in every direction except toward the harbor. In case of surprise attack, firing one of these weapons might not do very much damage to the enemy, barring an extraordinarily lucky shot, but the earsplitting roar would certainly rouse all the defenders.

One by one the five men surmounted the last rungs on one of the tall ladders poking up out of the outsized storage room on the stockade's ground floor, a large space which doubled as community meeting place until the colony could get around to building a church. As they passed through the trapdoor to the ramparts, Francis hoped to find the sentry vigilant, so they would not have to watch Miles Standish bawl the man out. Fortunately, the watchman had his eyes alertly fixed on the forest, either as the result of the Scotsman's dramatic arrival a few minutes earlier or perhaps in fear of Standish and his temper.

Captain Standish took a place near the sentry and began scanning the tree line himself. A short, volatile man in his thirties, with fiery red hair and beard to match his disposition, Miles Standish could be quite methodical, especially when it came to his arena of responsibility. A former English soldier, never a member of the congregation, he had been hired on in London to supervise the plantation's military defenses. Now the others stood quietly as he moved his eyes slowly across the edge of the forest, from east to west on each side of the settlement, then back again. David Thompson leaned his weary frame against the parapet and took the opportunity for another draught of water, which Delano handed him out of the sentry's supply.

"I see no savages," Standish said at last. "But that doesn't mean they're not there. More likely the opposite."

William Bradford only grunted in response. Francis knew the governor always took a cold view of the captain's bleak suspicions. The truth usually fell somewhere between Standish's pessimism and

Bradford's more hopeful outlook, though how Bradford could maintain hope in the face of so much personal tragedy was more than Francis could explain except for what had to be very great personal faith in the Almighty.

Standish spoke to the sentry. "Keep a sharp lookout. Our discussions here do not concern you."

A flash of resentment crossed the sentry's face, but he obediently walked away to the furthest corner and continued to scan the distant forest.

Bradford turned, with exquisite reluctance, to the bearer of bad news. "All right, Mister Thompson. Let us have it, if you please."

"Things is bad at Wessagusset, Guv'ner." His Scottish accent poured out so thick the Englishmen had to listen very intently, and Francis wondered if Philip could keep up at all. "That be why I come."

"Did Mister Weston send you?"

"Weston! We've not seen hide nor hair o' the man for weeks. He be out among the Indians, scrambling for beaver pelts."

"Who sent you then, Mister Thompson?"

"Why, I sent meself, sir."

"Who is in charge at the trading post in Mister Weston's absence?"

"No one's in charge o' the place, ever, whether Weston's there or whether he's not! It's a bloody—" Thompson again remembered his listeners. "Begging your pardon, gentlemen—it's a fearful chaos at Wessagusset, sir. And I come to you on me own prerogative."

"What is the problem, sir," Standish said, "in its essentials?"

"In its essentials, the problem? Flat hunger, Captain! That's why Weston's mad to go out on this beaver chase. What difference if we stack up every beaver's skin in the wide world if we're like to perish o' starvation?"

"We are not exactly thriving here at Plymouth either, Mister Thompson," Bradford said.

"At least ye have the strength to work." Thompson waved a limp hand in the direction of the surrounding fields. "I left men so weak they couldn't raise up to throw a stick on a fire."

"But what of the Indians?" Standish said. "Why have they followed you?"

"God knows. Maybe just havin' themselves a spot o' fun. On the other hand, maybe they want to cut me throat. I didna stop to ask, now did I? The savages, they look upon us with contempt, they do, 'specially them Massachusett buggers. Some o' our men be so far gone in starvation, they attached themselves to the Indians as servants."

"White men servants to a flock of savages!" Standish quivered with visible outrage.

"Aye. Boiling their porridge. Cleaning out their lodges. Bowing down in the mud to their shamans—all for a meager handful o' corn."

Francis spoke up. "Governor Bradford, perhaps we should offer the gentlemen shelter here at Plymouth."

"To eat up our own paltry supplies?" Standish snapped.

"They are our fellow countrymen, after all," Bradford said.

"They are not *my* countrymen," Philip said.

"The next ship should bring us new supplies from London," Bradford mused, thinking out loud.

"The last one didn't! Just a gaggle of empty mouths to feed."

"Including yours, Philip," Francis said.

"We must think of ourselves!" Standish insisted.

"God can make provision for us all."

"The good Lord may provide as He sees fit, gentlemen," Thompson said, "but I fear I've not conveyed the full measure o' folly. Now the savages refuse to barter corn anymore, as some o' our poor men has already traded the very trousers right off their spindly legs and don't have much left. So some o' our own more brutish sorts, the ones 'as got any strength left, are laying plans to take the Indians' corn by force o' arms. And by necessity they must needs move soon, gentlemen, whilst they're yet able. *That's* why I come to you."

His listeners looked at one other in bleakest distress.

Standish spoke first. "It would start a war. We could not survive a full scale war."

"Captain Standish," Bradford said, "at dawn tomorrow, take the shallop for Wessagusset with a few select men. Tell Weston's men there shall be no raiding of the Indians. If there is any such attack, it is my responsibility as governor of Plymouth plantation... to punish the offenders."

"To hang them, sir," Standish said with his usual sanguinary intensity. "I shall not mince words."

"I am sure you shall not, Captain," Bradford said dryly.

"Yes, sir."

"And put together a large bag of corn and a decent bag of our salted venison."

"We can't spare those."

"We must. We cannot issue threats without providing food to meet the immediate necessity."

The corn did not remain from last year's disastrous harvest but had been traded for from closer Wampanoag villages. The pair of skinny late winter deer had been shot by two of the town's designated hunters, which included Francis and Philip, though they had not brought down either of these.

"We still can't spare that much food, Governor," Standish said.

"You'll take care of that on the return journey. We have a long-standing agreement with the Indians of Cummaquid to sell us corn. In the light of what we have heard, you had best go to Chief Iyanough and collect what has been promised."

"I fear," Thompson put in, "ye may find your bargain is no longer in force."

"Our trade was negotiated by our Mister Winslow," Bradford said, "a particular favorite of Chief Massasoit."

"Aye, Iyanough and his people are part o' Massasoit's confederation, as you say, Guv'ner, but the prime troublemakers are the Massachusett, who are not, and they might wield more influence than you think, Cummaquid being closer to Massachusett land."

"All the more reason to hold Iyanough to our agreement. But not to fear, they want our trading goods as much as we desire their corn."

"But what if the savages simply decide to take what they want by force, Guv'ner?" Thompson said. "Your little party would be in grave danger."

This was too much for Standish. "If the Cummaquid savages have made us a promise, they shall keep it. That I guarantee. And do not fret your head, sir, about Plymouth men facing danger."

"In the spirit of gentleness, Captain," Bradford said, "gentleness and understanding, lest we foment hostilities ourselves. For your expedition, would Mister Cooke and Mister Delano here be acceptable?"

"Both are brave, reliable and good shots."

Delano swelled visibly at the captain's words, but Francis felt his own face turning red. He took no particular pride in the assessment, for qualities that seemed to contradict, in his mind, the New Testament ideals for Christian manhood.

"Very well," Bradford said. "Please choose your other men, but take Edward Winslow along as well."

"Winslow?" Standish said. "He is too weak and sickly, not as strong as these men."

"No, but he will do his duty. Mister Winslow is our best scholar in the Indian tongues and customs."

"We can take Hobomok for translator."

"Hobomok is away on his visit to Massasoit, and we cannot wait for him. Take Winslow, and be off with you as early in the morning as possible. Francis, if I may speak with you a moment..."

Standish saluted and went back down through the trap door with Thompson and Delano, who was promising the Scotsman to find him a bite to eat.

Bradford took Francis off to the corner of the roof furthest from the sentry, who persisted in diligent study of the forest.

Bradford stared out into the distance himself for a long time, then turned to Francis. "Brother Cooke, have you some objection to going along on this little foray?"

"Soldiering is not my cup of tea, sir."

"Captain Standish seems to think you have a certain prowess at it."

"I am sure you could easily find a man more suited, and certainly more enthusiastic, for a task of arms."

"It is your very lack of enthusiasm that commends you most strongly in my eyes, brother. Captain Standish is a good man, and a most competent military commander, but he has the weakness of bad temper. You are under his orders, of course, but I shall rest easier to send along a more temperate companion, a man of sound judgment."

"Mister Winslow is an even tempered man, sir."

"Even tempered, but perhaps too weak to assert himself in the face of Captain Standish. This is a delicate situation. After all, what is our most important relationship to these poor savages?"

"To win them to faith in Jesus Christ."

"Exactly, Francis. To win them, not merely by the spoken word, but by honest and judicial behavior."

Bradford briefly placed a grateful hand on his shoulder. Resigned that he could not escape the duty, Francis left to make his preparations.

CHAPTER 5

In Sight of Land

At dawn the next morning an armed party of seven men put out to sea in the shallop. Before the sun was well risen, the little single-masted boat had sailed out of Plymouth Harbor, rounded Saquish Head and Gurnet Point to the east, and headed north along the Atlantic shore in the direction of Wessagusset, deep in the Massachusett tribal territory.

Philip Delano sat in the back handling the tiller. As virtually the only man in Plymouth with experience sailing a small boat, presumably acquired as part of his mysterious but apparently privileged background, Delano fought to hold a steady course while instructing the hopeless landlubbers what to do with the lugsails, a process that often found him lapsing into French in his excitement. He sometimes handed the tiller over to Francis for a moment or two so he could haul on the sails himself. By late morning the wind and sea had settled out, and they were running well, sailing smoothly north along the coastline. What was unequivocal fun for the boyish and excited Delano constituted a bouncing agony for the seasick Englishmen, including Francis, who struggled to keep his unsettled stomach under control lest he fail to help when needed. Poor Edward Winslow lay stretched out and groaning in the bottom of the boat.

Nothing fazed the iron constitution of Miles Standish, however, and the captain marched briskly back to the stern and squatted down next to Philip and Francis.

"Mister Delano, there is a river emptying into the ocean about a mile this side of the landing for Wessagusset."

"I know the place, captain."

"We shall put in there and hide the boat."

Francis and Philip exchanged a quick look, prompting the captain to explain himself, doubtless a sign of his respect for the two men.

"We shall walk into Wessagusset from the forest, gentlemen," Standish said. "In military operations one always seeks to preserve the element of surprise."

The captain tried to keep his normally stentorian voice low, but it carried as far as Winslow, who propped himself up on one arm. "These are Englishmen, captain. We have not been sent to attack them, only reason with them."

This made everyone listen, so Standish roared out in his customary fashion, "Oh, they be Englishmen, all right, but would any man here want them living in our camp, where they could influence the young and the female?"

His listeners held their tongues, the only sound the wind beating against the sails.

"I thought not," Standish said. "These are Englishmen scarcely worthy of the name. Knaves who have debauched with Indian women, degraded themselves to the level of rutting beasts."

"We must try to reason with them as fellow countrymen," Winslow insisted, "despite their less than virtuous behavior."

"Oh, we shall reason with them, Mister Winslow. We shall reason with them most effectively."

* * *

Suddenly, without warning, the door to the hold slid back with a great noise. The passengers shaded their eyes with their hands, blinking painfully against the abrupt infusion of light from above.

"All right, you below," a harsh voice shouted, "ye can come up for a spot of fresh air, a few at a time. Women and children first, if you please."

Hester was sitting with her best friend aboard ship, an older woman named Elizabeth Warren, well over thirty, who presided over a brood of five daughters: Mary, Ann, Sarah, Little Elizabeth, and Abigail. The two women looked at each other with surprise and delight.

"They're letting us out of our prison?" Elizabeth said.

The Cooke and Warren progeny were already running noisily for the ladder before their mothers could stop them. Fortunately this seemed acceptable to the other passengers, since between them Elizabeth and Hester had the largest contingent of children. Other mothers followed with their own little ones.

Not having been out of the dark hold for nearly two months, Hester found direct sunlight extremely painful. It took several minutes for her eyes to adjust and staunch the tears running down her cheeks. She hoped the staring sailors would not misjudge her eye problem for weakness and melancholy. Knowing how the seamen held their human cargo in the greatest contempt, she had no intention of feeding their disdain. When able to look around freely, she saw other denizens of the hold wiping and shielding their eyes. Some of the sailors smirked, elbowing one another in the ribs, mocking the weak-minded fools who wept with joy at their fleeting release from captivity. Well, let them think what they would. What did it matter?

Clinging to one another like the blind men in the parable, Hester and Elizabeth began a slow circuit of the deck, determined to walk and walk until ordered back to the hold.

Elizabeth inhaled deeply of the clean air. "Smell that breeze, Hester! If that is not the breath of Heaven..."

"Certainly by contrast with the hold!"

Elizabeth wrinkled her nose. "Let us not speak of that place of woe."

Hester nodded in sympathy. The large main hold had been divided lengthwise by the hanging of spare canvas on ropes, with the men and boys on one side of the curtained partition and the women and small children on the other. None of the passengers had been above deck since embarking, except for some of the chief men for brief consultations with the ship's master. The captives did their best in matters of cleanliness and hygiene, but the stench became overpowering within the first week. Only the eventual and merciful deadening of the sense of smell, now proving to be only temporary, kept one from going mad in the close air.

"I wonder to what we owe this breath of freedom?" Elizabeth said, ever suspicious.

"I am too happy to ask."

"Do you hear?" a rough-looking sailor piped up, without bothering to keep his voice down. "The pretty one is French."

"Alluring wench!" his hairy companion spoke up, then shouted, "What you doing with a gaggle of English Bible-thumpers, girl?"

Blushing scarlet, Hester lowered her eyes to the deck as the other sailors laughed. She might look young, but she had been married a dozen years to a man twelve years her senior, having wedded him at sixteen. She deserved to be respected as a wife and mother, not degraded like a young street girl trawling a waterfront.

Elizabeth replied on her friend's behalf with a withering gaze that could burn through stone. The two sailors and their companions quickly busied themselves with their duties.

"Frightful beasts!" Mrs. Warren confided to everyone on deck and in the rigging far above. "I see more intelligent behavior from the smallest children down below!"

"Hush, Elizabeth," Hester said softly. "At least they have had mercy on us, letting us out for a bit."

By now the two ladies were making the aft turnabout just below the quarterdeck, where the ship's master stood aloof in the magnificence of command. At the moment he was staring at Elizabeth, perhaps wondering if he ought to bring her out on deck to bellow commands in the next blow. She dropped a quick curtsey, and he bowed his head, slightly.

Elizabeth gripped her young friend's arm tighter as they headed back forward and managed to speak in a tone somewhat below the level of cannon fire. "Mercy on us? My dear, you are such an innocent. Like many of your fellow separatists, you tend to ascribe mercy and other virtues to your fellow men where none exist. If Richard were with us now, he would soon sniff out the truth."

"And what truth would your husband scent other than this wonderful sea air?"

"Since our comforts have meant nothing to these scoundrels hitherto, Richard would guess our glorious captain yonder could have no other inducement than the scent of gold."

"Surely you do not suggest someone bribed him to give us a bit of fresh air. All our purses were plucked clean just to make this voyage in the first place."

"Just so. My dear, do you notice these birds, wheeling about the ship?"

"Seagulls. They fly everywhere in Holland."

"Indeed, as I hear your precious Holland is a land reclaimed from the sea."

"It is that."

"Seagulls are a coastal bird, are they not? They fish in the sea and prey upon its ships like the little thieves they are, but they nest on the land."

It dawned on Hester. "Land!"

"I take it we draw close enough to shore for our captain to be concerned that his travelers tell a pleasant tale to the elders of your sect. There are many other worshipers in Holland—and England too—awaiting transportation."

"You think we are almost there?"

"I do not think these gulls followed us from England, nor from Holland either."

Hester broke away and ran to the ship's rail. "Francis!"

Elizabeth chased and pulled her back into the authorized circuit of the deck before anyone could notice and object. "You miss your husband terribly, don't you, Hester?"

"My dear husband, yes, and my eldest child. I have not seen them these three years, since they left Leyden to sail on a tiny little ship, smaller than this one if you can believe it, called the *Mayflower*."

"How frightful! I cannot imagine."

"All this time, and no contact but a pair of precious letters."

"I am sure he hungers for the sight of you as well, your husband. A beautiful French wife for such a solid, hard-working Englishman."

"I am not French," Hester said, not for the first time in the course of their friendship. "I am Walloon."

Mrs. Warren waved a dismissive hand at this minor detail. A highly independent Celtic tribe scattered across northern France and the provinces around Brussels, the Walloons had more in common by blood and culture with their fellow Celts of Scotland, Wales and Ireland than with the French, but to Elizabeth anyone born in France, growing up in France and speaking French was French.

"Beautiful in any case," she said.

"Please do not feed my vanity, Elizabeth. I have more than enough struggles in that arena."

"As well you should, my dear. If betting were not a sinful practice for a Christian, I'd wager ye shall have another child nine months after landing and being with that husband of yours again!"

Hester covered a bright red face with both hands but laughed. "Elizabeth!" She soon lowered her hands though, whispering confidentially. "Well, I am certainly open to the idea!"

The two women huddled for a giggle when a loud cry broke out from the lookout's nest at the highest point of the main mast.

"Land ho!"

All the passengers on deck froze in place. New heads popped up out of the open hatch.

The ship's master shouted up. "Avast there, where aloft?"

"Land ho, sir," the cry came down, "straight ahead, two points to the starboard!"

After a moment's hesitation, all the women and children ran to line the railing on the right side of the ship. Unoccupied sailors did the same.

Hester glanced back and watched as the captain climbed into the aft rigging. He perched in the netting and shaded his eyes with one hand. She turned again to stare ahead in the same direction.

"Oh, dear Lord," Hester said, "can it be so?"

"I pray so, dear Hester. I pray so most sincerely."

They shaded their eyes with their hands. "I see nothing."

"The sailor is on a loftier perch than we," Elizabeth said.

Hester looked back to see men and boys running up from the hold to join the excitement. "I hope they leave us here until we see the land."

"Let them try to shove us back below," Elizabeth said with grim determination, but for the moment at least, none of the crew seemed interested in meeting the challenge.

Hester resigned herself to practice the virtue of patience. After years of separation, the endless weeks in the dark miserable hold, what did a little more time matter? Well, it did matter, every moment mattered, and she believed the Lord would understand.

Hester's children gathered round her, as did Elizabeth's, and the two women let them revel in the excitement without rebuke. Jacob seemed to be growing larger and heavier by the day, but at his insistence Hester lifted him up and propped him between herself and the rail for a better view.

The ship sailed on with nothing but sea ahead.

"Perhaps the lad was seeing things," Elizabeth said. "We all stand close to losing our minds, why not a sailor?"

"Now, Elizabeth, keep the faith."

"Talk about something."

"I beg your pardon?"

"Talk about something, Hester. Distract my mind, for pity's sake."

"Well..." Hester understood the need for diversion. Her friend did not want to break down in front of her children. Hester was not the only one anxious to embrace a long lost husband. "There was something you said a moment ago..."

"Yes?"

"We are not a sect," Hester said. "Our congregation. We are only poor Christians who want the liberty to govern our own church ourselves."

"My dear," Elizabeth said, keeping her eyes fixed to the fore. "If your people do not wish to bow the knee to the Church of England, that is none of my affair, nor my husband's. You have allowed us to join our fortunes to yours, and that is Christian enough for such as I. Ask a great bishop, however, and he would say you are a sect. There would be no better proof of the matter than a group of poor Christians wanting to govern their own church according their own principles. Having never been to England, child, you may not know this."

"I fled from France, and know their bishops' wrath, and their king's. But I would expect Protestant bishops to be more tolerant."

"Fat Protestant bishops are as fond of their prerogatives as any Roman. Poor Christians governing their own little congregation without answering to ecclesiastical authority?"

"We answer to God, and to His Word."

"You make revolution, Hester, and you do not know it."

"I suppose you are right."

The discussion went no further, cut off at the captain's shout, "Give the lad the coin!"

The ship's master saw land too.

CHAPTER 6

Forest and Fortress

They had not pulled very far up the river, using the oars, before Captain Standish spotted a good place to drag the shallop up onto the bank. Standish set Winslow to work with a branch, smoothing out the muddy footprints and drag marks leading up from the water. Though muttering under his breath against this childish game of war, Winslow performed the task compliantly enough. The others quickly cut down a quantity of brush with knives and a pair of hatchets, then covered the boat completely, disguising its hiding place among the trees.

Francis kept a discreet eye on the captain but saw nothing to complain of. He agreed with Standish on the necessity of taking every possible precaution. The Plymouth men had few dealings with the Massachusett tribe, who took no part in Massasoit Ousamequin's Wampanoag confederation. The Pilgrims had concluded a treaty of friendship with the latter almost as soon as they landed in late fall of 1620. The white men had subsequently learned how warfare among the so-called Indian tribes—a misnomer that tracked all the way back to Christopher Columbus—had been carried on since time immemorial, with raids and counter-raids, the stealing of women and children, and murderous conflicts over hunting grounds, fishing rights, the location of villages and cultivated fields, and sometimes over nothing at all save sheer hatred, revenge, or retribution for imaginary offenses great and small.

By the grace of God, the *Mayflower* landed at a time and place of relative stability and peace, thanks to the genuine statesmanship of Massasoit, who extended his customary tolerant policies toward the strange new pale-skinned arrivals. Considerable tension persisted between the Wampanoag and the Massachusett, however, exacerbated by the fact that the latter group had encountered an entirely different breed of white man in the persons of Weston and his gang, whom the Plymouth folk regarded, not without reason, as worthless idlers, fornicators, drunkards and thieves.

When Standish finally declared himself satisfied with the arrangements, he assembled the group.

"Very well, men," he said, "time's come to march, so light your matches."

The little company exchanged furtive glances of unspoken alarm. The muskets they carried could only be discharged by the application of fire. This fire was carried at the end of the match, a fuse composed of a length of rope or cord specially treated to burn very slowly, which each musketeer had to keep adjusting forward as it burned in the clamp at the end of the curving lever known as the serpentine. At the pull of the trigger, the burning end of the fuse would be plunged down through the touchhole into the gunpowder in the flash pan, which in turn ignited the main charge that propelled the ball out of the barrel. The gun could not be fired until the match had been lit from another source, which for the Plymouth militia was usually a recently invented tinderbox carried by at least one of the gun bearers, which Standish had fortunately snapped up in quantity along with the barrels of gunpowder and fifty muskets he had acquired in Europe, with every subsequent group of settlers under his instructions to bring along fifty to a hundred more, with powder, lead to melt into balls, fuses and tinderboxes. The long fuse cords were carried wrapped around each man's shoulder and lit at each end. In case the ignition of a shot blew out the business end of the fuse, it could be relit from the other end. Lighting the matches meant Standish wanted every man able to fire at a moment's notice.

"Come, come, gentlemen," Standish said, "our informer has given us warning about the Massachusett savages. We'd best be ready to shoot as the best guarantee we shan't have to."

True enough. Winslow, who refused to carry a weapon, looked primed for argument but held his tongue. Today all the other men carried tinderboxes, just in case, which they produced to strike a spark. Delano succeeded first, and the others lit from his flame.

Philip joked to Francis as they fired up their own matches last. "Perhaps we have to shoot some of your Englishmen also."

"God forbid."

"No?" Philip patted the coil of heavy rope he carried around his body in addition to his fuse, having brought it from the boat on the captain's instructions. "Perhaps we only hang them then."

"Please, Philip, this is not in the least funny."

Perhaps not, but one couldn't tell from the chuckling Frenchman.

* * *

Back in Plymouth, Governor William Bradford wrestled with anxiety and regret. If only he could have undertaken the mission himself… but that was impossible in light of his other responsibilities. Captain Standish was a good man, though rash, and his handpicked companions comprised the best the plantation had to offer, men of strength, courage, and spiritual maturity. Bradford could not afford to lose any of them, and he prayed for their safety on his knees.

Rising from his devotions, Bradford remained restive and unsettled. He consoled himself that God's power and willingness to answer prayer did not depend on the feelings of man, including the one doing the praying. Peace would come eventually as he sought the Lord's face. For now it was best to dive into work.

He left his house and sought out Doctor Samuel Fuller, a church deacon as well as the surgeon who had served as the colony's only medical officer since the beginning. The two men had been putting off the duty of going over the remaining supplies in the great storeroom up at the fort. Bradford thought the unpleasant task might occupy their troubled minds.

Bradford carried quill, ink and a scrap of vellum on which he took tiny meticulous notes as they went through the stores. The job completed, the two men sat down on barrels to ponder.

Fuller studied Bradford. "I know why we're here, Governor."

"Do you?"

"If we need to take in the Wessagusset men, you want to know if can we feed them."

"Can we?"

"Yes, indeed, provided they can eat gunpowder." Fuller gestured at the barrels stacked in the furthest corner from the outward walls. "We have plenty of that."

"Captain Standish's doing."

"He should have been in charge of buying the food as well, instead of those blockheads in London."

"The adventurers did what they thought best, to sustain their investment."

"Too bad they spent so much on English wheat seed, since they were told over and over it wouldn't grow in rocky soil."

"I know, I know."

In truth Bradford had little more respect for the expedition's London-based financial patrons than Fuller, but he felt a duty to defend their good name, out of propriety if nothing else. The congregation, weary from years of exile in Holland, fearful their children would grow up more Dutch than English, gratefully embraced investors willing to back them in forming a New World colony. They accepted entailing the profits of their own hard labors for years to come, assuming such gains should ever appear, which most of Bradford's people had long since begun to doubt.

"As long as we don't have to lie down in our graves because of their stupidities," Fuller said. "The blockheads are like all rich men, believing their judgment superior to that of all others."

The doctor had a point. The investors refused to entertain any suggestion from poorer men.

Two distinct types of moneyed blockhead—Fuller had used the term so often it sprang unbidden to Bradford's mind—sat on the London board. Each group shared the same prejudice but for different reasons. By far the greater faction consisted of wealthy merchants and bankers. In their view a chap with good sense should have been able to translate that wisdom into wealth, as they had. The tiny bloc of hereditary aristocrats simply had no patience for anyone with the arrogance and presumption to advise his betters.

Thus the adventurers could not be bothered to seek advice from anyone who had actually crossed the great ocean or had a go at planting a colony in unexplored wilderness.

The Pilgrim leadership, on the other hand, had read every published work on such matters as how to clear land or make contact with savages, interviewed anyone who might have anything worthwhile to say, and sought wisdom in prayer. Any thoughts or suggestions from them or pointed out from their researches, however, the financial adventurers dismissed as beneath contempt. In the hard school of actual experience, truth be told, all those books had proved as worthless and irrelevant as anything the investors had to say. Bradford suspected most of those authors were writing pure fantasy, to put a nice name to a collection of outright lies. If Bradford and the others survived, perhaps someday he ought to write an accurate account of such a colonizing endeavor. He had therefore begun to keep a secret journal that first freezing winter ashore, when everybody seemed to be dying.

In any case, before being dismissed from the meetings in London, the leadership had found themselves forced to accept the wealthy gentlemen's strictures and conditions in every particular. The poor believers were the ones who would be laying their lives on the line, but that counted for nothing against the all-powerful authority of money, without which the settlers could do nothing. If the adventurers picked up their bags of coin and walked away, the would-be colonizers could not make a move in any direction. The wealthy knew this and saw no reason to compromise their demands in the slightest. Those endless discussions going nowhere accounted for the *Mayflower* embarking so fatally late in the year. Once the exhausting debates finally concluded, the financiers would never have tolerated delay until the following spring, and truthfully neither would Bradford's own people. The brethren and their precious families had to get underway while they could.

"The wrath of God is one thing," Fuller went raving on, "the foolishness of man is something else entirely."

"Doctor, please."

"Forgive me, William. I do not mean to blaspheme, but these madmen in London almost drive me to it. Imagine, sending a ship loaded down with new colonists but no new provisions, and asking us to share our bounty with the new arrivals! Our bounty!"

"They won't make that mistake again. I wrote letters."

"We shall see." They both knew another ship was due soon and hoped against hope that Bradford's frantic epistles had achieved the desired effect.

"How is your chest of medicines?" Bradford said, changing the subject.

"Fairly bounteous. I re-supplied when that Dutch pirate dropped anchor here last year."

"Pirate?"

"All right, merchant then. I was defining the man by his prices."

Bradford was touched, having known nothing of the transaction until this moment. Since Dr. Fuller had not come to the council, he must have used some small hoard of his own money, hard earned but not bounteous by any man's definition.

CHAPTER 7

A Contrary Opinion

Captain Standish himself walked "the point of the spear" along the forest trail. He had been hired to lead this lot of lollygaggers, and lead them he would.

Francis glanced back at Philip, who took the equally responsible position of bringing up the rear. Certain brethren regarded the easily amused Frenchman as too lighthearted and irresponsible for such a trust, but Bradford and Standish saw the true depths of the man. Delano might break into laughter too readily for a more rigid English Protestant, but for now he embodied vigilance on two feet, peering round into the shadowed woodlands in all directions, walking backwards every few feet to keep an eye behind them. He happened to catch Francis's look and flashed his friend a quick grin, but his eyes moved on in unceasing search. Delano's example made Francis more diligent in his own looking about.

Francis kept his ears peeled too, as Hobomok had taught him. He heard nothing but the sounds of the forest, singing birds and chattering squirrels, the breeze rustling the budding leaves in the trees. Sudden silence or the song of the wind on its own would portend danger.

"Captain Standish?" Philip spoke in a low voice.

Something in his tone alerted their leader to put up his hand for a halt.

"Gentlemen, let's stop to rest for a moment." He spoke quietly as well. "And, please, don't make any sudden moves. Yes, Monsieur Delano?"

Philip approached the captain as casually as he could manage. "Sir, we're being followed."

* * *

After they finished taking stock, Bradford and Dr. Fuller paid a brief visit to the recovering David Thompson, who had nothing further to add to his story from the day before. Then they headed out to have a look at the fields. Some of the hardest-working men were out on the mission with Standish. Their absence magnified the lethargy of those left behind. The best remaining workers strove to keep the others going. Upon reaching the work line Bradford and Fuller stopped to chat with two of the most diligent, Richard Warren and a young man named John Alden, a newlywed thanks to the first romance to flower among the first comers aboard the *Mayflower*.

The four men had not been talking long when Mrs. Taylor walked past, herding her children back toward the upper gate. The widow lady and her flock had arrived the previous year on the *Fortune* and thus had no memory of the death and deprivation suffered by the *Mayflower* passengers during that first harsh winter, nor of the abundant harvest of 1621. She knew only the failed harvest of last year, for which she blamed everyone in Plymouth, not least her late husband who had brought his family to this vile wilderness but not lived to suffer the consequences.

"Hello, children," Bradford said. "Out for a walk, Mrs. Taylor?"

"We are that, Governor," she said. "I had hoped to see encouraging progress in these fields, but that is scarcely the case. This is work for stronger, more experienced men, and for oxen if we had any."

Bradford glanced at the position of the sun, well short of midday. "Perhaps the other ladies could use some help inside the walls."

"Everything is a great hardship, I tell you. You ask too much of us, sir. First we must go in out of this heat, to rest. Come, children."

The men watched her march the family back to the fort.

"Two weeks ago she was complaining about the cold," Fuller said.

"Perhaps if Mister Taylor had lived," Warren said, "the woman would be more agreeable."

"No, he would have run away into the forest."

"Next the men will be saying we ask too much of *them*," the governor sighed.

"Oh, that's already happening, I assure you," Warren said, "only out of your hearing."

"You have no idea how many come to me every week," Fuller said, "looking for any ground to excuse themselves."

"Their best medicine would be food," Bradford said. "The problem is mostly hunger."

"It may be," Warren said, "our people need their hearts fed far more than their bellies."

"I do not take your meaning, Mister Warren."

"I was a merchant by trade, Governor Bradford, before I joined my fate with yours, and I have spent many years observing human nature. Our problem here springs from holding these fields in common, 'for the community' as is said. However much work a man puts in, he will take back only what he needs for himself and his family. If the land were allotted on a private basis, so that every family tilled its own soil, then people could make some reasonable return on the sweat of their brows."

Young Alden looked surprised. "But surely such a base consideration would not apply to good Christian people!"

"I fear you betray your innocence, John."

"But, sir, the saints in Jerusalem held all things in common, in the Acts of the Apostles."

"Yes, and as I recall my New Testament, the rest of the Mediterranean was always taking up a collection for the support of the saints in Jerusalem."

"Enough, gentlemen, please." Bradford turned to Warren. "You know what you suggest is not permitted."

"Roman outposts used to have a saying, sir, in olden days. 'We are here, and the emperor is far away.'"

Squinting into the distance, Bradford changed the subject. "Look, there is the little Cooke boy, chopping away at a great stump all by himself, whilst his father puts himself in danger on our behalf."

"We shall go help the lad," Warren said.

The import of Bradford's words brought John Alden up short. "But surely, Governor Bradford, Mister Cooke and the others are not in very great danger, I trust."

CHAPTER 8

On the Horizon

The two Massachusett braves had picked up the party of white men as soon as they moved away from the riverbank and began thrashing noisily through the forest. Pecksuot, a warrior famous among the People for his gigantic stature, suggested using tomahawks to knock holes in the bottom of their hidden canoe. With a grunt his friend Wituwamat, a brave who inspired far greater fear for his sheer ferocity and great cunning, dismissed the idea as a mere boy's prank, unworthy of a warrior and serving no purpose.

They followed at a discreet distance, keeping the Bone Men in sight. Though the whites made a constant display of looking about in every direction, they never appeared to catch sight of their pursuers, a source of quiet amusement for the two braves.

Pecksuot knew Wituwamat would dearly love to attack with bow and arrows. Victory of two against seven would mark a great coup, but both warriors could see the five armed whites carried fire in their thundersticks. Knowing how much damage those weapons could do, they were content to follow, keeping the party under close watch.

Pecksuot understood why Wituwamat, though his hatred of the whites exceeded that of any other among the People, would hesitate to start a war on his own. The solitary murder of a lone English was one thing, the death of seven quite another. Such a step required reflection, deliberation, a decision by full tribal council. They did not have so much as initial approval from their own village chieftain and elders. The People would have to speak for war with a mighty voice—unless the blundering whites managed to start it themselves. That unspoken hope provided every incentive to search out what the pale fools were up to.

* * *

Returning from the fields, Bradford and Fuller were just reaching the upper gate when they witnessed a commotion on top of the fort. Since the frightened Scotsman's report, Standish had doubled the daylight watch. Perhaps bored with endlessly scrutinizing the surrounding forest, one sentry stood gazing out over the bay. Bradford was just at the point of shouting up an admonition when the man came alert, apparently staring at the ocean on the eastern horizon which on a clear day could be made out from the parapet, overtop the trees on the Cape Cod fishhook. He summoned his mate and pointed. The second sentry peered, then also came alive with excitement, bobbing his head up and down.

The first sentry hurried to edge of the stockade and shouted over Bradford and Fuller's heads for everyone to hear, "Sail, ho! Sail! A sail!"

Bradford underwent an involuntary shiver, as if the cry infused the air itself with new excitement and limitless potentiality. A heady moment of stunned repercussion crept dreamily past while the outcry went on and on. Then of a sudden all those not working in the fields—women and children, the aged and the ill—came hurrying and hobbling out of their nooks and hiding places. They shouted for confirmation from the parapet, then began beating a path down Town Street and out the lower gate toward the rocky shore.

Bradford and Fuller moved where they could gaze more easily into the northeast, toward the distant blue expanse where the larger bay merged into the sea.

"I can't see the least sign of a ship," the doctor said. "Not from here."

"Then it probably won't be here for hours. Everyone might as well keep working."

"Yes, of course. Good luck with that."

Bradford shook his head in resignation, then turned round to watch as word spread among the toilers in the fields. These tiny figures also began hurrying toward the shore, the responsible among them shouldering their tools, others flinging axes and hoes to the ground.

"Sam, find somebody with an ounce of sanity, and get a wheelbarrow out there to gather up the tools. Preferably before they sprout legs and walk off into the forest." Both men knew how badly the Indians coveted English tools, especially the big axes.

"Yes, Governor."

Fuller whistled off to perform this duty as Bradford sighed.

* * *

The last workers to receive the news were Richard Warren, John Alden and young John Cooke, cutting and chopping away on that huge stump at the edge of the tree line west of Fort Hill. A sudden change in wind direction allowed them to hear loud shouting in the distance without being able to understand the words. They turned to discover everyone in the fields running away from them toward Plymouth except for a few brave souls lingering to gather up armloads of abandoned tools. One of these spotted them and beckoned frantically.

John Cooke's heart leapt in his chest. There had never been an Indian attack since that one grim little skirmish when the first boatload of scouts went ashore from the *Mayflower*. He suddenly wished they had not strayed so far from the walls of the settlement. If the unfriendly Massachusett from miles north set upon them, he and the two men would never make it back alive.

Another distant man set down a wheelbarrow full of tools and ran partway down the slope in their direction, where he stopped, cupped his hands around his mouth and shouted.

"What is it?" Warren said. "Can you make it out?"

They listened intently.

"A ship!" the distant figure cried. "They say there's a ship coming!"

The three of them looked at one other in astonishment.

"A ship!" Warren said. "If it's English, it could be my dear wife!"

"And my mother!" John said.

They took a firm grip on their own tools and ran for the town.

"No more work this day," Alden said, sounding not at all displeased at the prospect.

CHAPTER 9

Death in the Swamp

The trail to Wessagusset led first through a series of hillocks in the area immediately bordering the river, then down into a dark and tangled marshland. The knowledge of being followed grew more oppressive and frightening with every slippery step. The treacherous footing forced the indefatigable Captain Standish to slow his pace, though he put on an outward show of bravado for the benefit of their shadowy pursuers as much as for his men. Francis Cooke felt thankful to ease up, whatever the reason. The pathway lay across muddy embankments barely protruding out of the muck and became quite difficult to discern in many places. One false step might sink a man into a bottomless morass.

Quicksand had been a fact of life in low-lying Holland, with nearly the whole Netherlands reclaimed from the sea. Especially out near the dykes, where the seepage of the tides did its work, ground as solid as a cobblestone street one day could be transformed overnight into an unsuspected gateway to death. People occasionally disappeared without a trace, though never anyone connected with the English exiles, praise God, and Francis wanted to keep that testimony unblemished. He once heard an educated sea captain declare quicksand could be found in all corners and countries of the wide world, lying everywhere in wait for the unwary. Francis felt a special horror of its menace.

By sheer coincidence Francis was pondering all this when the cry went up. Standish had stopped in his tracks and stood staring at something a short distance off the trail. The outcry came from the two men behind him, who followed his eyes and saw what the captain had spotted first.

"Is that a white man?" Standish said.

Francis and Philip hurried forward to look for themselves.

About three yards off the trail they saw the body of a man sunk up to the level of his chest in the mud, scant feet from a log which jutted out into the swamp from the point where its toppled trunk crossed the trail. The dead man made a hideous sight, bearded mouth wide open as if in a silent scream, black eye sockets fixed on the overarching trees that barred all sight of the heavens. The corpse had been there for some time. Insects and decay had long since begun their horrendous work. As Francis quickly looked away he heard one of the other men retching behind him.

Edward Winslow, the supposed weakling of the company, took action first. He walked out on the log and squatted down to take a close look at the dead man's face.

"It is a white man. One of the traders from Wessagusset. I've seen him before." The others shuddered at this challenging feat of recognition. "He must have fallen in and not had the strength to pull himself out."

Which meant the man died a slow death from starvation, screaming and crying for help until his strength gave out. A more horrible fate, Francis realized, than the quicker agony of choking in the bog.

"Poor fellow," Winslow went on, shaking his head. "I wonder what he was chasing, to move off the path. Some morsel of food, I doubt not."

"Unless the savages put him there," Standish said.

Delano knelt down to examine the ground for footprints. "No, captain, there are no tracks except ours."

"Why do we not see the dead man's? Savages know how to wipe the ground clean as we do!"

"We need to pull him out," Francis said. "Give the poor man a Christian burial."

"If he worked for Weston," Standish said, "he was probably a heathen. Why not just tip him over in the bog?"

Francis overrode the gasps. "Please, captain. We cannot do that to a fellow countryman."

"Oh, very well. We have more than reason enough to show respect." Standish lowered his voice. "Perhaps our faithful Indian pursuers are the very ones who did this thing."

* * *

Suddenly, as Wituwamat and Pecksuot watched, all the Bone Men except their leader and the man on the log jumped with fright as if they heard a war cry from a party of braves. They spun about, pointing their thundersticks as they peered ferociously into the darkness of the swamp.

Wituwamat grinned and whispered to Pecksuot, "They are looking for us."

"Now I know we are safe."

They managed to stifle their glee, and after a few moments of frantically looking about, the whites turned their attention back to the dead.

The black-haired man with the most colorful clothing handed his thunderstick to another tall man, then removed from about his shoulder one of the long thick English ropes so coveted by the People. He tied some kind of loop and crept out onto the log as close to the body as possible. Balancing over the quicksand, he shook out the rope. After a few tries he managed to throw the coil in such a manner that it fell around the dead man's neck and one shoulder. The black-hair squatted down and manipulated the cord until it slipped under the outstretched dead arm. He drew the knot tight, then quickly walked back up the length of the log.

All the English took a hand and began to pull. At first nothing budged as they strained at the rope. The two braves could barely contain the impulse to roar with laughter at the whites' lack of strength. Then they heard a sucking sound, astonishingly loud to be overheard from the distance where they watched. The party of English began to move steadily back. The dead body slowly emerged from the bog, and in a moment they pulled him up onto the trail.

Still curious, the braves watched as the Bone Men used hatchets to strip branches from nearby saplings, and in no time they were rigging a litter exactly of the type which the People used to carry their own dead and wounded.

Wituwamat caught Pecksuot's eye with a hard look. "Someone has been teaching them."

CHAPTER 10

First Reunions

Hester Cooke and Elizabeth Warren, their children, and most of the other passengers crowded the rail.

"Can you see?" Elizabeth said. "I cannot see a thing."

Hester wiped her eyes, laughing. "Perhaps we'd be able to see, if we could but stop crying."

"Yes, but praise God these are tears of joy."

Hester squinted for a long time, then pointed. "Look as far as you can... On a hill yonder, above the water... There, beyond the first line of trees... Methinks I see a square object."

"Really?" Elizabeth took a long time to find it. "Perhaps. It looks so tiny from here."

"Francis wrote they were planning to build a fort at the top of a hill."

"Is that what it is?"

"I don't know. Could the ship's master be bringing us right into Plymouth? How might he achieve such a feat?"

Hester's nine-year-old daughter Jane piped up. "Mother, it's called navigation!"

Hester hugged the girl extravagantly. "Indeed it is, my darling. Hooray for navigation!"

"Don't ye believe it, my dears," a crusty old sailor rumbled nearby, a dignified sort who had taken no part in the earlier crudities.

"Favored with a calm crossing, what we'd a done in the usual case is strike land, then sail up or down this coast a-searchin' for the right harbor. Taken days or weeks to find the place. If that thar be ye New Plymouth, 'tis only luck. And luck of such nature I've never seen."

"Then it was the hand of God," Jane said.

"After that last storm, little lady," the old man mused, shaking his head, "mayhap ye are right."

* * *

John took up a position just outside the lower gate while the others crowded the shoreline. The sun slowly crossed the sky toward the west. The ship, a mere speck on the horizon at first, tacked against the winds to sail a course into the bay. For once the colony had something to think about other than food, the lack of it and their hunger for it. John heard no complaints from the younger children, who joined their elders in watching without attempting to steal time for play. From atop the fort the leather-lunged lookout confirmed at last that the vessel flew English colors.

The anxious time eventually passed, and the ship trimmed sail as she came in from the sea and crossed the northern edge of the Cape Cod waters into Plymouth Bay. She slowly approached Plymouth Harbor, sounding for good haven in deep water before dropping anchor some distance out. That's when John ran down to the water's edge to join the others.

He could see movement aboard the craft, but she sat too far away for those on shore to identify the people lining the side of the ship. These waved excitedly, and John knew the passengers must have been released from their foul-smelling captivity below. What a difference it made to have a bona fide destination, a place to land. When the *Mayflower* had first dropped anchor, out at the pointed barb of the

Cape Code Fishhook, John and the others faced endless weeks of further suffering in the crowded hold.

Their scouting parties had eventually fixed the site of New Plymouth here, at a place deemed accursed by the Indians, where scant years earlier some mysterious disease had wiped out their late friend Squanto's village to the last soul. During the great die-off of the first winter, many speculated whether pestilence yet lingered at Plymouth. Doctor Fuller insisted their problem was lack of food and effective shelter against the bitter cold. By a disastrously unfortunate chain of circumstances, the *Mayflower* had landed in November, just in time for the onset of winter, with nary a shelter other than the ship itself and what they were able to construct ashore with their own inexperienced hands. That atrocious timing, John now understood, so costly in beloved lives, explained why the *Fortune* and now the *Anne* had set sail much earlier in the year.

Those ashore saw new stirring on deck as ship's hands lowered one of the boats. Crewmen scrambled down a webbing of rope, then assisted wobbly but enthusiastic passengers climbing down behind them, including three women but no children. The sailing master boarded last, discernible at this distance by the deference he received from all. No doubt he craved to hurry in and speak to the governor, but at least he had the decency to fill out this first boatload with anxious new settlers. Once he sat down, the oarsmen pulled for the land.

John strained his eyes along with everybody else, but no one could recognize anybody as the distance began to close. They would have to be patient a little longer, John more than most, for his mother would certainly not come ashore leaving any of her little ones on the ship. He knew her heart if not her face.

The oarsmen leapt out and dragged the boat up on the beach. The ship's master alighted first. Governor Bradford came forward to shake hands, and the two men engaged at once in conferral of the deepest solemnity. Bradford beckoned, and Dr. Fuller stepped out of the throng to join them. John turned his attention back to the boat.

Most of the passengers in this group were church elders, heads of families who had left their wives and children on board the Anne while they came ashore to shake hands and renew acquaintance with their fellow brethren of the old Scrooby congregation in Nottinghamshire. Of the three women, two were older ladies joining husbands, and their scenes of re-acquaintance were scarcely more emotional than the handshakes and occasional backslaps among the elders.

John's attention immediately riveted on the third lady in the boat, a quite striking young woman in her late twenties. The steersman displayed understandable if somewhat scandalous favoritism by sweeping the lady up and handing her down to a brawny oarsman, who cheerfully carried her ashore to spare her feet and skirts from a soaking.

This caught the attention of Governor Bradford, who broke away and ran to her, snatching off his hat. A sigh went up on every side as they closed the distance between them, but the governor only kissed her hand. It startled John to see a Plymouth man engage in such an aristocratic formality, but after Bradford kissed her hand, he clung to it. They gazed into one another's eyes, engaging in hurried, soft-spoken conversation. Then suddenly she threw her arms around him, and he returned the embrace, burying his face in her hair and cloak along with whatever embarrassment he might feel at this very public display of affection. The witnesses laughed, rejoicing for their governor's happiness, something all the people of Plymouth felt he well deserved, except possibly a few of the most rigid.

John knew who Alice Southworth was as well as any of the grown-ups. Word had gotten around how the governor had written the young lady to propose marriage, some thought with unseemly haste, after he became a widower. The letter had obviously found a willing heart, for here she was.

The death of the governor's wife had hung like a black cloud over Bradford and the rest of the colony ever since it occurred. The first death in the new land, it was the one people never spoke of, including Bradford himself, who had never uttered his first wife's name since and probably never would the rest of his days.

John recalled the incident with heartache. The *Mayflower* was riding on the dark waters of its first anchorage at the northeastern extremity of Cape Cod bay. When the passengers were allowed to come up from the hold for air, the only prospect before them was a bleak landscape already wintry and forbidding, a miserable trade for the cozy cities of the Netherlands. Bradford had gone off with the exploring party, which disappeared for days. The anxiety drove his wife Dorothy, already fearful and weak, into a yawning abyss of despair. One night she somehow managed to make it out to the deck, where she flung herself into the sea. She drowned before the sailors could manage a rescue. Ironically her husband returned safe with the others the very next day.

The colony never fully recovered from the blow, much less the governor himself, despite unspoken agreement never to discuss the matter openly. Adults sought to shield their children from the truth, though the latter found out everything almost immediately in the manner of children throughout the ages. A silence of respectability was soon enforced upon them with appropriate rigor, and now they never spoke of it either, except very rarely and secretly among themselves. Indeed the very youngest did not remember anything about it. The colonists and their governor hoped the tale would die with them. The poor woman's suicide left a black mark against their

Christian witness, most seemed to feel, a tragedy best forgotten if only it could be.

The previous summer John had been out in the woods working with his father felling trees when he chose to bring up the troubling subject.

"Father, do you think Mrs. Bradford went to Heaven?" he had burst out. The question had troubled him ever since her death, and his father was the only one he dared to ask.

Francis set his big axe down, made sure no one else was around to hear.

"Aye, son," he said, "methinks she did."

John's heart leapt with surprise and hope. He had always liked the timid Mrs. Bradford, and he feared a bad answer, which he would almost certainly have received from any of the elders, probably including Bradford himself.

"The apostle says nothing can separate us from the love of Christ," Francis explained, "which includes the sins and foolish actions of the believer, provided he or she is a true believer, which only God or oneself can know."

"Could a true believer take her own life?"

"There were some in the Old Testament who fell on their swords. Did they lose their redemption? We have no clear scripture that they did."

"King Saul was a bad man."

"He became a bad man, indeed, though he started out a man of faith, prophesying with the prophets. At the end, he and his armor-bearer committed self-slaughter after losing a battle. I do not believe that God wished them to do it, but they did."

"Mrs. Bradford hadn't lost a battle."

"Had she not? There are many battles in life, John, other than those against flesh and blood enemies. I believe Mrs. Bradford lost a battle against despair and sadness and worry. Terrible afflictions they are."

"We all despaired that first winter, Father, but we did not murder ourselves."

"No, praise God we did not, but neither have we the right to judge the weakness of that poor woman. The Tempter comes in many forms, sometimes as an angel of light, sometimes as the harbinger of terrible darkness. The grip of despondency can squeeze the life out of a poor soul. I've seen it happen, and I believe it happened to poor Mrs. Bradford. It led her to commit a great sin, but our Savior died for all our sins, past, present, and future, the great as well as the small. She may have died in a moment of weak faith, terribly weak faith, but no man can say she never had faith in Christ to save her soul, for that only takes a little mustard seed of faith."

John brightened. "There is reason to hope, then?"

"Every reason, chiefly that we have a great God, loving and forgiving as well as full of justice."

"But I have heard said a suicide should not be buried in consecrated ground."

Francis waved the objection aside. "Papist sophistry, carried over into the Church of England. All ground is consecrated to the One who created it."

"Then you don't think...?" John hadn't known how to finish the question.

His father laid a comforting hand on his shoulder. "The mind can become infirm as well as the body. The afflictions of life drove that poor lady to her desperate condition, set aflame by whatever fears and torments the enemy of our souls had sent into her mind. We'd best keep trusting in the mercy of God, as she did in all the best days of her life. The God of all the earth, will He not do right? The Lord will sort these matters out in mercy and justice, never fear."

They had never spoken of the matter again, though John had on a few occasions passed his father's thoughts along to other children, who found comfort in them too.

* * *

The trudging militiamen took turns carrying the litter bearing the dead man, an oppressive weight in more ways than one. The sickening stench of death was overpowering, and they lacked a blanket to cover the wretched fellow. Edward Winslow had made as to cover the body with his cloak, but the captain forbad it for reasons none could fathom and all resented. Standish insisted on taking his turn as a bearer, however, which no officer of any European army would do under any circumstances.

Standish was marching once more at the head of the column when they came upon Wessagusset. The whole group stopped as one, astonished at what lay before them.

The trading post stood in the midst of heavy woodland, which had not been cut away to clear a field of fire in case of attack. It consisted of a poorly built central building of wattle and daub rather than clapboard, thrown together at the bottom of a hill rather than on top, no doubt for ease of carrying water from the nearby stream. This unimpressive edifice lay surrounded by a small collection of rough shacks, hovels so primitive they made Indian dwellings seem triumphs of civilization by comparison. The traders had apparently started to construct walls for a stockade around the whole encampment but soon abandoned the project.

As for the traders themselves, Francis could see no sentries posted, no human activity of any kind. Then he noticed curious figures on the ground. At first he mistook them for odd shadows, deformities in the terrain, rocks perhaps. When one shape moved slightly, his eyes quickly sorted out the truth. The figures were men, sprawled out upon the earth. Francis felt a sharp pang of fear in his chest, the blood-freezing apprehension that they had arrived too late, that the Massachusett had already attacked. The feeling passed as the other bodies began to move, heads languidly turning in the direction of the intruders. Francis also realized that in the aftermath of a massacre some of the slain would be lying out in the bright sunlight. These bodies all lay or sat in the deepest shadow available, places of relief from the unseasonable heat.

Standish ordered his men forward. The shadow figures bestirred themselves, clambering to their feet. Francis had never seen a group of men so starving, listless, and devoid of the spark of life. Resentful eyes glared at the newcomers.

As Standish strode up the Wessagusset contingent drifted together in the manner of frightened sheep scenting a wolf.

"Don't you men have any sentries posted?" he raged. "We walked right up on top of you without so much as a shout of warning!"

One of the apathetic creatures scratched himself. "We wasn't expecting no visitors."

The fuming captain brought the column to a halt. "Is Mister Weston here about? We have matters of importance to discuss."

Another man answered from further back. "Weston's out wandering in the forest. Has been for weeks."

The statement confirmed the Scotsman's report, though Francis knew as well as Standish that it would have eased their unpleasant duty if Weston had happened to return in the interval since Thompson's flight.

"So who's in charge here in Weston's absence, if I may inquire?" Standish said.

Uneasy silence reigned until one tallish ragamuffin reluctantly separated himself from the pack. "That would be meself, I suppose."

"And your name, sir?" Standish said.

"John Sanders, acting governor of Wessagusset—in Mister Weston's absence."

"And I am Captain Miles Standish, of Plymouth."

As if they didn't know, thought Francis, quite certain the captain's reputation had preceded him.

Standish signaled the bearers to set the litter on the ground. When none of the Wessagusset men displayed the slightest interest, he stalked back and gestured at the corpse.

"Is this man one of yours?"

Sanders leaned forward a bit, then nodded. "Aye, going by what's left, that be Deaky Jones. We was wondering what happened to him."

Standish dripped scorn. "You were *wondering* what happened to him?"

"Aye, he set out one day and never come back."

"We found the man mired in the mud, not two miles from here. Don't any of you ever take a walk?"

Heads shook all around. One wall-leaning sluggard spoke up from the rear. "Nay, it's much too dangerous. As you can see."

"Poor devil," Sanders said.

While the Plymouth men were yet cringing at the callow response they heard the loud scream of a woman's voice.

"Deekee!... Deekee!..."

An Indian woman came running out the door of the shadowy storehouse at full cry, followed by two others.

The first woman flung herself down and gathered the dead man into a desperate embrace. "Deekee!... Deekee!... Deekee!" she continued to weep, more softly now.

Winslow caught Francis's eye. "It appears someone will miss him, poor soul."

The other two Indian women knelt beside their friend, supporting her with their arms and lamentations.

"I wonder why *she* never went out searching for him," Francis said to Philip too low for others to hear.

"Perhaps she was not free to do so," the Frenchman replied softly, with a pointed look at the filthy ruffians grouped behind Sanders.

The cries of the women had become too much for the acting governor, and he stepped forward, attempting to pull them away from the body. "Come on, now! That's enough of this racket! Get away, you wenches, give us some room here!"

The other Indian women attempted to drag the weeping girl off. She quickly broke free and scurried back to the dead man.

Sanders relented trying to interfere. "I suppose we have to dig a hole for him."

"Ah, Guv'ner," somebody in the crowd complained, "nobody round 'ere's got the strength to dig a 'ole!"

By now Captain Standish's exasperation had swollen to volcanic proportions. "We'll dig the hole," he roared. "Just show us where!"

* * *

Waiting to be rowed in took hours, delay all the more unbearable after the endless weeks at sea, but finally Hester Cooke and Elizabeth Warren sat in the ship's longboat with all of their children and possessions. Refusing to be separated had delayed their transport, but both mothers remained adamant on the matter. Now they moved forward at last, scanning the beach for familiar faces.

The weary sailors pulled at the oars, and the waiting figures ashore began to come into better focus.

"Look how thin is everyone," Hester said, her grasp of the English language loosening somewhat, as always happened at times of overwhelming emotion. "Nothing but—how you say?—the skin and the bones."

"And see the pathetic rags they're wearing," Elizabeth said. "Was there no one left in this colony who could ply a needle and thread?"

"Nor cook either."

"Perhaps they had nothing to cook."

Hester waved a hand at the greening hills and budding forests. "In this fertile land? There is always something to cook, the problem is persuading stubborn Englishmen to eat it."

Elizabeth chuckled in spite of growing anxiety. "We English are creatures of habit, are we not, Hester?"

"As you say."

"Do you see your husband and son?"

"Not yet, not yet."

"I do not see my Richard either."

* * *

The next approaching boatload held several women and a number of small children. John moved to the water's edge, where he peered out at the boat and instantly recognized his mother as the young woman seated in the midst with an older women on one side and her arm around a small boy on the other—his little brother Jacob, no doubt. John's heart jumped high and carried his whole body along. Hopping up and down, he began waving with both arms. His mother spotted him at once, bounding up so quickly she almost tumbled out of the boat, but the other lady grabbed her arm and pulled her back down.

"There is my son," he could hear his mother shouting. "My son John! John, John!"

After all those hours of worrying John and his mother had recognized one another at a single glance. No wonder Jesus taught

His disciples not to take thought for the morrow or the problems thereof. John filed the lesson away for future reference.

He splashed back and forth at the edge of the water, oblivious to anything except the approaching boat. Suddenly Richard Warren appeared at his side and waded up to his knees in the water.

Now the lady next to his mother took her turn screaming and jumping while the smiling Hester applied a restraining hand. "There's my husband!" the lady cried. "Richard! Richard!"

Mister Warren waved calmly, but John knew the gladness in his heart.

In a few moments the sailors alighted near shore and began to lift out the women and children. Hester fought off the brawny oarsman and splashed through the water with Jacob in her arms. She set the little boy down on the pebbled shore and swept her older son into a tight embrace.

John threw his arms around her and pressed his face into her neck. He felt the sting of tears in his eyes as he heard the familiar voice.

"My son, my son," she said, pressing her lips against his face again and again.

"Mother," he managed to say. "Mother."

Finally she pulled herself back, keeping her hands on his shoulders as she scrutinized him. He saw two little girls—his sisters— latch onto Jacob and stand shyly waiting behind their mother.

"Thou hast grown so tall, John," Hester said. "But so thin and ragged."

"Yes, Mother... it has been... difficult."

John became aware of Mister Warren again, off to one side where he stood wreathed in a seething mass of weeping, clinging, hugging females, the wife and five daughters he had spoken of constantly for the last three years. One Warren girl was standing back by now, however, who looked to be about John's own age or perhaps a year younger. She was openly staring, not at her father but directly at *John.* Puzzled and uncomfortable, he turned his attention quickly back to his own family.

"John," Hester said, "where is thy father?"

"Out on expedition, with Captain Standish."

"But he is alive? He is well?"

"Yes, Mother, Father will be back shortly, perhaps tomorrow."

"Praise God!" Sounding immensely relieved, Hester turned to the other children. "Jane, Hester, Jacob—do you remember your big brother, John?"

The two girls nodded bashfully, but five-year-old Jacob shook his head from side to side.

"Jacob, you were too little to remember John," Hester said, "but now you may renew your acquaintance."

"Where is our father?" Jacob said, staring at his newfound brother.

"He is out in the forest, on a mission with Captain Standish."

"But he will be safe?" Hester said, sounding apprehensive again.

"Quite safe, Mother. Captain Standish says our father is one of the best members of our militia!"

"Does he carry a gun?" Jacob asked.

"Certainly, Jacob. Our father is an excellent shot, one of the best Captain Standish has trained with the musket."

"Do you know how to shoot?"

"Of course he doesn't shoot, Jacob," Hester said. "John may be a big brother to you and your sisters, but he is only eleven."

"But I do shoot, Mother! Captain Standish taught Father, and Father taught me!" Noting Hester's concerned look, John hastened to add, "All the menfolk must learn. We need to be able to shoot for game, and for our protection."

"Surely the protecting hand of God counts for more in keeping His people safe than a gun," Hester said.

"Certainly, Mother, but Captain Standish says God gives some of us a good eye and a steady hand so we can shoot straight, and that is the best protection of all."

"Can I learn too?" Jacob said, impervious to Hester's disapproval.

Before she could reply William Bradford walked up with Alice Southworth on his arm. The governor doffed his hat. "Mrs. Cooke."

Hester curtsied. "Mister Bradford…"

"Please accept my profoundest regret for your husband's absence at such a happy moment. A matter of duty."

"My son was telling me."

"Francis and the others should be back in a day or two, no more."

"Knowing he is alive and well—it means more than I can say." Tears welled up in Hester's eyes, and the sight of them seemed to affect Bradford.

"John will show you to your house," Bradford said huskily. "If you require help of any description, please do not hesitate to tell me or any other member of the council." He bowed to her.

"Thank you, Mister Bradford. You are most kind."

As Bradford and Alice walked away, John knew his mother would do anything to avoid adding to the governor's burdens.

CHAPTER 11

Burial Party

The Plymouth men filled in Deaky Jones's grave with four rusty shovels acquired from the traders. Francis and the others fumed with outrage that none of the Wessagusset men attended the burial, not even Sanders, perhaps fearful of being saddled with some of the work. From the trading post only the three Indian women bore witness. The first girl tried to throw herself into the grave with her dead lover, but Winslow gently took hold, speaking soothing words in her own tongue, and was able to draw her back. She stood by weeping quietly, clinging to Edward as the other women helped bear her up.

Some distance away the two Massachusett braves who had been following since near the riverbank watched all this from hiding.

Pecksuot gestured toward the trading post, where the resident whites could be seen passing around a large jug. "These English drink strong water while their friend is buried."

"They drink strong water continually," Wituwamat said. "They poison themselves, and they seek to poison the People also."

"The strong water is good... sometimes."

"Do not drink it, my brother. It will make you weak and stupid, that they may slay you."

While he yet spoke, Wituwamat perceived how the leader of the scouting party regarded the other white men's laziness and drinking with a ferocity of contempt to match his own. Perhaps the Red Hair bore watching.

"Slay me? These cowardly English? Ha!"

Pecksuot burst out this last a little too loudly. Both braves hunkered down in the brush, but none of the whites so much as glanced in their direction. The pale-skinned invaders carried on, whether drinking or digging, as unobservant as ever.

* * *

Philip Delano held a rough cross fashioned of slender kindling logs at the head of the grave. Francis pounded it into the earth with his spade. The Plymouth men stood for a long moment in silence, broken only by weeping of the Indian woman.

"All right then," Standish said, ready to walk away.

"Someone should speak a blessing," Winslow said.

Philip gestured in the direction of the trading post. "They are the ones who should do it. He was their friend."

"They busy themselves with weightier matters," Standish said dryly.

"Someone should do it," Winslow insisted.

Standish nodded at Francis, already standing conveniently at the traditional minister's position at the head of the grave.

"Mister Cooke, if you please... A little prayer or something."

Francis glanced at Winslow, who nodded agreement, sweeping off his hat with the others as they bowed their heads. Francis followed suit.

"Our Father, we commit into Thy hands this our fellow countryman, whom we did not know. Yet Thou didst know him, Lord, as Thou knowest every one of us. We most earnestly hope that Mister Jones found mercy by trusting in Thy Son, though he did so only in the hour of his extremity. Indeed, as Thou art the One who inhabits eternity and didst create all worlds and time, I would go so far as to pray Thou shouldst move through the barrier of days and hours to make this so, for Thou art Merciful and Almighty to save, and no encumbrance can stand before Thee. Receive then this poor man's spirit into Thy heavenly courts for Jesus' sake, we pray in Christ's name. Amen."

"Amen!" Standish thundered. He clomped his hat on his head and marched back toward the traders as the others murmured their more restrained amens.

As Francis looked up, his eyes rested on Winslow and the Indian woman. Remarkably, she looked oddly comforted. Winslow nodded affably, Philip grinned while adjusting his hat, but the other Plymouth men were staring at him.

"You have some strange ideas, brother," one of them said.

"God is not a slave to time as we are, my brother, He is its Master and Creator. Prove me wrong from scripture," Francis said, "and I'll change my mind."

CHAPTER 12

Inventory

Hester and Mrs. Warren had come ashore with heavy trunks, one for each of their families, carefully supervised and protected by the women over the long course of the voyage. Hester was not about to let hers out of sight now. Once the sailors wrestled it to land without a ruinous dip in the surf, she took Governor Bradford up on his offer. Soon two rough bruisers in their mid-teens, the more diminutive but feisty Edward Doty and the taller and stronger-looking Edward Leister, were carrying the trunk up the hill. The latter boy stood out from the crowd as a very curious phenomenon, the only person Hester had seen in Plymouth with any meat on his bones. Both London lads, they quickly told her, had arrived attached as servants to the family of a Plymouth council member, Samuel Hopkins. Hester had never met Hopkins, meaning he came to this enterprise directly from England, as had the Warren family.

Hester was more than a little surprised that Mister Hopkins, who held no congregational position, never having been a part of the old church body from the rural village of Scrooby in Nottinghamshire, England, the people who formed the core group of settlers, had been permitted to take part in the civil authority governing the town. In Europe civil and religious authority usually overlapped, in Protestant regions as well as Catholic, but already in this tiny foothold of the

New World new approaches to many things were beginning to spring up.

Hester had a probing mind for delving into such unlikely matters. She could read and write, as could most of the other women she knew among the dissenters, except that in her case she was literate in French as well as English. Though invariably taught at home, there being no schools that would admit them, many Protestant women were raised to be able to read the Bible for themselves and not be dependent upon someone else for mastering the Truth, including their own husbands. This philosophy nourished curiosity and sometimes a startling spirit of independence among these ladies, and it certainly had in Hester's case. Otherwise, she would not have recognized that something unique in the world of politics was afoot in little New Plymouth. She pondered all this as she and the younger children followed John up the hill. The two Edwards brought up the rear, struggling mightily with the weight of the trunk.

"Our house is up near the fort," John was saying, "second down from the top of the hill. Captain Standish's house is the one right next to the fort on our side of the street. They wanted Captain Standish and Father to be able to come quickly in case of trouble. We're all to gather in the fort if there's an attack, but they want the most able men, the best fighters, to be able to get there first."

Hester found these excitable declarations more than a little disturbing, and she feared for their effect on the little ones. "But has there ever been such an attack?"

"No, but Captain Standish says the best way to stop one from happening in the first place is to be completely prepared. We know the Indians watch us from the woods, all the time. They know full well Plymouth would not be easy pickings."

Jacob only had eyes for his big brother, but Hester saw the girls casting uneasy glances at the high stockade walls enclosing the village.

Feeling a change of subject was in order, Hester said, "You admire this Captain Standish, don't you, John?"

"Oh, yes, Mother! Just wait til you meet him. Captain Standish is the greatest man I've ever known!" After blurting this out, John felt compelled to add, "Except for Father and Governor Bradford, of course."

Hearing groanings and thumpings behind, Hester looked back at the boys with the trunk. "Are you all right, young gentlemen? I apologize the trunk is so heavy. Perhaps we should find a wheelbarrow?"

"We're doing superbly, Missus," Edward Doty said, "if only Leister would keep 'is end 'eld up."

Edward Leister snapped back, "Don't you worry your 'ead about my end, Doty! Just keep your mind on your business."

"Young gentlemen, please!" Hester said, shaken at the depth of animosity between the boys and genuinely frightened they would come to blows.

"By rights we shouldn't be 'ere at all, Missus," Doty said quite conversationally, instantly dropping the quarrel, "we ought to be out on expedition with your 'usband and the others."

"Aye," Leister said, "as if Captain Standish would ever take the likes of ye along for anything important. 'e's completely 'elpless, Missus. Can't so much as catch a fish."

"'ow'd you like to find out who's 'elpless then?" Doty snarled as angrily as before.

Noticing her daughters' unwholesome fascination with the brewing clash between the two Edwards, Hester drew breath for further intervention, but suddenly a young woman's cry broke out from the doorway of the nearest house.

"Hester! Hester Cooke!"

Hester turned to see a very pretty slender young woman running out to meet her. With a shriek of recognition they threw their arms around one another. The two Edwards took the opportunity to put the trunk down and sit on it.

"Priscilla!" Hester cried. "Priscilla Mullins! You have grown so beautiful I do not know you!"

They clung for a long moment and then pulled back to examine one another's faces. Both had tears in their eyes.

"I am not Priscilla Mullins any longer, Hester. I am Priscilla Alden."

"Priscilla! You are not only a woman now, but you have found yourself a husband! God bless you."

Priscilla nodded happily. "A young ship's carpenter from the *Mayflower* crew he is, but a right Godly man none the less."

"I am sure you would choose no other. When can I meet him, Priscilla?"

"Soon, Hester. He is busy helping the other new arrivals for the governor. Your Francis and he have become great friends."

"Are they in good health, our men?"

"As good as any of us. Probably better, in your husband's case. He is strong, as is your son." Priscilla nodded at John, who reveled in her approval.

"Tell me true. Is Francis in danger on this mission that keeps him from us?"

"No more than any of us here, but danger is the constant measure of our lives, Hester. Why think you I was not down at the shore to greet you?" Hester shook her head, and Priscilla went on, "I was nursing those too ill to rise out of bed." Her voice faltered. "I have done so much nursing these last three years, but so many died anyway. Especially the first year. It was …difficult to bear."

Hester realized that only weariness could make her younger friend say such things in front of the children, and she drew her back into comforting embrace.

"Dear Priscilla. I am certain things will be better now. We must pray and be brave."

Priscilla pulled away and dabbed at her eyes. "Forgive me."

"Nothing to forgive."

"No, no, you are quite correct And you just crossed the ocean. You have earned the right to speak of courage." She turned to the two Edwards. "Come, lads, let's show Hester her new home."

The boys heaved up the trunk, and the little procession renewed its uphill trudge. Priscilla introduced herself anew to the younger Cooke children, knowing they might not remember her. Hester marveled at the young woman's gift for dealing with the little ones. Both little girls flocked close around her with conspicuous admiration.

Noting Pricilla's lamentable garment showed as much wear and tear as anyone else's in Plymouth, Hester racked her brain over the contents of the trunk, hoping she had included something fit for a wedding gift. The chest included a remarkable quantity of colorful new cloth. Perhaps they'd work together sewing Priscilla a new dress.

"The houses," Little Hester said, sounding dubious, "they look so... so rough."

"Your new house may seem a bit rough, yes," Priscilla said, "but it's bigger than any of us would have had back in England."

"We've never lived in England, Miss," Jane reminded her. "We've grown up in Holland."

"Jane," Hester admonished.

"No, no, you're quite right, Jane. So did I for the most part. I was younger than you when I last saw England."

"Was England good, missus?" little Jacob asked, to the astonishment of his mother.

"It was a beautiful land, Jacob," Priscilla said, "but we were not free to worship there."

"Why didn't we stay in Holland then?" Jacob asked, clearly no more enamored of what he was seeing than the girls. "We were free there."

"We were free, yes," Hester said, "but we could not earn enough to own our land and houses."

Doty piped up at this. "Sorry to burst your bubble, m'lady, but nobody owns nothing in this splendid borough neither! Everyone's required to 'old everything in common. Share and share alike, they says."

"One day that's going to change, Edward," Priscilla said.

"Sure it is. You was always good at ladling out children's stories, Priscilla! Very comforting."

"Stuff it up, Doty," Leister said, "Maybe Missus Alden's got privileged information."

"Stuff your own, Leister, or I'll stuff it for you."

"Would you boys please act your age?" Little Hester intoned.

The incongruity startled the boys, and they laughed.

By now the group was approaching the looming fort at the top of the hill. Hester glanced back at the waters of the harbor and bay spread out below them, reflecting the late afternoon sun. She noticed neighbors peeking out at them from various doors but recognized no faces. The children ran on ahead to look at their house.

"Priscilla," Hester said softly, "everyone is so thin and ragged here. Including yourself, my poor dear."

"We have been so short of food and cloth, Hester, but we shall do better now your ship has brought supplies."

* * *

Inside the large common room on the ground floor of the fort, Governor William Bradford and Doctor Samuel Fuller sat ashen-faced with the ship's master of the *Anne* and the church elders and deacons who came ashore with him. The latter brethren, gentlemen of long acquaintance stretching all the years back to Nottinghamshire, wore an expression of mounting bewilderment. Bradford stared at the bill of lading in his hand. The stricken faces before him trembled at his silent wrath, including the ship's master, no stranger himself to the perils of wielding authority.

"This, then," Bradford said through clenched teeth. "This is all the supply you have brought us?"

Fuller quivered at his side, no doubt tempted to set the air aflame with imprecation, but knew well enough to hold his tongue, at least for the present.

One elder spoke up, a good fellow named Richard Longtree whom Bradford had known all his life. "I take it we are missing something?"

"We are missing something that people can eat."

"Eat? You mean us to feed you? As you see," Longtree pointed at the lists, "we brought some barrels of flour, some large sacks of dried beans, a bit of this and that, and some seed for planting, but the adventurers in London gave us to understand that you could give us most of what we require out of your stored harvests. Til our own crops come in, of course."

Fuller spoke up at last. "Gentlemen, you were not led blindfolded up this hill. You've had a chance to observe the people of Plymouth— these walking skeletons. Not exactly thriving, I should say. Does the sight of us suggest we have much to offer in the way of stored harvests?"

"Please, Dr. Fuller," Bradford said.

"Our good governor fears lest I should rouse my passions to an unwholesome display," Fuller said. "Forgive me, gentlemen. Indeed, I find myself moved to the greatest extremity of passion whenever I contemplate the farsighted wisdom of those honest men of business back in London."

"I sent letters to London and to yourselves by every ship that landed on these shores," Bradford said. "Did none of them get through?"

"We did not see or hear of them if they did," Longtree said.

"They might have been withheld from us, perhaps," the youngest elder put in.

"By whom?" Longtree demanded.

No one answered, though Bradford knew what everyone was thinking. "I sent one by a Dutch trader that should have gone directly to Pastor Robinson in Holland."

"We saw it not."

Bradford sighed in resignation, casting another dark look at the lists in his hand. "Then of food that can be eaten, you carry nothing more than I see here."

"That's the lot, Governor," the ship's master said. "I couldn't very well bring more cargo than was put aboard, now could I? But it's all there that was put aboard, for what it's worth to ye."

"You have done your duty valiantly, Captain," Bradford said, "carrying our dear people across these stormy seas. We are more than thankful to have our brothers and sisters here alive."

The master nodded in satisfaction at the compliment, but Longtree was not appeased.

"William, I assure you, we had no idea, no indication whatever, how things stood here among you."

"The fault is not yours, Richard, nor any of the congregation's. If my letters did arrive in London, perhaps I failed to make myself clear."

"Oh, fiddle-faddle!" Fuller roared. "The late earl of Oxford himself could not impart more clearly with a pen."

"We shall need to go over these lists," Bradford said with preternatural calm. "By frugality and caution, exercising prudence, we must find means to feed the new arrivals and all of us until we do bring in a crop. Everyone here must contribute, new arrivals or not. When not working in the fields, we pursue hunting, fishing, clam-digging, and berry picking."

"The pursuits of a gentleman!" the ship's master joked, then beat a somber retreat. "At least—back home in England."

"If we do manage to stagger along," Fuller said, "pray God we have a better crop this year than last. If we suffer another failure, we shall perish every one."

CHAPTER 13

New Home at Journey's End

The two Edwards set the heavy trunk down behind Hester as she gazed at the house. The smaller children huddled close. Priscilla stood alongside with a beaming smile. Hester took a quick glance at John, likewise bursting with pride, then at the stricken looks on the faces of his sisters and brother.

The word "house" applied more by nature of function than by the standard of anything seen in Holland. This was a primitive structure, the sort of abode where one imagined some wild man of the forest might reside—a poacher's den perhaps. Roughhewn clapboards formed the four walls, any chinks filled in with wattle and daub. She wondered how the dried mud would stand up when the rains came. The roof rose to a high sharp peak, a contour at least recognizably European. Rather than boards or neat tiles, the roof was covered with what appeared to be long hay or swamp grass thatched together in thick bundles. John had already informed them excitedly that this technique had been copied from the local savages, and Hester dearly hoped it kept out the rain and cold as effectively as he claimed. She also decided to hold her tongue about the obvious fire hazard, at least for the present.

"Oh, John," Hester said, "you and your father built this?"

"With our own hands!" John glanced at the two Edwards. "But with the help of many others. We would help other families, and they would help us."

Hester leaned down to hug the boy, heartbroken to have missed three crucial years of his young life. "Then it is the most beautiful house I have ever seen."

The other children looked askance at this proposition but kept quiet for the moment, encouraged by Priscilla, who quickly touched a forefinger to her lips, a gesture Hester caught out of the corner of her eye.

"We were allowed to build ours among the first," John gushed, "and so large because Governor Bradford and the councilmen knew that all of you would be coming to join us."

"We are very grateful," Hester said, "to them and to you. And very proud."

"Come on, boys," Priscilla said to the two Edwards, "let's carry the trunk inside, where it will do them some good."

Hester and John led the little Cookes through the door. They looked the place over as Doty and Leister struggled in with the trunk.

The interior was a match for the crudeness outside. The central fireplace and coarse chimney bisected the space into two large rooms of equal size. The concept of windows apparently lay beyond the grasp of the amateur builders. Consequently, very little light penetrated, though there wasn't much to see if it did. The fixtures were few, primarily a table, benches, and some chairs. Furniture making would be a coming industry in the new world once society became more organized. Hester recognized the large metal kettle hanging in the fireplace as the one her husband and John had carried from Holland on the *Mayflower*.

All at once the longing for Francis swept over her, the intense feeling of emptiness and loss that had tormented her for three long years, made bearable only by the hope of seeing his dear face again. She could scarcely wait to throw her arms around him and feel his strong arms around her. She wanted to kiss him and kiss him and hear him promise over and over that they would never be parted again. It was intolerable she had arrived after this long wait to find him out in the forest somewhere, unaware she had come. How fervently she prayed he would make it safely through this last little patch of hours. She escaped unendurable yearning only by forcing her attention back to the present, rendered all the more poignant by knowing his hands helped fashion everything she saw.

The ceiling was a bit high in order to accommodate sleeping lofts in both rooms, situated just under the thatched roof and reachable by homemade ladders. She hoped this arrangement would be comfortable, but as weary as she and the children felt after the long voyage, she had no concern about any of them being able to sleep.

"Where do ye want this placed, Missus?" Leister said.

"Anywhere convenient, if you please."

The boys set the trunk down right where they were, but Priscilla intervened to thwart immediate flight. "Perhaps over against the wall rather than right in the middle of the floor, boys."

"Anything you say, Priscilla," Doty said saucily. They moved the trunk over to the wall.

"All right, then," Leister said, "we bid you good day."

"And joy of your fine new mansion, I'm sure," Doty added as they took their leave.

Leister began to chase Doty as Hester shouted after them. "Yes, thank you very much, young gentlemen."

"Young heathen, more like," Jane muttered.

"They'll come around," Priscilla said, ever the optimist. "They're good lads at heart, I think."

"You hope."

The two youngest Cooke children ventured forward as their eyes grew accustomed to the dim light. The continuing silence evoked nervous chatter from their older brother:

"Father says we shall build better furnishings when we have more time. He says with all the fine trees hereabout, what we need is a real sawmill to make lumber. He says maybe we can start one someday. There's not enough wind here to build the Dutch kind, driven by a windmill, but we can put ours over a running stream. Fast water will turn a great wheel that drives a whipsaw, the way they do it in England. John Alden says there ought to be a pretty penny in a sawmill." At this point the boy noticed one else seemed to be catching fire from his enthusiasm.

"Oh, Mother," Little Hester suddenly burst out, "it's awful!"

"What is?" John asked in genuine astonishment.

"This house," the little girl cried. "This so-called house!"

"Oh, no, no, my sweet," Hester said, taking the weeping little girl in her arms.

"It *is*, Mother," Jane said, fighting back tears of her own. "This is a terrible place!"

Hester freed one arm to sweep Jane into the same embrace. "There, there, my turtledoves, this house is not as terrible as the hold of a ship, is it? It is not filthy and smelling and pitching up and down on the sea as high as a mountain, is it?" She looked over at the astonished and disappointed John. "Do not worry, my son. These girls have fresh memories of the fine little cottages in Holland, that is all. You and your father have done very well. This be the first time in all our married years your father and I—all of us—have had a home we could call our own."

"Well, it's not really our own, not exactly," John said.

Hester straightened up. "What do you mean?"

"Oh, it's our house all right, never you fear. But the council decreed all the unmarried men should stay with families until we are able to build more houses."

"Single men? How many such are there?"

"Well, let's see." John started mentally counting up.

"No, son, I mean how many for this house."

"Well, we had John Alden, but he married Priscilla, and now they have a house of their own." The newlywed nodded happy agreement. "Edward Winslow stayed here for a time because his first wife died before we could build them a house, but he got married again, so he's gone too."

"But how many do we have currently?" Hester said.

"Oh, only one. Philip Delano."

"Philip!" Hester cried with genuine delight. "Ah, but he is a Frenchman. We can put up with him most charmingly."

CHAPTER 14

War of Words and a Little Something More

The two Massachusett warriors kept close watch on the angry confrontation between opposing groups of white men. They observed a great deal of talking and arguing, which they were not close enough to hear and could not follow in any case, knowing too few words of the white men's tongue.

Pecksuot crept close to Wituwamat. "I do not understand. The first English make no attack on the other English."

Wituwamat nodded. "No attack. They give every appearance of battle, but then they do not fight. They surprise the other English, but they do not shed their blood. First they put the dead one in the ground, and now only talk, talk, talk like the chatter of squirrels."

"Why did they hide their canoe before they walked the trail? If they would make no attack, why did they not come in directly from the Great Water?"

"They are cowards, I think. They dress for war, after their manner, but they do not choose to fight."

"The Red Hair does most of the talking."

"The Red Hair!" Wituwamat spat in disgust. "His face is full of anger, but he does not strike. It is said among the People he is the chief warrior of the whites, but I think he is only a woman and not a man."

"He is not only a woman, he is a very little woman!"

The two warriors chuckled.

"Come, we have seen enough." Wituwamat led his friend away. Neither man had any sense of the mortal danger inherent in what had been playing out before their eyes.

* * *

"You take too much upon yourselves, Standish!" Sanders shouted. "Ye do not have any authority over us!"

The captain fixed the trader with a steely eye. "We do not seek any authority over you, sir. We have only come here to make a statement, plain and simple. There will be no attacks on the savages, nor any taking of their supply except by trade."

"But I am saying you have no right to issue such a prohibition. We must do that which is necessary for our own survival."

"If you take any foolish action that stirs the savages to war, you endanger the survival of every Englishman arriving on these shores, now or in future. Our governor derives his office by charter from the king of England, and Governor Bradford intends to fulfill his responsibility to keep the peace."

"We are under separate royal charter."

"In this case, ours takes precedence." Angry murmurs arose from the sullen crowd gathered behind Sanders.

"Know this," Standish went calmly on, lifting his voice to address all the Wessagusset men, "if there be any here who are in danger of starvation, Governor Bradford offers to take you in at Plymouth and share our food, meager as it is. If any man feels he cannot survive in this wilderness or has no further wish to try, come to Plymouth, and we shall pack you back to England on the next ship, which is due shortly."

This offer served to quiet the discontent, and Francis saw thoughtful looks on many faces.

Standish let the proposal sink in. "But Governor Bradford also declares that any man who plunders the savages will face swift justice and sure, just as if he had robbed another Englishman."

"You threaten to bring us up on trial?" Sanders said, dripping sarcasm. "Have you built a gallows yet?"

"Not yet," Standish said. "But we have a good quantity of stout rope and an admirable number of trees."

As usual the captain practiced no discretion in his speech. Drunken anger seethed. Francis and Philip exchanged an apprehensive glance.

In the rear of the infuriated traders one extremely large man loomed above the others. In addition to his great height the giant must have been very fat to start with, being yet so large after all the starvation the traders had reportedly suffered. The huge man began pushing through to the front, rasping out a challenge as he came.

"Tell me something, little man."

The Plymouth men gasped. Standish's small stature abided deep in the territory of the unacknowledged and the unmentionable. Francis flicked his eyes from the angry heap of muscle shoving the other traders aside to look at Standish, whose skin was in the process of brightening into a flush to match his hair and beard.

It took only a moment for the big man to reach the front rank and heave Sanders roughly aside. He stood looking down on Standish contemptuously.

"Tell us," the big man said, anger quavering through his bristly croak of a voice. "Just how do you plan to enforce your high and mighty governor's decrees?"

"They shall be enforced by any means necessary," Standish said with admirable steadiness, not backing off an inch. "Including force of arms."

"Force of arms?" the big man demanded.

"Gentlemen, please," Sanders said, growing frightened.

"Now let me see if I got this clear," the big man growled. "You mean to say yourself and this passel of Bible thumpers is going to come up here and use the force of arms on *us*?"

"Somehow you have managed to divine my meaning splendidly, sir," Standish answered coolly.

"Think you could demonstrate this use of force on me, for example?"

"On you and any other loud mouth like you."

The captain's jibe galvanized his opponent into action. He charged forward wrathfully, swinging his huge right fist at Standish's head.

Francis started to move, convinced a single blow would kill the captain dead before them, but Philip stopped him with a hard grip on his arm. Francis understood instantly, though far from agreeing or approving—perhaps it was time to find out what their captain was made of.

First of all, he was made out of speed. He bobbed his head easily aside, so that the big meaty fist swung harmlessly through an arc of air without connecting. The force of the thrust unbalanced the attacker slightly. He had been drinking with his fellows.

The big man was already swinging the other arm wildly, but the captain dived underneath and bounced up quite close to the man, like a little rabbit popping out of a hole.

From this startling proximity inside the potential grasp of the giant's arms, Standish was already swinging his left fist around under his left side and upward, driving it deep into the muscle at the base of the man's rib cage. The sound rang out like an axe head being driven into a log. The air gushed out the big man's lungs. His face turned purple as he doubled forward, bringing his pained expression down within range of the smaller man. Standish threw a vicious uppercut with his right fist that smashed the big man's nose with another loud *thunk*. The giant's nose disappeared in an explosion of blood, and he toppled to the ground like a fallen tree.

The whole action took place in quicker time than it took to draw a breath. The large man lay on the ground gasping, fighting to breathe, gripping his ruined bleeding nose with one hand and his belly with the other. Standish stepped back, avoiding the mighty legs flailing at his feet, and stood over his attacker with fists at the ready. Soon it came clear the fallen had no plan to rise—and no capacity either.

Everyone else stood rooted in place, including Standish's own men from Plymouth.

Francis became aware of an animal growl buzzing through the other side's ranks.

"You can't do that!" one of the traders shouted, shaking his fist. "We outnumber you!"

The crowd took a step toward Standish. The man who had shouted was standing less than two feet from Philip but paying him no attention. Delano swung the butt of his musket and caught the shouter squarely in the teeth, sending him to the ground.

Two men tried to rush the captain. Reacting without conscious thought, Francis stuck his musket barrel out and tripped them up. Then he jumped over next to Standish and leveled the musket at the traders. The other Plymouth men trained their guns as well.

Philip stepped forward and placed the barrel of his musket against the cheek of the terrified Sanders. The man froze, knowing the big musket would take his head off.

"I do beg your pardon, gentlemen," Philip said courteously, "but if the matter has not come to your attention already, you will notice that the matches on these weapons are alight."

"Please," Sanders trembled.

"You only have five guns," someone muttered.

"Then which five of you will choose to be the first to die?" Philip asked, reasonably.

As this unfolded Captain Standish drew his sword. The factions glared at one another.

Standish gave an almost imperceptible nod to Philip, and the Frenchman backed off, though he kept the musket leveled at Sanders's stomach. With authority came responsibility, and since Sanders had been left in charge, he would catch one of the first balls if things went awry. Sweat poured down the man's face, and he was visibly shaking.

"So then," Standish said, the voice of sweet reason or at least as sweet as he could manage, "will you take Governor Bradford's gracious offer, or no?"

"I do not believe that any man here at Wessagusset wants to live with you people," Sanders said. Francis had to admire the man's nerve, speaking thus with the business end of a musket pointed at his belly. "But a number of us may want to go back to England, when that ship arrives."

Nearly unanimous murmurs of agreement arose at this. Most of these men had apparently seen quite enough of the New World with all its charms and supposed opportunities.

"But there shall be no molesting of the savages?"

"Nay. You have my word." Reluctantly given, but his word.

"And can you speak for all of these?" Standish said.

The others smoldered in silent, bitter endorsement. They clearly believed Standish and his brutes would not hesitate to hang them.

Standish sheathed his sword.

"Come on then," he ordered. "Our business here is concluded."

In the manner of more experienced soldiers, ingrained through the captain's long and repetitive training, the Plymouth militiamen backed off with their guns leveled. Standish sent one off to fetch Winslow, still occupied with the Indian women.

"Where now, Captain?" Sanders said. "Back to the comforts of home?"

"We go to pay a call at Cummaquid."

"Going to plunder the savages yourselves, are ye?"

Standish bestowed a look upon Sanders to make him yearn for the tenderness of a pointed musket. "We trade for our goods, Mister Sanders. You may not care for the settlers of Plymouth, nor our beliefs, but whatever you may think or say, we are not thieves."

Standish gestured for his men to fall in as he spoke his last to the resentful traders. "We shall send a message from Plymouth when the ship arrives. Any man who wishes to sail, let him come promptly."

Francis glanced behind them as the captain led the march back into the forest. He saw hatred in the sour staring faces, mixed with palpable relief at the Plymouth men's departure.

* * *

The little column of militia followed its wearisome reverse course through the swamps and forest and thence by river to the sea. Not a single native Indian witness had seen the Plymouth men strike with rigor and severity once they felt themselves sufficiently provoked. A deadly lesson went unlearned.

Its omission would soon prove costly to many.

CHAPTER 15

The New Land

The setting sun cast long shadows as John led his mother to the top of Cole's Hill outside the stockade walls at the eastern end of the settlement. Hester had asked to see the place on sudden impulse, and the short walk marked their first chance to be alone together in the course of a long hectic afternoon. Both seemed shy and uncertain, and neither spoke as they reached the summit.

Spread out at their feet lay the village graveyard, containing a heartbreaking number of burial places considering that only two little ships had discharged passengers in this colony before the present day's coming of a third. The graves lacked headstones or markers of any kind.

"Everyone who died is buried here?"

"Yes, Mother."

"But there are no gravestones! Not even wooden crosses!"

John hung his head. "So many people died that first winter. Captain Standish and the council decided we had better not mark the graves. Better not to let the savages know how many of us were dying."

"But we are strong now. You have built the stockade and the houses. Surely we could put up a few wooden crosses, if nothing else."

"No one thought of it, I suppose, marking the graves. We have had so much to do and so few hands to do it."

"Do you know where Sarah Eaton is buried? Which grave?"

"No."

Resting a hand on his shoulder to reassure the boy she intended no personal rebuke, Hester fell into reverie for a lost past.

"She was my oldest friend, John, a great lady of God. She took me in when I was nothing, a young Walloon girl on the run from the persecution in France. She treated me as a member of the Eaton family. She introduced me to your father."

"I do not know which grave, Mother."

"Did someone make a record? Of the graves."

"I doubt it. So many died, so many were ill... that first winter... I do not think it occurred to anyone."

Unable to speak, Hester attempted to hide her tears. She felt the touch of his hand on hers.

"I'm sorry, Mother. Whenever I used to cry about it, Father would say that we shall see them all again... in Heaven."

She tightened her arm around him, and he leaned against her. "Of course we shall... but we miss them so much in this life." She wiped her eyes. "John, why don't you leave me here for a bit? Go back and see about the children. I can find the house."

"Yes, Mother."

She hugged him tenderly, hoping to convey how very much she loved him and how joyful she felt to be with him again. She stood watching as he walked down the hill, grown so tall in comparison to the tiny boy she remembered sending off with breaking heart from Leyden.

* * *

At the bottom, John turned and found his mother watching him. She lifted a hand. He waved back, then passed through the lower gate into the stockade and started trudging up Town Street. He had climbed about halfway in the darkening twilight when a little girl with golden hair suddenly ran out from between two of the houses and stood blocking his path.

"Hello, John Cooke," the girl said, bold as you please.

She was a pretty little thing, a year or so younger than himself. He remembered where he had seen her before—near the group of tearful females gathered around the former London merchant Richard Warren. At that time, he recalled, she had not been busy with the others kissing and hugging her long-separated father. She had been staring straight at John! And with the same odd expression as at present.

"Hello," John said tentatively.

"My name's Sarah. We came over on the *Anne* with your mother."

As if any other ships had arrived recently, John thought but did not say so out loud. "Yes. You're one of Mister Warren's daughters. He was on the Mayflower with my father and me."

"Really? That explains everything!"

"I beg your pardon?"

"What I'm doing here and so forth, it's becoming quite clear."

He felt his face grow warm. "I suppose I was rather stating the obvious."

"I'm teasing you, John, I have a bad habit of that. Never mind. I only meant, we obviously know one another's family history, so we can dispense with all that."

"Why aren't you at home with your family then? You ought to have enough to talk about." Without going out bothering strange boys, he wanted to add but again held his tongue. He edged away from her and resumed his journey up the hill. To his horror she fell in beside him.

"I couldn't stand it in there for another minute," Sarah said. "My sisters are all crying their eyes out wanting to go back to England."

"Already? They haven't been here a day."

"I know."

"Well, my brother and sisters were doing exactly the same thing, although they didn't keep crying about it. My mother wouldn't let them."

"How, by punishing them? With my sisters that would make them cry more."

"No, no! She comforted them."

"Oh. She's good at that. I observed her in the hold, many times. She's the one first told me about you."

Having no ready response to this brazen assertion, John ventured, "How about you? Do you want to go back?"

"Not at all. My sisters are silly. That's why I had to get out of the house. I don't want to go back to England. I like it here!"

"But how do you know? You've only been here less than a day yourself."

"I'm the sort of person who knows what I like, that's how."

By now they reached the front of the Cooke house.

"I'm home now," he said, struggling with a strange constriction of the throat.

"I think you must be a very brave boy."

"Good night then." He bolted for the door.

"Good night, John."

Quickly pulling the door closed behind him, he caught a last glimpse of her staring at him more intensely than ever.

* * *

Hester lingered on top of Cole's Hill as dusk faded into night. Gathering her wrap around her shoulders against the chill, she wept softly as she carefully walked among the graves. Most of the dead from the *Mayflower* were women. From the little John had told her, she had no doubt Mrs. Eaton and the other ladies had sacrificed most of their share of what little food they had for the sake of their hungry children. Their starved bodies left them little protection against disease and winter cold. As thin as all the survivors now looked, what must the condition of these poor women have been?

It was almost more than Hester could bear. The courage of these faithful, loving mothers deserved a memorial that would stand until the trumpet of God summoned forth all the dead bodies from the earth and the sea. Yet these burial plots remained unmarked.

She became slowly aware of the wind plucking at her hair, and she turned to gaze out toward the east and north. Lightning played in the distance, illuminating dark clouds gathering over the ocean. As the wind rose, she heard the rumble of thunder. A great storm was approaching, marching toward the little colony over the cold Atlantic, perhaps a twin for the raging tempests that made their life miserable aboard the *Anne*.

Hester needed to get back, but she took another moment to let her eyes wander back across the landscape leading inland from the sea. Enough light shown from the moon and stars, not yet covered by the impending storm, to illuminate the wide cleared fields stretching out in all directions from the stockade. She could scarcely imagine the never-ending work required for Francis and John and the others to complete all this without oxen or horses or any other beast of burden to help them. Add to all this the building of the clapboard houses, plus the fort and town walls constructed out of felled logs, and what had been accomplished in less than two and a half years was almost unimaginable.

Hester lifted her gaze to the line of forest beyond the fields, now reduced to a threatening ring of deepest black. The wind grew stronger, the thunder louder and more frequent. Yet she stood in place transfixed and thoughtful.

Out beyond her to the west lay a dark virgin continent, already known to be vast, though how vast no man could say. Embracing it, taming it—merely exploring it—would consume many more lives than of those lying at her feet. Yet she could not let herself be overwhelmed with fear. With God's blessing and protection, dear Francis would soon return safely, and they would be back in one another's arms.

Jesus taught long ago that life should be taken one day at a time. The difficulties of a single day were sufficient unto themselves without bogging down in a morass of worry and fear. She determined more than ever to meet each new morning with God's help, armed by prayer and His Word, enabled by His power and His Spirit to face life as it came. Otherwise these dear sisters would have died in vain.

Hester turned and hurried down the hill, hoping to make it home—home!—before the rain began to fall. As she passed through the lower gate, a guard admonished her to make sure to be inside the stockade by sundown in future, as that's when the gates were supposed to be closed. The new arrivals had clearly thrown the town into a certain amount of confusion, exacerbated by the absence of this Captain Standish of awesome reputation and the discipline he customarily imposed. The guard spoke kindly, though, and she thanked him sincerely.

As she hastened up Town Street toward the house, it stuck her how extraordinary it was that indeed she already thought of this roughhewn place as home, despite the initial dismay of her youngest children. They would change and adapt, she felt sure of it. The night suddenly flashed bright as day from a bolt of lightning, followed almost instantaneously by a shattering thunderclap. She began to run.

CHAPTER 16

A Night among the Savages

In the midst of the raging downpour Philip Delano finally spotted where they needed to land. He did so long after nightfall, contrary to all his confident promises, recognizing the cluster of savage lodges only when a particularly terrifying flash of lightning providentially lit them up. He shouted the good news to the others as he fought to turn the rudder for shore.

Francis shook with terror that the next blazing bolt would hit the shallop. From his childhood in England Francis remembered seeing the body of a farmer shortly after the tree he stood under had been struck by lighting. The poor man had been left blackened and steaming, agony branded on his face, which for some reason had not been burned out of recognition like the rest of his charred remains. Francis shuddered at the memory as the cold rain poured over them and lightning struck afresh.

To make matters worse, the boat was nigh filling with water. Francis bailed with the others, struggling to stay afloat as Philip drove the tiller for the shoreline.

The roar of the surf slowly grew louder than the storm, and suddenly the shallop hurtled down through the high breakers, plunging faster and faster through a surge of white foam. A big wave caught them then, and they sped in toward what Francis hoped was a sandy and welcoming beach, carried in the curl and crest of the swell.

A sky-rending flash exposed the big grin on Delano's jolly upturned face, reveling in the wild velocity of the ride.

The boat suddenly heaved with impact against a submerged rock, the loud splintering crash centered right under their feet.

The shallop lifted off at once, wobbling madly as if ready to break into pieces. Francis prayed the water would prove sufficiently shallow to allow them to scramble ashore. He had not swum in years and did not trust his skills to rescue any man who could not.

"Now!" Philip cried.

"Out of the boat!" Standish shouted at the top of his drillmaster's lungs.

More terrified of the captain than the storm, every man except Philip leapt over the side, keeping a tight grip on the gunwales with at least one hand. Francis was relieved to find his feet touching bottom at a level that left the shortest man, Standish, with his head well out of the water. Then a wave broke over all their heads, nearly capsizing the boat. All managed to hang on except poor Winslow, who was swept in toward the beach, sputtering and waving his arms in the foam as he disappeared from sight.

"Up on the shore!" Standish commanded. "Run it up! Quickly, lads, fast as you can go!"

The men needed no persuading. They ran the shallop up out of the water until the bottom scraped.

"Higher up, higher up!" Standish shouted. "Or the high tide will sweep it back out to sea!"

Philip leaped out to join the push, and they kept going, shoving and dragging the boat up until they felt thick grass underfoot, and only then was Standish satisfied.

Philip clambered back aboard to roll, tie, and hide the sail in the bottom. Others helped make the shallop fast with ropes. Standish paced around, examining the hull. Standing nearby Francis could see enough damage to have sunk them in moments if they hadn't been so close.

"Make it secure, lads," Standish said. "We'll have to leave it here til we come back from Plymouth with proper tools—and our friend John Alden who knows how to make boat repairs."

Philip began to pass weapons down to waiting hands, along with small bundles of trade goods.

Suddenly Francis remembered Winslow, totally forgotten in the excitement. He turned and ran down to the shore without bothering to explain himself. He moved south, in the direction of the tidal flow, and by the next flash of lighting he saw Winslow on his hands and knees in the shallow water, trying to crawl ashore as wave after wave swept over him. Francis dashed out and pulled him to his feet, practically carried him up on the shoreline.

"Let me rest, let me rest," Winslow begged.

When they reached the rain-beaten grass, Francis allowed Winslow to sink down on all fours again. He squatted down beside the bedraggled man, trying to protect him as best he could while Winslow coughed up seawater. They were already soaked to the skin by means of total immersion, but wind and downpour lashed them anew, intensifying by the moment.

"We need to move, Edward."

"Just a moment, please."

Standish came upon them leading the others. "Excellent, Mister Winslow, we didn't want to lose you."

"Thank you, Captain," Winslow managed to gasp, looking and sounding like a half-drowned kitten.

"We'd best seek shelter."

"Very well." Thus urged by the captain, Winslow allowed Francis to lift him back to his feet.

Over the noise of the storm, a clamor of voices arose from further inshore. Standish's hand dropped to his sword, which he had strapped on at some point after landing the boat.

A stream of excitable humanity poured out of the sodden and windblown darkness—the inhabitants of Cummaquid, mostly youthful braves but a few young women too. The Indians carried bear and deerskins over their heads as protection against the downpour. Before the white men absorbed what was happening, each found himself bracketed by a pair of the savages, spreading the skins overhead and sheltering the Englishmen far more effectively than one of those storied new modern inventions back in the England of King James, the umbrella. This wind would have torn any of those flimsy devices to pieces, but the animal skins kept them protected from fresh torrents as the Indians ran them off in the direction of the village.

Captain Standish tried to refuse the help. "No, thank you. I'm already drenched in any case," he said, marching along. His two protectors would not take no for an answer, however, and they stretched out a deerskin over his head and walked beside him, though he was so short they had to hold the skin low, allowing the rain to stream down their own faces.

The hasty wet retreat toward the village became a source of the greatest amusement for Winslow, seeming to bring him back to life. Francis continued to hold him up as two braves spread a huge bearskin overhead. They moved fast, Francis almost carrying Winslow anew, the man's feet barely tapping along the ground. Nearly everyone was laughing by the time they reached Cummaquid, the friendly Indians loudest of all.

They slogged past huts where women, sleepy children, and the elderly packed the doorways, watching curiously. The entire population looked friendlier by an incalculable degree than the white traders at Wessagusset, and Francis hoped Captain Standish managed himself well enough to sustain this frame of mind.

The exuberant welcoming committee led the whites to a central hut considerably larger than the others, then stood aside to allow their guests to go in by themselves. Francis looked around curiously, never having entered an Indian lodge before. He wondered if this were some kind of village meeting place, equivalent to the common room back at the Plymouth fort. The space was indeed quite large, with enough room for several times their own number to sleep. Francis wondered if anyone had been moved out for the white men's convenience. A fire burned briskly in the midst, providing a great deal of welcome heat.

It touched Francis how the commitment of these poor people to hospitality, without benefit of the Bible and its admonitions, put many Europeans to shame. He moved to the fire with the others, all anxious to dry out and stop shaking—all except one, that is.

Standish prowled about looking the place over with meticulous scrutiny. In construction the round house was not totally dissimilar to one of the rectangular homes at Plymouth, except that it extended much further in diameter, with a rounded rather than peaked roof curving overhead. The sides were constructed of small trees and branches rather than English clapboards carved and shaped out of logs by axe, hatchet and saw. Mud and daub had been spread thick to form the surface of the Indian walls, whereas at Plymouth it was only used to fill the occasional chink or gap. The finished work looked solid enough, and the hut certainly held the heat. Smoke from the fire rose to exit through a hole overhead, and surprisingly in the absence of a chimney, most of it did just that. There must be some kind of flap arrangement above, on the outside, for very little of the heavy rain fell through, though enough to cause continual hissing in the flames.

The walls were hung or lined with various tools and implements, all of a practical rather than decorative nature. On one side of the hut, nearest the fire, a collection of jars and cooking implements stood lined against the wall, so clearly someone did live here in addition to any communal function.

Francis felt quite surprised at the comparative tidiness. Like most Englishmen he identified savagery and primitive conditions with disorder. Yet the worst filth and disarray witnessed so far on this expedition belonged to the drunken white men of Wessagusset.

The front door flap was lifted aside, and a tall savage in his fifties made an impressive entrance accompanied by two braves. The sopping and disheveled Winslow advanced to greet the man in his own language, then introduced him as the village leader, Chief Iyanough. The captain walked forward to greet him courteously, Francis was glad to see. Winslow conducted the conversation, translating for the benefit of the others.

"Hello," the chieftain said. "I greet you, English friends."

"Hello, Chief Iyanough," Winslow said, "we are honored to greet you as a friend as well."

"You have ventured out on a night when you should have stayed in your lodges. Now you are wet and cold."

Francis often wondered if the Indians truly spoke as eloquently as Winslow always made them sound in translation. To find out he would have to steal a page from his son John and start taking language lessons from Hobomok. Perhaps he needed to make the time, as his boy had.

"It was our duty to come out," Winslow said.

"What duty calls you out in such a storm? I would not expect you to act impetuously, as those other English are wont to do." The chief gestured vaguely north.

Standish ignored the compliment, perhaps offended at a savage presuming to draw judgmental distinction between Englishmen. "Mister Winslow, tell him why we are here, if you please."

"Chief Iyanough, we have come because you made a bargain with our Chief Bradford to trade for corn."

Iyanough conferred with the two other Indians, probably elders of some kind. Francis hung in suspense with the others, waiting for the answer. Fortunately, it was not long in coming.

"Your chief Bradford promised us trading goods for our corn."

Winslow gestured toward the bundles resting next to wet English boots. "We have brought the goods. We are ready to trade."

Iyanough nodded with satisfaction. "Very well. But men do not trade in the darkness." He gestured toward the piles of bearskin along one of the walls. "Strip off your wet clothing, and wrap yourselves in the furs. Lie down and sleep. We shall trade on the morrow."

"What did he say?" Standish said, so sharply that Iyanough looked at him in puzzlement.

"The chief will not trade tonight, captain," Winslow explained. "He thinks we should all take our rest first, then trade in the morning."

"We are not here to dance at his convenience! We have a long walk in front of us back to Plymouth. If we traded now, we could leave at first light."

"Captain Standish," Winslow said with a forced smile that belied his words, "we need that corn. If we wish to make a good trade, we should follow their customs. The chief and his people have shown themselves most friendly in taking us in. I think we should be wise not to jeopardize our situation."

Though Francis could see the captain turn red in the face of this quiet rebuke, Standish was also sharp enough to see the wisdom of it.

"Very well, Edward. Tell him we shall be happy to trade in the morning."

"Chief Iyanough, our captain thanks you for your hospitality. We are most grateful to the People for giving us shelter from the storm. We shall be happy to trade tomorrow, at your convenience."

"Good night, then," the chief said, then turned around and left, his two elders trailing behind him.

The veil of strain and tension lifted somewhat in the wake of their departure. A couple of fellows began following the chief's advice regarding their wet clothing.

"Just a moment, men," Standish said. "We can't just go tottering off to dreamland like a flock of weary children."

"Why not?" Philip Delano said. Standish glared at him in an attempt to make the Frenchman uncomfortable, but he was game or defiant enough to ask again. "Why not, Captain?"

"Because we are not passing the night at our Aunt Matilda's. We are soldiers in alien territory, and none of us is going to sleep a wink without someone among us standing guard."

Audible groans arose from the troops. The captain forged on unabated. "We have a choice of how to carry this out. Each man stand watch for an hour and wake the next. Or we can cast lots for the duty, and each winner take two hours, allowing some to have a full night's sleep."

Only Standish would describe the one the lot fell on as the winner rather than the loser, but there was no doubt he would risk a turn, not excluding himself from the lottery by reason of rank.

"Perhaps we should do it by voluntary action, Captain, working it out among ourselves," Francis suggested. "How would it be if I take the first watch and stand two hours?"

The others stared as if he had taken leave of his senses.

"Are you sure, Francis?" Philip asked.

"I take time to fall asleep," Francis explained, "but when I finally do, I don't want to wake up again until I have to."

"Very well, Mister Cooke," Standish said, "but a good soldier should train himself to fall asleep at a moment's notice."

"You can wake me to take the next watch, Francis," Winslow said. "Two hours, and then—shall I wake you, captain?"

"Very well," Standish snapped. "And I shall prod Monsieur Delano when my duty is done. That will get us through till sunrise."

Standish grabbed one of the bearskins and curled himself up in it before the fire without removing his wet garments. While the others stood there watching, he was as good as his word, falling into contented snoring almost immediately. The other men looked at each other, wondering if Standish was only pretending, but Francis somehow knew he was not.

Most of the weary militia undressed, draping their wet clothes on sticks pushed into the ground near the fire, then rolled up in the bearskins. They fell into exhausted sleep almost as quickly as the captain.

Winslow hung back to whisper with Francis. "Why do you have trouble falling asleep, brother?"

Francis shrugged, feeling vaguely ashamed.

"There is a verse I have committed to memory," Winslow said. "from Paul in Philippians four, 'Be nothing careful, but in all things let your requests be shewed unto God in prayer and supplication with giving of thanks.'"

"I do all that, John. I know worry is a sin, but I have my weak flesh to contend with."

"God is not finished with any of us." Winslow patted his arm. "Don't worry, Francis. That ship she's coming in, it will be much sturdier than the old *Mayflower*. The Lord will keep them safe. Here, let me build up the fire for you." He did it quickly. "When this burns down to about here, that should be two hours."

"Thank you."

Winslow soon undressed and collapsed in a place of his own, rolled in the fur, and if he was not immediately asleep, he gave every appearance thereof.

For all his words about taking time to fall asleep, Francis feared to sit down lest he doze off. He inspected the door of the hut opposite the one the chief had entered and found its covering tied down from the inside. Then he walked over to the front entrance, drew the flap aside, and stood looking out at the falling rain.

* * *

As the rain continued to fall outside, Hester observed no water dripping through the thatched roof. Perhaps the construction of her new home was more substantial than one might expect by the inevitable comparison with the sturdy little houses back in Holland. She had little problem herding her sleepy younger children upstairs, where she hugged and tucked them into bed quite close to the slanted thatch ceiling of their sleeping loft. The steady rainfall made a comforting sound in contrast to the retreating thunder. They all fell deeply asleep before she reached the ladder to climb back down.

She found John cleaning up the dishes from their modest supper. He had caught some crabs the previous day, and that blessed coincidence allowed him to present the others with a little feast of welcome. She found him pouring the shells into a bucket. "We save the husks," he explained, "for fertilizer and other purposes."

He carried the plates to another, larger bucket containing water.

"I can do that, son."

"We have had to do such things for a long time, Mother," he said, but he did allow her to take over.

"I know, and I am proud of you for it. But now we can be a family again, and we shall all do our fair share."

"I'm sorry we didn't have more crabs." The little girls and Jacob had still looked hungry at meal's end, though they had enough courtesy not to ask for more.

Hester waved the apology aside. "Shellfish tasted very delicious after shipboard fare." In memory of the dead women of the *Mayflower*, she had made sure to eat her own share. The children might go a bit hungrier than strictly necessary, but she believed they needed her to stay alive.

"Father always says he is very lucky to have a French wife to do the cooking."

"Oh, does he now? Well, I am a Walloon as he well knows, so most of the French would not consider me truly French. But I suppose I can cook."

"When you have something to cook," John said rather morosely.

Hester chose to ignore his obvious worry. "Don't you remember my cooking?"

John shook his head no. "I suppose you would have served vegetables with a meal like this, not just a pile of shellfish."

"It is good to have vegetables, yes, but your shellfish were very splendid. Do we not have any vegetables in Plymouth?"

"Most of the gardens did not grow very well last year."

"Perhaps they need a woman's touch."

"Father isn't bad as a gardener himself. In truth ours grew better than all of the others, but then the councilmen enforced the equality rule."

"What is the equality rule?"

"It's actually not the council's fault, but the decree of our backers in London."

"But I do not understand."

"All the vegetables were taken up and distributed equally, whether someone worked hard at his own garden or not. In consequence, all the vegetables were gone long before winter. We need to plant again soon, but father wonders if it's worth the trouble. And so do I."

Hester put an arm around the boy to comfort him. "We must not give up, John. I am sure that if we work hard, everything will come right in the end."

"But if there is no reward for our hard work?"

"There shall be reward."

"I do not see how. No one does. It is as if whatever a man gains with his own hands is taken away from him and scattered to the winds."

"Changes will be made."

"Truly?"

"I am sure of it. Men cannot live in a state of foolishness forever."

The thought seem to cheer the boy a bit. She could almost hear the gears of his mind grinding, like those of a Dutch windmill, as he considered other elements of the problem. The studious look on his face reminded her powerfully of his father.

"Some of the seeds we brought on the *Mayflower* don't take root over here," he said. "Some do, but some don't. They grow stunted, or they don't grow at all. Father says we have different air and soil than we had in Holland. Or in England either, so they say."

"What is the main crop we are growing, in our fields?"

"Corn."

Hester scrunched up her forehead. "I do not know this... corn."

"Neither did we, but it's a most useful crop. It's a strong green standing plant that grows straight up, and the edible part grows out in ears. We harvest the ears, eat some, dry some for winter, cut the kernels off for cooking in stews and drying. The largest part of the kernels we grind into meal that can be used somewhat like flour."

"I see what you mean by useful. But is corn the only crop that is grown in these large fields?"

"No, there are three, but they all grow together. When the corn plants grow to the height of a man's hand, then we plant beans at the base of each plant."

"Ah, so the vines will grow upward twisting themselves around the corn plant."

"Exactly. Father always says you know your way around a garden. We also plant squash at the base of the corn as well. The beans twine upward on the corn and the squash grow outward on the ground all around the base."

"How did you know to do all this?"

"We learned it from the Indians. Squanto showed us how to plant, weed, the entire process the first year we landed. He's the one insisted you have to plant the beans, otherwise the corn grows less healthy and you'd soon wear out the soil. No one knows why, but it seems to be true."

"Squanto?"

"He was an Indian whose tribe, the Patuxet, lived in this very place, a large group of them. Years ago, he was stolen away by white men and sold into slavery in Spain. He escaped and somehow made his way through France and across the channel to England. He made powerful friends, learned our language, and was able to catch a ship for home. But when he arrived here, he found his whole village had died from a pestilence."

"How terrible!"

John nodded agreement. "Chief Massasoit of the Wampanoag suffered him to live on the site by himself, and then one day we showed up. He chose to teach us, to give us every kind of aid. We should not have survived without him, I can tell you that. Father says his behavior was noble of him, since it is likely his tribe caught their death from white traders and their ships."

"No one can know that."

"No, but Doctor Fuller has always suspected it. If Squanto thought it, he never said so."

"I look forward to meeting this man."

John shook his head sadly. "You can't. He died the beginning of last winter, of a sudden illness."

"I am so sorry. Did he put his trust in the Lord Jesus?"

"Yes, it seems he did."

"Then I shall meet him in Heaven." She could tell her son had a great fondness and gratitude for this so-called savage, who sounded nobler in heart than many Europeans she had encountered. "What else do the Indians eat, besides this corn?"

"They shoot deer, turkeys, ducks—with their bows and arrows. They catch fish. They dig up eels out of the mud along the shore. Squanto taught us to do all of that."

"But surely these people, they have other plants and trees they eat the fruit of. Perhaps there are vegetables that grow here which do not grow in Europe."

John wore the stunned look of one whose mind had never considered such an obvious question. "I do not know. We never asked."

"Perhaps it is time someone did. But for now, it is time for a certain weary young man to go to bed."

"Yes, Mother."

They hugged again and kissed, then Hester watched as he climbed the ladder to take his place in the sleeping loft. For all his independence and sophistication on certain matters, right now he looked like nothing more than a tired little boy, and she guessed he would fall asleep almost instantly.

When he disappeared, her shoulders sank a bit. She had been displaying more courage and optimism for the boy's benefit than she actually felt. The rain beat down outside as hard as ever. She walked over, opened the door, and stood staring into the sheeted downpour.

"Oh Lord God," she prayed softly, "thank you for bringing us safely to this place. Now help us and protect us, please. And bring my dear Francis safely home, for Jesus' sake."

CHAPTER 17

Return, Reunion and Renewal

The rain stopped falling before dawn. While the Englishmen shared a most welcome breakfast of corn cakes and honey provided by their hosts, the sun warmed and dried the ground. Animal skins and blankets were soon spread out, and the trading took place outside, before the entire village, with every man, woman, and child watching in a state of enthrallment.

Francis never failed to be touched with pity by the excitement that a few baubles and trinkets, a few colorful ribbons and bits of dyed cloth, engendered in these poor childlike people. As soon as this thought occurred to him, however, he immediately chided himself for pride and conceit. The Indians possessed enviable skills for staying alive in a wilderness that easily made his own people look like fools. He also remembered Christ's teaching that a man must have the faith as of a little child—the trusting heart of one—in order to experience salvation at all. These so-called savages were potential brethren in Christ, already closer to God in some respects than the drunken reprobates back at Wessagusset. He had no business looking down on them.

The village chieftain Iyanough was made of sterner stuff than most of his villagers, not to be swayed overmuch by colorful beads and other cheap trifles from Europe. He accepted a measure of these for the happiness of his people, but he sought more useful treasures.

His stance exasperated Standish, one practical man bumping up against another, and both drove a hard bargain, fraying the nerves of poor Edward Winslow, dried out at last, who had to do the translating. The chief eyed Standish's sword hungrily, as well as the muskets, but on these the captain unsheathed a will of iron, unmoving as the earth, and even a bargainer as sharp as Iyanough was forced to pull back. Standish stood ready to provide tools, but never the more dangerous weapons, though he refrained from taxing Winslow and the chieftain further by stating the matter so indiscreetly. Francis thought the native tomahawks and knives of sharpened stone looked sufficient for most purposes, but the Indians were deeply impressed with the fine-edged steel blades of European implements. Eventually they settled for three sharp knives, two hatchets, and a whetstone, in addition to an impressive quantity of the trinkets, ribbons, and colorful beads that wrought so much excitement. The Plymouth men for their part got away with all the cornmeal they could carry on their backs, including Standish, who bore a burden as large as any of the taller men.

With a regretful glance back at the shallop, sitting forlornly awaiting repair, they set out through the forest. The budding leaves of an early spring dripped from the previous night's downpour, and the men slipped and slid in the mud underfoot. Iyanough had offered shelter for another day or two to allow the trails to dry, but Standish would not hear of it, to the satisfaction of all his men except Winslow, who made no bones about enjoying every moment he spent in the presence of the natives. After stumbling on for a couple of hard miles, Francis began to wonder if they had been too hasty, but their captain marched relentlessly forward, allowing them to pause for a five minute rest once an hour. Standish was one of those strange people who seem to have a timepiece built into their brain, as accurate as any great town tower clock back in England or Holland. He had demonstrated this ability so many times that Francis had no doubt about their schedule and the duration of their rest periods. As the day wore on, Standish began to call for rest twice an hour, then thrice, as the burden on their backs became a growing misery. No man complained about pushing on, remembering the Scotsman Thompson's tale of pursuit by the Massachusett war party, their fear newly reinforced by the memory of Deaky Jones's body in the swamp. None of the militiamen wanted to risk the woods after dark.

An Indian guide from the village had been offered but refused with thanks. Francis knew the way home. At the warrant of the Plymouth council, he and John went out hunting at every opportunity to break away from the tedium of the cornfields. Many men and boys yearned for the same escape, but Francis along with a few others had earned the privilege with the accuracy of his eye and the alacrity of his and John's attentiveness to everything Squanto and then Hobomok had taught. By now he and his son knew enough to go out without a guide, frequently wandering far afield in pursuit of game. Thus every time the column reached a fork in the trail Francis was able to point them in the right direction without a moment's hesitation.

It occurred to Francis that if trouble were brewing, he would have to forbid hunting trips to John for a time, and he himself should probably go out only with Hobomok or in company. Hobomok would be no problem, but a group of white men tended to frighten off the game. Francis had learned to tread lightly from his Indian teachers, but most of the colonists, with the exception of Philip Delano, who had mastered the tricks of the poacher's trade as part of that same mysterious past wherein he had learned to sail, either would not or could not walk quietly. On their present trek the heavy-tramping Plymouth column had not seen so much as a rabbit, not to mention a deer, but only a few outraged squirrels brave enough to bark at them.

The captain's duties in the settlement had kept him from doing much wandering himself, but by the time they came within shouting distance of Plymouth, he was familiar enough with the land to know it.

"Not too much further, men," he declared. "Just over that next hill, and we're home!"

If he intended to lift their spirits he failed, for the men plodded on in the same state of weary stupefaction.

At the moment Philip was on point. Knowing how close they were, he had drifted far ahead. Francis watched as his friend disappeared into the trees to climb over the rise.

Suddenly their world shifted in a moment of time.

Philip came running back down the hill, waving his hat and his musket while shouting at the top of his lungs—in French.

"The man's gone daft," somebody said. "What's he saying?"

"Philip!" Francis shouted. "English! Speak English!"

"The ship!" he shouted. "The ship! The ship! The ship!"

Everybody began to run. Before Philip could turn around others were speeding past him.

The corn on their backs became as light as bags of feathers, as did the formerly burdensome muskets in their hands. Their legs pumped through the final borders of the forest. Standish ran as hard as any, one hand gripping the pommel of his sword to keep the blade from tripping him up. Philip ran just as swiftly, though lacking the motivation of Francis and the captain, miserable for beloved faces long unseen.

Francis burst out of the trees as he crested the hill, the land-clearing process having moved this far north, and the welcome sight of Plymouth lay before them, with an English ship larger than their old *Mayflower* riding at anchor some distance offshore.

The running men scarcely paused to drink in the truth of what they saw. They ran down the hill, then started across the cleared fields toward the stockade. Francis was aware of joyous runners to his left and right, but his long legs ate up the ground, putting him out in the lead. Shouting workers converged from the fields to join them, surging *en masse* for the fort.

Some from the expedition now tossed their bags of corn aside in order to make better time, causing Standish to roar with displeasure, bellowing on the run for men from the fields to pick them up. But not Francis—he kept running full out, not even slowing when a strong breeze plucked off his hat. His heavy burdens did not impede his progress in the least. The pain in his lungs must belong to some other man for all it affected him. Where his strength came from he did not know nor did he care. Excitement wrought strange consequences at times, lending a fearful man courage or a weak starved skeleton the strength and endurance of a Samson.

Now a cry went up from one of the sentries on the roof of the fort. "The scouting party, ho! Captain Standish is returned! He and the militia approach from the forest! They're coming on foot, from the north!"

* * *

Hester lifted her eyes from sewing a new shirt for John.

"What was that?"

Her breath tightened. Her heart leapt. She almost fainted as she shot up out of the straight-backed chair, casting the new shirt aside.

Sudden fear overwhelmed her. Something terrible must be wrong. All day she had been running outside to look for the shallop approaching from the sea.

But the sentry was bellowing something about men coming from the woods.

In a matter of seconds Hester plummeted through a crisis of belief. The shouted words should not be true. Some fearful misadventure had occurred. The party was returning without her husband! He'd been lost in the raging ocean, which had sought to destroy their family so many times before. Or he'd been slain by savages! The scouting party returned, carrying his broken body on a litter.

Then in an instant she swept all these evil forebodings aside and was running out the door into sunlight. The shouts and scurrying of her own excited children barely registered as she passed through them like a bolt. On some level she heard them running behind her, shouts of "Mother, Mother" pursuing her up the hill as she passed through the western gates beyond the fort. They cried out, but for once in all her years of responsible and caring behavior toward her little ones she paid them no attention.

The new arrivals from the *Anne*, caught up in the exhilaration, including those not looking for missing husbands or fathers, easily swept to the head of the pack as people converged on the upper gates from all directions up and down the Street and from the fields. It was hard to credit that long weeks of the vile food endured in the hold of the *Anne* had left the passengers better fed and with more energy than those who dwelt at Plymouth, but that seemed to be the case.

Hester fought through the teaming mob at the gate, then stopped so abruptly that some of her little children collided into her, which she did not so much as notice. She stood at the edge of the crowd with both hands to her face, peering desperately downhill as seven approaching men outran the gathering workers. The runners looked white and weak and tottering and thin as everybody else in Plymouth, but they ran as if touched with supernatural power, including the little red-bearded man with the sword, who was only being outrun now by... by—by the tall man out front!

"Francis!"

Hester screamed with joy that echoed out to the trees and hills. Her cry startled and embarrassed some of the more austere English people around her, but she left all modesty behind as she began to move toward him. She had to prove this was no dream. Stumbling forward, she wiped tear-blinded eyes, keeping them fixed upon him, the dear, strong, long-separated husband of her youth, her tender lover and the father of her children.

She began to run, the tears now coursing down her cheeks, and then it was that Francis saw her.

She ran crying his name over and over but did not know it.

He stood stock still, as if doubting the evidence of his own eyes, and let the others run past. Still looking at her, he calmly prepared for her arrival by setting down a huge heavy-looking bag he was carrying roped to his back and leaning his frightful-looking musket against it. Then as he straightened back up the familiar grin spread across his face, and he began to move toward her again, now walking slowly and deliberately.

She ran into his arms. She gripped him desperately, her face a fountain of happy tears against his chest. She could feel his ribs and how much weight he had lost since the last time she saw him nearly three years ago in Holland, but he had the lean hard physique to sweep her off the ground and swing her about. Her weeping mingled with laughter as her feet flew in a ranging circle a foot in the air.

She became aware that he was repeating himself too.

"Hester, Hester, Hester, Hester..." As if he could not believe their good fortune either, as if the litany of her name would make it all true.

Then he did a startling thing and set her back down on her feet so he could kiss her on the mouth, the sort of thing that Godly Christian English couples did not do in the sight of strangers and the church, but he did it anyway, and she responded. He bent down to her, and they plunged into the depths of a long passionate kiss she had hungered for the full three years they'd been parted.

The spell was broken all too soon. Francis pulled back, and they looked at each other as if they had never been apart, with all the promise of future joy and tenderness, stretching down the length of all their years to come. Then her husband bent down and began to hug their children. Hester stepped back to give them access to his arms and put her own arm around John who had walked down with the others to watch the jubilation.

"Something must have happened to the shallop," John said. "I hope it didn't sink. We need it."

Hester nodded, scarcely thinking about the matter. The boy was undoubtedly right, but the important thing for her was the boat's precious human cargo.

She saw Barbara, an attractive, unmarried young woman Hester had gotten to know well in the hold of the *Anne*, walking down the hill to greet the man who was her fiancé, the gentleman she had crossed the sea to marry, Captain Miles Standish. Showing considerably more public dignity than the already married Cookes, the little red-haired man went down on one knee and kissed Barbara's hand. She pulled him to his feet, however, and enfolded him in a chaste hug. Hester could see that Barbara was crying, though undoubtedly with joy. Standish's face reddened, but if he felt any embarrassment he soon forgot about it, and the betrothed couple stood holding each other as the tide of excited humanity swept around them.

* * *

Wituwamat and Pecksuot watched from the edge of the forest. They had followed the Red Hair and his party ever since they left Cummaquid. Late the previous night it came to Wituwamat that they might have made a mistake giving up on their surveillance at

Wessagusset. He chided himself for being a poor hunter. He had gone soft on his prey because he had no respect for the quarry. He might hate the Red Hair but should have kept an eye on the man, no matter how many boring Bone Men activities he and his friend were forced to witness. And so he had dragged Pecksuot out of his dry place before dawn. His explanation turned aside the initial complaining, and Pecksuot came along willingly enough.

Now they lay on their bellies under a tree at the edge of the hill, keeping the whites under watch. A group of startling size milled about near the huge lodge on the crest of the opposite hill. The Red Hair and his party attracted great attention. Men embraced their women and their children. Men took the hands of other men and occasionally embraced them too.

"Look how many," Wituwamat said. "Their numbers are greater than any three villages of the People."

"It is a big village, but only one. The People have many villages."

Wituwamat shook his head, gesturing toward the great canoe floating out in the water. "More of them have come."

"They are few, and the People are many."

"But if they keep coming, soon they will be many, and we shall be few."

"But what can we do? The two of us?"

"We must persuade others!" Wituwamat said. "Before the land is overrun!"

Wituwamat led his friend back and away. He was glad he had come to see this sight. He had many things to ponder, and soon he would have many words to speak, and not only for the ears of Pecksuot either. From what he saw this day, he knew they needed to take up the bow and tomahawk, they and many other warriors.

Otherwise, the People were doomed. Their survival might well depend on him.

CHAPTER 18

A Time to Love

Hester heard it was Elder William Brewster himself who suggested performing the weddings outdoors. His stature and spiritual authority carried the day at once, holding any consequent murmuring to a bare minimum. Certainly, as a tiny number of her English friends whispered, a church seemed the appropriate place for a marriage ceremony, but then Plymouth did not have a proper church, now did it? Just the storage room on the ground floor of the fort. These complainers had forgotten or never knew that nearly all separatists had forbidden church weddings at first, there being no scriptural record of such, though widespread demand was slowly producing more and more church weddings in separatist congregations all over Europe. Furthermore, the outdoors seemed a perfectly valid substitute for the scriptural tradition of weddings at home, such as the marriage in Cana of Galilee where Christ performed His first miracle by turning the water into wine. The open air seemed particularly suitable since the entire colony wished to attend. After their long confinement below decks, Hester and her fellow passengers from the *Anne* certainly had no objection to fresh air under any circumstances.

Everyone, including Captain Standish and his own bride-to-be, insisted that Governor Bradford and Alice go first. The poor man certainly deserved his happiness and that without delay.

Since the governor obviously could not perform his own marriage ceremony, Elder Brewster did the honors, his strong lay preacher's voice easily carrying to the outer reaches of the crowd of witnesses, which included every man, woman or child in Plymouth except for the watchful sentries on duty at the top of Fort Hill. By some miracle the men washed ashore with the shallop had been spared any suffering from colds and fever. Priscilla's truly ill patients managed to rouse themselves from bed at her word and Dr. Fuller's that fresh air and warm sunlight would do them a world of good. Hester strongly suspected little was wrong with anyone at Plymouth that couldn't be cured with a few good meals.

Besides the glories of impending spring, another major advantage of holding the wedding outdoors was that, in contrast to a church meeting, the women and children did not have to sit on the other side of the aisle, separated from the men. Husbands and wives stood together, holding their children, as Bradford and Alice exchanged their vows. Hester and Francis traded meaningful looks at several points, and she was certain they were not the only couple who took the occasion for the unspoken renewal of their own promises of love and sanctity and devotion. She noticed Priscilla wiping her eyes more than once. She did it one-handedly, never releasing her tight grip on her husband John's hand with the other. Richard Warren suddenly put his arm around his own wife's shoulders. She looked up into his face with the greatest affection.

Hester gazed fondly at wise old Elder Brewster, for he had almost certainly foreseen all this. A wedding was not a time to separate women from men, but to bind them together more strongly than ever, both relative newlyweds like the Aldens and Winslows and those like the Warrens and Cookes who had been married for many years.

Soon Governor Bradford took Bible in hand in his role as magistrate and performed the same marriage service for Captain

Standish and his Barbara. This time Hester watched the proceedings with her children, as the captain had requested Francis to stand as part of an honor guard of ten. The militiamen stood at attention, five on each side of the happy couple, holding their guns at port arms. Hester thought the honor guard silly and pretentious, especially after having picked up the musket behind her husband's back one night and realizing how heavy it was—she could barely lift it. Though the ceremony was brief, less than a quarter of an hour, unlike the interminable papist weddings she had occasionally witnessed in France as a girl, she had no idea how Francis and the other men could hold those weapons in salute for that long without wavering the fraction of an inch.

John and Jacob were clearly bursting with pride at the sight of their father, and surprisingly Hester found herself coming around, won over as completely as her boys by Francis's military bearing. She saw how the other members of the colony stood a little taller at the sight of those ramrod straight men with their big guns, though they lacked red coats and white vests, their only uniforms the best clothing they owned, the patched and cleaned-up raiment of humble working men. It occurred to her that perhaps Standish knew what he was doing after all. The little ceremonies of order and governance might carry more importance in this wilderness than on the other side of the Atlantic.

CHAPTER 19

A Time to Gather

Over and over during her first days in Plymouth Hester heard assorted variations of a single mysterious refrain: everyone would know corn-planting time had arrived when the fish began to run. When she sought explanation for this odd turn of phrase, people only chuckled, including Francis and John making no further answer than a cheery, "You'll see."

Then one bright morning Francis, after dropping pointed hints on the advisability of eating the heartiest breakfast possible, headed out to the fields early. For once John lingered behind to help Hester with the younger children. These were awakened, dressed with haste, and served corncakes made with their family's share of the Cummaquid corn.

Enlightenment came with a booming cry from the sentries atop the fort. "The fish!"

Hester looked at John. "You knew it was today."

He grinned back. "It starts around the same time every year. Squanto taught us when to expect it." He turned to the younger children, "Come, let us finish quickly."

Though the little ones no more understood the excitement than their mother, they made quick work of the food.

John swept up some netting he and his father had diligently repaired and kept next to the door along with some sharpened wooden stakes and a hammer. Bundling all these in his arms, he herded the family outside, up the hill and out through the upper gates of the stockade. He ran them through the fields toward the forest, moving so fast that Jacob could hardly keep up. Before they reached the trees, Hester picked the little boy up in her arms and carried him.

"Slow down, John, please," she begged, fighting for breath.

"We need to stake out our spot!"

John led them to a tiny forest clearing where a gleaming brook coursed over rock ledges to form a series of steep cascades leading downhill from somewhere higher up, making its brisk way toward some distant and unseen outlet to the sea. It was a large, fast flowing stream, about four yards wide in this spot and perhaps two feet deep at most.

Hester and the children came to an abrupt halt, awestruck at the sight before them.

An enormous number of fish were in the process of leaping from one level of the creek to the next, their silver bodies flashing in the dappled sunlight as they fought their way upstream. There must be scores of them, maybe hundreds. As Hester stood and stared with her little ones, John was pulling off his boots. He hammered a stake into the ground not far from the edge, attached one end of the netting, and then stepped boldly down into the water, wading across to the other side. One of the leaping fish hit him square in the side of the head, causing his sisters to cry out, but he only grinned back at them. He clambered up the opposite bank and drove another stake to anchor the far side of the netting.

Then he waded back, out into the middle of the stream. Most of the fish sailed right over the netting, but it served as an effective trap for dozens of the others. John began to seize the entrapped fish and flip them out onto the near bank, where they landed at the feet of the others.

"Jacob!" he shouted. "Move those fish away from the edge, so they won't flop back in."

Jacob responded enthusiastically, flipping the writhing fish back onto the grassy floor of the clearing well away from the water. The little boy quickly understood the nature of the problem when a couple of the larger fish managed to launch themselves back into the flowing stream.

"The rest of you come help me!" John shouted. "Please, Mother!"

Taking off their shoes, Hester waded in, followed by the girls. The icy cold of the water hurt. Fortunately it wasn't very deep, though it came up over her knees and was very swift. She had to fight to stay on her feet. Following John's example, they began to scoop fish, cupping both hands underneath the scaly bodies and flipping them onto the bank. It took practice to gain anything like John's proficiency, but soon they began to improve. Jacob ran around on the edge, delighted with his responsibility, herding the flailing fish away from their only escape. Not many eluded his vigilance.

Moving her eyes up the stream's incline, Hester could see and hear other people wading into the cold water, staking out their fishing grounds. She questioned John about why they didn't all work together.

"Every house stakes out its own place," John explained.

"Well, then, do we keep all these fish for ourselves?"

"Need you ask, Mother? No, the fish will be divided equally."

She noticed people upstream who were clearly not working as energetically as the Cooke clan. The few women and children she could see only stood on the bank and watched their husbands and brothers, not so much as securing the catch as Jacob was, scurrying around on his little legs. "I see what you and your father mean... it is most unfair."

John laughed. "Welcome to Plymouth."

The first one knocked off her feet in the fast-flowing stream was not Little Hester, whom Hester was more concerned about, but the one year older and much taller Jane. She looked as though she were about to cry when it happened, but her big brother picked her up.

"Don't worry, Jane," John said, "it happens to everyone eventually." She bent quickly back to the task.

It was backbreaking work, for they had to remain mostly stooped over except for the strenuous upsurge when they flipped each net-trapped or hand-caught fish toward the bank. Hester knew they would have to take a rest eventually though some of the precious fish would inevitably escape.

* * *

Before long the fish they had gathered must number in the hundreds. Jacob seemed happy to reign over his little domain. Ordinarily, Hester would have expected him to demand to be part of the "fun" of being in the water, but John kept paying the odd compliment that made the little boy swell with pride, thus keeping him content on the bank. Hester marveled at the maturity of her elder son being so thoughtful toward the little fellow. Yet John was not a grownup quite yet.

"John, we must have a rest," she finally said. "or we shall wear ourselves out."

"But it's the height of the run, Mother!"

Jane squinted at John as if he were a slave driver.

"We need a respite," Hester said, "or we'll be good for nothing."

"All right, perhaps in a bit. Then we'll take turns, perhaps?"

"Fine, but your sisters will rest first."

"Very well."

The girls gave their mother a grateful look.

"Do we have enough salt to preserve this quantity of fish?" Hester asked.

"We don't preserve them, Mother. These fish are for the corn planting."

"What?" said wet shivering Jane.

"Squanto taught us," John explained, keeping up his rhythm of flinging fish onto the bank. "You dig a little mound for each corn plant, and you bury some fish at the base of each mound. He said it gives the corn plant the food its roots need to grow strong and tall."

"I have never seen so many fish in my life." Hester said. Her own fish flinging had unquestionably slowed down, as had the exertions of the two girls.

"They only run once a year," John said, "right at the time for the corn planting."

"Ah, then it is a provision of God for our good."

"The fish were running a long time before we arrived, Mother. That's how the Indians have always known when to plant."

"But it is God's provision still. Our Lord loves the Indians as much as He loves us."

John was sufficiently shocked to stop and look at her. "I've never heard anyone say that."

"It is most clear from God's Word. I will show you verses tonight."

"I thought God only loved the elect."

"God loves the whole world. Besides, who says red people cannot be numbered among the elect? Do you think Christ died only for sinners with fair complexions?"

At this point Hester peremptorily ordered the weary girls out of the water for a rest, brooking no dissent from John.

"Go sit in the sun, Jane. Try to dry off."

Hester was considering whether to go home for blankets when Philip Delano burst out of the woods carrying an armload of that very article on top of a stack of huge woven baskets. The baskets solved the mystery of how to transport the fish back to Plymouth. She wondered if they had been procured from the Indians or if the settlers had learned the craft of basket-making themselves. There was so much she did not know and yearned to learn about these folk whom most Christians of her acquaintance referred to as "savages" without so much as a fare-thee-well. She had yet to see her first, though everyone claimed they were always watching the white people from hiding. Personally she found this idea absurd. The Indians surely had more important things to do than gaze upon the pale strangers in their midst, and she thought the English flattered themselves.

"I am so sorry, my beautiful ones," Philip was saying, "I had to help your father clear a last corner of the fields that our most wise and farseeing councilmen require for the new planting, and I have not until this moment had the time to come fishing with you."

"Where is he then?" Jane demanded.

"He has dismissed my lamentably inadequate efforts most scornfully in order to send me ahead." Sizing up the situation before him, Philip approached the rock where the girls sat and placed blankets around their shoulders, then rubbed their frozen feet with big gentlemanly hands long since hardened and calloused into those of a working man. He accomplished all this with his customary patter of charming jokes, then turned toward the stream. "You'd better take a rest as well, *mon chere*." He removed his boots and waded into the torrent as Hester was only too happy to climb out. "How about you, John?"

"I'm fine," John said through gritted teeth. Philip took his word for it, taking over the place alongside. John seemed to take new vigor from Philip's example.

"How about you, little man?" Philip asked. "Should you not take a rest?"

"I'm fine!" Jacob sounded exhausted, but Philip took his word as well. Hester realized the success of the corn crop must depend on acquiring a tremendous quantity of fish. There could be no other explanation for this amount of hard work and determination.

Pulling a welcome blanket around her, taking care to tuck in her feet, Hester sat in the sun with her daughters. By now they were all as wet as Jane or nearly so. Closer upstream she saw a new group of women and girls watching men and boys fish. Over the noise of the torrent she heard them shrieking with the glee of excited spectators. Somehow John never suggested this option existed for the Cooke family women. She smiled at how much he had come to resemble his father.

It suddenly occurred to Hester that she had no idea how long this phenomenon of the fish run would last, so she asked Philip.

"It varies, but usually a week to ten days." The girls groaned, anticipating days of agony, but Philip soothed their worried minds. "For some reason the fish, they run heaviest on the first day, which is why the Indians put all of their people into the streams, as do some of the more cruel among ourselves." He laughed, though no one else did. "But do not worry. The fish will soon thin out, and after two or three days the job can be handled by a few strong boys like Jacob."

Jane and Little Hester heaved visible sighs of relief. Hester felt the same.

"But by then," Philip added, "we shall be busy with the planting, which will make us yearn to be back at the fishing!" He took a moment to allow the girls to groan again before adding, "But do not worry, that is not for the ladies. Nor little children, just big grownup fellows like John."

"Lucky me," John said from the middle of the stream.

As her daughters rejoiced at their reprieve from another backbreaking job, Hester wondered what there was about planting that she and they could not handle. With no additional information forthcoming as Philip busied himself in the stream, she rose and walked over for a closer look at the accumulating fish. They appeared to be a kind of herring, though one she had never seen, slender bony things without much meat. The largest looked completely unsuitable for human consumption, which was probably fortunate for the corn but quite the opposite for people hungry in the here and the now. Feelings of hunger could not be satisfied by the prospect of a good harvest in the autumn. With more women newly arrived, including at least herself trained from childhood in the highly adaptable cooking of France, she and the other ladies of the colony had a duty to help find a solution. Just because this land did not produce a steady supply of what cantankerous Englishmen were used to eating did not mean there was nothing else here to eat.

All the more reason she longed to make friends with some of the Indian women—to find out more about their foods. As a Walloon, uninfected by any sense of loyalty to French culture, which continued to dominate the minds of French Protestants like Philip even after being forced to flee the mother country for their lives, Hester took satisfaction in something her mother had told her in childhood. The French had stolen all their good ideas about preparing food from the Italians! Yet her mother did not deny that the French adapted and developed what they stole. In matters of cuisine the French were quite flexible and highly innovative, unlike a certain more stodgy nationality Hester could mention. The Indians had taught these English to catch fish, hunt, plant corn, possibly weave baskets, and much else. Francis and John surprised her nearly every day with the latest allusion to something they had learned from Squanto or Hobomok.

She wondered afresh why no one had bothered to question the Indians more closely about their bill of fare. Corn itself was new to the English, and now they would attempt to grow it in vast quantity, well beyond the efforts of the natives. The cornfields surrounding Plymouth were as large as European wheat fields. There had to be other foods in this land that the English didn't know about yet, and Hester was determined to find out as soon as she got the chance.

CHAPTER 20

A Time to Plant

The planting began the next day after the fish commenced their spectacular run. Francis and Philip disappeared at sunrise, marching off with spades on their shoulders and a huge basket with the household's initial fish allotment carried between them. The precious seed corn would be distributed at the direction of the council when they arrived in the fields. John headed for the forest to join those, mostly other youngsters, assigned to the second day of fishing.

By mid-morning Hester had enough of sewing clothes and wanted to investigate the other kind of sowing. The English tongue could be so odd sometimes, with the same sound having radically different meanings depending on how it was used. She had learned the language as a girl, after her arrival in Holland, where she landed amongst these kindly refugees from similar persecution against religious dissenters in England. Though she did remarkably well, she knew she had not mastered the tongue completely and probably never would. Philip maintained English had two or three times more words in its arsenal than French or German, perhaps more than French and German combined. She could well believe it but had no idea how one could know such a thing. It was not as if anyone had ever compiled a list of all the words and their meanings, which would probably not be a bad idea, come to think of it. It would save her constantly having to ask, guess or remain in ignorance every time she heard a new one.

Doctor Fuller claimed there had been a wealthy aristocrat under the reign of Queen Elizabeth and the early years of the present English king, a secret scribbler who invented hundreds of words on his own, using them in poetry and plays he put forth under an assumed name to avoid family disgrace for dallying at such lowborn endeavors. If only the English demonstrated that much invention in their kitchens!

Putting such scholarly musings reluctantly aside, as one prone to them since learning to read, Hester yielded to Jacob and the girls' pleas to walk out to the forest. After a night and morning to rest their backs, the girls now regarded the fishing as rather fun, though perhaps without Jacob's keen enthusiasm to have another go at the process.

They reached the familiar clearing and found the stream being worked by a small group of highly efficient young men and boys including John. The lads had strung much more elaborate netting, and the arrangement made trapping the fish easier, though without any relief for the backbreaking labor of bending and tossing them up on the bank. As Philip had predicted, the leaping fish were not as numerous as the previous day. The boys looked startled when Hester volunteered herself and the girls to help, but John deflected the ladies to carrying a load of fish to the fields, a task more in line with the other young gentlemen's expectations. Jacob begged to resume his duties from yesterday, and Hester agreed, leaving him in the keeping of his brother.

The Cooke ladies managed two baskets, Hester carrying one, Jane and her sister bearing the other between them. Fortunately the fishing spot lay not very far from the area of the cornfields where they found Francis and Philip hard at work, a matter of divine providence as the heavily burdened Hester and her daughters believed, since the men never knew what part of the field they would be assigned to when they showed up for work in the morning. Hester had heard Philip complain more than once how this often meant spending the better part of each new morning repairing the shoddy labors of less diligent workers from the previous day.

Both men were exceedingly glad to see them, having nearly exhausted their complement of fish. Francis had scarcely opened his mouth to say thank you when an unpleasant-looking Englishman ran up from nearby. Hester did not know the man, so he must be one of the English who joined themselves to the Leyden group on one of the two previous ships, in the way Mrs. Warren and her flock had crossed aboard the *Anne*.

"'ere now," the unpleasant man protested, a Londoner to judge by his speech. "Ye cannot dispatch yer women folk to bring ye fish without sharing with the others! Who do ye thank ye are?"

The man scowled at Hester and the girls as if they had committed the unpardonable, which was a good thing for him because he missed the downright ungodly male expressions glowered in his own direction. Francis's face flushed deeper than his sunburn, and for an instant Hester feared he would actually strike the man, with Philip happily following suit. She watched her husband draw a slow fuming breath before he spoke.

"Certainly not, brother," Francis said with studiously controlled courtesy. "We share and share alike around these parts, do we not?"

"Indeed we do, sir," rasped the un-brotherly brother. "If ye choose to dispatch yer womenfolk for this unladylike task of bringing fish, then ye must not take sole advantage of it."

The impertinent grumbler was making matters worse, to the point that Hester questioned the welfare of his soul. By now Philip looked downright murderous, as if ready to make the destiny of the man's soul an issue of immediate concern, but Francis continued to play peacemaker.

"I have set no such burdens on my wife and daughters, sir. They are only trying to help."

"Then they can help one and all." Without another word, the unpleasant man turned and beckoned. Other men approached, none of them familiar to Hester, and soon scurried off with well over half the fish.

"Mother, look," Jane grumbled. "Those men haven't exhausted their fish nearly as much as father and Uncle Philip have!"

"Ssh, quiet, my dear."

"But it isn't fair!"

"No, Jane, it is not," Philip said, for once too softly for his voice to carry, "and sadly many of those fish will be wasted, either because they will not be properly planted or they will not be guarded vigilantly enough in the nights to come."

Though Philip sought to make her and the girls feel better after their humiliation, the guilty thought plucked at Hester: why had she looked around for her husband when they stumbled out of the woods with their boodle of fish? Why had that seemed the natural thing to do rather than simply take the basket to the first men she saw in the fields? Perhaps there was unacknowledged sin in this, a failure to live up to proper standards of community virtue, though frankly she could think of no scripture to prove it. She had simply looked for those of her own household without thinking.

"If you please," Hester said, putting self-accusation aside for later, "show us how you plant. Perhaps we can help you with that as well."

"I think not," Francis said quickly. "It might cause more resentment."

"Come, Francis, no harm in showing them," Philip said.

They all moved over to where the two men had just been working. Hester happened to glance toward the stockade and was astonished to see Governor Bradford and Doctor Fuller standing very close at hand, watching them. They must have seen everything that just occurred, and Hester blushed to think she and her girls had unwittingly instigated such a mortifying exhibition. If the governor thought them blameworthy, however, he hid his feelings well, lifting his hat and making a slight bow in her direction, looking as kindly as ever. As the two older gentlemen turned their backs and walked away, heads bowed in conversation, Hester's ears burned at the possibility they might be discoursing on the greed and selfishness of the Cooke family.

Her daughters had already focused their full attention on the work of the men, and she joined in, trying to look equally innocent. Her husband must have sensed her discomfort, for he gave her a quick comforting squeeze with one arm. Philip explained the corn planting process with his usual charm and volubility. Hester felt grateful as the endearing Huguenot caught her up in his own enthusiasm, pushing everything else out of her mind.

Philip described how they planted the corn in long parallel rows that ran the width of each section in the fields. The beloved Indian Squanto had shown them how far the plants should be set apart from one another to leave plenty of room for the squash that would be planted last. He taught them to leave half again that much space between the rows to create walking room so the corn, bean and squash plants could be tended and harvested.

"But we start with the corn." Philip used his spade to dig a shallow hole. "You place one to three fish at the bottom, depending on the size, and cover them over." He showed them how to plant the seed corn and cover it with sufficient soil to raise a little mound overtop. "You do exactly the same for each separate plant. The decaying fish provide food to make the corn grow tall and healthy, just like these beautiful children of my dear hosts the Cookes, whom I must look upon every day with great envy in my sad unmarried condition." The girls giggled.

"What did you mean about being vigilant in the night?" Hester asked.

"Ah, starting tonight we must set a guard about the fields. Unless they are protected, we shall never harvest a crop from all this hard work."

"Protected from what?" Jane said with big rounded eyes.

Philip and Francis glanced at one another, and the Frenchman left it to her father whether to let slip the unvarnished truth.

"Protected from wolves," Francis said. Little Hester ran to her mother's side as he hastened to explain. "It's nothing much to fear, really. But until the fish have had a chance to rot, the wolves will try to steal in and dig them up. A few beasts gorging themselves could limit the crop. A whole pack would destroy it completely."

"But aren't they dangerous?" Jane said, taking the words right out of Hester's mouth. "Do you have to fight them off?"

"They are rather shy creatures, really," Philip said. "Some bonfires and a few loud fellows with the lungs of leather are usually enough to frighten them off."

"Usually?" Hester said.

"Well, perhaps one has to discharge a musket now and then. Just to frighten, of course. No point shooting something that is not good to eat, *non*?"

"How do you know a wolf is not good to eat?" Little Hester said.

"You have me there, little one. Perhaps we should put the issue to the test." The eight-year-old looked torn between laughing and crying.

"Please, Philip." Francis turned to his wife. "We should return to our work."

"Come, daughters," Hester said, then to the men of her house, "are you sure there is nothing we can do?"

Francis glanced around at the other men toiling all over the fields. None was entertaining womenfolk, and the closest wore frowns of disapproval.

"Perhaps you should come back at end of day, Hester," Philip suggested. "I should be glad to keep an eye on your children for a time. Perhaps your husband could show you around a bit before we fall upon our suppers."

Francis lifted his eyebrow at this, but Hester made haste to say thank you and accept. Time alone with Francis had been almost nonexistent except for the dark hours after the children had gone to sleep or before they woke, a time when the weary parents craved sleep for themselves.

"Excellent," Philip said. "Then afterward some of us must return to spend the night in the fields."

"Could we?" Jane asked, any fear of the wolves dissolving into excitement. "Are girls allowed to shout at them?"

"No entreaty of man nor command of king has ever prevented *mademoiselles* from lifting their voices whenever they choose, my pretty one," Philip said. "The decision is up to your good parents."

"We shall see," Hester said. "For now we need to go home." As they turned away, she spoke to the men. "I'll send Jane back at midday with some dinner."

The two men stood watching mother and daughters walk back toward Plymouth.

Philip said, "I wonder what it shall consist of?"

"What?"

"The dinner. I do not think your beautiful bride perceives the full extent of our deprivation."

"She'll find something, you'll see."

"Then she had better send enough to feed all." His hand swept across the fields.

"No, when we see Jane coming, you and I shall walk nonchalantly into the trees and partake by ourselves."

"An excellent plan. Quite devious. Are you sure you have no French ancestors?"

CHAPTER 21

Encounter at the Tree Line

The more reliable men, including Francis and Philip, strove mightily to keep all hands working until dark, but weary workers began to dribble away long before sunset. Francis remonstrated more than once, only to be ignored or fended off with the bitter question, "Why?" No one dared explicate the question aloud, but he knew its full bleakness well enough—why slave to the point of exhaustion with no direct benefit to oneself or one's family?

"Because without a good corn harvest the whole colony will perish," Francis answered.

"We're perishing now!" one ragged cynic threw back over a retreating shoulder. The would-be farmer and his companions in exhaustion thus deserted, shaking their heads in wonder at the steadfastness of dreamers. Men drained of hope were in no mood to hear further promises of theoretical but so far imaginary benefits for the community at large.

Philip unleashed a loud stream of French invective at a fellow Huguenot leaving early, but the Gallic version had no more impact than the Anglo-Saxon. More honorably, several younger men including John Alden labored on unwavering in the fields, somehow finding reserves of inexplicable strength in knowing what had to be done for Plymouth to have any hope of survival. Philip quickly organized these to dig in the same section, on the theory they would make more progress planting in concert than singly on widely separated tracts.

At long last the shadows began to grow longer, and Francis looked up to see Hester walking down the hill from the town. He and Philip, tired as they were, had attained a certain proficiency, and they managed to shovel half a dozen mounds each in the time it took her to reach them.

Philip raised a rakish brow. "Where are the children?"

"I left them with Priscilla. You're off the hook, Philip."

"Unlike the delicious perch you provided for our noontime repast." Philip swept off his hat for a quick bow. "For which I thank you, kind lady."

"The perch weren't exactly hooked," Hester said.

"How so?" Francis said. Hidden among the trees according to plan, he and Philip had been too busy wolfing down the startlingly fulfilling meal Jane brought to ask any awkward questions at the time.

"We followed the stream down to its mouth, by the edge of the bay, and found a tidal pool with these lovely perch frolicking about, pretty as you please. We were able to obtain six."

"And how, pray, did you obtain them?"

"We happened to take one of John's little nets along."

Philip grinned at Francis. "You see? French blood!"

"Walloon!" Hester said. Delano always insisted her beauty and good judgment proved there had to be French aristocracy somewhere in her ancestry.

All seriousness and concern, Francis ignored the japery. "I trust you weren't seen, and a good thing it is!"

"Why?" Hester asked, clearly puzzled at his sternness.

"Because, dear lady," Philip explained, "if you had been caught with the six perch, they must needs be divided amongst all Plymouth, just as with the loaves and the fishes, though I doubt they should have fed so many as when our Lord did the dividing."

"A little catch of fish, they too? You are joking."

"Not at all. Ask your husband. When he and your son go out and shoot a deer, does the Cooke household receive the benefit of their skill and daring? No, my dear, the equality rule applies in every sphere. The carcass must be divided equally among all the households in our fair town."

"But that's different. Francis is an excellent shot."

Francis lowered his eyes. "Please, Hester."

"He is an excellent shot, according to John," Hester rolled right over her husband's modesty, "and thus a designated hunter. When he and John go out they are hunting for the entire village. Besides, a deer is a very large thing, and six perch are so very small."

"Madame," Philip said, "your logic is impeccable as always, and I am very much on your side, but unfortunately the principle is considered the same for six little fish as it is for a deer. As has been decreed by our wise and prosperous masters far away, we share and share alike."

"That is absurd. I am glad no one saw us then."

Philip shrugged. "The favor of God."

"I did give a couple of perch to Priscilla."

"Well, there you are. The spirit of the law has surely been fulfilled."

"We must try to obey the rules," Francis felt he had to say, though without fervor.

Hester stood pondering, the unfairness of this enforced equivalence no doubt brought home more powerfully than ever. Francis fancied he saw an all-encompassing comprehension dawning in her troubled eyes at last. He knew she would turn aside now from any expression of its enormity, turning the matter over in her active mind for days to come, in the long process of forging an opinion of her own. She was not the kind of wife to be told what to think by a husband, however much she loved him. Oddly, but secretly, Francis took pride in this.

"Philip," she turned to their houseguest, "if you go home you will find a squirrel stew in the pot. John managed to kill a nice couple of fat fellows, which I boiled with some wild herbs and carrots that I found overlooked in the garden behind the house. The children have eaten, and you had best get your share before some lunatic distributes it out to the wide world."

This jibe startled Francis—perhaps she had formed an opinion already! Well, if ever such rapidity were justified…

"Hester, we did not make these silly regulations," he said.

"No, but as men perhaps you should be doing something more about changing them."

"I shall look forward to dining on your masterpiece of cookery later," Philip nodded toward the tree line, "but now we need to build our bonfires for the night."

Hester turned to look in the same direction. Youngsters were streaming out of the forest with arms full of branches and small logs. Francis could not see John, who was probably out doing a substantial portion of the chopping.

"So that's where John fled after eating his supper," Hester said. "He didn't bother to explain. He just ran off."

"We all have our duties," Francis said.

"I have so much to learn."

"Go home and eat, Philip," Francis insisted. "There are hands enough to build the fires."

"Very well. Thank you. Thank you, both."

* * *

Hester was deliberating whether to take Philip's abandoned spade in hand to help her husband as he bent down to put the finishing touches on the mound at the end of a row, but he rose and put his arm around her shoulder.

"Come, my darling, let us walk."

He handed off the tools to John Alden, who gave a quick nod of encouragement and understanding. "I shall see to the fire and take the first watch."

Hester glanced back as they walked away. "Has Mister Alden had his supper?"

"I know not." He led her off, and she allowed it.

They walked slowly, as if out for an evening stroll in a Leyden park, where the gardens were as well planned but considerably more imaginative than the squared up straight-line symmetry of the corn plots. For the first time Francis took the time to explain exactly what the men were doing in the fields and why. Hester had already picked up a certain amount of this knowledge, and he seemed happy to fill in the gaps as best he could. She had grown up tending vines, herbs and vegetables in tiny household gardens. His own experience as a gardener had come in the years since the Mayflower voyage, a duty she knew he would gladly relinquish to her more experienced hands. Neither of them understood farming of such great extent, the faltering and slapdash enterprise they saw all around them as they walked. Hester said its scale compared to anything she had ever seen in France.

"I only hope it yields a sufficient harvest this year," Francis said, "worthy of the amount of land we've cleared."

"Why should it not?"

Francis shrugged. "I am no real farmer yet to be sure, but I've learned a harvest grows out of more than seed and earth. It takes knowledge and hard work, and proper work requires the most diligent and careful attention to details and practical matters of every description."

As they traversed various sections Hester could with her relatively untrained eye discern striking contrasts between one patch of ground and another. Where Francis and Philip had been working this day the rows were long and straight, each planted mound pitched a precise distance apart from the next. The mounds themselves were virtually identical, no doubt formed exactly as their Indian teachers had shown them. This uniformity did not hold sway throughout the breadth of the fields.

"These are not all the same," she said, indicating a sweeping span of crooked rows. The mounds themselves diverged exceedingly in size and placement.

"I know." She heard the exasperation in his voice. "If the mounds are too small, the bud will pop up before it can take root. If the mound be too large, the plant is buried too deep to reach the sun. You wind up either with a weak and sickly plant or none at all. Hours of hard toil for nothing if it isn't done properly."

"But why bother to do it wrong?"

"Men are indifferent. Some are weak. Perhaps more than a few are lazy."

"But shouldn't something be done?"

"I know not what can be that has not been tried already. Remonstrance is certainly more than useless."

"What can we do then, we who care?"

"The most important object is to plant the corn seed in the few days we have. If we finish the greater work, perhaps some of us will be able to come back and correct at least a portion of the mistakes." He sounded doubtful by his tone. "There is so much to be done, and so few of us willing to put the full effort into doing it right."

"Why are the days so shortened?"

"Squanto taught us that all the corn must be planted within less than two weeks after the fish run begins. Otherwise you might not be able to bring in the full crop before the first freeze comes upon us in the autumn."

Half-worried he might go hastening back to his shovel, Hester asked about the clapboards used to build the houses.

"These fields were thick with trees when we landed. John Alden was a carpenter and shipbuilder by trade when he left the Mayflower crew to join us."

"I suspect Priscilla may have been a motivating factor."

"No doubt, though Captain Standish had his eye on her as well."

"I suspect the better man won."

Francis left that comment alone. "Brother Alden had more knowledge and experience to supervise the construction than anyone else. He was also a most effective and patient teacher when it came to showing those of us completely devoid of useful experience how to do everything we had to learn. What a frightful process! Exhausting beyond anything you can imagine. Still, we managed to build all you see from the timber provided by these fields and forests." Eagerness beamed from his face. "Once more settlers come, I've been thinking a man could do well running a sawmill. Many towns and houses to be built, and people will want proper lumber and plenty of it. They won't be contented with boards roughed out by the axe."

"John said something about that."

"Yes." Francis grinned. "The boy seems excited by the idea. Of course, neither of us knows anything about building or running a saw mill."

She squeezed his arm. "You can learn. Anything is possible in this new land."

"That's as I see it too, Hester! We've talked it over with John Alden, and he grasps it as well. All you need is a good fast running stream to drive the wheel, perhaps beside a little waterfall for more pressure. You could set up grindstones as well. Then you could handle lumber year round and grain at the harvest! But the main thing would be the saw. Once people begin to arrive in great numbers, the demand for lumber will be—well, there's simply no limit to it!"

"It sounds wonderful."

"John and I have been combing the forest for a likely spot, when we're out hunting. We've found several."

They were just reaching the edge of said forest when Francis suddenly stopped, hesitating before walking in among the trees. She looked up at his face, concerned at the troubled new look she saw.

"Of course, all that must wait til one can feel safe out there," he said.

The sinking sun cast ever-lengthening black shadows across the cornfields. Forbidding darkness already reigned among the trees. Hester could hear the wind whistling through the bows overhead. She heard the distant hoot of an old owl somewhere, that fierce and implacable harbinger of night, bestirring himself to the hunt. A shiver ran down her spine. She nestled tightly to her husband's side.

"There are dangers?"

"Absolutely, and you and the children must never forget it."

"But we are at peace with the Indians, are we not?"

"Only with our Wampanoag neighbors by formality of treaty, not that we are at sword's point with any savage people of course. But sometimes distant tribes send hunting parties to Wampanoag land. War parties, too. One never knows. Until we number far more, it's best not to hazard overmuch."

She moved round to gaze up at him. His arms went around her. She felt his strength and hugged him back. Their physical connection transmuted the leaden dross of fear into an opulent tenderness.

"We have not been alone enough," she whispered.

"I know."

She lifted her face up, and he bent his down and kissed her powerfully on the lips. She hugged him tighter, as if to prevent his ever being torn away from her again. After long moments she bent back slightly to study his face by the ebbing twilight.

Though her eyes were closely focused, she caught a glimpse of movement at the right edge of her vision and turned her head slightly to look.

The dark figure of a devil materialized out of the darkness, standing only a few feet away, watching them. It was of the size and shape of a man, but warped, distorted by odd protuberances that stuck out strangely from its head and body. Horns, without a doubt. Old tales from childhood flashed through her mind, of demons rising out of the earth to drag unwary sinners down to Hell, stories her Protestant mind had hitherto dismissed as Romish superstition.

Hester screamed.

Francis whirled about, stepping in front of his wife to protect her as his hand flew to the knife in his belt. Then he saw the source of her fright and immediately relaxed.

The devil walked forward a bit, and Hester saw it was a man after all. The horns were a handful of large feathers stuck at the top of a thick lock of hair on a mostly shaved head. The bodily protrusions were nothing more that a bow, a quiver of arrows, and a lance carried in his right hand.

Hester became aware of movement behind her and turned to see figures running in their direction from the fields, hands filled with tools as weapons to the battle. Hester rued how loudly she must have screamed. By now everyone had heard the Scotsman's story and knew the purpose of her husband and the others' trip to Wessagusset. People were nervous and justifiably so. She felt instantly embarrassed to be the source of a false alarm.

Francis cupped his hands to his mouth and shouted. "Nothing to fear, gentlemen! My wife has never seen one of our Wampanoag friends before!"

The headlong rush ceased at once. The men and youths went back to preparing and lighting their scattered bonfires. Younger boys turned back again from headlong retreat to the fort. She could hear chuckling and laughter, which she much preferred to anger over her stupidity.

"Don't worry, my darling," Francis said, "it is a mistake anyone could make. You mustn't be frightened." He turned to the Indian, who stared at her with eyes so wide that the whites of them stood out sharply against the growing darkness. "May I present Hobomok, ambassador to Plymouth from Massasoit Ousamequin, great chieftain of the Wampanoag? Hobomok, this is my woman—my wife—who has come to join us from across the sea, along with my other children."

"How do you do, Missus?"

Hester stepped out from hiding behind Francis's back. The frightening barbarity of the man's scarred face made a startling contrast to his formality of English expression. "I am very well, Mister Hobomok. And yourself?"

"I am very well, Missus." Hobomok turned to her husband. "I bid you good evening."

"Good evening, my friend."

They watched as the Indian walked off toward the stockade, stopping occasionally to say hello to the boys building the fires. One and all seemed glad to see him.

"I'm glad he's back," Francis said. "He can help oversee the rest of the planting."

"You call him an ambassador?" Hester asked.

"As much as any European. He lives among us most of the time in that very role. All the local groups and villages for miles around," Francis explained, "are part of a confederation, each village or clan with its own chief man, but ruled overall by the great chieftain of the Wampanoag tribe, Massasoit. Almost at once, when we landed on these shores going on three years ago, Massasoit made a treaty of peace with us."

"And this Massasoit has proved reliable? Trustworthy?"

"Indeed he has. His word, once given, has proved far sounder than that of many English gentlemen and professing Christians. Massasoit can be trusted completely, we find, though he remains obstinately impervious to the Gospel."

"Perhaps he has found certain Christians untrustworthy, as you say, and why then should he trust the Christian Gospel?"

"That may indeed be the root of it, but we of Plymouth, beginning with Governor Bradford on down to the least of us, have always sought to deal with him and any of his people as honorably as he has dealt with us."

"And Hobomok lives with us at Plymouth?"

"It is to our advantage, believe me, though he also keeps an eye on us, I suppose. He's here all the time except when he goes home to consult with Massasoit or see his wife."

"His wife! He has children?"

"I believe he does, yes."

"But could they not live with us too?"

"It has been discussed, but some of the brethren felt their presence might be disturbing to our own women and children."

"Oh, I think not, Francis, I believe it would be wonderful to make their acquaintance. Think how much we could learn from Mrs. Hobomok!"

What Hester saw most clearly from his puzzled expression was that this opportunity needed to be pursued with some diligence, or nothing would happen. As absurd as her first encounter with a native had been, she was determined to do better in the future.

CHAPTER 22

Village Meeting

Out in the vast forests, from one scattered village to the next, the People grew weary from planting corn, especially the women and children who traditionally bore the greatest part of the burden. The warriors lent desultory help, of course, but they worked with bow and tomahawk close at hand, in case warning came of nearby game or approaching enemies. The elder women joked knowingly with the younger that such alarums had a way of turning up just at the depth of the tedium, allowing the braves to scamper off to their fun, leaving the women and the young to bear the heat and misery during the long hot middle of the day. Indeed, the men sometimes disappeared for as much as a week, though the crisis, whatever it was, always seemed to pass as if by powerful magic as soon as the planting was finished. Then the men would come creeping back, a little shamefaced perhaps, but usually with a large taking of game to justify their absence. The ensuing feasting on deer, turkey, rabbit, and the occasional lean, winter-depleted bear usually mollified the wives' resentment, or at least it did after the passage of a day or two of chilly feminine silence, sufficient to make the point. Yet the older women wisely advised daughters and granddaughters that the unfairness of it all was not worth begrudging, since the men were never going to change.

A couple of planting seasons back, when a certain startling rumor first arose regarding the Bone Men, the Wampanoag women could not believe their ears. The reaction in Cummaquid was the same as in all the villages. By twos and threes, beginning with the youngest girls, women would slip away and take the long walk south to establish the truth of the matter with their own eyes. Yet their testimony upon returning was not believed, and others had to go look for themselves. Eventually everyone believed it—among the strange new tribe of English the men and boys did the planting, with scarcely a woman or little girl in sight! This practice had not changed in the least now white squaws from the third great canoe had taken the places of the first winter's dead. The occasional woman or girl had been observed weeding or hoeing during the growing season, some claimed, but if any English squaw attempted to make the occasional effort during the planting, she did not last long or was quickly driven away, as if women's involvement were somehow a thing of dishonor.

To the warriors and hunters, of course, this astonishing behavior only reinforced the womanish reputation of the Bone Men. The more mature among the Wampanoag women had to agree. Which was better, to have more help in the fields, or to have strong arms that could bring home game and protect the village from marauding enemies? Most young women granted the truth of this as well. Though a little more help would be appreciated, they wanted their men to be men. Stirrings of discontent moved among the braves that perhaps the Massasoit had given his hand of friendship to the English too readily. If their men were weak and effeminate to this extent, perhaps it were less trouble to drive them back into the sea than to put up with them.

The peace with the whites marked one of the few occasions when some of the villages—generally those with younger and perhaps more reckless leadership—regretted the great Massasoit held the tribal authority he did. It had been recognized years ago, however, that sometimes a decision involving all the People had to be made quickly rather than argue the controversy out village by village. The chief of chieftains rarely used this power, but once he did there remained not very much anyone could do about it. Either plead for him to change his mind, or wait for the next generation to replace him. Gossip had spread that the Massasoit's sons, especially the eldest, did not hold with this particular decision, though the old man had been such a good chieftain that no one wished him ill over one possible mistake.

In the customary pattern of things, some form of alarming news came to the Cummaquid cornfield this very day. Shortly after the sun had reached its zenith, most of the men suddenly threw down their tools, picked up their weapons, and ran off into the forest. The women looked at one another as if to say, "There they go again."

After the sun had moved a bit, however, the women were astonished to see most of the men come trailing back into the field and returning to the work. Reluctantly perhaps, but they did it. As for the alarm, it proved authentic enough. A boy had spotted the approach of two warriors of the Massachusett tribe, but they turned out to be alone and wanting to parley. Rather than decide the matter himself as the warriors seemed to wish, Iyanough had decreed the whole village would meet to listen to their words after sunset. The Cummaquid men said the Massachusetts seemed astonished at this, not understanding that the Wampanoag tended to make important decisions with the consent of the entire village rather than blindly follow the dictates of chief and elders, the tendency of certain other tribes no one had the rudeness to name. The two outsiders were especially surprised that the women and children would be allowed to attend, as many as wished to do so after their long day's labor.

* * *

When the time came after supper, only a few of the very oldest people and the very youngest children chose to roll up in their blankets for the night. With the exception of these and a few extra watchers whom Iyanough set on guard duty out in the woods against the possibility that the two visitors were part of some ruse to cover an attack, all the others gathered in or around the great lodge. In truth most of the People of Cummaquid felt more distrustful of the Massachusett than of the Bone Men, who seemed harmless enough and had a reputation for honest trading. Yet all were willing to hear their visitors out. By custom the elders and strongest braves took the best places on the ground around the fire. Then the women and children swarmed in. The lodge quickly became quite crowded, with a large number of the young and female forced to remain outside, watching and listening as best they could.

A low murmur of excitement filled the meeting room as Iyanough's woman built the fire to a hot brightness against the chill of the night. When finished, she moved back and took a place among the women lining the wall. Plucking a brand from the fire, Iyanough lit a pipe, then passed it ceremoniously to the two visitors, who puffed and passed it on to the encircling elders until it came back to the chief. If the Massachusett braves felt impatient their stony faces did not betray it.

Finally Chief Iyanough rose to his feet, and all whispering ceased at once. He introduced the guests as Wituwamat and Pecksuot, two valiant warrior-hunters of the Massachusett, who had been traveling about speaking to the villages of their own tribe regarding an important matter. Now they thought time had come for discussions with the Wampanoag.

Every eye fixed on Wituwamat as he rose to his feet. No one wondered that he turned out to be the spokesman. Though shorter than his gigantic friend, he looked fiercer. Out of politeness his listeners tried not to stare at the many scars on his muscular body. Whether from war or the hunt, he carried them proudly as marks of honor, and as he began to speak his inherent ferocity caused most of the village to believe they came from battle.

Wituwamat spoke eloquently, so that his opening formalities of greeting and compliment were well worth attending. He rehearsed names of elders and warriors he had only just met, alluding to accounts of their prowess renowned among his own tribesmen. These courtesies impressed his audience almost as much as his skill with words. He praised everything from the leadership of Cummaquid to the beauty of its women, always good for a laugh and for putting everyone at ease. He laid it on so thick that some of the older and wiser began to worry about what all this was leading up to, certain that whatever it was, it was not going to be good.

They were right.

"My friend Pecksuot and I have begun to walk the forest paths among all the villages of the People. We purpose to speak our minds to all the encampments of the Massachusett and to all of yours and to those of every tribe with an open heart to listen to our words. We do this because we perceive a great danger that confronts the People, a new danger that appeared on our land about thirty moons ago, a threat worse than any monster crawling up out of the Great Water." He looked around at the rapt faces, as if wondering if he had to say it. "This danger is the English. The white-skinned strangers. Those you call the Bone Men."

Perhaps it was the mention of the monster that inspired the laughter. Everyone had heard childhood stories about monsters that came out of the water to devour disobedient youngsters, though the tales usually involved a long deep lake somewhere far to the north or west rather than the Great Water itself. The more likely source of the mirth, however, was the very idea that those pathetic ragged skeletons represented any kind of a menace, something to be mentioned in the same breath as a monster. Although the laughter consisted only of a few stifled giggles, Wituwamat appeared taken aback, but he quickly regained his composure.

"The Bone Men have colorful clothing!" someone said.

"Even if it is falling apart!" someone else added.

This fed the laughter.

Looking resigned, Wituwamat concentrated his attention on the serious men, the elders and young braves who were not smiling. He nodded sadly. "We receive the same response from our own People, unless we are able to make them think. But why can you not see the danger, my brothers? Another big canoe has come from across the Great Water, bearing more than a hundred new whites, including many children, including many women young enough to bear more children. Do you not understand that the sea will cast up more and more of these English on our shores? They will shoot the game. They will continue to cut down the trees until there will be scarcely any trees left."

"There is much game, Wituwamat," Iyanough scoffed. "There are many trees. We have shared the land with the Massachusett and many others. Why should we not share with the English?"

Among the Wampanoag an orator could only continue uninterrupted as long as his words held everyone's attention. Once someone felt free to speak up, the assembly quickly became a forum for open discussion, and Wituwamat had unknowingly crossed that line by the absurdity of his claim. He accepted the change in the atmosphere graciously, clearly prepared to give an answer to one and all.

"We must not share with the English because once they are many, they will take everything. It is their nature."

"We have found them friendly, and honest traders," one of the elders said.

"That is not who they truly are. You have not encountered the man Weston and his group of mangy dogs. Observe them, and you shall know the true nature of the English."

"Perhaps there are many kinds of English, as there are among the People," one of the women said. "Some are honest, and some are not."

If surprised at one of the women speaking up, Wituwamat did not show it. "Your English only do right while they are few and weak."

"But your English of the man Weston are much fewer," a young brave said. "They should act better than ours if what you say is true."

"Have you not heard how when the great canoes first came, the whites stole young men away, placed them in bonds of iron and carried them off beyond the edge of the world?" Heads nodded. Indeed everyone had heard of this, and only Tisquantum the Patuxet had ever returned alive to tell the tale of strange lands beyond the horizon. "That is the true nature of the whites. They are thieves, liars, menstealers and killers. Do not be fooled because those you know pretend to be weak and friendly."

"If what you say is true," Iyanough said, "what do you declare that we must do?"

It was Pecksuot who answered, clearly exasperated by the course of discussion. "The time has come to shed blood!"

Most of the women gasped, but the sound faded in the gathering silence. The gravity of the proposal demolished any impulse for murmuring and whispers. All eyes swept back to the orator.

Wituwamat savored the impact while he studied their faces.

"My brother is right," he said. "When my people the Massachusett learned that the Weston traders had decided to steal from us, we were more than ready to shed blood."

"So we have heard," Iyanough said, "but did not the other English put a stop to the stealing before it took place?" As with everything the strange newcomers did, chatter about the Wessagusset confrontation had been dispersed far and wide.

"They did this only to save themselves."

"Whatever their reasons, they did it."

Wituwamat disparaged the objection with a sneer. "My friend and I witnessed all. The little Red Hair knew the traders were too weak to fight. It is an empty thing to make bold threats against enemies too sick to get up on their feet."

"They were only sick from drinking too much strong water," an elder said. This raised another laugh though the elder himself did not crack so much as a smile.

"It matters not," Wituwamat said. "None of the English has yet been seen to fight, despite any idle tales we may have heard. They are weak and cowardly for now, but they must be killed before they grow in numbers. How could they ever be defeated, with their long knives and thundersticks, after they become more numerous than the People? As they grow in numbers, so shall they grow in boldness, and then it is the People who will die. They must be killed, my brothers. That is the only answer, and it must be done now while they are at their weakest and their numbers are small."

Further silence ensued as everyone chewed this over.

Iyanough spoke, as was his place to do. "Have you spoken of this to the Massasoit?"

"Why? Can the people of Iyanough not think for themselves?" This skirted the boundaries of insult, evoking a general guttural sound very much like growling. Wituwamat hastened to add, "Can the people of Cummaquid not take action on their own?"

"I will only say this," Iyanough said, rising to his feet with great dignity, "which you may carry back to any other of the Massachusett who share your opinion. My people of Cummaquid are proud to be Wampanoag, and the Massasoit is the great chieftain of all the

Wampanoag. Our village will not join in killing unless the Massasoit declares the will of all the Wampanoag that we must take the warpath."

"We Massachusett are not Wampanoag!" Wituwamat snapped, clearly angry that the tide had turned so quickly against him. "We do not bow the knee to the Massasoit!"

"Then you are free to act for yourselves. We shall not. I have spoken."

The last words formally ended the meeting, and the villagers began filing back to their homes, quietly discussing everything they had witnessed. Curtly rejecting an invitation to stay the night, the exasperated Massachusett braves stalked off in anger and frustration.

They had no way of knowing that Iyanough had already sent off a night runner with a message for the Massasoit.

CHAPTER 23

Town Meeting

Word came as dawn broke over the sea, before the exhausted and sleeping had time or inclination to crawl out of bed for work. Loud pounding by the Edwards Doty and Leister provoked in turn the irritable or anxious opening of every front door in Plymouth. The boys' excitable words conveyed the astonishing news that Governor Bradford and the council had called a town meeting to begin in one hour. The governor insisted everyone attend, each man, woman, and child in Plymouth except for the ill, the sentries and a skeleton watch in the fields to run off any wolves bold enough to approach after sunrise.

At the Cooke house Hester struggled to bestir the children into reasonably presentable condition. "What do you think this is all about?" she asked her husband.

"I know not," Francis said, pulling on his work clothes and old boots so he could go straight to the fields from the fort. "But it must be important to take time away from the planting. I can't imagine the governor will allow it to take long, though."

Philip Delano smiled mysteriously while he sipped a cup of fresh hot tea brewed from the bounty Hester had carried over from Holland.

"What do you know, Philip?" she demanded.

"Nothing. I know nothing." He withered under her inquisitorial stare. "Well, I really do know nothing, but let us say, perhaps I have a hope."

"And what is that?"

"The hope that perchance we are about to have all our wishes come true."

Hester noticed a certain dawning of the light in Francis's eyes. but that was all she was able to pry out of either for now.

* * *

Before the hour was up they were seated on the roughhewn benches in the meetinghouse, the women and children divided from the men just as for a worship service. John Cooke sat with his father, as he had Hester's first Sunday morning in Plymouth, which arrangement no one seemed to find remarkable. She had her other children by her side.

Judging by remarks overheard as people filed in, nobody else knew any more about the purpose of this most unprecedented conclave than the Cookes. Governor Bradford rose to his feet and gestured for silence. Elder Brewster opened with a brief prayer, then gave the floor back to the governor.

"My dear friends," Bradford said, "please do not be concerned, we shall have you back at your labors as quickly as possible, but what I have to say is important, involving the most momentous decision we have undertaken since signing our compact of self-government on board the old *Mayflower* after she dropped anchor out in the bay."

Fevered whispers rose and fell as Bradford waited anew for their undivided attention.

"The council has called this meeting for the purpose of dealing with a matter which has been the subject of more argument and contention than anything else since we first set foot on these shores almost two and a half years ago."

Glancing across the aisle, Hester saw Francis and Philip exchange a look of satisfaction. John put his hand on his father's.

"As you know," Bradford went on, "the adventurers in London, when they put forth the initial financial investment to underwrite our efforts here, did specify that all lands should be held in common. Each man and each family would undertake whatever effort was needed to grow a crop, and our harvests would be gathered into the common storehouse, to be distributed to each family according to need. The excess would be applied to cover the investment and take common profits."

Hester noticed astonished and apprehensive faces throughout the congregation. According to her understanding, the financial arrangements had never before been discussed so openly, however much people might grumble in private.

"There is nothing particularly remarkable in this arrangement. It is known as farming in common, though perhaps more frequently practiced on the continent of Europe than in our old homeland of England."

With this breakthrough into public discourse, Bradford visibly relaxed, walking around and looking at his listeners' faces as he spoke.

"Well," he said, "it was a lovely theory. But as so often happens in this harsh world, theory has come crashing shipwreck on the hard rock of disagreeable reality. The fact is, our harvests have been so poor we have no excess to apply toward the investment. As for a profit, we have not reached the point of being able to feed ourselves adequately through the winter. In these circumstances the word profit strikes one as little more than japery, and not very amusing japery at that

"If our friends and neighbors aboard the *Anne* had not brought at least some food to help feed themselves until harvest time, we should be in great difficulty indeed. As matters stand, we must be vigilant in the distribution, and we must be diligent as well in hunting, in fishing and clamming, in gardening, and in gathering fruits, nuts, greens and berries from the forest."

The grim truth he described sent most eyes downward, but Hester and the men from the Cooke house kept looking at the governor, who paused to smile slightly with the air of a man about to deliver the good news after laying out the bad in all its harshness.

"The council members and I have been at pains to steer a course out of this dilemma, and therefore, after much prayer and many hours of discussion, we have decided upon a new policy, and we have decided unanimously."

People looked up again, curious and surprised.

"We have determined that from henceforth our cultivated land will be divided up on the basis of private ownership."

Bradford waved down a loud buzz of astonishment and frenzied whispering. Many of the hardest-working men, including Francis and Philip, gestured and called for silence as well.

"The councilmen have been working on the division for days. Captain Standish and his helpers have been out by the firelight overnight, planting stakes in the cornfields, and they are prepared to show the demarcations."

There was shouting now, but Bradford spoke louder yet.

"The land has been apportioned by families, with one acre of ground assigned for each man, woman, or child in that family. Single men and any others without families have been assigned one acre each. Though we have not the power of charter yet to make it true in law, the land thus assigned will be treated in all practical respects as the private land of that family or individual. Anything grown thereon will be considered the private property of that family or individual, except for a tithe of ten per cent which shall be paid into the common storehouse of the colony, in accordance with the example set for Israel in the scriptures. The expenses of government and the repayment of our common debt will be paid out of the storehouse."

"Ten per cent won't be enough for all that!" a man shouted from the rear and Hester turned to find it was none other than the unpleasant fellow from the day before. "How can you do all you claim with only the tenth part?"

"We discussed that. We determined that if God Himself, in His word, should be satisfied with the tenth part, it would be most unseemly for a government of man to demand a greater."

"But the debts?" the argumentative Londoner objected.

"In the place where we stand today, after two harvests," Bradford said, "not a farthing has been paid on the debts to the present hour. And that is with the common storehouse taking *everything*. We hold that ten per cent of something is greater than the whole part of nothing."

A second man raised his hand. "But, Governor, is it quite fair to allot a full acre to children, the same as to the fully grown?"

"They eat as if fully grown, sir, sometimes more. And they can do work to match, most of them, if they exert themselves."

Another man followed up on the last. "Fair enough, but do you assign a full acre for a babe in arms, or a child too young to work?"

"We do," Bradford said. "The smallest babe is fully human, and thus we make our assignments, one good English acre for each living soul in the colony. Our Lord said, 'Suffer the little children, and forbid them not to come to me, for of such is the kingdom of heaven.' We can do no less than He commanded. The children represent the future of our colony, sir, the youngest of them as well."

The Londoner was not finished. "But do you have permission from the adventurers to make these changes?"

Hester saw Philip look as though he'd like to throttle the man.

"We do not," Bradford said, "and we do not have a year to exchange letters with London. We here are the ones who face this wilderness. The elders agree that this decision is ours to make."

The London man leapt to his feet. "But surely you have taken too much upon yourselves! Such a drastic change should be submitted to a vote of every man in this plantation."

Bradford waited pointedly until the man sat back down before proceeding. "This we also discussed, my brother. When we signed our compact on the Mayflower, we covenanted ourselves to live by representative government. Your councilmen and I have voted that this division of land is our best course, and we believe we possess all legitimate authority to render this decision. If you or any man feel that we have wronged this colony, you have the power to replace us at the next election. But as for now... the land will be distributed privately."

"How about the gardens?" someone shouted. "The fishing and the hunting?"

"The same principle of individual effort will apply. Household gardens belong to that household, though as with the acreage we require the tenth part of the crop for the common good. Every man is henceforth free to use his time as he will, and anything he hunts, grows or catches will be his own or his family's. The only exception will be that we shall continue to send out members of the militia, our best shots, to hunt game for the town, which shall be distributed as before. These men, however, will also be free to go out hunting on their own, for the good of themselves and their own families."

By the storm of disagreement that broke out in murmurs and shouting, Hester grasped how radical, indeed how revolutionary all this seemed in comparison with all that had gone before.

"We do ask," the habitually peaceful and quiet Bradford raised his voice above them all, "that you inform the gate sentries of your destination and expected duration on every occasion when you leave the proximity of the town. We ask that women and children not wander out of sight except in groups and then only in the company of two or more armed men."

"But why?" Priscilla asked, the only woman who had spoken up, though so softly that Hester would not have heard her if seated any further away.

The governor heard the question though. "Merely a precaution, Mrs. Alden. And hopefully only a temporary precaution at that."

In all the braying excitement nobody else was paying much attention to this exchange, and Hester saw her shipboard friend Elizabeth's husband rise to his feet, flagging for attention with his arms.

"Mister Warren?" Bradford said.

Hester quickly understood why the governor gave him the floor. Like his wife, Richard Warren commanded a bellow powerful enough to quiet a mob. "Thank you, sir, I should like to get something straight, if you please!"

"Certainly, sir." Bradford smiled as the meeting was intimidated into silence.

Warren lowered his voice. "Let us say that by due diligence, hard work, and the favor of Heaven, a harvest is brought forth, more than enough to feed those who tilled a particular parcel of land. Would the excess belong to that family or single person?"

"It would, sir."

"And would the owners then be free to do anything they choose with that excess crop?"

"They would."

"Would the owners then be free, for example, to trade with the Indians for beaver skins and such other goods as they might wish?"

"I do not see why not, sir."

This exchange brought fresh gasps from most of the ladies, so used to sharing and sharing alike, as far back as Holland, but most of the men looked by contrast utterly delighted, with the contented but slightly guilty look of the cat that had swallowed the proverbial canary.

"And if those furs and other goods were shipped back and sold in London," Mister Warren went on, "the profits would belong to those who grew the original crop, would they not?"

"Indeed they would, sir."

"Thank you, Governor Bradford. I believe I have the picture now."

And so did everyone else as Warren sat down beaming with satisfaction. Hester could almost hear mental wheels grinding in calculation, especially on the other side of the aisle.

CHAPTER 24

The New Era Begins

John Cooke witnessed powerful change at once, from the moment everyone hurried out the upper gate to inspect his or her allotments in the fields. He could see it by the spring in people's steps, by the outcries of enthusiasm or sporadic disappointment as families and individuals discovered which tracts had been assigned to them.

It turned out the process of allotment had been going on for days, well before the final decision was taken in council. Miles Standish and two men he had trained as a surveying team, beginning with lessons in the hold of the *Mayflower*, had surveyed and laid out the farmland from the beginning. No one had suspected their true purpose in re-surveying the fields in recent days, using the customary stakes and rope and studious calculation. Not a word had slipped out concerning the council's secret deliberations. Everyone had assumed the new survey had something to do with the vast expansion of newly cleared land, and this was certainly true as far as it went. Governor Bradford, Elder Brewster, Doctor Fuller and Captain Standish made the specific allocations to families and individuals, with the final say reserved for the governor. Beyond his indispensable mathematical and mapping skills, the professional soldier's presence at the grim center of potential controversy made it unlikely some grumbler would openly challenge the land committee's allocations. Nobody wanted to pick a quarrel with Miles Standish.

Whatever the reasons for the captain's original inclusion, John believed he had played a most active role in the specifics of distribution. His father and Philip agreed. They held this opinion as a logical conclusion based on incontrovertible fact.

Long before this new decision about private ownership, particular men had a tendency to work in particular sections of the fields, either by assignment from the leadership thenceforth continued or by outright personal choice, as with his father and Philip, who enjoyed one another's company and preferred to work together as much as possible. Consequently, the task of clearing had been carried out most efficiently in the places where the hardest-working men had undertaken the challenge. These men and boys tended to cluster in groups, as did the laziest, most shiftless and worst complaining in their own. Later, when time came to plant, the diligent returned if at all possible to the acres they had cleared themselves. Philip had been known to drive off certain fellows who attempted to work land he and Francis and John Alden and Richard Warren had prepared, though how he managed it without coming to blows comprised another element in the on-going mystery of the man. Whether by charm or occasional intimidation Philip had proved sufficient to his purpose.

Thus by an inexorable process the poorly cleared ground came to be the most improperly planted. The same listless and slow-learning hands that failed at digging up stones and roots also made a subsequent botch of spading the soil. Now everyone quickly discovered how the worst tracts had been assigned precisely to those who worked them so poorly, while the best had also been signed over in large degree to the workers responsible. Knowing their man, Francis and Philip suspected the captain had largely brought this about, however much his punitive impulses had probably been mitigated at least to some extent by the governor.

John suspected an appeal to Bradford regarding the demarcations would prove useless, partly because the governor undoubtedly sympathized with the hardest workers, among whom he could properly count himself, and partly because the nearest approach to any sort of police enforcement in the colony resided precisely in the persons of Captain Standish and his loyal militia. General opinion quickly attributed all this distributive justice—or injustice depending on one's point of view—to the hand of Standish alone, Bradford being regarded as too kindhearted for such retribution. The Cooke household doubted this, knowing full well the core of steel within the meek-seeming governor.

The prior inequity between work and its outcome had created a fountain of bitterness and recrimination that poisoned the equal sharing of the prior two years' harvests. The most industrious hands had managed to put more land in order than their share in the distributions, so at least some of the best soil now turned up in the portion of the worst workers, though this beneficence did little to stifle the initial murmurs and bellyaching, which always grew quiet, however, whenever Bradford or Standish passed by. Though his father maintained his customary attitude of compassion toward the foolish and irresponsible, John noticed Philip suppressing a smile every time a complaining voice was heard.

The Frenchman made bold to raise the matter with Elder Brewster as that aged gentleman passed by with a spade on his shoulder, heading for his own acre.

"Some of the brethren seem a bit put out," Philip said with a twinkle.

The old man lingered a moment, his kindly face crinkling into a contemplative smile. "I have always found our Lord's parable of the talents to be rather hard words, when the poor anxious fellow suffers having his one talent taken away and given to the braver and more diligent. Yet perhaps Christians can use a hard lesson occasionally. A man's behavior bears consequences, and we need to find this out if we are to live our lives aright."

"God forgive us then," Francis said, "for we all make mistakes."

"God forgive us indeed." Brewster gazed off across the fields. "Yet mistakes can be rectified, if we become aware of them soon enough to make a change. Surely that is one manifestation of God's grace."

Philip looked a little sheepish and less self-satisfied as the elder walked on.

On the far side of Mister Brewster John was astonished to see one of the laziest men in New Plymouth chopping and digging at a huge immovable tree stump that had broken up the straight rows of corn through two plantings and harvests. It was a wearisome job long postponed by all who confronted it, but now the land belonged to the gentleman, the same ugly old stump made an obstacle not to be tolerated for another moment.

*   *   *

John wished he could stay to help his father and Philip, whose acre was contiguous with those of all the Cookes, but for the present he had to hurry out to take his part in the fish gathering. At the stream the boys labored on in a tumult of excitement over the new rules, discussing and arguing over what they would mean. Soon competition arose concerning the fish, with each boy striving to put aside the best for his own family's corn plants. Captain Standish came by, however, and called a halt to the clamor before open fighting could break out. The fish, he said, would be distributed as before, to all who needed them in the fields.

"You men are like the hunters who go out on behalf of the entire plantation," the captain said. "You heard the governor explain the matter. This endeavor of yours is a special one, like that of a hunting party, and the work of your hands will benefit one and all without consideration."

However this may have violated the logic of the early morning meeting, the bickering died out at once, possibly because all the boys felt so honored that Standish had addressed them as men. He moved on, doubtless carrying the same message to all the fishing spots. John felt more admiration than ever as he watched the red-haired soldier walk off into the trees. Then he thought of something and ran after him.

"Captain Standish?"

Standish halted and turned about, impatient as always to his duty. "Yes, Mister Cooke?"

"Forgive me, sir, but with all your and the governor's other duties, how will you tend your own acres? Perhaps I could help you."

Standish regarded him for a long moment with the greatest solemnity. "Thank you, John, but do not worry. The governor and I both have new wives, and we plan to work them like Indian squaws."

John stared at him, then laughed when the red beard split open in a grin.

"But the governor and I shall take note of the offer for future reference."

As Standish marched off, John somehow was not completely convinced the captain was only joking about working the wives. Yet he knew their acres would be farmed if the two leaders had to ply their own spades and hoes by moonlight. No special consideration would be expected or received.

By midday the boys took time to eat meals brought from home, necessarily small, but they did so in turns so the work of accumulating fish continued unabated. When his chance came round, John took the opportunity to walk back to the fields for another visit with his father and Philip. They had no time to talk, however, and John did not press the matter. The two men seemed to be working more industriously than before and clearly did not wish to waste any time. Slightly put out by their unaccustomed brusqueness, John walked off to eat by himself, moving past clusters of frenzied activity, people who appeared to be working as hard or harder than his father and Philip, including many for whom this comprised a whole new experience. No one greeted or appeared to notice him as he passed.

He headed for the area at the edge of the forest where the process of clearing had abruptly halted the day the fish began to run. Taking a seat on a fallen log, he pulled a small wrapped bundle out of his pocket. Inside were two hardboiled eggs and a small leathery piece of dried venison, prepared as Squanto had taught them.

As he peeled an egg, striving to control his ravenous hunger so he would not wolf down the meal but take time to savor food as his mother taught, John gazed out across the fields. There was something strange about the sight, about all the people so hard at work, but he felt so weary from his morning's endeavors that he could not put his finger on it.

He saw the same formerly lazy man still beavering away at his stump—alone as before. This struck John as extremely odd. By now the man should have called for help. Shading his eyes, John could clearly see that sufficient chopping and digging had been accomplished that two or three extra men ought to be able to wrench the thing out of the soil, but the man appeared to be hacking the stump's root structure into pieces small enough to pull it out on his own. John wondered why. He thought about going over to offer assistance but knew he had to get back to the stream. It was well past noon by now. Surely someone would offer to help the fellow soon.

Then it struck John what else was different about the activity in the fields. The surprise hit him so hard he almost choked on his first delicious bite of egg. There were women and children everywhere! And they were not merely standing around watching either, or bringing food and drink from the town to feed their men. They were working! Hoe and spade in hand, mothers and children were digging mounds and planting seed, and some of them had already gained an expertise to compare with that of their husbands and fathers. John saw one tiny little boy running back and forth to a wicker basket of fish, readily providing a fish whenever his parents needed one. All at once he turned to survey the plots of Governor Bradford and Captain Standish. Sure enough the governor was teaching Mrs. Bradford how to dig a planting mound, and Mrs. Standish was already working by herself, no doubt pending the captain's return from the stream.

"Hello, John Cooke."

He almost jumped in fright, but quickly saw it was not a real threat but only that little package of blonde trouble, Sarah Warren.

"Mind if I join you?" she said, bold as ever, then took a seat beside him on the log before he could answer. She sat extremely close, which for some reason made him extremely nervous though at the same time oddly excited. He was of an age where he could not understand how Edward Doty and Edward Leister and the other older boys could let themselves be so raised up or cast down by a look or a word or the absence thereof from some young lady. He looked all around, hoping no one would see him sitting with Sarah, but everyone seemed too busy with his or her own tasks.

He turned back to find her staring wide-eyed at the size of the egg.

"What kind of egg is that?"

"Wild turkey. The hens only nest once a year, in the spring. Hobomok taught me how to find their nests."

"You didn't steal them all, did you? The poor hen."

"A hen lays one egg a day but doesn't start sitting until she's filled her clutch. That's when you can take a few, when she's off about her business. You don't want to take them once she's sitting, she'd kill you."

Sarah laughed. "But you wouldn't take them all."

"Not unless something's happened to the poor hen." Such as you've just put an arrow through her, he refrained from saying. "One always leaves a few eggs so there'll be new turkeys."

"They're very big eggs."

"Have you had your dinner?"

"We had a bite, yes," she said, looking away.

"Why don't you take this second egg?"

"No, thank you," she said primly, eyes averted.

"Go ahead, Sarah, I'd like you to have it."

She turned to look at him, and for a moment he thought she was going to burst into tears. "Very well. Thank you, John."

John wanted both the eggs for himself, of course, but found some inexplicable satisfaction in giving one up for her. He reached into his shirt for the sharp hunting knife he carried tucked in his belt, and sliced her off a piece of the venison without asking.

Her eyes widened. "You carry that big knife?"

"It's a useful tool."

"But why do you keep it hidden?"

"For safekeeping," he said vaguely, handing her the slice of meat.

"What is it?" she said, inspecting it dubiously.

"Deer meat. Venison."

"Old?"

"Smoked, dried out and salted to preserve it."

She took a tentative bite, and he almost laughed as she struggled to tear it with her teeth. "A bit on the tough side."

They both chewed studiously. "The Indians say that's good, though. Keeps you from eating too quickly."

"It's like eating a shoe."

"Keep chewing. Softening it up brings out the flavor."

"You're right," she admitted.

They sat contentedly, alternating bites of meat and egg.

"This egg is as good as any chicken egg," she said. "Maybe better."

"Father says hunger enhances one's enjoyment of almost any food."

She looked at him closely. "It's been terrible for you, hasn't it, since you've been over here?"

He stared down at his feet. "It's been difficult, but the hunger wasn't the worst of it." Something about her attentiveness drew forth words he never planned to speak. "That first winter, the cold cut clear through to your bones... You felt as if you were freezing into ice. So many people became ill. So many died. That was the worst of it, all the dying and nothing you could do about it."

"I'm so sorry, John."

He glanced at her, read nothing in her solemn little face but unadulterated sympathy, then turned his eyes to look out across the fields toward Fort Hill. "We landed at the onset of winter. Most of the ladies and small children continued to live aboard the Mayflower while we tried to build houses. Most of us had never built anything in our lives. Thanks be to God that the ship's master was willing to wait until spring to sail back to England. He was a kindly man, name of Christopher Jones."

"He probably did not do it out of kindness," she said.

"What do you mean?"

"My father says the winter storms at sea are worse than what we endured on board the *Anne*. Your Mister Jones was waiting for clearer sailing."

"Perhaps so, but he was a kindly man in any case. I remember when we had finally managed to build the first common room up there," he pointed, "where the fort is now. It was a very difficult task in the dead of winter. Felling the trees, splitting the logs into clapboards, all the rest. It had to be done in harsh cold and deep snows, with the freezing wind plucking at you every minute of the day. At night we'd row out to the Mayflower and spend the night aboard. The plan was, once the common room was built, the men and the stronger boys would sleep there, spending all our time ashore to get more done."

"You were one of the stronger boys, then." She spoke as if it were a given.

"I suppose. I remember when the common room was finished. We were too weary to be happy. We simply bedded down for the night. I remember going to sleep on the ground with the others, dead tired. I was awakened in the middle of the night with my father shaking me. The whole place was on fire."

Sarah gasped. "Was anyone hurt?"

"No, thank God, we all got out safely. But our first fort, our first completed structure at so great a cost, burned down to the ground on the first night. The ship's master allowed us to sleep back aboard the Mayflower."

"What did you do?"

"Started over the next day. Carried off the ashes and rebuilt it from the ground up, only larger, less flimsy. This time we used logs, no clapboards, which burn more readily. You haven't lived until you've had to cut logs and drag them uphill in the depth of winter. We had to arrange ropes and pulleys. It was a nightmare."

"Weren't you discouraged?"

"Of course we were, but it was either start again or give up. That's what Mister Bradford and Captain Standish said, and everyone agreed."

Sarah shook her head. "After such a terrible thing... Weren't some tempted to think the hand of God was against you?"

He shook his head. "No. The hand of the Devil perhaps, but mostly the hand of man."

She looked at him sharply. "What are you saying? What caused the fire?"

"No one ever knew for sure, but my father believes it was deliberately set."

"By one of the savages?"

Another shake of the head. "By one of our own."

"Oh, surely not! How could you know it was not one of the savages?"

"There were no tracks or slide marks in the snow outside. If it was deliberate, it was one of our own."

"By why would someone do such a thing?"

"To force us to go back to England, or Holland as the case may be." John did not rule out members of the Leyden congregation for suspicion, and he wanted Sarah to know that he did not distrust the families that came directly from England, like hers, any more than those he had known as a small child during the Netherlands exile.

By her expression he thought she understood his point. "No one was ever brought to justice?"

"Never, and if anyone had reason to confess, he has resisted the impulse successfully."

She followed his gaze out into the fields. John thought he could see every whole family from Plymouth except his own.

"Look," she pointed, "here come your mother and sisters."

This uncanny junction with his own thoughts startled him. Sure enough, he saw Hester and the girls heading down the hill from the fort, Jane holding little Jacob by the hand. "What are they doing?"

"Coming to work, I should imagine, or at least to see if your father will allow them to help. Your mother probably noticed that nearly every other woman and child in Plymouth is already out here."

"I see that."

"We Warren girls were the first ones!"

"But why? I don't understand. Every suggestion the last two years that the women and children might be able to help out a bit in the fields has been resisted, complained of, or completely rebuffed."

Sarah laughed. "That was before families started working for themselves!"

"I beg your pardon?"

"My father declares there shan't be any more bad harvests, from this day forward."

"How can he be so sure?"

"Because now you men have some help. And enthusiastic help at that."

"Well, we can certainly use it."

"Please. You're just playing innocent, aren't you?"

By way of answer he broke out in a smile that seemed to please her.

"Of course you are," she said. "My father says you and your father were foursquare for the change to private ownership."

"I can't count the times I've heard your father's speech, Sarah, and he's right. Now the men who work the hardest will reap the reward of their own hard labors, and any who shirk will pay the price."

"Well, do you think the ladies are any different? One of those acres over there is mine, and everything grown on it will go to benefit my own family and myself. Why should we leave it to our father to do all the hoeing and planting for seven acres just because he's the only male? It would be absurd."

"Of course."

"How about your household? Do you think your father and Monsieur Delano will allow Mrs. Cooke and the girls to help?"

John grinned. "I don't think there's any doubt."

"I probably should be back at work myself. They'll be looking for me." Sarah stood up.

"Have another slice of venison first."

"All right." She sat back down as he cut. She sat closer than before.

CHAPTER 25

A Troubling Incident

It was on a Monday morning, the fifth day of the fish run, that the incident occurred which Hester singled out in her own mind as the beginning of the troubles that almost destroyed Plymouth. No one else knew of the matter outside the Cooke household, but it carried extraordinary meaning for her because it involved Francis, a good and Godly man as she had always known him to be since before their marriage.

Within the congregation Francis might not be greatly reputed for religion, for he was a quiet sort who spoke rarely and refrained from judging others or showering them with unsolicited advice. Any who doubted his maturity in Christ should only observe the tenderness and resolve by which Francis sought to raise up his elder son and other children in the nurture and admonition of the Lord.

The openness and lack of severity in her husband's outlook, Hester believed, made possible his capacity for his forging genuine friendships not only with the French patrician Philip Delano and the London tradesman Richard Warren but also with such as Hobomok and the late Squanto, whom others deemed mere savages, however indispensable to the life of the colony. As Hester had been able to piece together the spiritual aspects of his story, Squanto—or Tisquantum, to use his true name—had first heard something of the Gospel from Roman Catholic monks who aided his escape from slavery in Spain and then further Truth from the benevolent Protestant men in London who befriended the homesick and befuddled man, eventually buying his passage aboard a ship returning to America.

Among his more recent English friends in New Plymouth, Tisquantum had spoken in a manner signifying the requisite childlike faith in the Savior not long before illness struck him down the previous November. Francis, who knew the man well, consequently saw all Indians as men, whatever their spiritual condition, and not inherently inferior to whites in any sense, only different. Francis had told her recently that all true friendship was rooted in equality of respect, in spite of any difference in riches, education or natural condition.

"After all, I might not have been so close to Philip if we had met while he was being driven about in a great carriage with a purse of gold on his belt."

"You are friends only through his misfortune?" Hester had teased.

Francis laughed. "I hope not, but our mutual poverty certainly makes for a great leveling factor."

"But Philip shows himself friendly toward all men."

"So he does, but in his former station across the sea this would have passed as mere condescension. However pleasing he might find true friendship with such as we are now, the great gulf betwixt common folk and landed gentry would have stood between us. His new and inferior stature has been a blessing for us at least, if not for him!"

This sentiment typified the open heart of Francis, as well as his inclination to think matters through for himself. Hester believed True Religion, the faith revealed in the Scriptures, was itself a matter of the heart and mind—of belief—not of keeping laws nor of following rules and regulations, for all the good works, piety and self-reformation of man, no matter how well intentioned or vigorously pursued, suffered the pollution of sin and human pride, which rendered them as filthy rags before the perfect holiness of God. This is why the Son of God went to the cross, that all who put their trust in the Lord Jesus Christ and His atoning sacrifice and triumphant resurrection should be cloaked in His perfect righteousness by faith, receiving at once the free gift of salvation, encompassing forgiveness of all sin, eternal life and the indwelling of the Holy Ghost.

All Protestants supposedly believed in justification by faith alone in Christ alone through grace alone as the crucial central doctrine taught throughout the Bible, the Word of God being the sole loadstone and guide for all those who sought to reform Christianity ever since the time of Martin Luther. The Old Testament, the very repository of God's Law, described the Lord raising up David the shepherd boy who became King and ancestor of Christ, as "a man after Mine Own heart." David, as with Abraham before him, was a man who "believed God, and it was imputed to him for righteousness."

Yet Hester knew certain of the more recent reformers, not only exalted theologians and scholars but also many everyday saints sitting in their pews, had become in their own way as legalistic and pharisaical as any Romanist—and sometimes worse. She felt it was this all-too-human judgmental and rule-enforcing tendency, in some measure, that prevented her husband the recognition he deserved. Yet Francis was content to remain an unassuming man, walking humbly with his God. She bore what she dared hope was a Godly form of pride in him for this humility, and if others failed to grasp his potential, so much the worse for them.

She inwardly admitted, however, her own capacity at times for straying into a judgmental outlook inappropriate for anyone but God. Perhaps it was fear of this propensity that hindered her fully recognizing the incident for what it was that sad Monday morning. If she had, and if she had urged Francis to deal with it, perchance their state of affairs should not have become as dangerous as eventually it did.

* * *

The conflict had its origin in a matter of timing. When a fish run began, most of the action took place in the first five days, after which the number of leaping fish fell off precipitously. Unfortunately, in this year of our Lord 1623, the fish did not have the courtesy and good sense to launch their activities early in the week as they had the two previous years, but rather on a Thursday. Consequently, the fish would continue running well come Sunday.

The muttering began before the sun went down on Friday, the day of the surprise town meeting. The planting proceeded briskly with an ardor born of unbridled enthusiasm. The untried women and youngest children quickly mastered the process, goaded by frantic husbands and fathers. Francis marveled to Hester how some of the least adept men had been transformed into most diligent planters and teachers of planting. Such was the alteration wrought by the mere possibility of profiting personally from the labor of one's hands. Everything Richard Warren had predicted came to wide-ranging fruition in a single day, but the secular prophet himself drove the sometimes-flagging efforts of his own wife and children too relentlessly to take much satisfaction in his vindication. Urging the youngsters on, Mister Warren set a blistering pace to follow, as did Francis and most other fathers.

As the Lord's Day loomed, the saints began to question whether it would or should be kept as every other. As with most reformers of their time, the separatists of Plymouth tended to a very strict observance, taking as their pattern the nation of Israel's Sabbath keeping by the law of Moses, as a day devoted to God, a day when no work or travel was to be done except within very strict limits of absolute necessity.

The Church of Rome, for all its strictness in some arenas, such as forbidding the Word of God to the laity, had been lax on the Sabbath for centuries. As long as people showed up for morning mass, the priests did not much care what they did the rest of the day. On Sunday afternoons the village squares of Europe filled with the stalls of merchants and wagons of farmers marketing their wares. The Lord's Day became something very like a weekly festival, especially in the larger towns, with games and celebration and no little drunkenness. The Church of England had carried over such Romish practice after King Henry the Eighth broke with the Pope. On all this the English reformers, in their zeal to purify the Church of England, took a dim view, a very dim view indeed, as they did of most things which gave people worldly joy.

In this and innumerable other respects, the Plymouth believers made a remarkable contrast with their long-faced brethren back in England. They favored the colorful clothing remembered from the reign of Queen Elizabeth, when the first trickle of flight to Holland began, and saw nothing wrong with looking as bright and happy as God's beautiful creation. They wore black for funerals. Indeed their partiality for brightly colored fabric had turned out quite the advantage in their trading with the Indians. Such cloth was one commodity massively replenished by the *Anne*, in exultant response to private letters sent back to Leyden on board the *Fortune*. The purchasing of such cloth had been done in small or greater quantities by the new arrivals themselves, such as Hester in outfitting her own trunk before embarking from the Netherlands, and not by the London adventurers who insisted on keeping a controlling and parsimonious hand on the more important general supplies, such as food, seed for planting and other commodities.

Sunday morning services in Plymouth were lengthy and appropriately uncomfortable, but the afternoon became a time when children felt free to run and play, when people visited one another for conversation or a shared meal, when married couples could seek out time and place for a sweet interval of unaccustomed privacy. No one engaged in wrestling matches, selling goods or cockfighting, but otherwise these few brief hours bore an undeniably festive or at least restful air.

What the people in Plymouth did *not* do of a Sunday was work. The Old Testament pattern prevailed. Except for survival-related matters that couldn't be helped, such as feeding one's family or caring for the ill, the day set aside for worship and rest was not a time when work should be performed.

Yet as Sunday approached no one wanted to lose a full day's effort in the fields. Philip reminded all who would listen of Christ's declaration that the Sabbath was made for man and not man for the Sabbath. To his manner of thinking, continuing the planting fell under the auspices of legitimate emergency and was thus allowable. Richard Warren took up this reasoning ever more vociferously, filling the spring air with condemnation of the hypocritical religious leaders of Christ's own day, ceaselessly constructing new burdens of law too heavy for men to bear without lifting a finger to help them.

Christian people no longer lived under the Law after all. If they did, the Sabbath would be observed on the last day of the week instead of the first. The Bible had never explicitly changed the day. The early Christians had done so in commemoration of Christ's Resurrection, and no one now pined for the old Hebrew practice. It would do no harm in these present circumstances to work through one solitary Sunday. Such a decision surely fell under the purview of legitimate Christian liberty.

Others in Plymouth, indeed most of the others, were not so sure. The highly persuasive Delano and Warren had well-deserved reputations as silver-tongued devils, further suspect because neither sprang out of the original Scrooby, Lincolnshire, congregation that had fled England for Holland in the first place. Yet it was all too likely most people secretly yearned to be brought fully over in mind and heart to their happier and certainly more convenient opinion. After all, if Sunday observance proceeded as usual, guards would have to remain posted on the perimeters of the fields to frighten away the wolves or other predators. From this it was but a short step to one and all continuing to work the soil as usual.

A number of the most faithful, including Hester, saw the controversy as something very like a sort of cosmic test. If the believers demonstrated a willingness to honor the Lord in the face of all human logic, He would bless them and the fruit of their hands that much more fully. Somehow the planting would be wonderfully completed though they took time out for God as usual. Naturally, Warren and Delano and their followers tore at their hair in frustration at this womanish assertion—as they saw it—but insults alone could not carry the tide.

Neither under such conditions could every man be allowed to follow his own conscience on the matter, which was Philip's fallback position. The people of Plymouth formed a community, a Christian community at that, and such anarchy could only result in chaos and bitterness among the brethren.

Thus the decision fell at last, as all matters of contention eventually did, upon the weary shoulders of William Bradford and the council. So soon after the major decision about private ownership, another visitation by the specter of controversy came as most unwelcome indeed, but the men had no choice but to deal with the matter, meeting by candlelight after their own long days in the hot spring sun. The discussions went on for hours over two nights, Hester reliably heard from other women, with Elder Brewster leading the charge for the Sabbath and others, generally younger, arguing just as strenuously for an exception. Captain Standish, perhaps more sensitive on this issue to his status as an outsider, held his tongue for once, though the younger men imagined he supported their view.

Eventually Bradford managed to hammer out a compromise, though only by Saturday evening, when messengers were dispatched throughout the village with the news. The Sabbath would be observed as usual, with a full morning worship service and no work in the fields afterward, but any boys who volunteered would be permitted to spend the day at the streams, continuing to collect fish. Naturally every young man in the community chose the fish, except for those like John Cooke, whose mother forced him to attend worship before finally releasing him, in response to his ceaseless pleas and against her better judgment, to bound off for the forest.

As with most political compromises, no one was completely satisfied. Bradford came in for a full barrage of criticism, both to his face and behind a back bent and exhausted from working on his land. The frontal attacks ceased for good late Monday afternoon when a self-appointed faction arrived to remonstrate that the governor's actions had tempted the young into a maelstrom of loose living and sin. Not yet having eaten his supper, he drove the complainers from his house with roars, imprecations and the shaking of clenched fists, shocking proof that sufficient pressure could impel the mildest and most even-tempered of men to distraction and wrath.

Alice Bradford told Hester later how the loss of his temper made her husband yearn to lay down the burden of his responsibilities. Let someone else try to be governor for a while, he fumed, and see if they could do any better. Naturally, once calmed down and fed, the guilt-ridden Bradford felt compelled to make the rounds asking forgiveness of everyone he had frightened, but Alice barred the way to their door with the interposition of her own body. Rather that cast her physically aside, he listened to reason and retired to their bed. In any case no one gave him any more grief over the Sabbath decision.

Francis took no position on any of this, being able to see reason on both sides. Meanwhile Hester and Philip went at one another with relish, in the French style. Philip accused his friend only half-facetiously of not having the courage to confront his wife. Hester knew that was untrue, having faced contradiction from that stubborn but well-beloved direction on many prior occasions. No, Francis simply could not make up his mind and was no doubt relieved when leadership settled the matter. That was the purpose of a governing council after all, though Hester thought he looked a tad wistful early Sunday afternoon as he watched John trotting off for the woods.

Francis managed to hold himself in check throughout the rest of Sunday, though he joined his colleagues in casting an envious eye at the fish every time some of the boys brought in fresh loads for overnight safekeeping within the walls.

Hester joked to Priscilla and some other ladies that a race would be run at dawn when each man sought to claim his fair share. Her remark intended in jest provoked no laughter, only chilly acknowledgement of truth. Her friends' silence sent coldness over Hester, a nameless sense of dread she could not well explain.

*   *   *

Hester woke before sunrise Monday in an empty bed. She clambered down the ladder to find Francis pulling on his boots near the door. John had awakened—or been awakened—as well, struggling sleepily in the last stages of dressing.

"You are going out *now*?" Hester yawned.

"Have to," Francis said. "Philip has already left. We lost a day's work yesterday, and we need to be at it."

"Let me make breakfast. I have some eggs and turkey hen remaining."

He shook his head. "No time, but thank you. We can make it til midday before we eat."

Young John's eyes did not exactly gleam with eager accord, but neither mother nor son would raise an objection in the face of such urgency. But something else mattered more to Hester than physical sustenance.

"What of our devotions? Shall we read a verse or two at least?"

As a family they had always begun their day with Francis reading a passage from the Bible followed by a brief prayer, the little ceremony joined by such of the children as needed to rise early. John had told her how they had always done the same as a houseful of bachelors. These days, the duty of saying the prayer revolved according to Francis's whim, and some of Hester's favorites were those spoken by little Jacob.

Today, however, Francis only shook his head again. "No time. We shall have devotions tonight, after we return from the fields."

She started to say something more, but he snapped a quick look in her direction. The irritation in his eyes froze her tongue. Francis was not an ill-tempered husband under normal circumstances, but he clearly had no tolerance at present for further discussion.

An uneasy Hester watched from the doorway as her husband and eldest child disappeared into the darkness, hurrying up the hill to lay claim to their proper portion of the Sabbath fish. She pulled her shawl more tightly around her shoulders. The chill she felt came out of more than the cold air before sunrise. This was the first occasion she could ever remember her husband taking no time for God. Later, after serving hot eggs, a little dark turkey meat and a fragment of corn cake apiece to Jacob and the girls, she took a few moments for scripture reading and prayer before they went to join Father and John in the fields.

It was good she did, for all returned home that night too weary for anything but eating small supper and toppling into bed. So much for the postponed devotions. Despite any satisfactions pertaining to a long, hard but extremely productive Monday, she lay awake for a time knowing the day had not begun well, had not begun well at all.

CHAPTER 26

A Dangerous Mission

Wider events in Plymouth soon thwarted Hester's naïve hopes for a more settled life following the frenzy of planting. The pessimistic words of her own mouth came true with a vengeance as the experience of gardening herbs and vegetables in Holland proved woefully inadequate to the backbreaking labor and constant attention required in caring for young corn by the acre. The hungry wolves from the forest proved themselves unusually aggressive this year, and for more than a week large numbers of Plymouth folk had to spend sleepless nights out in the open. The lookout required became more demanding, Francis pointed out bitterly, as the new landowners began limiting their vigilance to their own acreage without regard for their neighbors'.

The two previous sowing seasons had been neither as extensive nor as efficient, and a few guards and bonfires scattered around the perimeter had been sufficient to protect all the cropland. Now the appointed guards and militia were posted out as before but no longer trusted to do the job. Old hands and new alike, budding farmers who had never in all their lives possessed anything beyond the clothes on their backs and a few household goods, sought to make sure of their property by personal surveillance. Observing this, the perimeter guards tended to drift over to their own acres. These disquieting alterations comprised the earliest public hint of any negative consequence to the new private arrangements.

By the end of this troublesome beginning, when the buried fish had decayed sufficiently to cease attracting the predators, members of each household had been out in the fields every night for days, protecting their own acres, without any compensating relief from the unending toil of the daylight hours. Eyelids grew heavy. Tempers grew short. At one point Hester and Priscilla found themselves snapping at one other until they realized what they were doing and fell into one another's arms, first laughing then weeping in genuine spiritual distress for the direction the whole colony seemed to be heading.

The fertilized earth, nurtured by warm sunlight and spring rains, brought forth sprouts of corn with astonishing speed. What sprang up with greater rapidity, alas, was a wide variety of choking weeds. The hard drudgery of hoeing out these interlopers became a daily portion of new agony for bent backs and aching muscles. Both Francis and John attributed the shortfall of the previous year's crop, in part, to the failure to protect many of the young spring plants from being strangled in their earthly cradles by the more vigorous weeds, a failure due almost completely to the prior lack of sufficient and effective workmanship. This year proved far different as the laborious output of women and children came into practice.

Amidst these changes, the number of quarrels and outright feuds breaking out formed into a darkening miasma of the gravest foreboding for the women of Plymouth. The ladies spoke with growing urgency among themselves. If they broached such concerns at home, however gently, most of their husbands refused to acknowledge any problem save in the overactive female imagination. Hester, Priscilla and others thus found they had no recourse but to take their mounting anxieties to God in fervent prayer.

* * *

Less than a week after the local Indian villages called off the wolf watch as no longer necessary, with Plymouth immediately following suit, Governor Bradford and Doctor Fuller took time from their own work for an appraising walk through the cornfields. They were brought up short when young Edward Doty came running down from the upper gate.

"Sir! Sir!" Doty gasped between labored breaths, "Begging yer pardon, Guv'ner, but Captain Standish says come at once, sir, and you too, Doctor Fuller, if you please!"

"What's this all about, son?" Bradford said.

"Take a breath, boy," said Fuller.

"Don't know quite what it's about, sir," Doty gasped, "except for old 'obomok just turned up looking like 'e's seen a ghost and run straight to the captain..."

The men made for the stockade at once.

* * *

Within the hour Edward Leister came puffing down from Fort Hill to summon Francis Cooke from his hoeing. Closely questioned on the way to Miles Standish's door, the boy babbled with agitation but knew only that the elders needed to meet with Francis at once and it had something to do with Hobomok.

Leaving the wheezing boy outside, he arrived to find an extremely gloomy council gathered round the captain's long table. Every eye followed Francis as he entered the room.

Off to one side Edward Winslow perched on the hearth of the central fireplace, elbows to his knees and face buried in both hands. He appeared more stricken than the councilmen. Hobomok was nowhere to be seen. Francis fixed an apprehensive gaze on the grim men at the table.

"Gentlemen, please. What's wrong?"

It was the governor who spoke. "Brother Cooke, we have received word from Hobomok that Chief Massasoit has fallen gravely ill."

Francis immediately understood the tension and melancholy on every countenance, especially Winslow's. "Is it very serious, do you think?"

"So serious," Doctor Fuller said gravely, "that he is not expected to live."

"As you know, Francis," Bradford said, "we credit Massasoit with keeping the peace between our peoples. Should he die... we cannot know what would happen."

"What would you have me do, gentlemen?"

"The council and I have determined that we must try to help. We shall send of our stock of medicines to see if we can provide any remedy for his condition. Doctor Fuller has volunteered to go himself, but as he is our only medical officer, it is felt we cannot spare him."

Bradford paused, and all turned to the doctor, who kept looking at Francis.

"For some time, Mister Cooke," Fuller said, "I have been undertaking to instruct Mister Winslow in basic medicine, knowledge that might prove useful to him in his role as our translator and chief ambassador to the savages. Between now and tomorrow morning, he and I shall go over the nature and application of all our medicines as I provide him with samples of each to carry with him to Massasoit."

Francis nodded.

Bradford picked up the thread. "It is felt that Captain Standish should stay close to home in such dangerous circumstances, and that in any case it would be inappropriate to send a minister of healing as part of anything resembling a military expedition. Mister Winslow will be going back with Hobomok, but we also want to send along another man, someone with a sound mind and a strong body, who also happens to be a crack shot. Just in case... as we should say."

Francis grasped their intent long before the governor stopped speaking. Every man gazed expectantly in his direction. "Gentlemen, I am deeply involved in farm work right now," he stammered, "with my whole family."

Answering the unspoken question, Bradford said, "I should have preferred to send a single man, Mister Cooke, but you are better qualified than any who came to mind."

Francis thought of Philip, of course, but he had to admit his best friend manifested a certain spirit of impulsiveness that went far toward justifying the inbred suspicion an English council would naturally feel toward a Frenchman under the best of circumstances. He quickly pored over a mental list of the other bachelors in Plymouth, much as the councilmen undoubtedly had. The unmarried ran a pattern from young men and mere boys to a few older widowers, from those too young to be trusted with important decisions to those too weathered with age to walk the distance required for the journey. Francis had to admit he could not think of any he felt could be trusted with such heavy responsibility. For all his discomfort with anything that smacked of vainglory and pride, the obvious contrast with his own relative eligibility closed about him like a snare.

"I trust your good wife will understand the necessity," the governor was saying. "We shall see to it that she and your children receive any help they might require in your absence."

"If necessary, Mister Cooke," Standish spoke up, "I shall put your fellow militiamen out to help your family. In the meantime, they have Monsieur Delano."

"I shall be happy to explain the situation to Mrs. Cooke," Bradford said. "Perhaps coming from me..."

Francis straightened his posture to a more military bearing. "I think you exaggerate my gifts, Governor Bradford, but I am most willing if you gentlemen feel I am needed. You need not trouble yourselves with my wife, though. She will undoubtedly receive my selection as a great personal honor, as do I."

* * *

"Francis! I simply do not understand this at all!" Hester cried.

Philip and the children had cleared out fast. Francis dearly yearned to be with them under the night sky, listening as Philip pointed out constellations or told marvelous stories to distract attention from the storm inside the house.

"I suppose the governor and elders find that I am a judicious man," he murmured.

"And are there no other judicious men in this colony?"

"You would be surprised, my dear."

"And did these wise men provide any other reason?"

"Well, they say I am—nothing!"

"No, go ahead, please. What do they say you are?"

Oh, how he regretted starting down this particular road.

"Please," she said. "Tell me."

"They say I am a good shot." He spoke scarcely above a whisper, but she heard well enough.

"I see," she said, cloaking herself with an unlikely and most unconvincing composure. "And most important of all, is there not a judicious man and a good shot in this colony who does not have a newly arrived wife he has not seen in three years and four little children who depend on him?"

"Hester, you mustn't worry. We treat with the savag—the Indian people constantly. This is simply a more important emissary than usual."

"Then why does it matter, your skill with the gun?" Whenever Hester became excited, her French accent strengthened, charming and touching his heart all the more by the affection and concern thus revealed.

"Oh, perhaps we shall need a little hunting done, one never knows. You mustn't worry."

He felt guilty and frustrated to the most extreme degree in thus misleading her. He knew they had every reason in the world to worry, not only for his own but for all their lives.

What would happen? He could scarcely conceive of the question, much less the answer. What would happen to them all if Massasoit should die?

CHAPTER 27

Through a Landscape of Sorrow

Francis and his companions for the journey rose long before dawn, but Hester was up before them. Edward Winslow and Hobomok reported to the Cooke house to find a hot breakfast of corn cakes and honey, tea, and slices of cooked salmon. Hobomok ate with relish, complimenting Francis on his woman's cooking.

Philip and John climbed down from the sleeping loft just as the men were finishing their meal. The time had come. They held hands for prayer, the Frenchman leading, and Philip's eloquent words encompassed every concern of Hester's and more. She squeezed his hand in gratitude as they said amen.

The men shook hands all around. Francis grabbed hold of his son for a hug, then turned and held Hester for a long moment. Pulling away, he paused outside the door to give them a jaunty wave. Then he followed his friends into the darkness.

"John," Hester said, "why don't you go back to bed and see if you can get a little more sleep?"

"All right, Mother."

The boy climbed back up the ladder, surreptitiously wiping his eyes as he went.

Hester stood in the doorway with Philip as they gazed down the dark Town Street. A distant lantern flickered as one of the guards let the three men out the lower gate, where they felt their departure less likely to be observed.

She wiped her own eyes. "Philip, I put some food aside for your breakfast."

"I shall wait and eat with you and the children." He followed her lead, speaking in French as they nearly always did when alone together. He placed a tentative, comforting touch on her shoulder. "Hester, I went to the council last night and tried to persuade them to let me go in Francis's place. As I am a single man, without responsibilities..."

"Oh, Philip, why didn't they?" She immediately felt guilty. How could she be so eager to expose their friend to danger rather than her husband? She started to apologize but Philip lifted his hand with a graceful aristocratic shrug.

"Who can say? Perhaps they trust your husband more than a mad frog, though they would not be so impolite as to say this aloud."

"I had no right..."

"Do not think of it."

"Thank you for trying, dear Philip."

"It was nothing. But you must not worry, my dear. God will keep him safe."

Under normal circumstances, Francis found few delights more invigorating than a day in the woods, far from the backbreaking work of builder and farmer.

But today was different.

The Plymouth envoys were already deep in the forest as the sun rose behind them. Hobomok had led a blistering pace from the first, and Winslow muttered more than once that the man must be able to see in the dark like a cat. Sticking close in the hindmost position, Francis steadied Winslow whenever he stumbled. They made a gloomy little column as the earliest daylight began to penetrate the trees. Winslow's personal agitation apparently canceled out any temptation to gape at the many sights that customarily appealed to his naturalist's eye. He blundered along, snapping twigs with his feet, leaving all observation to his companions. Not being a hunter, he undoubtedly failed to pick up what was immediately apparent to Francis.

It was too quiet.

As the sun rose higher, and stronger light filtered down through the canopy of growing leaves overhead, Francis missed the full cacophony of the usual springtime sounds, the cries of birds and squirrels, the buzzing of insects, the thrashing of large game flushed out by the approach of man. To a visitor fresh from a large, noisy city the normal background din of the woodlands would probably compare to the total silence of an empty cathedral. To one accustomed to the forest, including such a neophyte as Francis regarded himself, its noise this day lay under some mysterious but unmistakable restraint. The babbling of brooks, the very wind in the trees seemed strangely subdued.

After Winslow spoke up a few times, he caught on to the reticence of his companions and joined their fellowship of silence.

They went mutely on, mile after mile. Perhaps it was only preposterous fancy, but to Francis it seemed the whole world had put on a mantle of grief. In the eerie and oppressive stillness a pall of mourning seemed to cast a darkening shadow across the superficial brightness of new green leaves and blossoming flowers. As if the forest itself and all its creatures wept for the plight of Massasoit.

Francis prayed they were not too late.

At midday they suddenly heard a terrible sound, a ghastly wailing chorus as if of ghostly wolves or some stranger and more monstrous beast, crying out somewhere close ahead. It made the hair stand up on the back of Francis's neck. After hesitating a moment, they crept ahead along the trail. The sound became less unearthly, its origins unmistakably human.

Hobomok held up a warning hand to bring them to a halt. Francis signaled Winslow to keep still and stole silently forward to join the brave where he squatted behind a tree peering into a clearing.

There next to a babbling brook a small group of Wampanoag, probably a family or perhaps two families—they could see two adult couples, an old woman, and several children of various ages—lay crumpled over the ground, on their knees or prostrate. They wept, all of them, pouring out a mournful keening more intense than that of the grieving Indian woman when the Plymouth militiamen carried the body of Deaky Jones home to Wessagusset. These poor souls were too caught up in lamentation to exercise rudimentary caution against the possible approach of an enemy. Their wailing cut Francis to the heart, not only with sympathy but also with fear.

"Stay here," Hobomok whispered. "I go speak with them."

Francis wanted to watch, but he heard noises from where they had left Winslow, who had grown impatient and was now approaching. Francis hurried back in a crouch, grabbing the younger man's arm a bit more tightly than necessary.

"Wha—?"

"Ssh," Francis held him in place.

"What is it?" Winslow whispered.

"A group of Wampanoag. In mourning."

Even by the dim green-tinted light of the burgeoning forest, Francis could see Winslow turning pale.

Hobomok came hurrying back.

"They say Massasoit already dead."

The three men straightened up to full height and stood pondering.

Winslow spoke up first. "How do they know?"

"They just get word. On the trail."

"By runner? Special messenger? Drums?"

"No, they meet other People who hear Massasoit die."

"Then no one actually saw Massasoit's dead body, with his own eyes?"

"No, not see, only hear."

Francis immediately saw what Winslow was driving at. This dissipated his exasperation when the impulsive scholar strode boldly forward to speak to the mourners himself.

Francis and Hobomok followed along and watched as Winslow quickly established a deep rapport with the bereaved. He might not have picked up anything from the Indians about hunting or stalking an enemy, but he had absorbed much else. He spoke their language fluently, effortlessly establishing himself as a compassionate listener, and they were not shy about breaking off their grief for a few moments of sympathetic conversation. Whatever he said in response appeared to give them hope, and they pulled themselves to their feet. They could not have looked at him with more adoration, Francis thought, if he were an angel of mercy sent down from Heaven. And indeed perhaps he was.

"What did you say?" Francis asked when Winslow came back.

"Oh, I merely pointed out that forest gossip is no more reliable than any other. I told them we shall go and look upon the Massasoit for ourselves. If he be truly dead, we shall join the People in mourning, but if not, we shall try to help him with our medicines."

Francis and Hobomok exchanged a look. If the old chief had actually died, the safest course would be to break off the mission, return to Plymouth and await developments. Winslow had taken that option off the table at a stroke. True, he had only given the promise to a small group, but word of it would spread far and wide, the more so if they failed to follow through.

"He's right," Francis said to Hobomok. "We have to go see for ourselves."

"I go alone, bring you word. You return to Plymouth."

Francis shook his head. "No, if he's alive, Edward is the one who can help."

"I shall go with Hobomok, Francis," Winslow said. "You go back."

"Don't be absurd."

They withdrew as the Indians waved and shouted. Francis did not understand their words but grasped the import readily. He walked away deeply touched by their excitement, their hope that some strange magic of the white men might be able to help their beloved chieftain.

Francis prayed it were only true.

CHAPTER 28

The Duel

The news of Massasoit's illness spread quickly in Plymouth. Most households made the quiet decision to keep the women, girls and youngest boys within protective walls, at least for the present. Members of the militia, including Philip, were posted out on patrol or guard duty with primed muskets and lighted matches.

John spent a long hot morning hoeing weeds alone in the Cooke section of the cornfields. Just at midday, by which time he had somewhat relaxed in regard to any real possibility of imminent attack, he noticed a sudden stirring of puzzling activity.

At the end of the walking line between rows of plants, he saw a small group of men and boys gather, confer, then head for the northwestern edge of the surrounding forest. Curious, he paused to watch and soon caught sight of other fellows walking off in the same direction.

He searched out Richard Warren in his family's acreage and was surprised to find him surrounded by his daughters as if nothing were amiss.

"Mister Warren, do you see?" John gestured toward other men hurrying into the woods. "Where is everybody going?"

"Girls!" Warren said sharply. "Find your mother and go back to the house at once!"

John experienced anew the cold touch of fear.

"But, Father!..." Sarah, of course. One severe parental look sent the others scampering, but she followed them only at further command and with the most unconcealed and disputatious reluctance.

"Stay with me, John," Warren said, "we had best investigate."

John shared Mister Warren's alarm. To the northwest lay a secondary trail leading down from Massachusett territory before cutting southwest toward the Massasoit's village. John's fears for his father's safety burning brighter by the moment, he hurried along in Warren's wake, joining other men and boys as they converged from all directions.

Plunging into thick bush well beyond the tree line, John scarcely noticed the branches and briars tearing at him as they passed. Then he realized the other fellows were talking and laughing as they went, laying aside at least in part their long day's burden of disquiet and apprehension. They sported the demeanor of young boys unexpectedly liberated from school or chores, out for a lark in the warm springtime sunlight. His worst fears calming, John followed along with the most intense curiosity.

He and the others soon arrived at the apparent destination, which proved not to be a swimming hole or fishing spot, where John and his mates would have been heading in such a mood, but a small clearing in the woods, a flat, mossy patch of ground well lit due to a paucity of overhanging tree branches. If John had known this was where they were going, he could have led them an easier path, without having to plunge through dense undergrowth like a herd of wild pigs. But he had not been consulted, as boys of his age generally were not on any occasion.

At the center of the clearing stood Miles Standish, ready to preside over the impending festivities. Judging by his immaculate appearance, the captain also knew the easy trail to this location. He waited impatiently as late arrivals joined the other spectators in forming a circle around the perimeter of the tiny glade. John started to ask Mister Warren what was going on, but then the situation became all too clear—a test of manhood had been prepared that he had previously encountered only in history or the tall tales of Philip Delano. The dapper Frenchman himself, absent from patrol with the obvious complicity of the captain, gave John a friendly wave from the other side of the clearing. John suspected Philip was not only one of the first to arrive but perhaps a chief instigator as well.

A few feet on either side of Captain Standish stood young Edward Leister and Edward Doty, stripped to the waist and holding swords in their right hands. The weapons were long thin rapiers in the French style—dueling swords, not the heavy broad-bladed English man-killers such as the captain carried on his belt. These could be equally deadly, of course, with the right kind of thrust at a vulnerable spot, and they could put out an eye in a heartbeat.

"All right, you fellows," Standish said, only loudly enough to be heard plainly by those in the clearing, "this is the gentleman's answer to settle the long-simmering dispute between you. I shall serve as referee and judge. You shall commence fighting only at my word, and when I say break, you shall cease fighting and separate immediately. Agreed?"

Both boys nodded, glaring at one another with hatred. Their bearing gave John a qualm the other spectators plainly did not feel. A quick survey of the onlookers revealed only mild amusement and anticipation. John wanted to cry out that Christian men should not stand idly by a potentially murderous situation, but he could not engage his tongue. He feared rendering himself absurd before every man and boy in Plymouth, a diminishment in reputation he could ill afford. If everyone else went along with what was about to take place, why not he? Elder Brewster and Bradford were absent, his father far off on his mission, but other men watched who certainly knew their scriptures better than John could claim. Who was he to raise a protest?

"This duel is not to the death," Standish was saying, "but by the rule of first blood. The first man to draw blood wins, and the fighting shall cease at once. Are you ready, Mister Leister?"

"I am."

"Are you ready, Mister Doty?"

"Just say the word, cap'n."

This provoked laughter all around, though John felt too horrified to join in.

He heard a noise behind him, as of an animal in the bushes, but everyone else was too engrossed to notice. John turned to look. There, almost directly behind him, peering out through parted leafy branches, loomed the white stricken face of Sarah Warren, gasping at the sight before her.

"Very well," Standish said calmly. "On guard!"

John whirled back toward the duelists. They went at each other with a passion.

John had never seen a sword fight before, but Leister and Doty must have been practicing somehow, for instead of the untamed awkwardness he expected, the boys displayed what appeared to him a considerable expertise. Steel rang on steel, and the two Edwards drove each other across the clearing. At first the bigger Leister drove Doty back, almost to the edge of the battleground, and then Doty came to life, driving his opponent back with an equally aggressive attack.

John turned to check on Sarah, but she was gone. Attending to the fight again, he felt relief at her departure. She had no business seeing blood flow. He was not sure he wanted to see it himself.

Only Standish and Philip ventured to cry out advice for the fencers. It occurred to John they were probably the only ones who had ever witnessed such a contest before. The other men and boys were in the same new boat as he and kept silent.

The echo of clashing swords sang through the trees.

* * *

The Massasoit's village consisted of more dwellings, contained more people, and covered more ground that any other Indian community the white men had seen.

The two Englishmen and Hobomok walked in from the forest without challenge, though Francis had little doubt everyone knew they were coming, probably since not long after they set out before sunrise.

As if by signal, the people of the village flooded out of their dwellings and pressed in upon the visitors. They looked a bit more sullen than usual though perhaps only worried. Francis heard none of the customary laughter and joking, but he also saw no manifestation of the intense grief afflicting the group encountered in the forest. This gave Francis hope, and as they moved toward Massasoit's large central dwelling, he allowed himself to believe the great chief might not be dead, at least not yet. The unmistakable sound of keening women arose from the great lodge, but Francis guessed that if the man had truly died these cries would be louder and the whole village so engaged.

A number of young braves stepped out of the throng to bar their path. Grim faces harsh with antagonism, their abrupt shield wall of muscle and brawn caused Francis's heart to pound in his chest. An older man, however, no doubt one of the tribal elders, stepped in front of these. He appeared a kindly man and addressed his remarks to Winslow in a friendly tone.

Knowing Francis had made no effort to learn the Wampanoag tongue as had his son John, Hobomok moved close to whisper a running translation.

"Greetings, Englishman," the elder said.

"Greetings, my friends," Winslow answered in their language, loudly enough to be heard by all. "My brothers and I have come to learn of the great Massasoit Ousamequin." His use of the plural "brothers" explicitly included Hobomok and caused a ripple of approval to pass over the multitude. "We have heard bad tidings."

"Yes, friend," the elder said, "our great chief lies at the door of death. That is why you hear his women weeping."

Winslow spun toward Francis and spoke in English before Hobomok could translate, "He still lives."

"Praise God!" Francis said.

Winslow turned back to the elder and resumed in the Wampanoag language. "Would it be possible to visit our friend the chief?'

"He is very ill, nigh unto death."

"We have brought medicines, all the medicines known among our people. Perhaps we may do some good."

This suggestion brought about a flurry of talk, with other elders stepping forward to discuss the matter with the first. Loud argument broke out on every side, with everybody taking one position or the other. The controversy was growing more vociferous when a wiry old man, covered with paint on his face and body, emerged from the lodge and pushed through the swarming villagers as if they were so many disobedient children. Plunging into heated argument with the elders, the painted man had the look of some devil in a nightmare. This had to be the village medicine man, no happier to have his professional competence questioned, at least by implication, than any European surgeon would have been under equivalent circumstances.

Francis guessed the painted face and body were intended to frighten off the illness, an idea Doctor Fuller would probably have considered no more ridiculous than certain misguided practices of his own supposedly enlightened colleagues.

"What's going on?" Francis whispered to Hobomok.

"Some say, ye might poison Massasoit."

"That's ridiculous! We'd never get out of here alive."

Hobomok nodded. "That is what the other people say."

Displaying no shortage of courage, Winslow stepped forward to join the fray, both speaking directly to the elders and arguing vociferously with the painted shaman. The shouting flew too fast for translation, but by the look on Hobomok's face he seemed to be both enjoying himself and filled with admiration for the scholarly Winslow, who would not back down an inch despite his frail appearance.

Finally the first elder held up his hand and shouted for silence. He did not receive the instant obedience Massasoit would have commanded, but the arguing slowly died away before the man's stern gaze. "Very well, young Englishman, you may come in. I think the great chief will be glad to see you."

"Wait out here, Francis," Winslow said, handing over his pack and the extra musket he had been obliged to carry, much against his will. Not only did its burden violate his conciliatory style of life, but he scarcely knew one end of the weapon from the other. Standish had insisted, however, and the captain could be more than persuasive.

As Winslow turned to enter the lodge, the medicine man made as if to accompany him, but Winslow insisted he remain outside. The first elder gave the requisite order, leaving the enraged witch doctor fuming and Francis the only available target of his resentful glares. Francis met his gaze steadily while shooting up a silent prayer for protection against any invisible devils that might have formed an alliance with the painted one.

Winslow went in by himself.

Time passed. It was the shaman who finally looked away.

* * *

The two Edwards fought with the energy and outrage of insulted youth. Their mutual abhorrence, simmering for years, blazed with a white-hot ferocity. The swords clashed furiously as they drove each other back and forth, one duelist gaining strength or footing, then the other. To John it was clear the boys were trying to kill each other, not merely inflict an honorable wound. He felt astonished that none of the watching men, professing Christians all, stepped forward to intervene, even to prevent a murder. Most of the spectators seemed to regard the action as sport, as if those steel blades were not utterly real and sharply pointed. Yet for all his horror and apprehension, John could not tear his eyes away.

By now both youngsters were beginning to tire, but the thrusting and parrying went on, though at a perceptibly slower pace.

Suddenly John was distracted by another sound from behind him. He turned to behold the bushes part in a different place. Sarah poked her head out once more, looking relieved to find both combatants alive and unwounded.

The leafy branches continued to move, and John realized someone else was emerging from behind Sarah. She must have run off to locate a personage with the authority to stop the fight, most likely the governor or perhaps Elder Brewster if she had not been able to find Bradford.

The figure of enraged and offended rectitude who materialized out of the brush, however, was not the honorable William Bradford or Elder Brewster. It was in fact John's mother, followed by her best friend Priscilla Alden. Both women paused for a quick breath, as if questioning the proof before their outraged eyes that whatever report Sarah had brought them was all too true. For one long merciful moment only the gaping and slack-jawed John was aware of the ladies' presence, but that changed in an instant.

Hester screamed.

Not only screamed, but screamed loudly enough to wake the dead.

John was already swinging his head back toward the clearing to watch the reaction.

Nearly every man started with fright, then froze, including Edward Doty, though not Captain Standish and not Doty's furious opponent.

The hate-crazed Edward Leister took his opportunity for an undefended forward thrust. Doty saw it coming at the last instant and tried to move left, but Leister's blade pierced him through on the right side, a few inches below the armpit.

The boy gazed down with a stricken, utterly surprised look on his face as blood began to pour out of the wound. Leister drew back for another thrust, one that would surely kill his opponent.

Now it was Hester Cooke's elder son who shouted at the top of his lungs, for John was the only spectator still looking at the duelists.

"No!" he cried, but Leister paid no mind. The blade thrust forward, headed straight for Doty's heart.

CHAPTER 29

The Gift of Healing

Coming from the bright spring day outside, Winslow had to wait a moment for his eyes to adjust to the darkness of the lodge. His sudden appearance muted the weeping of the women. He stood without moving until he could see Massasoit lying on his bed of royal bearskins, surrounded by four ladies of various ages ranging from nearly the chief's own to the youngest, who appeared scarcely twenty, if that. Whether these were wives or merely female relatives of some sort, Winslow did not care. The patriarchs of the Old Testament took multiple wives after all, though the practice had been discouraged in the New. The women moved politely aside as he approached.

He knelt for a closer look at the wily old heathen for whom he felt so much genuine affection.

The old man's face was covered with perspiration. He looked terribly ill. Lifting his eyes, Massasoit recognized Winslow, and his lips parted in a weak smile.

"Ed...War...Wins...Low. My young... white... brother..."

The weakness of the noble Massasoit's voice nearly broke Winslow's heart. "Massasoit Ousamequin, our own chief Bradford heard that our brother was ill, and he has sent me and my brothers to see if, by the help of our God, I should be able to heal you with our medicines."

"My thanks to you... my young brother... and to your chief Bradford... Now Ousamequin knows that you love him."

The old Indian could not have used a more powerful word. Winslow thought of the love of Christ for all mankind and of himself as a messenger of that love, and it was all he could do to keep from bursting into tears. He knew the value of keeping his composure, however, and waited a moment before he spoke again.

"We do love the great Massasoit, all of us, and now with your blessing I shall need a place for my brothers and me to prepare our medicines. We shall do our best to make the great chief well."

"Yes. We put you... in the next lodge." Massasoit made a weak gesture with one hand, and the eldest woman immediately scurried outside to convey the chief's command.

"Now, my dear old friend," Winslow said, "what seems to be the problem?"

* * *

Leister's rapier was heading right for the unprotected Doty when Captain Standish, undistracted by the arrival of hysterical women, stepped forward between the fighters and intercepted Leister's blade with his own. Standish swept his heavy broadsword upward with sufficient force to fling the foil clean out of Leister's grip, and it went spinning over the clearing, causing wary men to dodge frantically before it clattered to the ground. The quickness and power of the action exhibited the sheer physical strength of the little man.

"There, there, Mister Leister, you have drawn first blood. No reason to carry your victory further. Gentlemen, I declare Mister Leister the winner!"

Doty swayed on his feet, holding his side with his left hand as blood flowed out between the fingers, but he had no intention of standing still for a decision he considered an outrage.

"Just a minute, 'ere!" Doty cried. "This weren't my fault. It was that screamin' female! She distracted me, she did! It ain't fair, not a bit of it!"

"Rules are rules, Mister Doty," Standish said calmly. "Let that teach you to keep your mind on your business, no matter what the distraction."

The captain's very placidity seemed to drive Hester to distraction.

"What do you men think you are doing?" she shrieked.

John noted the flush on his mother's brow, backed off a step or two. He knew what his mother, normally the gentlest of women, was capable of in a state of high dudgeon. He feared her indignation had never soared higher than at the present moment.

Meanwhile Priscilla rushed forward, snatched one of the discarded shirts, balled it up, and began pressing the cloth tightly against Doty's wound. He winced with pain, then slowly dropped into a sitting position on the ground as she supported him.

"'old on there," Leister said. "That's my shirt!"

Priscilla shamed him to silence with a single withering look.

"You did this without Dr. Fuller present?" Hester demanded.

Guilty eyes dropped to contemplate the mossy ground. John realized the doctor had not been summoned because he would have put a stop to the whole business.

"Someone run and fetch him!" Priscilla said.

One of John's friends welcomed this occasion for flight, but Standish stopped him with a word. "Don't bother. We shall carry young Mister Doty to the fort. It's only a scratch."

A scratch that continued to bleed rather prodigiously if Priscilla relaxed her pressure.

As men hurried to grasp the wounded boy, Hester placed herself before the captain, and John was astonished to see him flinch, though slightly.

"Captain Standish," she said, "What did you think you were doing? A duel? I cannot believe that a mature leader as intelligent as yourself would sanction such a thing!"

"Mrs. Cooke," Standish said in a sheepish tone that quite astounded Mrs. Cooke's son, "it is a perfectly honorable means to settle a longstanding..."

"Honorable! I cannot believe such an expression would come out of your mouth, sir." She swept a furious gaze across every face, and few there were with courage to meet her blazing eyes for long. "And I cannot believe the rest of you could stand around and watch this blood sport like Nero on his throne and not one of you is Christian enough—nor enough of a man!—to speak out against it!" By the time her look fell upon her own guilty son, John abode in deepest contemplation of that small world of enthralling interest just in front of his own toes. "John Cooke!"

Oh, Lord, deliver me from the wrath to come.

"John Cooke, get thee back to the fields! You should be ashamed of yourself, and all the more should be all these grown men, so-called."

"All right, Mrs. Cooke, that's enough," Standish said.

"Enough?"

John looked up, terrified his mother was going to slap the man.

* * *

Francis passed an extremely nerve-racking interval waiting outside the lodge. Villagers of all ages milled about, at a polite distance initially, though soon gathering their courage to creep forward and reach out to touch him, his clothing and his equipage. They showed special interest in the guns. A few snarls from Hobomok served to keep the curious away at first, but Francis was soon enveloped, no doubt because he made a genuine effort to show himself friendly.

"Hello. Hello," Francis babbled intermittently. "No, no, I have to hang on to these... No, no, can't let you open the bag, important medicines inside.... Does any one of you speak any English? No? Sorry I haven't learned a word of your pleasant-sounding tongue. Hobomok has tried to teach me, but I have a bit of a tin ear, I'm afraid, unlike Mister Winslow who is inside there speaking with your great chief... It is certainly a privilege to be here among you, and it is my hope that we can help our old friend... I hope that we shall all be friends..." Poor Francis felt he had never strung more words together in his life—for listeners, alas, who in all likelihood did not understand a single one.

Hobomok stood grinning at him, no doubt for being absurd, but Francis hoped his friendly tone would communicate something aright. He kept his tight grip on the bags and the guns.

Then an old woman emerged from the chief's lodge and spoke with the elders. The first elder barked an order. Other women ran to clear out an adjacent hut, and then he and Hobomok were escorted inside and left alone. They rid themselves of their burdens and sat down on blankets that the women had apparently prepared for them. By now Hobomok's mood seemed to have soured, and they waited in silence.

Francis felt quite worried indeed by the time Winslow finally joined them, looking quite relaxed. In fact the younger man seemed downright chipper. He dropped down onto a third blanket, and they put their heads together, speaking quietly after Winslow warned that some of those outside only pretended not to understand any English, making Francis regard himself that much more of a fool. These purported savages frequently demonstrated a far greater learning facility than most white men did for any of the native languages.

Francis really did have a tin ear, but he thought most of his white brethren simply didn't want to be bothered. A bookish soul like Winslow might be fascinated by the scores of Indian dialects they already knew about, but most English folk expected that if the savages had anything important to say, they ought to learn to speak the King's English like gentlemen, and the same went for froggy Huguenots and other foreigners to boot.

"Well?" Francis said.

"The chief is very ill." Winslow broke into a grin. "But I think perchance we shall be able to do him some good." He gestured for Francis to pass him the medicinal bag and began to root inside.

Winslow's confident assurance surprised Francis, who had observed over a lifetime how most applications by doctors of reputed medicines had little or no effect upon the patient except perhaps to usher the sufferer into eternity more speedily. Among the people of Plymouth, European medical science carried not only the ancient taints of alchemy and outright charlatanism but most of all the stain of sheer ineffectuality. Fortunately their physician Doctor Fuller had proved himself more competent than most.

"You really think you can help?"

Winslow nodded. "Several days ago, the village had a great feast to celebrate the first successful hunt of the springtime. Massasoit Ousamequin apparently ate himself into a state of prostration. And he has not been able to have a bowel movement since."

Francis was incredulous. "You mean he's... he's...?"

"The man is constipated."

"And he could die from this?"

"Absolutely. I apologize for speaking of something so indelicate."

"Edward, as long as you can help him, I do not care in the least."

"Neither do I, Francis. I seem to recall a place in the Gospels." He thought for a bit. "Matthew Chapter Fifteen—and also Luke Chapter Seven, I believe. In any case, where Christ mentions the food passing through us needing to be cast out into the draught. Our Lord was a bit less squeamish on matters of the body than we, it seems. But never fear..."

Francis gazed at the bag. "You have a laxative in there?"

Winslow plucked out the packet he was looking for and held it up in triumph. "Indeed we do!"

Hobomok did not completely follow what they were talking about, but their improving mood lightened his own, and he lay back on his blanket.

"I shall mix this up at once," Winslow said, "and then I'd like to get it and a bit of soup into him as well. Priming the pump, so to speak."

"What kind of soup?" Francis said.

"Well, chicken soup would be best, but since we don't have time to re-cross the Atlantic..."

"Would a duck serve?"

"Yes! In lieu of a fine English chicken, a nice fat duck would be just the thing."

"Hobomok," Francis said, "would you know the nearest place to bag a good duck?"

The Indian shook his head. "I ask." He sprang up and went outside.

Francis watched as Winslow unwrapped a mortar bowl and pestle out of the bag. He emptied some of the contents of the packet into the bowl and began to grind the material into a fine powder.

"What is it?"

"Senna leaves mostly, with a bit of ash tree. I am quadrupling the recommended dosage. Ought to do the trick."

"God grant."

"I shall need some water heated up, Francis, to make this into a tea. Then you best go see about that duck."

It was unnecessary to obtain a brand from an existing village fire. Francis built a stack of wood and kindling from the hut's supply, then struck a flame from his tinderbox. Picking up an old brass kettle as good as any back in Plymouth—proof of Wampanoag contact with European traders years before the Mayflower arrived—he was just setting water to boil when Hobomok returned with a young boy to serve as guide for the duck hunt.

Francis found it hard to believe Hobomok could not have guided him or found a duck on his own. The brave probably thought he needed to stay near Winslow and his irreplaceable patient. This perception shook the serenity Francis had been able to attain. Fresh waves of fear swept over him, gripping his heart more strongly than ever—but he had to push on.

* * *

The two insistent women would not be denied entrance, and now Hester and Priscilla stood near Bradford, who watched the proceedings nearly as anxiously. Edward Doty lay on a strong table as Dr. Fuller prepared to tend his wound, Miles Standish at its head in case the boy needed to be held down. The doctor's operating theater was a separate enclosed space facing east toward the town on the ground floor of the fort. A substantial portion of Fuller's implements and medicines were kept here, a secure room walled off at the rear of the large storage area where church and town meetings were held, rather than at his home, as would have been the case anywhere in Europe. Since the fort would serve as the last redoubt of defense against attack, Captain Standish insisted this was where the primary facility for treatment belonged, and Fuller had gone along with this logic, though grumpily.

Though the crude, hinged windows Fuller had demanded prior to construction were now hooked open from the inside, miniature trap doors cut into the thick logs of the eastern wall, he had to light candles for additional illumination, since the afternoon sun now stood on the opposite, western side of the fort. Examining Doty's wound carefully, he saw that the sword thrust had passed through the flesh on the boy's side, along the surface of the rib cage, grazing the bone painfully but not penetrating. A wound below the ribs would have been much more dangerous, the doctor knew.

Back in England and Holland, Fuller had acquired a reputation among other physicians for eccentric ideas. One of these was an obsession with cleanliness quite unknown among his contemporaries. He could not prove the matter nor explain it, but in his mind he associated disease and infection with filth. He found confirmation for this in his studies of the scriptures. In the Old Testament books of the Law, God gave Moses detailed instructions on various matters that struck many as purely arbitrary. Unwilling to ascribe capriciousness to the Creator, Fuller suspected many of these mysterious commandments had something to do with good health. Human waste, for example, was to be gathered up once a day and transported outside the camp, to be buried far from the place where the children of Abraham lived or drew their water. Since the walls of Jerusalem contained a "dung gate" in the time of Christ, Fuller concluded that this practice had been continued long after the Jews occupied or built cities in the Promised Land. This system stood in shattering contrast with modern London, where the streets reeked with human and animal filth that choked every gutter. A growing population had transformed the mighty Thames River into an open sewer as with the Tiber of Rome centuries earlier. Fuller had done his best to impose the Old Testament system on Plymouth. Given the prior history of disease in this location, which the native tribes considered accursed, the governor and council had backed him up.

In keeping with his obsession, Fuller's first act in treating Edward Doty was to scrub his own hands with soap and water, a source of great bemusement among his colleagues back in Europe, a practice he patterned after the ritual cleansing enjoined on the Jews. After cleansing his hands, Fuller used fresh soap and water to do the same for young Doty's puncture wounds. Fuller tried to keep his anger over the duel in check, but gently as he strove to wash the wound, the boy moaned in pain.

"Now this is going to hurt a bit more, I'm afraid, but it'll be over in a moment."

One of the medicines Fuller had brought across the sea was a large supply of a mysterious fermented liquid that had been brewed far stronger than any spirituous liquor he had ever encountered. The sharp odor filled the room as soon as he uncorked the bottle. Fuller could not imagine taking so much as a sip without risk of death—yet it seemed to have quite positive effects on cuts and wounds. He poured some of the foul brew on a clean cloth and washed the wound again as gently as he could, though the boy cried out so much that Captain Standish had to hold him down.

"Are you going to have to cauterize it?" Standish said.

Doty's eyes bugged out in fright.

"No, Captain, that probably won't be necessary, but we shall have to see if any signs of corruption appear later." Fuller had learned this trick from the same Gypsy who sold him the elixir. Washing a wound with the medicine seemed to be as effective in preventing infection, at least in some cases, as searing the wound with flame or a red hot iron, the common treatment which had been in use, primarily to prevent gangrene, since the time of the Roman legions.

"You won't have to burn me, sir?" Doty said.

"I cannot say yet, son, we shall have to wait and see. But we have a better chance if I pour some of this in."

"All right, sir."

Fuller poured a small draught in a tiny cup.

"Better bite on that belt for a bit."

Standish stuck a piece of leather belt between the boy's teeth. Fuller positioned the bottle over the entry wound, used his fingers to pry it as wide as he could, and poured some of the liquid in. The boy screamed louder than before, but it was muted as he bit on the cowhide.

"Now the other side, I'm afraid, and then it will be over."

Doty managed to roll over with his own strength, and Fuller poured in another hefty dose. The results were the same.

"Brave lad. I've had grown men pass out from this treatment. Now can you sit up while I bandage it?" He placed a pad of clean cloth against the wound and began the process of winding a long strip of cloth around the boy's body to hold it in place. The custom of the age would be to keep wetting the bandage down with water, but Fuller had found the healing process seemed to work better if bandages were kept dry and changed often.

He had learned from Edward Winslow that the local savages treated wounds in a similar manner, except they usually placed a piece of tree moss betwixt the bandage and the wound. This horrified Fuller initially, with his fear of dirt, but he had by now heard manifold reports that the tree moss seemed to prevent corruption and speed healing. He could only conclude the moss contained some medicinal element, and he had gone so far as to acquire and keep a fresh supply for himself, just in case, though so far he had never encountered in Plymouth a wound severe enough to entice him to the experiment.

By now Hester Cooke was stalking up and down like a caged lioness ready to pounce. Fuller had never actually seen a lioness, caged or otherwise, but he had read enough to form a picture in his mind. As he bandaged, the cat found its roar.

"I cannot believe to see such a thing in a company of the saints," she burst out at Bradford. "To be fighting the duel!"

Here she let loose a long stream of French before lapsing back into something they could more or less understand. "Is it that we are here to do, to take all the worst things of Europe and plant them here in this wilderness? I have been so naive to believe we are here to plant the Gospel of Jesus Christ and to water and grow His church! Instead we come into the woods and what do we find but fighting of the duel with swords and the cutting to blood?! And with my little son watching with all the other stupid fellows who ought to be old enough to know better!"

Here she fixed Standish with another accusatory gaze, but he did not meet it, concentrating instead on the repair work.

"This is not what we wish our children to see," she went on, "such terrible things!"

In the meek silence that followed this outburst it was young Doty who spoke up. "I'm sorry, Missus, it was all me own fault, mine and Leister's. We be the ones that got into this fight."

Hester was having none of it. "And where, pray tell, did you and the other young blockhead acquire the swords for this dangerous game?"

"It's all part of our training, ma'am. From the captain."

"Ah, from the great captain." She turned again to Bradford. "He not only trained them to play with the swords, he was acting as the referee!"

"Mrs. Cooke," the governor answered, "if you could but calm yourself..."

"Calm myself! I fear it is difficult to calm myself, sir, as it will be for every other lady in Plymouth, if I know them as I do."

"I need no convincing in that regard," Bradford said in the tenor of a man who did not necessarily look forward to going home himself. He cast a hard look of his own at a Standish too fascinated by the ministrations of the doctor to notice.

"Then I trust you will have the little word with our glorious Captain Standish about this disgraceful... about this terribleness!"

"I shall speak to him, dear lady. I promise."

"Come, Hester," Priscilla pleaded. "Let us go." She took hold and dragged the fuming Hester away.

The entire male contingent breathed a sigh of relief at their departure, except for Doctor Fuller, who finally let a long suppressed smile break forth on his face.

CHAPTER 30

The Proper Use of Various Weapons

Francis followed the Indian boy along well-hidden but passable trails, through an increasingly marshy terrain of copious trees, thickened by nearly impenetrable brush. The lad looked both younger and smaller than John, but wore that same familiar aspect of solemn gravity, which this harsh land seemed to impose on children, growing them up so tragically before their time. Or perhaps the youngster only carried the pervasive burden of anxiety regarding the beloved Massasoit. Francis made to offer a few words of reassurance when they first set out, but the boy gave no indication of comprehending a single word of English.

They moved quickly, rapidly covering a distance of at least a mile from the village. The boy glanced back occasionally to make sure he had not lost his charge. This would have been quite a merry chase, Francis thought as they trotted along, if the outcome of the old man's crisis did not hang over them like a Damoclean sword. He and the boy were not exactly running, but Francis could not recall the last time he had moved so far so quickly.

He was determined not to humiliate himself by stopping for a rest. He was just at the point of surrendering this resolution when the boy plunged off the trail into the bush, which slowed their progress. Francis watched his step. The dense plant life grew out of wet, swampy soil that lay interspersed with muddy pools. The boy was leading him deeper and deeper into another one of the many swamps that dotted the forests for miles around. No obvious path or trail presented itself to a less seasoned English eye, but Francis reckoned the boy knew his business. He made sure to follow him with absolute precision as the boy made eccentric and unexplainable twists that violated any notion of traveling in a straight line. The gruesome fate of Deaky Jones loomed large in Francis's mind.

Suddenly the boy held up his hand, and they came to an instantaneous halt. Francis listened intently. After a moment he heard it clearly, some little distance to the front, the congenial quacking of a tremendous number of ducks. He nodded at the boy, who smiled and resumed leading him forward, both moving stealthily as death.

Ahead of them loomed a natural barrier, a kind of embankment that rose up higher than a man's height out of the surrounding swamp and extended as far as Francis could see to either side of them. When they reached it, the boy dropped to his belly and crawled to the top. With a wayward thought for the state of his newly re-sewn and freshly washed clothing, followed immediately by the happy realization that he no longer had to launder them himself, Francis flipped the carrying strap over his shoulder so the big gun hung down his back, dropped to his hands and knees, and followed the boy's lead.

They squirmed to the top and slowly lifted their heads to look out over the edge. Francis almost gasped at the sight. Before them lay a large pond or small lake of the purest blue water, quite unlike the muddy swamp pools they had been tracking through and around for the last quarter hour. He wondered how such a marvel could exist in this place. The water must come from some deep spring far below the ground, but how had the embankment come to be, protecting this astonishing body of azure luminosity from all the surrounding impurity? He could only shake his head in awe at yet another of the Lord's natural created wonders.

More important to their current necessity, the smooth surface of the pond supported an immense company of ducks swimming back and forth, ducks of every color, size and description, a veritable conclave of the species duck. Francis could not begin to guess at the number, but they made an impressive flock. He glanced over at the boy, who grinned at him with all the joy of childhood, the solemnity of the day momentarily—and reassuringly—forgotten. He nodded and slipped back down the bank, where the boy joined him.

Francis brought the gun over into his lap and reached into the leather pouch on his belt. He knew he would have only one shot before every duck in the pond took wing at the noise. For this reason he had waited to load the firing pan with fresh, dry powder at this last possible moment. He carried out the process as the boy watched intently. Francis would have preferred to empty the barrel out as well, tamping in a new charge, ball and wadding, but this noisier step could not be taken without greater risk of giving themselves away. He could only hope the musket had kept the barrel's contents dry, and he fortified that hope with a quick silent prayer.

Francis had friends who believed effectual prayer could only be accomplished at a proper time set aside for devotion and with a formality appropriate to the awesome dignity of the Living God. He tended to take Hester's line of focusing more on the scriptures portraying the Lord as a loving Father rather than a terrifying Judge, though both concepts were equally Biblical.

In any case he agreed with her at least in theory that the Apostle Paul's admonition to pray without ceasing meant staying in touch with God not at some special hour but throughout one's day, as she did with much greater dedication than his own practice, sending thoughts and requests winging Heavenward along with appropriate praise, in good times and bad, but especially as some need or problem arose. She seemed to breathe out prayer as a part of her very being.

Though he would probably never admit it to other men, he had learned much from his dear wife of how one should at least attempt to live in this attitude of constant unbroken connection with Christ, in the same way the Spirit of Christ abided in constant unbroken connection with those He indwelt.

After preparing the firing pan, the next step was using the tinderbox to strike a light. He did his best to time the striking of the flint to coincide with one of the crescendos of quacking and honking from the other side of the embankment. Worried about the moisture in the swamp, he managed to spark a flame after only two tries. As the boy gaped in wonder at the device, Francis applied the little fire to both ends of the fuse coiled round his shoulder, then quenched the tinderbox and put it back in his pouch. He carefully attached one smoking extremity to the serpentine lever that would plunge the burning end down into the firing pan when he triggered the mechanism.

Because of endless training and repetition, the process had taken less than a minute though he exercised extraordinary care to do it right. When ready, he nodded to the boy and they slithered back to the top of the embankment. He wished it were possible to fire from flat on his belly, but that capacity would have to await future developments in firearm design. He might be able to fire from a sitting position, bracing the musket on his elbows and knees, but the safest recourse, the one he had most often practiced, was a standing position. Signaling the boy to stay on the ground, he waited for a nod of understanding and then slowly and carefully raised himself to his feet behind a large tree growing out of the embankment between him and the pond.

Moving ever so noiselessly, he slid around the trunk until he had an open view of the water. He lifted the musket into position, bracing it against the tree for extra stability. It was quite heavy, and though his arms had developed more muscle than he ever could have imagined back in Holland from the constant use of shovel, rake, hammer, saw and ax, he did not want to hold the gun in place for long.

He had no desire to shoot a bird on the wing either, though he had seen Standish and Philip do it, and he had once managed to do it himself out of more than a dozen attempts. The firing of a matchlock musket was always an adventure, that was the problem, and the slightest hesitation between the fall of the serpentine and the ignition of the charge in the barrel could throw one's timing off completely, especially against a moving target. He had seen Hobomok hit flying birds with a bow and arrow, a feat of timing and hunter's skill that put them all to shame.

The present game was not some ground-running wild turkey moreover, but sleek and fast-flying duck. Francis had no desire to accomplish a trick shot that would make him a legend among Massasoit's people. No, he had every intention to violate a hunter's code already a byword the world over. He sought out the proverbial sitting duck, the fattest one he could spot.

An easy target waddled nearby, a mother duck with a flock of ducklings, but he declined to deprive the young of a loving parent and allowed her to move into the water with the little ones trailing behind her. Then he spotted a fat mallard unconnected with the rest of duck society. The fellow sat napping on the bank, not bothering to look around. A poor bachelor destined to pay the ultimate price for his independence.

Francis slowly and carefully squeezed the trigger. The lit fuse dropped into the firing pan, setting off an explosion of white smoke. Time seemed to crawl through an excruciating pause. The quacking and honking began to rise to new levels. Wings began to beat. Francis thought at first he had a misfire but held the gun steady. Unfortunately for him the mallard was slow to react in the second or two available. When the prime charge fired he had not moved an inch.

Hundreds of ducks rose into the sky.

The Indian boy leaped to his feet and ran toward the fluttering mallard. The lad was screaming words that Francis naturally could not understand. The shot had severed the duck's neck, taking the head clean off, and now the headless body was hopping about, just like a chicken after its fatal visit to the chopping block. The boy managed to reach it, shouting, before it flopped out into the pond. He snatched the legs and held it up triumphantly for Francis's inspection. He was looking at the white man with awe and overpowering respect. Francis was apparently destined to become a legend in spite of himself.

As he walked down to join his new friend, Francis decided he would never tell anyone he had been aiming for the duck's fat body and had only taken off the head by sheer luck or, as he preferred to think of it, divine intervention.

* * *

Once they returned to the communal nursery set up in the Aldens' home, more or less on a permanent basis, Hester and Priscilla focused on the day's children and kept further roaming and exasperated thoughts to themselves, despite relentless questioning by Jane Cooke, Priscilla's designated helper for the week. There were fewer babes and toddlers on hand than usual, as most of the women refrained from working in the fields, though some had dropped off children anyway in order to work undistracted at their vegetable gardening or other tasks within the palisade. By the time the sun sank below the western tree line, the little ones began to be collected by grateful mothers. These were full of questions too, but Priscilla and Hester remained intractably evasive, as frustrating for themselves as for their friends. The tale of the duel and its aftermath had already blanketed Plymouth in any case, but Hester held her tongue, fearing her temper might flare up once more to the detriment of all.

Once the babies had all been picked up and the Cooke daughters sent ahead on their own, Priscilla drew a shawl around her shoulders against the cool evening air and accompanied her friend up the hill. They walked in silence. Both knew they had to put a supper together for weary households, but each still felt a continuing need for fellowship with the other.

They stopped before Hester's house and for a time stood silent watch as the gloaming darkened into full night. The breeze from the sea plucked at their hair.

Hester rubbed at her eyes with a quick movement, embarrassed at the sting of tears welling up. She wished to be more in control of herself in the presence of her dearest friend.

Priscilla touched her arm. "Perhaps the men are right."

"Oh, Priscilla, the men cannot always be right about everything! Surely you have been married long enough to know that."

The younger woman giggled, dropping the commiserating hand. "I think I knew that well before my marriage."

"Those boys could have been killed out there. The Doty boy could still die."

"Possibly," Priscilla admitted, "but I think not. Doctor Fuller is a skilled surgeon."

"The men seem to regard it as nothing more than a harmless game. I am surprised they were not placing wagers."

"Who says they weren't?"

Hester sighed. "What do you know about this great Captain Standish that everyone seems to admire so extravagantly?"

"I only know that he is an experienced soldier. He fought in the wars with the greatest bravery, they say, and knows how to train men and lead them. He was hired right before the Mayflower sailed from England, to be in charge of our protection."

"Recruited by the adventurers in London?"

"No, hired on by Governor Bradford and Elder Brewster. It was one decision they insisted on making themselves. Perhaps the adventurers had won so many of their demands by that point they could spare the good grace to yield on something."

"Not unless they thought our people had finally been pushed to the point of walking away." Hester had heard plenty about the adventurers from Francis and Philip, who would never credit those prideful, petty-minded scoundrels with good grace over anything.

"Perhaps you are right. But everyone says Captain Standish is a very fine man."

"Do you think him a Christian man?"

"He has never joined our church, though he always attends most respectfully. I have heard whispers that perhaps he is Catholic, but if that is so he has never done anything to evince his Romanism."

"I care not if he is the most faithful Protestant in the world, if he exercises an influence of spiritual darkness on this colony."

"Oh, Hester, I do not think that is the case. He is a good man after his own lights."

"That is *his* opinion, to be sure."

"Even if you are right, Hester, what can we do? As women we are not permitted to speak up in a meeting, to express an open opinion."

"I believe you saw me expressing an opinion today!"

"Yes, and you may suffer for it!" Now Priscilla was the one at the point of tears.

Hester put an arm around her. "We have the option that Godly women have always had. We can pray."

"We do pray!" Priscilla snapped in a distraught tone that seemed to imply '*and what good is it doing?*'

Hester hugged her tighter. "We pray, and we wield an influence on our husbands."

"John and Francis? You think we can persuade them?"

"One has to be subtle, of course. No man is keen on a nag. But we can influence them. Gently influence them by modest and Godly behavior as the apostle says, and perhaps we may help bring them around on matters that need to be made aright."

"And they can speak up in the meetings, if need be!"

"Of course."

"Oh Hester, it is plain you have been married longer than I!"

"We must move carefully though. Our husbands are good men, but as Sarah Eaton used to say, all men respond better to woman's influence when they do not know it is being exercised." After her screaming fits at Standish and Bradford, Hester felt a certain lack of credibility in defending the virtues of quiet modesty, but Priscilla looked at her with awe.

"Hester, you are subtle as a Jesuit!"

Hester laughed. "More subtle than I showed myself today, I trust."

"Quiet influence. That is what we women have to fight with. I am glad of it, dear friend. What we do is better than fighting a silly duel with swords."

"In the battles we fight," Hester said, "there is often more at stake."

CHAPTER 31

The Warning

The entire Wampanoag village erupted with commotion when Francis and the boy returned so soon after their departure. It was a joyless tumult at first, no doubt due to lingering anxiety over the great chieftain's illness, but rose to a happier frenzy as the young guide excitably told his tale. Francis had no idea exactly what the boy was shouting at the top of his lungs—a hunting yarn no doubt including an exaggerated account of his impossible shot. Francis felt guilty to see fear rising in the eyes of so many, but now at least no one attempted to lay a hand on his gun.

The boy seemed disappointed the villagers avoided touching the duck as well, perhaps out of fear that some strange magic might rub off, with unpredictable consequences. Francis laid a hand on his little friend's shoulder as they walked, hoping to insinuate the boy would abide under his protection against any act of resentment or envy after the white men had withdrawn.

* * *

Weak and ill as Massasoit remained, he sent one of his ladies out to discover the cause of all the excitement. When informed Winslow planned on cooking the soup personally, he had the Plymouth visitors brought back to his lodge. His women were powerfully curious to watch a white man cook, a procedure so at odds with the Bone Men's incompetent reputation. In fact Edward Winslow brought to bear considerable skill at cooking for any man, but especially an Englishman, a talent for which Francis had often felt thankful when Edward had been an unmarried housemate, though never so thankful as on the present occasion.

As Winslow proceeded from plucking the duck to cutting it up, Francis began cleaning his musket. Captain Standish had pounded into their skulls that guns had to be cleaned as soon as possible after use to prevent the buildup of powder residue in the barrel and mechanism, though in this case Francis had only fired once. As he worked, he leaned forward to ask a question.

"Did he drink it?"

Winslow, focused on his culinary performance, looked up with a puzzled expression.

"The laxative, brother," Francis said. "Did he drink it?"

"Oh, yes. Drank the foul brew down every drop."

"When?"

"Soon after you left."

Francis felt troubled at this. "Shouldn't there be... results by this time?"

"My dear fellow, not necessarily. Has to work through the system. If he's been impacted these several days...could take time. That's the purpose of this soup, to give him a push from the other end, so to speak."

Francis glanced over at Massasoit, who lay as sickly and perspiring as before.

Winslow's cheerful face showed little concern, and Francis concluded he had no choice but to nurture the same kind of confidence within himself. This would render the passage of time more endurable than its opposite, which was to feed the worry beast, an inclination to which Francis was all too well disposed. With a sigh he drew back and sat on a blanket to watch the artist at work.

Winslow began to engage the women in conversation as the pieces of duck simmered in the water. Francis understood nothing, of course, but Winslow used the same tone one might use politely inquiring after the well-being of children or such like. Prying a response out of the ladies proved quite difficult at first, but Winslow's brazen normality, his evident certainty that all would be well, gradually drew them out.

Francis studied the kettle where the duck was beginning to boil, a larger item of European metalwork than the one he had used to boil water for the laxative tea. It struck him with more force than ever before how much red man and white had been influencing one another since their earliest contact. The scholar's dream of the unaffected savage dwelling in the purity of nature had ceased to exist the moment the first white man stepped upon the shore. Francis had heard of bookish men in Europe who took umbrage at the so-called lost innocence of native peoples, as if civilization itself were a form of corruption.

As a Christian man who read his Bible, Francis thought all that was nonsense. The heathen dwelt in terrible darkness awaiting the light of Christ, Who would not only redeem them to forgiveness and eternal life but also help bring out the best qualities they already possessed. And they did have many wonderful qualities. After all, how would he and his fellow believers have survived without the practical knowledge acquired from these pagans, however devoid of revealed Truth in the spiritual realm?

His own compassion was far more engaged with the problem of literal rather than philosophical corruption, especially contamination by the terrible diseases that had slain countless millions on the other side of the Atlantic. The kidnapped Squanto had returned from escaping slavery in Europe to find his Patuxet village, located exactly where the English had built New Plymouth, wiped out to the last soul. Francis knew Doctor Fuller suspected some white man's contagion as the culprit. The surgeon theorized that whites built up protection over time against their own familiar pestilences, though neither he nor the great medical faculties of the continent had the slightest idea how this worked, neither as to what caused the diseases nor how the human body developed the capacity to resist them.

Contagion operated through mysterious and invisible processes no one understood. Epidemics had swept across the world for centuries, but medical men knew from ancient texts that each successive wave of a particular pestilence somehow claimed fewer fatalities. This held true for a vial of wrath as lethal as the Black Death itself. Every ensuing visitation of that hideous affliction carried off ever fewer victims than the nearly world-destroying outbreak of the Fourteenth Century.

However Europeans developed bodily strength to resist the shadowy unseen killers that stalked their populations, the Indians had no protection at all against childhood fevers rarely fatal to whites. The suspected power of white man's disease to ravage the native tribes was a major reason Francis and Winslow had breathed potent sighs of relief to learn that Massasoit's only problem was severe constipation.

When Winslow determined that the duck had cooked through sufficiently, he took the chunks out separately and cut away the bones, slicing the cooked meat into small pieces. Once all the meat was back in the broth, he added vegetables brought to him by the women as requested: red tomatoes, a little onion, dried beans, carrots, young green beans, some green leafy vegetable that Francis could not identify. These Winslow added, then built the fire a little higher and sat by stirring the pot. He pealed and sliced up a considerable quantity of what were apparently potatoes, though unlike any potato Francis had seen before, added the slices, then put aside a quantity of the previous harvest's corn kernels which he said he would put in last, since corn took less time to cook than the other ingredients.

Before long the mildly boiling kettle wafted out a savory aroma that made Francis's mouth water.

In the event, relief came without having to prime the pump. Massasoit suddenly cried out. Two of the women rushed to his side, helped him to his feet, and aided him in walking, very quickly, out of the lodge and into the nearby woods.

Francis and Winslow looked at each other.

"Perhaps it's working," Francis said hopefully.

"Perhaps it is." Winslow grinned.

Massasoit was gone so long, however, that they both began to worry.

Just as Francis was thinking seriously of going out to see about him, the old man returned, still between the two women though not leaning so heavily on their support. He wore a weak but unmistakable smile of relief on his face. He nodded, which communicated everything required, and resumed his place on the royal bearskins.

By this time Winslow was ready to serve the meal. Francis had heard rumors, though not from Winslow, that some Indian groups ate by dipping their unwashed hands into a communal cooking pot, but that was apparently not the custom of the Wampanoag. Winslow selected one from a number of small bowls and filled it from the kettle. The patient sat up and began to wolf down the soup, bowl after steady bowl with scarcely a pause between. The hungry Plymouth men looked on a bit wistfully, as did the women, but the stew had been intended as medicine for the sufferer, and as treatment for the sufferer it all went down. Francis hoped this display of the same gluttony that brought on the initial crisis would not have the same result again. Winslow had better leave some of the laxative behind with appropriate instructions.

At last Massasoit leaned back with a sigh of satisfaction and an empty bowl. He regarded his visitors with a sharp and calculating eye, then spoke a peremptory order that sent all the women scurrying outside. He waited a moment, smiled, then barked another command.

Francis thought or possibly imagined he could hear the faint sound of soft moccasins retreating from the outside walls. With eavesdropping an obvious concern, the aged chieftain beckoned his rescuers to sit closer, though Hobomok stayed where he was, smoking a fragrant pipe with the serenity of a man who already knew everything about to be said.

"Ed-ward Wins-low, we know you and your Eng-lish brother have taken your lives in your hands to come to me in my illness." Massasoit spoke in a voice scarcely above a whisper. Winslow translated for Francis. "Had I died, you perhaps would have died as well. Yet you came knowing this. I was sick unto death, but you saved me."

"As I have said," Winslow replied with equal formality, "when we heard our friend was ill, we could do nothing else. Our chief Bradford and all our people felt the same. We are most gratified that our great friend did not perish, and we thank our God for his healing."

Massasoit waved a hand to dismiss the sermon. Clearly, he credited the undoubtedly brave but ever opportunistic white men, not their God. Francis caught the full meaning without translation. The languid gesture struck him as very far removed from a savage pagan given to paint and feathers, calling to mind another type of reprobate entirely, supposedly civilized men with less excuse, such as that one loud mocker of religion who seemed to inhabit every English village, or worse yet the proud but secret European atheist, lurking bitter, rebellious and undetected in the bowels of church or university, yea sometimes at the very pinnacle of politics, society and wealth. Nurtured with all comforts and benefits in the very bosom of Christian heritage, these foolish and ungrateful vipers had no excuse, and their foot would slide in due time.

With prescient insight Francis saw Massasoit Ousamequin not as a true worshiper of nature spirits and graven idols, but as a comparable worldly cynic who believed in nothing he could not see, hear, smell, taste or touch. Such men ever refused to credit that other men might be motivated by anything beyond their own material self-interest, such as a genuine belief in supernatural religion. It was the same skepticism that left so many learned and prideful men, wise in the knowledge of the world, with the greatest fund of book learning, completely helpless and devoid of wisdom when it came to understanding the most powerful movements in human history. With the obstinacy of Pharaoh these often denied the miraculous even when God sent it knocking at their doors, and Francis wondered if the old chieftain would react according to type, denying the evidence of his own eyes if and when the decisive supernatural event came into view.

"You have saved my life," Massasoit went on, "and it may be I shall be able to do you a like service and save the lives of all your people."

He paused to give Winslow, whose throat had obviously gone dry, the time to translate this startling assertion. Massasoit fixed Francis with a hard stare before proceeding.

"I have something to tell you which is of the greatest importance. You must listen closely and carry my words back to your chief Bradford."

"Very well," Francis said, nodding agreement after translation. The chief had apparently marked him out as the older and more sober man, the warrior, whose word might be taken more seriously by his tribal leadership than that of the tenderhearted Winslow.

"There are two braves of the Massachusett tribe, who dwell to the north. Their names are Wituwamat and Pecksuot."

"Wituwamat and Pecksuot," Francis repeated.

"These braves are full of hatred toward all white men. They go from village to village, not only among the Massachusett but also among my people and others. They say all the tribes must go to war against the whites. They say we must kill all of you. They say we must make this war before it is too late. Otherwise, the land will fill up with the whites, and the People will be driven away or destroyed."

"But, Great Ousamequin," Winslow said, "Can you not prevent this war? Your people and ours have always been friends."

"I am not a king as you English have a king," Massasoit replied, displaying remarkable political sophistication for an illiterate heathen. "Nor a *gov-ven-nor*."—he astonished them further by assaying Bradford's official title in English—"When it comes to the warpath, I have great influence, greater influence than younger and more impetuous braves might wish. But I have not power to make a law the People will obey forever. Each village is free to make its own choices under its own chief and its own council."

"I believe you have more power than you credit," Winslow said.

Bristling slightly, the chief kept his grim solemnity fixed upon Francis. "I have called for peace, and the villages of my people may well listen to me – for now. Had I perished, I know not what would have taken place. You two might have been only the first to die."

"God grant you live to keep the peace," Francis said.

Another dismissive wave. "I shall do my best as long as I can. But I have no influence over the Massachusett, none at all." He paused to let this sink in. "And should they fall upon you, without doubt some among our villages will join them. Perhaps most, if the Massachusett win a great victory with their first attack."

Francis remembered the listless drunkards and unfinished stockade up at Wessagusset. A successful massacre there could set the whole country ablaze against Plymouth. The sooner the pathetic traders were packed off to England aboard the *Anne*, the better one and all could sleep. But he also knew their departure would not end the danger, not according to what he was hearing now.

"Chief Ousamequin," Francis said, "you know our Governor Bradford has the greatest respect for your wisdom. In this matter of Wituwamat and Pecksuot, what would you advise us to do?"

During and after translation the old chief kept looking steadily at Francis. "There is only one thing you can do. You must seek out Wituwamat and Pecksuot. Arrange a meeting as soon as you can."

Heart sinking, Francis knew what was coming next.

"Yes!" Winslow burst out naïvely. "We seek them out, we extend the hand of friendship. But what can we say to them that will put this matter to rest?"

"You say nothing, for it serves no purpose. You lure them to the meeting, and then you must kill them."

CHAPTER 32

Council of War

The deliverance of Massasoit at death's door instantly transformed the mood of the Wampanoag from deepest grief to an ecstasy of joy. Yet the next morning, as the good news continued to spread through forest and village, Francis and Winslow walked back to Plymouth under a greater cloud of woe than when they set out the previous day. Hobomok did not share their disquiet in the least. In fact his customarily stony visage took on a downright cheerful aspect. He had received Massasoit's ferocious counsel with the same equanimity in which it had been given and would doubtless have been quite astonished to learn of the inner travail churning the hearts of the two Englishmen.

Francis could only imagine what his scholarly companion must be feeling. Given his love for the Indians, Winslow doubtless carried a far greater burden than himself. Both knew Massasoit's advice had not been lightly tossed off, but rather set before them with every degree of seriousness demanded by very real dangers rapidly impending.

When the great chief uttered his implacable words he had seen the sharp look that passed between the two white men.

"Yes, my friends," the old man had insisted, using the most profound word for friendship available in his native tongue, as Winslow pointed out later. "You must kill them. Sometimes men with thick skulls cannot be persuaded, and you can only bash them in before they smash your own. These two I named are such men. You *must* kill them. You have no other choice."

A long restless night and half a morning later, this grim admonition still echoed through Francis's memory with terrible reverberation. He saw nothing but sinister possibilities and unpredictable consequences on every hand, no matter what they decided to do.

When they finally came in sight of Plymouth, Francis broke their long silence. "We must show ourselves lively, Edward."

"I know it."

In other words, they could not let on by a sad demeanor that there existed any sort of problem. Their only public sentiment must be relief and rejoicing for a job well done. The dire forewarnings of Massasoit must remain for now a matter of secret deliberation by those only who needed to know. If word went out to the community at large, it had to come from those elected for such responsibility and not by way of two mere emissaries.

Winslow's ability to shuck off his long face and put on a smile proved the superior gift as Francis could only plod alongside, all his worry and confusions continuing to roil. An anxious throng converged upon them for the happy news before they had marched halfway through the cornfields. Loud and widespread joy broke out as the good word passed, though no English group could ever rise to the raptures of the Wampanoag.

Allowing Winslow and Hobomok to do most of the talking, Francis nodded and grinned with the discomfort of a man forcing himself to smile on the outside while trembling within. For a born politician like Philip, this self-division comprised an essential element of his capacity for leadership, the hiding of personal fear to keep up the spirits of others. Francis had to labor mightily to carry out such a ruse. Or at least so he flattered himself.

Perhaps he was a more talented deceiver than he imagined, as his only failure came with Hester. She could still read his moods without difficulty after three years' separation. Rushing up to hug him, she then pulled back and studied his face. A flash of understanding passed between them, and he saw her perceive in an instant that something was wrong. She also understood it was important not to reveal it, so she took his arm after he had hugged his children and walked him to Bradford's house, embracing him again before he and Winslow went into immediate private consultation with governor and council. The couple gazed at each other as the front door closed between them, and Francis gave her a quick nod as if to say, *I'll tell you later*.

He reflected that he might be the only husband in Plymouth whose desire to talk things over with his wife was well nigh as strong as her desire to know what was going on. So much did he prize her wisdom.

* * *

The meeting went longer and grew more disputatious than Francis feared.

"But surely we are not in real danger of a war," Bradford was saying. "Massasoit has always been strong for peace between our two peoples."

By now the weary Winslow had sunk into the dispirited misery of a hireling tutor trying to make headway with a particularly obtuse child. Francis noticed the warlike Standish shaking his head in sympathy for the aggrieved scholar. Though the governor was not exactly a man of the sunniest disposition and outlook, given the anguish of his recent past, Francis knew the problem here was not any inherent density of his reasoning powers but Bradford's strong personal inclination to transcend the doctrine of total depravity by somehow believing the best of all men. Very rarely did the governor's optimism get the better of him, but this might be forming up as one of those occasions.

"But Massasoit is in a sharp predicament here, Governor," Winslow explained with exquisite patience. "The troublemakers are not his fellow clansmen. Massasoit has influence over his Wampanoag tribe alone, and what he wields is precisely that— influence, not command. If the Massachusett should decide to attack, Massasoit seems to doubt whether he can hold all the Wampanoag villages in line, if indeed it comes to war. As for the Massachusett themselves, the great chief's words have no importance at all."

"But it's madness!" Bradford shouted. "It brings to mind the warring tribes of Scotland!"

"Oh, it's worse than that," Standish put in quietly.

The governor stared at Winslow as if desperately hoping for a contrary response. "And the chief feels that our only choice...?"

"Kill the troublemakers," Winslow said without joy.

"And these men would not be open to suasion of any sort?" Bradford turned toward Francis.

"I could not understand the man's words without translation," Francis replied, "but his tone of voice was unmistakable. Kill the men who are stirring up the strife. I regret to say it, but that is his advice. His only advice."

"And good advice it is," Standish said. "Spoken by a red man or not."

"Good advice you say!" Bradford said. "I cannot think but that there must be some more honorable course. Some method of communicating through kindness and negotiation."

"Kindness and negotiation?" Standish spat out. "My dear sir, you know so little of hate. Where hatred burns strong, kindness and negotiation will only be perceived as weakness, and thus fan the flames to a greater conflagration when the fatal hour comes round at last. The only persuasion these savages will grasp is the shedding of blood. And if we do not act to spill theirs first, it will be our own that pours out upon the ground, our blood and that of our children. We have the great chief's own word for this."

"The chief's own word, you say?" Bradford said. "What about the Word of God? How could we countenance such a murder?"

"The Word of God is very fine for a Sunday morning, Governor! But here we face a matter of life and death!"

Standish might roar, but Bradford was prepared to roar back. "The Word of God is for all days, sir! And its issues are the very essence of life and death!"

Standish strained forward, his face red, but Winslow sat close enough to lay an admonishing hand on his arm. The captain looked down at this foreign object, as if to sweep it aside like a beetle, but the very pause enabled him to bring himself under control. He spoke more calmly, looking each of the elected representatives in the eye.

"My dear sirs... it has never been my practice to argue the fine points of theology, and I do not propose to begin now. But could it not be that this sudden warning comes as it does – and at the time it does – *now*, when we can draw the sword against the danger, by the Providence of God?" Standish brought his burning gaze back to their leader. "Aye, sir! By the very hand of Divine Guidance! I do not speak of murder, Governor Bradford. I speak of a military act. To strike before the killing blow can be struck against us and against our women and children. As I read my Bible, the children of Israel knew how to heed a timely warning, sir."

"Please, Captain, the appeal to scripture is not necessary to validate every point."

"I seem to remember that somewhere... Augustine... of Hippo... argues the right of Christian men to fight a just war."

Francis thought Standish stumbled slightly because he nearly said *Saint* Augustine. He thought he saw Bradford smile just as slightly in response, a welcome lightening of mood if true. Augustine, for John Calvin and most of his successors, was considered the paradigm of a supposedly more Biblically-based theologian, before the Roman church went down into its medieval bog of corruption and heresy. Francis had heard and read Godly separatist thinkers, however, who claimed Augustine was the very source and poisoned fountain of all the papist distortions to come. In any case, despite these dissenting views, an appeal to Augustine's opinions had been considered legitimate for most Protestants from the time of the former Augustinian monk Martin Luther.

Since the time of Calvin, debates between Protestant and Catholic scholars—all too rare these days, when religious conflict between professing Christians was more likely to culminate in blood, imprisonment and the stake than in gentlemanly and bookish discourse—had all too often degenerated into each side going back and forth with competing quotations from Augustine and other ancient authorities, especially the so-called church fathers from the second century and later. Francis believed many of these, including Augustine, had handled the written Word of God quite loosely, ever prepared to spiritualize, distort or otherwise reject any Biblical passages that contradicted their various philosophies, presuppositions and burgeoning traditions.

Since all believers in Jesus Christ were saints according to the scriptural usage, of course, Francis saw nothing wrong with referring to any Christian by that title. At present, however, far more crucial challenges loomed than fastidious issues of religious nomenclature. As usual Francis did not envy the governor his responsibilities.

The latter's reaction brought Francis out of his theological reverie and back to the present.

Bradford shook his head. "It would be a grave undertaking. I will not sanction it on my own authority nor that of the elders."

"The longer we wait," Standish said, "the greater the danger. And if word should leak out, as surely it will..."

"I will not act on my own, sir!" Bradford shouted. "Nor will the council!"

"You acted so on the matter of private land!"

"That was land! Here we are speaking of human life! This matter must be debated, understood and decided openly! By all our people!"

CHAPTER 33

Doubt and Disquiet

By the time Francis reeled out of the barking dog pit otherwise known as a committee meeting, he imagined he knew how a man must feel after a beating. Not that any anger had been poured out on the two unwilling bearers of the day's evil tidings, at least directly. In truth the chief men's solicitude sharpened the sting of Francis and Winslow's unpleasant duty almost unbearably. They had to go over the same scant information again and again, as if confronting a phalanx of devilish lawyers frantically searching for an escape clause. Only the imminent collapse of the witnesses finally induced Governor Bradford to gavel the proceedings to a close.

It was well after dark when Francis finally staggered the few steps to his own house. He tottered inside to renewed embraces, worried faces and a strong silent handshake from Philip, offering unspoken support amidst predicaments yet unexplained. Hester's quiet solace shown through in concerned looks, a gentle touch and the rapid placement of a warm aromatic bowl before his starving nose. She had managed a delectable rabbit stew—John had once again made good use of his trusty bow and arrow, the second bow since the first one prepared under Squanto's tutelage, with the boy's archery brought to some degree of mastery under Hobomok's. The meal helped put to rest the memory of having to sit watching as Massasoit slurped up all the duck soup for himself.

Naturally John and the other children longed to hear all about their father's latest adventure, but Hester shooed them off to bed, assuaging their disappointment with promises that he would regale them on a more convenient and well-rested tomorrow. The adults lingered over cups of the precious tea, their conversation pointedly limited to the banalities of the Plymouth workday. Questions on the Indians did not arise, however difficult for Hester and Philip to hold them back. After a few witty comments on the chaotic leaves in the bottom of his cup, the Frenchman excused himself and climbed aloft. Whatever Philip's kindly expectations in leaving the couple alone together, Francis was too exhausted for spousal sharing. Hester gave the tea implements a quick wash, and they crawled off to their own sleeping area beneath the slanting roof on the opposite side of the house, that small distance their only provision for marital privacy.

Francis slept as soon as his head fell on the pillow, and given her own fatigue, Hester soon followed. Hours later they awoke at the same moment in the deepest darkness sometime before sunrise. This was their customary private time, sanctified by long familiarity and more than a decade of preserving a curtain of silence around the marriage bed in a tiny house increasingly filled with lively children. The three-year disruption had not impaired their tender and passionate symbiosis in the least. Hester felt certain she was with child again, just as Elizabeth Warren predicted, but as it would take another month or so to know for sure, it served no point to raise her husband's hopes and attendant worries aforetime.

Afterward, Francis lay back on his pillow and told her exactly what was going on. They spoke in hushed whispers, careful not to let their voices rise.

He told Hester the entire story, including a brief account of the debate within the council.

* * *

By some not-so-mysterious process word of the menace made its way into every household during the night. Everyone in Plymouth knew everything, it seemed, in time for the next day's work in the fields. It soon became obvious to Francis and Hester that the council had lingered after his departure and decided to put out the whispered word themselves for the precise purpose of widespread discussion. Yet the women and children insisted on resuming their field labors as before, in spite of dangers known and unknown. The tiniest landowners, the smallest children capable of tottering about and understanding speech, such as might have been spared the appalling truth by the reticence of concerned parents, raised questions when they noticed the increased numbers and steadfast vigilance of Standish's guards on the perimeter, all those hard-eyed men with guns, dry powder and smoking matches, gazing warily into the depths of the forest. The grim men on the parapets likewise surveyed their surroundings with unyielding concentration rather than their customary languor, another conspicuous transformation.

Bradford and the council set a new town meeting for the following day. They would have preferred more time to accommodate private deliberation, but sheer urgency cried out for immediate action—or so it seemed.

Hester for one doubted the immediacy of the peril. As Francis told the tale, the two hostile Massachusett braves had been endeavoring to raise their fellow savages against the whites for quite some time, thus far without success. It was only the ludicrous episode of Massasoit's constipation that brought the news to Plymouth now. Hester feared they were being rushed into precipitate action. She believed Christians tended to make their greatest mistakes when they felt hurried, when they did not take the time required to gather the facts about a matter and seek God's will. She had made such mistakes herself.

Now obviously life often threw up quandaries that had to be decided quickly. Meeting such challenges was one of the purposes of developing Godly wisdom. In the present hour Hester stood firm on the ground of God's sovereignty, on the power of the Almighty to arrange circumstances to produce a sufficiently timely warning. She simply did not believe the threat comprised the kind of desperate emergency that called for making a decision as hastily as everyone demanded, especially to set in motion so fatal and irrevocable a course.

The people of Plymouth worked through the day in a state of distraction, often breaking off in pairs or small groups to worry and belabor the crisis that filled every mind with apprehension. Hester held a quick parley with Priscilla and found the younger woman in complete accord. They agreed to meet before supper for prayer, as prelude for pointed discussion with their husbands. They hoped Francis and John would feel led to speak up in tomorrow's meeting.

The plan to wait, however, soon took flight in the face of opportunity.

Shortly after breaking off with Priscilla, Hester noticed Francis walking off into the trees by himself. After making sure of her children at their tasks, Hester followed, hurrying between the long rows of sprouting corn and plunging into the forest at the same place.

An odd sound, a faint ringing and rasping of metal, led her to him. A hundred paces into the trees, she found him sitting with his back toward Plymouth on an old log beneath a large spreading oak. He was sufficiently experienced a woodsman now to hear and recognize her approach, but he kept up the methodical stroke producing the metallic noise. In one hand he held a huge pointed knife, not his hunting knife but an implement she had never seen before, and he was using a whetting stone to sharpen the edge.

Glancing over his shoulder at her, he turned back to uneasy perusal of the forest and its shadows.

"Hester, you should not be this far from the stockade. The Indians..."

"If I am in danger, then so are you." She took a seat beside him.

"Let us go back then." His hands ceased from their well-practiced business.

"Nay, Francis, let us sit a moment, please."

Enveloped by the soft resonance of the forest, they sat staring into its loveliness. She saw old trees and young leaves and bright splashes of springtime light, but when she glanced at his hard alert face and restless eyes, she knew he saw a world of threat and mortal danger that lay beyond her capacity to perceive amidst so much beauty. This wilderness life had deepened him, had transformed him from a soft man of Europe into a hardened survivor, imbued with a touch of this untamed land's violent ferocity. The sudden insight both thrilled and frightened her, this newness in the man she thought she knew as she had known no other. She realized she could not presume his routine agreement with her on the matter of the proposed attack on the hostiles. Her uncertainty involved this change within Francis, based on all he had been through, not merely the combative influence of the warlike Standish or bloodthirsty Massasoit.

As if to underline the point, his hands went back to work with the whetstone. The blade flashed and gleamed in the dappled light as he sharpened its point and edges.

"This is a fine old log, isn't it?" he said. "A nice place to sit."

"Yes."

"I wonder what made it fall. No savage chopped it down, you can see the roots there. Something made it topple."

"Perhaps lightning."

"No evidence of burning. Perhaps it just got old and tired, or got hollowed out by termites, though it seems solid though."

The thick moss on the ancient trunk made their seat more comfortable.

"What kind of knife is that?" she said.

"It's a dagger. A present from the captain for doing him a service once."

"I might have known."

"Both edges have to be sharp on one of these, along with the point. I find I like sharpening steel. The motions are the nearest thing to wool combing I've done these three years." He spoke ironically, but with a voice tinged by mild regret for his lost profession. Those days before the *Mayflower* were simpler for him, she knew, without the necessity for life-and-death decisions, but also without much in the way of excitement.

"It is for killing, the dagger?"

"It is for defending one's life. And the lives of those one loves."

"I did not know you had it with you, in the fields."

He lifted his shirt briefly to reveal a leather scabbard strapped over his shoulder to hang under his arm, a buckskin contraption of Indian workmanship, though the weapon had come with Standish across the ocean. "I keep it about my person when the times call for it, though secretly, not to spread alarm."

That he would be armed without her knowledge nearly brought a sob to her lips, but she choked it down, knowing the secret owed more to her lack of observation than a husband's deception, for his explanation made perfect sense, given the number of women and children in the fields who were distressed enough by the sight of all the men with guns.

"How do you think the vote will go?" she said. "No one has talked of anything else all day."

He shrugged. "Who can say?"

"But what do you think? Shall we take up arms against the Indians?"

"On the advice of Chief Massasoit." The whetstone slid against the blade, over and over. "But only against a pair of troublemakers."

"And we shall kill them?"

"These two men... they are trying to raise the rest of the savages against us. If enough villages rise, they are numerous enough to kill us all."

"But is this the proper manner for the people of God to meet such a challenge?"

His hands paused. "I don't know."

"Surely we have come to this wilderness to bring light to the darkness. Surely we must first try to reach out to these men in the love of Christ."

"Our course has not been decided yet. It will be debated openly and then voted upon."

"But I shall not be able to cast a vote, nor say a single word. Nor will Priscilla. Nor will any of the other women."

"I know." He took the stone in the same hand as the dagger and put his free arm around her.

"Please, Francis. Someone must speak up for the souls of these Indians, however misguided and murderous they speak. Perhaps it is only, how you say, Big Talk. Someone must point out we need to act as Christians."

He bent down and held her, speaking softly into her ear, which trembled as much as the rest of her was trembling.

"This I well know, Hester. Believe me, I know."

CHAPTER 34

The Consent of the Governed

Beginning with the solemn and lengthy opening prayer by Elder Brewster, the tension and gloom of the town meeting made a bleak contrast with the preceding glorious occasion. All children had been kept out except for a privileged and mature few, mostly from the Mayflower, including John. Many of the women had leapt at the chance to mind the banished youngsters, but John could look across the aisle and see his mother perched next to her friend Priscilla. He had no success catching her eye, so intently did she follow every word.

With a sigh he brought his own attention back to the so-called "debate," one-sided as it was. Speaker after speaker cast up great towers of rhetoric upon a foundation of ostensible and so far unbroken consensus, much to the satisfaction of Captain Standish. John assumed that whatever the captain wanted to do was probably the right action, but he could not remain untroubled by his mother's reservations and haunted look. From a nearby pew the unhappy Edward Winslow easily read which way the wind blew, and he maintained a morose silence.

Governor Bradford presided without the slightest indication of his own opinion. Now he recognized John Alden.

"Brethren... and sisters," Alden said, in the day's first acknowledgement of the ladies' scanty presence, "I am as troubled as any of you by the dangers we face. But I am most troubled that we might be guilty of a hasty decision. This matter cries out to be taken before the Lord more comprehensively than we have had time to do. All the people of this plantation should bow the knee before our Father and seek his will."

"We have already prayed!" an impatient male voice shouted.

"We have prayed, brother, but we have not prayed our way through to the peace that passeth understanding. I believe that if we shall have exercised our faith in a proper manner, the Lord Himself will teach us what choice we should make, and it may be some wondrous course we have not thought of, a solution that does not involve the shedding of blood. We are God's people, and our steps should be in accord with God's nature, His love and His holiness. We should exercise the greatest possible care before we act in a worldly and ungodly manner ourselves."

Disapproving murmurs made evident the deep unpopularity of these expressions. The tide of grumbling swept poor Alden from his feet with a reddening face, but when John Cooke glanced over at Priscilla he saw pride shining from her eyes and from his mother's too.

Miles Standish bounded off his bench in the front. "My friends, John Alden speaks to the higher truths of theology, and he does so effectively. Perhaps he should consider a call to the ministry. But our situation is urgent and our danger immediate. We have neither time nor leisure to engage in a lengthy, mystical investigation of every alternative."

"God can give us more time if we ask Him!" Alden piped up from his pew, impressing John with his strength of mind in the face of such blatant disrespect for his sentiments.

"God can do anything He chooses," Standish said, "but sometimes He gives *us* the responsibility to choose—and to act. When

I was engaged to join this expedition, to help you plant an English and Christian foothold in this wilderness, the duty given to me was for the military security of the colony. As your duly appointed military commander, I urge that we give heed to the warnings of Massasoit, and to his advice as well. His plan is a wise one. The danger we face can be averted if we act to cut off the demagogues before they succeed in their devices. But we must act quickly!"

The captain sat down. Sobering thoughts furrowed every brow. The ensuing silence grew protracted. Any further misgivings remained unspoken. John sensed an air of unanswerable finality creeping over the room. Yet Bradford waited patiently to see who else would rise to speak, if anyone.

John was astonished when his own father stood up. Every waiting face turned in his direction. Francis had a reputation as a silent man, a listener and a thinker. If he chose to speak in public, it was an occasion of the greatest personal significance.

"I agree with John Alden," Francis said. Audible gasps arose on every side. He waited before proceeding. His son thought he paused out of bashful hesitation, but the effect was as dramatic as the greatest orator's.

When Francis went on his voice rang out firm and steady. "In circumstances as serious as these, human logic is not the most reliable guide for our conduct. Oft times the Lord's will flies in the face of human logic, we have all seen that. Indeed, it is in the very nature of the Gospel, the eternal Son of God dying for the sake of sinful man, a concept so contrary to reason it takes divine intervention to open our sin-blinded eyes to see the truth of it. As the heavens are higher than the earth, so are His ways higher than our ways, and His thoughts above our thoughts. As our brother says, we need to continue in prayer, and we need to wait for clear guidance. We must assure ourselves that the steps we take are taken only in faith that fully relies upon God, not in desperation or self-will. Let us remember Paul's word to the Romans, 'whatsoever is not of faith is sin.'"

Francis sat down to the deepest silence yet. John thrilled at the deference with which the words had been received, in contrast to the blatant disrespect young Alden provoked. He felt proud though he had no idea whether his father or the captain had the truth on his side. Across the aisle he could almost feel the warmth of Hester's gratitude to her husband for taking a stand for caution in what might well prove a losing battle.

Standish spoke out once more. "I would direct a question to Mister Cooke."

As the governor did not intervene, Francis stood up again. "Yes, Captain?"

"All our people know you are one of our best-trained militiamen, Mister Cooke, and an expert shot. My question, sir, is this. Would your opinion on this matter cause you to refuse duty if we vote an action with which you disagree?"

Francis thought for a long moment before answering. "I urge upon this body that we should wait. But in the case as you put it, I would have no choice but to do my duty."

"Thank you, sir. I would have expected no less," Standish said, remaining on his feet as Francis sat down. "Gentlemen and ladies, I know the hearts of these two who have spoken out for caution, as well as one who has kept his reservations to himself." He bowed his head in Edward's direction.

"Mister Winslow, Mister Cooke, and Mister Alden are three of the finest men in Plymouth, men with good and valiant hearts. But speaking as your military advisor, I believe they are wrong. This colony faces a great danger, growing more deadly by the hour, and it is imperative that we take preemptive action before the two hostiles can gather forces to strike a murderous blow against us, or against the reprobates up at Wessagusset, for that could only lead to our own slaughter. Every argument on every side has now been brought to the floor. You have heard most of the councilmen and elders recommend Massasoit's plan, and I urge you most sincerely that this is what we should do." He sat down.

Bradford looked around carefully, but no one else chose to speak. "Very well. All sides have been heard. I see no reason not to proceed to a vote. All who favor the recommended course of action, signify by raising a hand."

Hands did not shoot up all at once, as John had seen in other meetings on more trivial matters. The votes came slowly and deliberately, one man at a time. John strained his neck looking all around. Philip Delano raised his hand. In the end the only men he could see not voting aye were Winslow, Alden, Elder Brewster and John's father.

The majority was so clearly overwhelming that Bradford spared the dissenters from having to raise their hands. Nor did he lift his own.

"Very well," he said. "The motion is carried."

Across the aisle John saw his mother put her face in her hands.

CHAPTER 35

Ruffled Feathers and the Smoothing Thereof

The meeting broke up quickly for so momentous an occasion. Few lingered outside to chat in the bright sunlight. Most households regrouped at once and made for the fields.

Francis and Hester consoled each other with a long silent embrace, then he let her go retrieve the younger children. He stalked into the cornfields in a kind of mental fog, John tramping along at his side. Francis set his face as flint against all disapproval. None of those voting for the plan spoke to him except the irrepressible Philip. It was as if Francis and John Alden and Edward Winslow—no one could summon up any hard feelings against William Brewster—had stolen away something precious merely by urging delay for additional prayer and deliberation. So be it. If unanimity came at the price of good conscience, so be it. He met silence with a deeper silence of his own.

Though despair of making the slightest bit of difference had sealed Edward Winslow's lips in the meeting, his sentiments were by then all too well known, as Captain Standish had acknowledged. Since word of the aggressive plot seeped out, Winslow had spent the intervening day and night quietly but frankly averring to all questioners that Massasoit's scheme was a bad idea, though coming from a man he admired. Given Winslow's well-known affection for the savages, the voting majority tended to disparage the value of his skepticism.

As for Alden, he could be easily dismissed for youth and its attendant enthusiasm, no doubt fed by his beloved Priscilla. The prevailing gossip singled out the younger wives in Plymouth as the one group most opposed to a resolution by armed might—an excellent demonstration, as if any were needed, why women should never be entrusted with the vote.

Francis was a different story, an older and well-respected personage known by all as a man who thought for himself.

* * *

The entire Cooke family kept to themselves throughout the course of the day. In late afternoon a well-armed Philip took the children off for a lark, attempting to stamp a few eels out of the mud down at the shoreline. At sunset Francis and Hester walked home arm in arm, entered their empty house, and closed the door behind them.

It was relatively cool in the dark interior and silent. Francis threw himself down at the dining table. Hester built up a small cooking fire and put on the kettle to make tea. She set two cups before them and sat to his right, holding his hand as they waited for the water to boil.

"Thank you for trying, my darling," she said softly. "I was very proud of you."

He knew what she meant but could only shake his head, ashamed of his failure to be more persuasive.

Much later, after the children and Philip had returned, been fed delicious cooked eel and crawled off to bed, Hester and Francis were sitting at their table for another cup of tea when the knock came at the door.

"That will be the captain and the governor," Francis said. "Had to wait for cover of darkness, like Nicodemus coming by night."

Hester had to stifle a giggle in spite of herself. "I'll put on more water."

Francis opened the door to prove himself prophetic.

"Brother Cooke," Bradford said, "I wonder if we might have a word."

Francis glanced back at Hester where she bent over the fire.

"Alone, if you please," Standish added, earning a stern glance from the governor.

"We may speak out back," Francis said.

He closed the front door on his wife and led them around the house to the vegetable garden.

"Looks to grow into an extraordinary garden, Francis," Bradford said. "You should be proud of your womenfolk."

"I am that, sir, thank you."

Standish dipped his head in the direction of the house, where Hester could be heard pottering about. "Any trouble with Mrs. Cooke?"

"She is not the portrait of happiness just now, but no trouble."

"Women! They can be wonderful, but we cannot let their frailty constrain us from making our own determinations."

Francis barely constrained the fire that flared in his bosom. "Captain Standish, I am happy to obey you in all matters military, but I shall thank you to leave my domestic arrangements alone."

It was too dim to see the captain flushing red as a beet. Francis fancied he could feel the heat radiating from his trembling and furious silhouette, but he no longer cared.

Bradford stepped in before Standish could make things worse. "The captain intended no offense, I am sure. Our ladies seem to believe Mrs. Cooke strongly opposes the course of action proposed... which has now been voted to carry out."

"I have already given answer as to my willingness to do my duty," Francis said coldly.

"You gave a manly answer," Standish said, not only mastering his temper but attempting to smooth things over, "to which I raise not the slightest doubt."

Francis turned to Bradford. "As everyone apparently seems to know, my good wife raises the same objection I thought you and I agreed upon. How does taking this action comport with Godliness? With the Indians, how does this course not set back the work of the Gospel, possibly for years? And let us say we carry out these murders with the most brilliant success. Would we not plant a seed for future wars and conflict?"

"No Christian could take this course without agonizing over all the dilemmas."

"I beg to differ, Governor. Methinks some if not most have voted this rash action without agonizing in the least. In pleading for more time to pray, I should very much crave to see a bit of agonizing done, a great deal more in fact than has been, if I judge correctly."

"I think you underestimate our people, Francis."

"I hope I do, sir."

"Beg pardon, gentlemen!" a tinny youthful voice interrupted. Startled, they turned their eyes and squinted, barely making out the wide expanse of young Edward Leister lumbering toward them from the street. He came with all the satisfaction of a diligent seeker finding his quarry at last.

"Yes, Master Leister," Bradford said with chilly decorum, "you have a message?"

"Not exactly," Leister admitted sheepishly, "or only one from meself."

"And that would be…?"

"Well, governor, sir... Captain Standish, Mister Cooke..." Leister twisted his hands in the faint starlight.

"We're occupied here, so if you'd be so kind as either to spit it out or come back later."

"It's only I wanted to ask the captain." Leister turned and blurted out to Standish. "Please, sir, may I be allowed to go along on the mission? I've been training very well, and I have a strong arm, and I be young and unmarried if you please, sir. Proper fodder for soldiering as is said."

Francis winced at the pathetic boy's ridiculous martial enthusiasm and would have wagered the governor's reaction was something very like his own.

Still failing to grasp he had interrupted crucial proceedings, Leister forged on. "Please, sirs, this may be the closest I can come to going off to war, as the good captain did at my age."

Francis could take no more. "Son, this crisis is not a proper time for boyish enthusiasm..."

The resolute object of the callow youth's high regard made amends for whatever humiliation Leister felt at this objection with boyish gusto of his own. "Indeed I did go soldiering at an age not much older than yourself. It is a manly vocation for any young man." The captain turned to the others. "Young Mister Leister does have a strong arm and courage, as he proved in his duel with Mister Doty."

Typical Standish, Francis seethed within—breezily unapologetic for what remained a sore point for many in Plymouth, especially on the distaff side of the aisle.

"I drew first blood, gentlemen," Leister boasted. "Right quick too!"

That wasn't how Francis heard it from John. The warlike and experienced Massachusett braves would prove far more dangerous adversaries than poor little Edward Doty, and he hoped Standish had the good sense to fob the boy's offer aside.

"The captain is free to pick his own party," Bradford said. No hope coming from that quarter.

"Than I can come?" Leister pleaded.

"Of course you may, my boy." Standish clapped Leister on the shoulder. "I intended to ask you all along."

"Oh, thank you, Captain! Thank you, Gov! I'll go begin me preparations at once! Oh, and sorry for the interruption!" He hurried back to the street and down the hill.

"Well, now that's settled, I gather you won't be needing me along," Francis said.

"I need you, Mister Cooke."

Francis sighed, finally admitting to himself that the runaway horse of military action could no longer be reined in. "The lad raises another issue of importance to my family. Why am I perpetually the only married man sent off on these hair-raising adventures?"

"There'll be two of us, Francis," Standish said. "I am a married man now too."

"So you are, Miles." Francis heaved another sigh. "So you are."

CHAPTER 36

Invitation to a Killing

They slipped quietly from one dappled shadow to the next, following the fresh tracks of the stag. Then Wituwamat abruptly stopped and held up a warning hand. Two-dozen paces behind him Pecksuot obeyed the signal instantly, slipping behind a tree to remain hidden.

Pecksuot moved his eyes carefully over their surroundings but saw nothing out of the ordinary. He looked back in the direction of his friend, who had lowered the hand but otherwise stood in place, motionless as a suddenly alerted doe in that frozen instant before bursting into flight. Pecksuot, normally the bravest of men, scarcely breathed, striving mightily to suppress an unexplainable sense of dread that slowly enfolded him in its grasp. Perhaps one of the nearby trees housed or sheltered a powerful spirit.

Whispering wind tugged at the overhang of green leaves. Their rustling hiss made his unmoving stillness seem more protracted. Pecksuot fell into the odd stupor of a man caught in a daydream. Memories of long-ago events poured through his mind with the quickness of birds frightened out of hiding into flight. On the wings of this waking vision he seemed to pass through his own life with the fleetness of a running deer. The countless flowing days and moons carried him from childhood's carefree playing before his father's lodge to the here and now of the warrior's walk. As the vision passed it struck him how death lurked close at every turn. It struck him how much for granted he had taken the gift of life, this journey through his allotted and irrecoverable span of years.

If he knew without doubt that some powerful spirit were indeed reaching out to warn him through these feelings, he would tuck tail and run like a coward. He would run away to some far place and never return.

But then he thought, *What shameful weakness, giving way to such foolishness!* Especially in the presence of such a stalwart friend and lifelong guide as Wituwamat, a man never given to doubt about anything. Pecksuot forced himself to cast off his strange passing notions.

Suddenly a dark manlike figure stepped into a wide shaft of light some distance in front of Wituwamat. It raised a hand in formal greeting rather than friendship. This happened so quickly that Pecksuot almost jumped in womanish fright behind his tree, but then he recognized the dark figure as the treacherous Wampanoag brave Hobomok, well known by sight and deeply hated by each Massachusett.

As soon as he recognized the man, Pecksuot plunged out of hiding and strode forward to join his companion, earning a quick glance of disapproval from Wituwamat. But why? Pecksuot felt confused. Meeting the Wampanoag here might be their chance to be rid of him, perhaps plant his dead body in a bog to fertilize cranberries. Then he realized Wituwamat had probably wanted him to remain concealed for just that purpose, for the tactical advantage of a hidden partner. Well, too late now. He liked Hobomok knowing he faced them both. Increasing the man's level of fear would help rob him of his fighting skills, which Pecksuot had no doubt were negligible at best. How could any warrior stay sharp while spending so much time among the bungling whites?

"Greetings, warriors of the Massachusett," Hobomok said, speaking first as was his place, being the one who initiated the contact. The man exuded nothing but confidence, Pecksuot had to grant him that. They would soon put this self-assurance to the test.

"Why does the running dog of the white men stand in our path?" Wituwamat said.

"I have sought you out, but not as emissary of the English," Hobomok mildly replied. "The words I bring come from Massasoit Ousamequin, great chief of all the Wampanoag."

"How do we know the 'great chief' would speak through such a woman?"

Pecksuot reeled with surprise at the level of Wituwamat's scorn, beyond all bounds of common politeness, demanding the satisfaction of honorable combat. If positions were reversed, the two Massachusetts would already be attacking knife in hand.

Hobomok's stony face betrayed not the slightest disturbance. "You will know because the Massasoit has sent his warriors to keep me company."

The rustling noise scarcely surpassed that of the wind and the leaves, but all around them figures arose out of the shadows, arrows notched to their bows.

Pecksuot realized he and Wituwamat were the ones who had walked into a trap. They had been too intent on tracking the stag, and he knew his friend was probably kicking himself inwardly, though outwardly he remained as calm as the wily Hobomok. Pecksuot fingered his own knife, planning to take some of the attackers with him if it came to that.

"What would the Wampanoag say to the Massachusett then?" Wituwamat asked.

"Not to all the Massachusett, but only the two of you. The Massasoit declares the English know what you are doing, how you go from village to village, striving to plant the seeds of war."

"Perhaps the English know because the Massasoit has told them."

"Ousamequin declares the English want to meet with you. They will send the Red Hair to deliberate whether there can be an agreement to make peace."

"The Red Hair is nothing but a little man who talks very loud. Why should we meet with him?"

"Are you afraid to meet him?"

Wituwamat visibly bristled. He thus failed, Pecksuot realized with a sinking heart, to maintain the self-mastery Hobomok had shown in the face of far more insulting provocations. Could it be that the older Wampanoag was the better man after all? He would need to ponder this later.

"I am not afraid of the Red Hair!" his friend shouted. "Nor of all the English! But I will not go to their village!"

"The Massasoit has told the Red Hair to meet with you at Wessagusset in three days time, when the sun reaches the middle of the sky."

"I do not like this," Pecksuot said. Wituwamat gave no sign of hearing.

"How can the People listen to a call for war," Hobomok said reasonably, "if you are not willing to parley with your enemies when they wish to? For myself I believe you are afraid. I believe you are the women here."

Pecksuot lifted a cautionary hand to his friend's arm, but Wituwamat was already shouting.

"Very well! We meet with the English as you say, but if we cannot make peace with these Bone Men, will the Massasoit call for war?"

"Ousamequin will consider what to do after you have met with the English."

Without another word Hobomok and the other Wampanoag braves faded back into the forest. Wituwamat was breathing as hard as if he had been in combat. As both men knew, now Wituwamat had given his word, it could not be taken back. They must parley with the Bone Men in three days time. Pecksuot thought perhaps they had just been through a sort of battle, and he very much feared Wituwamat had lost.

CHAPTER 37

Preparations

Francis and Philip watched the tattered men of Wessagusset gather up their possessions to make the long walk down to Plymouth. Some of the wretched traders cast resentful looks in their direction but made no argument, for Captain Standish had once again insisted his men keep the matches lit on their muskets, purportedly for protection against Indian attack. Even habitual drunkards and good-for-nothings knew how much damage a huge musket ball fired at close range could inflict. All inhabitants were being impelled to leave Wessagusset but given the option to join themselves to Plymouth if they wished to remain in the new land. Surprisingly, more than a third made this choice despite the stern requirement to lead sober lives and maintain regular church attendance.

The *Anne* waited at Plymouth, ready to make sail for England as soon as its scruffy passengers arrived. The ship's master, homesick for civilization, had only remained this long because of Bradford's assurances the departing traders would arrive bearing pelts or other goods to pay for their passage. Francis felt relieved to witness the truth of this. Every trading man, including the most pale, starved-looking and ill, came dragging a rolled burden of animal skins ready to be hefted on his back. Francis knew these riches had survived only because the local Indians placed a higher value on foodstuff. The canny savages probably calculated they would be able to appropriate the skins anyway once the white men perished from hunger.

An impressive new and recently trained company from Plymouth stood off to one side, comprised of single youths plus a few married men, primed to bodyguard the Wessagusset wastrels on their way through the forest. The traders muttered in dread of this long march, resentful that the English ship had not been brought up the coast for their boarding convenience or that they were not at least being carried south aboard the shallop, now fully repaired under the supervision of John Alden. The two groups from Plymouth, both the escort company and the ambush party, had each been far too large for transportation in the little boat, so it had been left at home. No one felt particularly inclined to press this obvious explanation on the complainers, especially since most of the traders had shown so little gratitude for the gifts of food from the colony's sparse stores that had kept them alive since Plymouth had been forced to take a hand in their fate.

Standish clumped up to Francis and Philip. "No sign of Weston," he fumed. "Not a man jack among them has a clue where he is."

"Don't worry, Captain, I am sure he will turn up," Philip said.

"Yes, I am quite sure he will! And we in Plymouth shall have to take care of him, no doubt."

Knowing how thoroughly Standish detested the man, Francis and Philip grinned as the captain stomped off.

Since his arrival the year after the Mayflower, Thomas Weston had been a constant thorn in the side of all the righteous at Plymouth. A master of sharp practice himself, he naturally turned a blind eye to thievery, false dealing, and immoral behavior on the part of his men. He traded beer and spirits to the savages without a qualm, cheated them whenever possible, and nearly always told lies, especially when deflecting blame for his own faults onto others. Fortunately most local Indians had come to see the two groups of white men had little in common, this because the Plymouth folk had resolved to maintain fairness and honesty in all their dealings with the native people—at least until today.

"Glad to be headin' back to England meself!" a huge man shouted at his bemused observers. Francis recognized him as the big fellow Standish had punched in the nose during their last visitation. "Happy to leave this infernal wilderness to the savages and you Bible bashers! We'll see what ye can make of it other than your own graves! We shall see!"

"Come on, come on," another trader urged, anxious not to attract attention from the volatile captain.

A glance from Standish served to quiet the big man, and he lined up with his companions in misery.

"Our lads will have to help them with those bundles before they reach Plymouth," Francis said.

"Too bad then," Philip said. "I should say, carry them yourselves or leave them behind."

"That would not exactly comport with, 'as ye would that men should do to you, so do ye to them likewise,' my brother. Our friends will help them, have no doubt."

Philip sighed. "All the more reason to be glad we stay here."

"I had rather carry a thousand burdens."

"I know."

The traders fell into place, ready to move out.

"Going back to England," one dissipated cove muttered to anyone who would listen. "It's the right thing to do, I guess. Seeing the old home country, it'll put a spark in me like I've not had in many a day." No one seemed to care so he shut up.

Standish walked to the front of the column and loudly professed his admiration for the military precision of the Plymouth men at its head, rear and sides. He signaled the point men, and the leading group set out, the traders slogging in their wake until the last of the new militia brought up the rear. John Sanders, Weston's underling who commanded in the great man's absence, came up for a final word.

"That's all of us, Captain, everyone accounted for but one. Weston's still out among the savages provided he's not dead. As far as I'm concerned ye can do anything with Wessagusset that ye like. Put it to the torch, for all I care." He bent over to heft his bundle.

"Put your dainties down, Mister Sanders. You're not going anywhere for now."

Sanders stared at Standish as if he had gone mad. "But...but, what do you mean, my dear sir?"

"Our best scholar in the Indian languages is detained at Plymouth." Detained in the sense of hoeing his corn patch at the side of his wife, for Edward Winslow refused to have anything to do with the day's proceedings, and Governor Bradford himself had not been able to change his mind. "We need a man who can speak a bit of the Massachusett tongue."

"Please, Captain! I have no part in this!"

"Don't worry, Sanders, you'll be protected if anything should go awry. But we need you to facilitate our discussions."

"But I'll miss the ship! I can't let the ship sail without me!" The distress in the man's voice was pitiable as he watched his companions disappearing into the forest.

Standish had little compassion to spare. "The ship will wait until we arrive safely back in Plymouth. We have letters to write and put aboard after today's business is done."

These assurances seemed to fall on deaf ears. The remaining witnesses suffered the mortification of watching Sanders begin to weep.

"Please, Captain. I beg you. I want to go back to England. I want to go home."

"For God's sake, Sanders, try to play the man. I know how difficult it must be, but only for a few hours."

* * *

Pecksuot and Wituwamat had not come far from their home village when they perceived they were being followed. They stopped to allow their pursuers, who were making no particular effort to hide themselves, to catch up. Soon two boys appeared on the trail, and Pecksuot recognized them as two of Wituwamat's nephews, Wantusso and Miktanni. They approached with a grin, and though Pecksuot knew they were young, well under twenty harvests, the boys stood almost as tall as their uncle. Despite their friendliness, Wituwamat put on a mask of grimness, so Pecksuot did the same.

"Uncle!" Wantusso said. "Where might you be heading this warm spring morning? A new fishing hole perhaps?"

"You know very well where we go," Wituwamat said sternly. "And why."

The whole village and probably the entire Massachusett tribe knew where they went and why—to parley with the Bone Men—but the boy kept smiling. "You have some distance to travel, wherever you are going."

"We thought you might enjoy some company," the shy Miktanni put in. Pecksuot thought he saw affection in Wituwamat's cold eyes, but only for a moment.

"I thank you for the thought, for I know it is only for our good, but I want you to return to my brother's lodge and wait for us there. We shall bring you word of all that happens."

"Please, uncle," Wantusso said, "let us walk behind you. You are less likely to be attacked along the trail if there are four of us."

Wituwamat glanced at Pecksuot. Both knew the boy had a point.

"You can have no thought of attending this parley. It is for braves alone."

"Then why did the chief not send a larger delegation, with other braves and some of the elders?" Miktanni said.

"Because the English have asked to meet with the two of us, and the chief made clear when I asked him, if it is any of your concern, that for now the matter does not involve the entire village but only us two."

Pecksuot searched Wituwamat's rigid warrior's face in vain for any resentment of that dismissal, which had certainly increased the possible danger to themselves. If Wituwamat chose to drive his nephews away, he would do it for their own protection, because otherwise he would probably appreciate the company as much as Pecksuot, though he would never let on. He avoided weakness in part through shunning any outward sign of weakness. This made him a difficult man to know or understand, though the nephews and many others stood in awe of him for his indisputable hardness and courage.

"Then let us escort you to the meeting place, my uncle," Wantusso said. "Four bows and knives are better than two. Please!"

Wituwamat sighed, by which Pecksuot knew he was going to relent. "Very well, but you must do exactly as I say."

"Yes, uncle!"

"We would think of nothing else."

The boys' joy soon faded. Once they took to the trail, the young men seemed to walk with the same wariness and apprehension that had afflicted Pecksuot for the last three days.

As for Wituwamat, though, he strode boldly on toward Wessagusset, doubtless completely confident his spineless pale-skinned foes remained harmless as ever.

CHAPTER 38

A Time to Kill

The little band reached Wessagusset well before midday, as Wituwamat wished, allowing ample time to observe from hiding. If the English had any other reception planned than one of their endless talk dances, unlikely as that might be for such cowards, he felt sure the whites would not be able to mask their intent. Pecksuot tended to agree with this. The four Massachusetts concealed themselves behind trees and thick foliage to watch.

The most startling thing they saw was how little there was to see. The unfinished stockade and crumbling lodges lay in worse condition than ever, but more remarkably the listless ragged men idling about in the shade, often with their dishonorable female companions from among the People—these were all gone. For days rumor had swept through the forests that Weston's fools planned to use the huge canoe waiting at the larger white man's village to go back across the Great Water whence they came. Now Pecksuot knew this must be true, for the small huts all stood open and empty. The central lodge of the trading post was not large enough to conceal more than a few.

The only two white men in sight stood at the open front gate. Having seen Plymouth, the older braves understood that a gate was supposed to provide entrance through solid walls surrounding a white man's village. Since the walls here had never been completed, except nearly so on the opposite side of the settlement not far from the creek, the gate rose in solitary splendor like some strange totem to hopeless incompetence. Pecksuot wondered if the whites ever bothered to close its massive doors since any enemy could simply walk around. He recognized one of the white guards as Sanders, the stingy and disagreeable man who did the trading whenever Thomas Weston was absent, nearly all the time these days. Unlike Sanders, the missing Weston carried out his lying and cheating with verve. The People preferred him because at least they knew where they stood and also found the scoundrel somewhat amusing. The single aspect in favor of Sanders was that he could sometimes be intimidated in a manner his chieftain could not.

The other white man looked familiar, and Pecksuot realized he had been among the party that the Red Hair had last led to this trading post. He was a youngish man, dressed in bright colorful clothing, and he appeared strong in body. He looked calm and relaxed next to Sanders, smiling and gesturing as he talked, but Pecksuot noticed how he carried his thunderstick in a state of readiness, and how his eyes swept the woods, never bothering with so much as a glance at his companion. Pecksuot could see the little whiff of smoke rising from the burning cord that somehow made the thunderstick do its deadly business. He felt more confident knowing Wituwamat's nephews would be waiting here with bows at the ready. If the boys had to let arrows fly, they would be accurate.

The gaudily clad man kept up his friendly-seeming conversation with Sanders, but the latter appeared more fidgety and irritable than common. Wituwamat signaled for the others to keep watch as he stole off to the right. Pecksuot knew he was going to make a full circuit around the trading post. If men lay in ambush among the trees, whether white or Wampanoag, they would not escape his discovery.

Their friend and uncle's departure nudged the others to a higher level of uneasiness. The late morning crawled as the sun made the slow climb to its apex. After some time Wantusso asked if he should go check on his uncle.

"No," Pecksuot said. "Keep waiting."

The ordinary sounds of the forest held steady, neither rising nor falling. Then with the faintest rustling of brush Wituwamat finally reappeared from the left. He nodded to indicate he had seen nothing amiss.

The sun stood overhead now. The time had come. As Wituwamat and Pecksuot rose, the boys moved up beside them.

"Where have all the white men gone?" Wantusso said.

His uncle made a gesture of contempt. "To flee back across the Great Water. It will be a shouting day when all the whites have done the same—if any still live."

Wantusso indicated the central lodge. "Uncle, we want to come with you."

"No. You boys stay here in hiding, and watch."

"We are not boys, but men!"

Wituwamat looked them over as if with fresh eyes, and Pecksuot could see his pride in the youngsters.

Miktanni spoke up before he could rebuff them again. "Please, uncle, four to go to that lodge will be safer than two. You and Pecksuot are great warriors and hunters who can look out for yourselves. But I entreat you, do us the honor of accepting our help, however unworthy. Please, suffer me to ask this, for we are your family."

This was the longest speech the cryptic Miktanni had ever been known to make, and Pecksuot knew by Wituwamat's proud smile that he would honor the occasion.

"Very well. But keep your wits about you. Stand behind us, and do as we do." He turned and led them out into the warm sunlight.

* * *

Philip Delano had spent most of the morning standing around with the insufferable Sanders not only because he was the most experienced hunter among the Plymouth men, though Francis was rapidly catching up, but primarily because he was the man best able to hide his emotions and play a cool hand, whatever the game. He felt fairly certain he had picked up the Indians nearly the moment they arrived, all four of them. He felt more confident they remained unaware of being under his observation. Sometimes the savages had contempt for whites surpassing the arrogant disdain most Europeans felt toward them. This was fine with Philip, for an overconfident opponent had already half-lost.

He kept up a running conversation with Sanders, trying to keep the fool calm and amused, but it was impossible. The man had all the bravado of a rabbit. Philip kept talking anyway, trying not to observe too obviously when the second biggest but probably most experienced Indian went off to circumnavigate the outpost. The fellow was good, for he disappeared completely, and Philip did not pick him up again until he arrived nearly back at his starting point.

Come on, you murderous heathen, he wanted to shout, *let's get this over with.* He felt relieved when they finally emerged, then appalled to see how young the two boys were, scarcely four or five years older than John Cooke. Perspiration broke out on Philip's brow. As the Indians approached he swept off his feathered hat for a small bow of homage, using the gesture to dry his forehead. The visitors gave no indication of appreciating his good manners.

"Gentlemen, I bid you welcome," he said with as jovial a formality as he could manage, controlling his voice with more effort than he would ever care to admit. Sanders translated.

"We have come to parley with the Red Hair, as the Massasoit and our own village chieftain have requested." The scarred savage who did the scouting was clearly the headman, at pains to make clear he had not come of his own accord.

"Our captain awaits your pleasure within."

Then Sanders piped up on his own, gesturing at the boys. "Wituwamat, this meeting was only for you and your friend, Pecksuot."

Philip understood enough to feel enraged beneath his placid exterior. He knew if the Indians picked up on the danger and ran, they might never be caught. He gave the interfering Sanders a look that could burn through armor.

Wituwamat displayed no hint of suspicion. "These are my nephews." He actually smiled. "Strong young braves to give me courage to stand up to the fierce Red Hair."

Rewarding this insulting jest with what he hoped was a convincing laugh, Philip fumed as he led the way to the large central hut where all the trading was done, pulled the door open, and bowed all four Indians inside. For a moment Sanders looked to remain out in the fresh air, but Philip propelled him indoors with a shove. He himself lingered to draw the door shut behind them. He softly dropped a heavy bar into place, using the two hasps on either side of the door that the Plymouth men had mounted not five hours earlier, while the traders were still lining up to leave. By any outward indication the four Indians failed to notice they were now trapped. The room was surprisingly dark considering the poor construction of the walls and thatch ceiling. The Indians stood letting their eyes grow accustomed to the gloom.

* * *

As Philip leaned back against the barred door, Francis stood in position on the left side of the hut, behind and to Standish's right as the captain waited about two thirds of the distance straight in from the entrance. As the newcomers' eyes adjusted to the mottled light, they found white men lining the walls on all sides, outnumbering them at least five or six to one.

Francis watched the eyes of Pecksuot and the unknown boys dart around the room. The intricate shadow patterns rendered the grim white men's faces as barbarous, devilish and menacing as those of any painted savage.

If the ringleader Wituwamat felt the least intimidated, he gave not the slightest sign.

The translator Sanders visibly trembled by now, in fact shaking like the proverbial leaf.

So quivered as well the overgrown boy Edward Leister, feebly supporting himself against the lodge wall on Francis's left.

Standish took a couple of steps forward. Not to be outdone, Wituwamat marched proudly up to confront him from mere inches away.

Towering over the smaller man, the Indian looked the captain up and down, an arrogant smile curling on his lips.

Light reflected off the large knife that hung on a cord around Wituwamat's neck. Though stretched up to his full height, Standish only came to eye level with the blade.

Wituwamat did not say a word, so the captain spoke up. "We have heard that you are trying to make trouble for us."

Philip pushed Sanders forward so hard he almost fell down. Licking dry lips, the resentful wobbler managed to croak out words in the Massachusett tongue. Only later under unsympathetic questioning would the exact meaning of his sentences come to light.

"Wituwamat," he tried to warn the Indian, "they know you have been trying to raise a war against them."

Wituwamat kept his glare on the captain as he spat out something unmistakably defiant.

"He's come to talk things over peaceably, Captain," Sanders offered in dubious paraphrase. "That's why he's here."

Standish spared a skeptical glance for Sanders, then went back to meeting his opponent's fierce stare. "Sanders, if I find out you are not translating accurately, I give you my word you will never go aboard that ship. Do you understand me?"

"Yes, captain."

"Now tell him we have heard of his idle words, and we believe that empty words can be dangerous. We cannot allow our families to be threatened, and I am sure he would feel the same."

"Back away, and get your people out of here," Sanders said instead. "Don't you see they're going to kill you?"

Wituwamat only laughed.

"I said nothing in the least amusing, Mister Sanders," Standish said. "Now tell him what I said. My exact words, if you please."

Before Sanders could pull himself together for this duty, Wituwamat spoke up in broken but clear English that came as a surprise to everyone, including his own companions. "Empty words? We hear... of *your* empty words... cap-tain."

"Oh, speak ourselves a little of the King's English, do we?" Standish said.

"You speak big strong words... but you are only... little man!"

Wituwamat roared with laughter at his own wit, joined by the other Indians, probably without understanding the joke.

Standish's face went purple with rage. He moved with blinding speed. His right hand shot out and snatched the knife hanging around Wituwamat's neck. Grabbing it by the handle, he jerked so hard the rawhide cord either snapped or came loose at the knot.

Before Wituwamat could react, could stop laughing long enough to register astonishment, Standish drew back with the knife and plunged it up to the hilt in the Indian's bare chest.

"Uncle!" one of the boys screamed in his own language.

Wituwamat gasped and staggered. Standish maintained a tight grip on the knife. He pulled it out of the wound and stabbed the man again and again, driving him backwards.

Francis had no idea how the Indian stayed on his feet, why he wasn't already dead. He must be tremendously strong.

Every set of white hands without a gun produced a blade. Violence erupted throughout the hut.

Pecksuot shouted something as the white men converged on them. As the boys stood their ground behind him, he managed to snatch his tomahawk out of his belt and swing at the head of an attacker, but the white man dodged, absorbing a glancing blow on his shoulder. Otherwise the stroke would have split his skull in two.

Drawing his knife left-handed, bellowing at the two boys, Pecksuot spun to face in Francis's direction, lifting the tomahawk to throw it right at him. The space between them momentarily cleared. Both their weapons were traveling fast, the gun rising and leveling, the tomahawk arcing back for the throw.

Francis was faster though it seemed to take forever. Musket braced against his shoulder, he pulled the trigger. The tomahawk was still moving back as the burning match plunged downward to ignite the powder in the firing pan. Amidst all the shouting and flailing the gap between the two men remained open.

No delayed ignition this time. The gun went off with a roar. The huge ball caught the Indian square in the chest. Francis was astonished when the impact lifted the gigantic Indian clear off his feet. He flew several feet backwards to slam against a post and slide down, tomahawk and knife still in his hands. The body twitched a bit, but Pecksuot was dead before he hit the ground. The shot had blown out his heart.

This was merciful compared to how it went for the others. Someone snatched up Pecksuot's tomahawk and began to use it on one of the Indian boys, who were both screaming.

Philip and other men with guns shouted to move out of the way so they could get a shot, but it was too great a risk in the whirling chaos.

Suddenly the second Indian youngster, wounded and bleeding, squirted out from a mass of attackers and ran staggering for a poorly daubed area of the back wall. He began to claw through with his hands, in a diagonal straight line from where Edward Leister still stood as if paralyzed, jaw agape. Francis didn't know how this could be happening, but for the moment all the white men were busy hacking away at the other three Indians, including Pecksuot's dead body. Wituwamat and the other boy somehow went on fighting and struggling, absorbing wound after wound.

Francis had only vague awareness of all this as he tried to force passage through the mob. He watched with horror as the second boy's desperation combined with the shoddy construction to make a breach in the wall. In no time the youngster was able to claw a hole large enough to clamber through.

Standish somehow noticed this too and pointed, roaring at the top of his considerable lungpower, "Leister! Don't let that one get away! There can't be any survivors!"

His cry brought the English boy to life. As the Indian youngster's moccasins disappeared outside, Leister ran and dodged across the room and ducked through the opening right behind the fugitive.

* * *

After emerging from the hole the Indian youth called Miktanni turned and staggered toward the Wessagusset creek, out behind the only nearly completed wall of what passed for a stockade. This gave him little trouble as he went out quickly through one of its many gaps. Then he ran for the stream and the woods beyond. Whether he fled only to stay alive or also to carry word of the white men's treachery back to his tribe, no one could say, least of all Edward Leister.

Already fighting for breath, Leister struggled not to fall any further behind. He could not believe how fast this Indian ran while bleeding from so many wounds. He ducked through the same gap in the stockade and pursued, yelling for help continually as he was unaware whether any other Plymouth man had come through the walls behind him, though he thought not.

He reached for the knife in his belt, almost fumbled it away but contrived to hang on. It was only a rather flimsy kitchen knife "borrowed" from his master Mister Hopkins, but now he needed a real weapon he cursed himself for not acquiring a better. His clumsiness grasping his weapon cost delay, allowing the quarry to gain that much more ground ahead.

The wounded Indian boy might have made the trees if not for the little Wessagusset creek. He had to slow down slightly to pick his way down the steep bank. This allowed Leister to put on a lung-searing burst of speed to bring himself close. As the Indian was just reaching the bottom, Leister launched himself over the edge of the bank. His hands managed to grasp and trip the boy at the ankles, but the impact caused Leister to lose the kitchen knife. The Indian hurtled forward into the creek bed, grunting as he landed hard on an area of flat stones where the steam flowed strongly only a few inches deep.

Not thinking now, only reacting, Leister swarmed forward on all fours to wrap his arms around the other. The blood made his almost naked foe slippery. The young savage rolled over on his back and managed to snatch up the hunting knife hanging around his own neck.

He pulled back to stab, but Leister slid forward over his body, trying to pin him down with his weight, and seized the wrist of the knife hand with both his own. Each of them was screaming in his own language. The Indian was very strong, as well as desperate, and Leister had the terrifying thought that the savage would make short work of him if he were not already so terribly wounded. He might do it anyway. They wrestled desperately in the shallow flowing stream, out of sight of the stockade, which the Indian all at once seemed to realize, for he stopped yelling and put everything into the struggle. If he could stab the white boy and reach the trees, he would get away. He clubbed at Leister with his free hand but was unable to reach his head, only landing hard thumping blows on the bones and muscles of Leister's arms and shoulders, causing him to grunt with pain. Leister kept screaming, frantically trying to summon help.

"Help me! Help me!" Leister bawled. "I've got one here! He's trying to get away! Help me!"

He felt himself weakening while the Indian seemed to grow stronger. Their battle went on and on.

Suddenly Leister heard noises. Men were stumbling down the bank behind him, splashing through the water. A booted foot came down on the Indian boy's knife hand. A strong hand gripped the back of Leister's shirt and pulled him back off the boy. For a frightening moment he thought it must be other Indians. Then his eyes traveled up the leg that belonged to the booted foot, and he saw it belonged to Philip Delano. The Frenchman placed the barrel of his musket against the Indian boy's head and tripped the fuse. Nothing happened. The powder in the firing pan had either gotten wet or fallen loose in the chase. Other white men shoved Leister aside and fell on the Indian, pinning him down as he screamed. Knives flashed up and down at terrible slanting angles, splattering curls of bright red ghastly in the perpendicular yellow sunbeams. Then someone must have struck an artery or the heart itself, for blood erupted in a great fountain of released pressure. Some of it sprayed Leister right in the face. His clothes already drenched red from his opponent's earlier wounds, he stumbled and fell further back, gasping to breathe. The knives kept stabbing away until all signs of life ceased.

The water flowed deeply red from where the Indian boy's body lay unmoving. Then two of the men seized the ankles and dragged it out of the brook.

Edward Leister sank down in the damp sand at the water's edge and began to weep.

Philip knelt close alongside to put a consoling arm around his shoulder.

"You did very well, Edward. That one would have gotten away if it hadn't been for you."

Leister put his face in his hands and sobbed more bitterly than ever before in his life.

CHAPTER 39

Aftermath

Inside the shadowy lodge the smoke of gunpowder hung in the air with the odors of blood and death. Francis could hear the ragged breathing of his companions over the pounding of his own heart. More than one man ran outside to be ill. He wondered why they bothered. The room could scarcely be more defiled.

He turned his eyes away from the three bleeding husks that used to be men and a boy. The other Englishmen averted their faces as well. Someone dropped a knife on the floor of soft dirt, which was already absorbing the blood. No one would need to mop up.

Captain Standish sprang to life first. "All right, men. Well done. Well done." The others turned dull stupefied eyes in his direction. "But now we have more work to do. Come help me."

Standish seized one wrist of the dead Wituwamat. Two men roused themselves to take the other, and the three of them dragged the body outside. Francis followed. The least he could do was help dig the graves.

Instead, Standish directed his helpers as they hauled the corpse over to a log, flipped it over, and placed it face down across the rough bark. Standish pulled the corpse back slightly by the ankles, hooking Wituwamat's chin on the far side of the log, then flipped the long black hair forward, baring the back of the neck.

Francis watched in lethargic confusion.

"One of you fellows," Standish said, "go get that pike."

"We bury them?" Philip asked as he walked up from the brook.

"Not this lot. We dump the bodies in the woods and let the dead bury their dead."

Through a nightmarish haze Captain Standish could be seen taking a good sharp English axe in his hand. When Francis realized what was happening he tried to shout but made no sound.

Standish grasped the wooden handle in both hands and lifted quickly and powerfully, the steel axe head flashing upward into a stream of sunlight, then descending at top speed toward the bared neck.

Francis snapped his eyes shut but heard the loud sharp smack as the blade penetrated through flesh and bone into the log.

* * *

The bodies disposed of, the men formed into a column.

"Are you ready to beat that drum, boy?" Standish said.

"Aye, sir." Edward Leister swallowed hard but seemed to have pulled himself together under the captain's ministrations.

"Beat it loud. I want to be able to hear it."

"Yes, sir!"

Leister's shirt was still red with the dead boy's blood, but Standish himself had dipped a cloth in water and washed Edward's face, praising his courage all the while. Now the young man stood near the head of the column, military drum belted to his waist, a drumstick in each hand.

Francis had noticed a pair of such drums as part of the captain's unending supply of military accoutrements. Standish must have put the two Edwards to work learning to play, perhaps as a means of deflecting their pleas to train with the militia.

Standish walked along the line, passing close to Francis and Philip. "Keep your matches well lit, gentlemen," he said. "I expect no further trouble from the savages, but one never knows."

By this time Francis had found his tongue again. He indicated the front of the column, where one of the men stood holding the horrific trophy aloft on the point of an iron pike. "Is that really necessary, Captain Standish?"

"That one was the chief plotter," Standish snapped. "We need to make an example."

Philip glanced at Francis with a tiny shrug as Standish strode off to take his place at the point of the column.

"Forward...march!"

The drumsticks hammered away as they set out. Men stepped lively to the music. Now Francis thought he knew the real reason Leister had been brought along. The boy played without holding back. The cadence invoked the parading, all-conquering armies of Europe, every breast swelling with pride and military bearing. Francis found himself carried helplessly away by its power, as unable to resist his emotions as any of the others. The thunderous drumming echoed through the woods as they marched.

Francis forced himself to his duty, especially to vigilance. The drum proclaimed their coming from afar. In spite of any serene confidence on the part of the captain, no one really knew how the savages would react.

* * *

It would be hard to determine later, but perhaps what got the terror rolling with such power, other than the killings themselves, was the simple fact that the tribes had never heard an English drum before. And such a drum it was! The more primitive drums of the locals were nothing to be ashamed of, but the craft of English drum making was something else entirely. The tapping of the snare skin detonated with a deep sinister sharpness never heard before in these parts. It must have fallen upon uncivilized ears like pounding footfalls of doom.

For once in their lives the two Edwards had managed to keep a secret. Their practice at the drums had always been carried out in a forest gully they found that trapped sound and stifled echoes. The boys' motive had been to hide out as they struggled to develop their skill, whether for fear of mockery or envy by other boys they knew not—probably both. Thus unknowingly and in secret they empowered a major component of the captain's strategy to intimidate the natives with dark ritual. Standish meant to flaunt a savagery so excessive it would shock the savages themselves into permanent quiescence.

* * *

The People had drums of their own, of course, not only for communication but also as a mainstay of various celebrations, often frenzied, involving harvests, fertility rites, and preparation for war. Since their warfare depended on ambush and stealthy attack, however, they had no concept of armies advancing openly with banners and music to inspire themselves and frighten their enemies.

It was thus understandable how all who heard the menacing rattle of the drum felt the cold grip of fear. When a few curious souls cautiously approached and peeped through the trees, they were horrified to see what one of the white man was carrying near the vanguard of the procession.

The warriors of the People, in certain tribes at least, counted coup by lifting the scalps of their enemies. Most had heard of such things though never witnessing the practice themselves. But these cruel English took the whole head!

The watchers could scarcely refrain from screaming as they took to their heels, carrying the tale back to their villages.

Massachusett braves found the mutilated bodies by mid-afternoon. They fled in horror and terror.

The fame of the terrible deed soon spread in all directions, with the speed and destructiveness of a forest fire.

* * *

Word reached the village of Massasoit Ousamequin well before sundown.

From inside his hut the great chief heard a distant disturbance. At first he thought it was only children playing, hardly worth the trouble to go out and rebuke them. Then he recognized the sound of adult voices shouting and crying. The rising wall of noise came at his lodge like a mighty wave thundering toward a shoreline, gaining power as it rolled.

He flipped aside the thin blanket that had replaced winter bearskins over his door and stepped outside to a prospect of complete pandemonium. People ran in circles of aimless panic, sobbing and screaming. He saw mothers snatching up small children and fleeing into the forest, with older children wailing lamentably as they tried to keep up. Old men and old women went limping into the trees, leaning on sticks or each other. An ancient crone on a pallet pleaded for someone to carry her, but her relatives had already fled.

The great chief strode to a young brave and seized him by the arm with an unbreakable grip. "What is happening, young brother?"

"The English!" the boy cried. "They are going to kill us all!"

CHAPTER 40

Consequences

Governor Bradford walked the master of the *Anne* down to the waiting long boat from the ship.

"Thank you, captain, for anchoring with us as long as you have."

"I felt it was my duty, sir."

Bradford smiled. "We appreciate it in any case."

"I do not envy you, sir, you and your people. Your hardships..."

"If you might convey the truth of our situation to the adventurers in London, that would help us."

"Consider it done, governor."

"And one more item, if you please." Bradford drew a newly sealed letter out of his cloak. "If you could carry this letter for us."

The captain looked at the address. "John Robinson, in Leyden, the Netherlands."

"The pastor of our home church. To catch up our congregation on all that has taken place in the last year."

The captain tucked it away. "In London I'll post it for Amsterdam."

"If you don't mind, captain, aren't you headed there yourself, after London?"

"Yes, sir." The ship's master nodded with understanding at the importance of what was entrusted to him. "I shall wait and carry it myself then, directly to Holland."

"Thank you, sir." The men shook hands, allowing Bradford to pass over a gold coin, which neither was crass enough to mention. "And God protect you on your voyage back."

The captain glanced at the skies as he pocketed the money. "Springtime is here. Better time for a crossing going back then when we left."

"God grant it may be so."

The sailors pushed off the shoreline as soon as their master boarded. Bradford studied the glum passengers crammed into the boat. Despite Standish's fury at his treachery, no one had wanted to keep Sanders around, and he had been permitted to join the last stragglers from Wessagusset. Any joy or relief at departure scarcely touched their long bitter faces. None of their companions who had chosen to remain bothered to see these off.

As the rowers pulled for the *Anne*, Bradford wondered if any of his own folk wished they were heading back for London or the Netherlands. In spite of everything, he thought not. They had all been given the chance and refused. After all, if no one from the *Mayflower* had chosen to leave on the *Fortune* after that first tragic year in Plymouth, when they had well and truly starved for months on end, he could judge with some assurance that he and his people had come to stay.

* * *

The Plymouth settlers may not have chosen to leave, but an extraordinary number took time from their labors to watch as the *Anne* tacked out through the bay toward the open sea. Some watched for a few moments. A few walked north to a place far enough and high enough to see the ocean, where they kept vigil until the sails disappeared from view. Whatever other meaning it carried, the *Anne*'s departure severed the last link with former days. Humanly speaking, the people of Plymouth stood totally alone.

Alone, completely cut off from the outside world, and in danger.

Hester Cooke was surely not the only one praying, she firmly hoped, though she herself did so out of persistent uneasiness over the previous day's actions, which others saw as a triumph, a veritable and unmitigated victory from the very Hand of God.

Yet judging by appearances a surprisingly large number did not take time to pray silently in their hearts as Hester did. They were too busy at work. To bring in a successful crop some arduous chore always had to be done. She knew secret resentment had developed over taking so much time out for the Lord's day though none would say so openly. How else to explain so many growers caught "taking walks" in their fields on recent Sundays? Elder Brewster had felt obliged to address the matter in a sermon. Sabbath breaking had never been a problem before, Hester had heard, back when the inhabitants farmed in common. The challenge then had been to provoke workers to the fields on the other days of the week.

As she had both heard and observed with her own eyes since arriving, work stirred deep resentment when required by force of authority to benefit the community. But as the means to personal advantage and potential profit people seemed to thrive on the same exertions, though the performance remained as backbreaking as ever, indeed more so as it became more difficult to acquire help from a neighbor.

This narrow concentration on tasks at hand, Hester thought, explained the widespread relief at having the problem with the Massachusett troublemakers so permanently and indeed fatally resolved, as was thought. Once Standish and his men returned late yesterday afternoon, nearly the entire colony had breathed out a great exhalation of relief and resolved to move on, not only without remorse but with outright happiness and a not inconsiderable pride in a job well done.

Francis had displayed none of this triumphal spirit and refused to speak of what happened to anyone, including her. Last night she had expected they might lie awake for hours, but both had fallen immediately into the deep sleep of complete exhaustion. Early morning had brought no change in his willingness to talk about what happened. He fended off all questions from their children or anyone else. Whatever feelings might be churning within, he kept them to himself and went about his work. For once she found his dear face impossible to read.

Doing her best to shake off her troubling thoughts, Hester returned to her weeding.

* * *

High atop the fort the two duty sentries could watch the departing ship longer than anyone else in the immediate area of Plymouth. They took turns gazing seaward so as to keep one pair of eyes on the forest.

Wherever they turned or looked, they avoided the southwest corner of the parapet. Fortunately it was downwind most of the time. The stench would probably go away completely within a few days. They speculated over whether any of the savages had crept up to see what was exhibited there. No one could know for sure. Captain Standish had declared they wouldn't dare come so close, not yet, but they would in future. He planned to leave the gruesome thing right there on its iron pike for many years to come, long after it withered into a skull, as a warning to any savage who thought of plotting against Plymouth.

* * *

John was working near his mother and the other Cooke children in the late morning when he looked up and saw Hobomok come stalking out of the woods. John lifted his arm in welcome, but the grim-faced brave marched on toward the fort without appearing to see anybody and without returning any of the many greetings.

People looked at each other in bewilderment as he passed.

Hester walked over to John. "Have you ever seen Hobomok so unfriendly?"

"I think he looks worried, Mother. Anxious about something."

"The events of yesterday?"

"I doubt it. His feelings were the same as the Massasoit's."

By now they were joined by Priscilla Alden, who overheard John's words. "Yes," she said, "and Hobomok is usually the friendliest of men."

Not long afterward boys came running out of the gates to summon the town council.

"John, go find your father," Hester said.

* * *

Francis was admitted to Governor Bradford's house simply by showing up, aided by the coincidence of arriving at the same time as Captain Standish, who pulled him inside. Bradford had already sent for Edward Winslow.

All listened with bleak faces as Hobomok described the terror engulfing native villages for miles around. Francis heard with a steadily sinking heart, though he had no idea how many of the others shared his reaction. Some did. Winslow's eyes filled with tears, and he could not bring himself to respond, not so much as to ask a question.

Hobomok was a man of few words, and the recitation of the facts soon came to an end.

The council members kept silent, most with downcast eyes.

Finally it was up to Bradford.

"I am very sorry, Hobomok, but I do not see there is anything we can do."

Hobomok looked from face to face, and Francis felt his own burn with shame as he met his frequent hunting companion's eyes. Hobomok turned and left the meeting without another word.

Silence hung heavy in the air until Captain Standish spoke up. "Please remember, gentlemen, Massasoit and Hobomok were enthusiastic participants in our actions. Massasoit gave us the plan of attack fully formed, and Hobomok baited the trap."

This was cold comfort in light of what they had heard.

"That may well be," Winslow spoke up at last, "but it will quickly be forgotten. I fear we shall bear the entire burden of the blame." He proceeded to argue that he ought to be sent out to do anything possible to assuage the spreading panic. Bradford and the council refused, not willing to risk the young man's life in circumstances both volatile and unpredictable.

Francis slipped outside to find Hobomok, but the man had already disappeared. The sentries recounted the sight of him running back into the forest whence he came. They had never seen the Indian move faster. He suspected Hobomok ran propelled by grief. The same emotion kept Francis from approaching Hester before returning to the council.

* * *

By early afternoon word of what was happening among the Indians spread all over the settlement. Many heard with undisguised satisfaction and few with the trepidation of the Cooke family. John bent to his work, hoping someone would figure out what to do. He had no doubt they ought to do something, if their profession of Christ meant anything at all. He knew his father and Winslow were not as coldhearted toward the native people as others. They would come up with an answer if the council did not, and John wanted to help.

In the event it was not his father who sought him out but his mother.

She came with Priscilla, both women wary to avoid scrutiny.

"John, do you think you could find Hobomok? Where he went?"

John leaned on his hoe. He knew his father had made no attempt to follow the Indian. But John knew a bit more about Hobomok's habits than anyone else.

"Yes, Mother. I think I can."

"Then you must lead us to him."

"Lead whom? You and Priscilla?"

Priscilla touched a cautionary forefinger to her lips. "Did you see where Hobomok went back into the woods?"

John indicated the place. He did so far more precisely than the sentries had been able to do for Francis.

"We'll meet there then," Hester said, "in half an hour."

"Mother, I don't think this is a good idea. We should talk things over with Father."

"Not now, John. Let's slip away one by one, so as not to be observed."

They separated. John made a quick but fruitless search for his father, who was probably still at the governor's house. He dared not consult any other male authorities, lest he land his two favorite ladies in hot water. If they had some folly in mind, he prayed he could talk them out of it.

* * *

Whatever the women were up to, John resolved they would not enter the forest without some protection. He went to the hiding place for his bow and quiver of arrows. Waiting for his mother at the rendezvous, he sharpened his hunting knife.

Upon arrival she surprisingly made no protest at the sight of these weapons. Yet he knew they counted for laughably little in his young and inexperienced hands. Under conditions of the gravest danger, one boy and two unarmed women comprised a delegation from the uttermost frontiers of lunacy. That is how the captain would regard it, and so would his father. After Priscilla showed up with an Indian water skin strapped across her back, he tried to make the women see reason.

"What exactly are we planning here, Mother?"

"We need to find Hobomok."

"But why? What can we do, if the militia cannot do anything?"

"We must show him—how you say it? We must show him that we care. That we are not unfeeling monsters."

Her words shook John to his core. Had she cut to the heart of this matter? Might something so uncomplicated have indeed driven Hobomok to distraction and flight? Could it be he simply thought none of the English had the slightest concern for the fate of his people?

"Very well," John said meekly, all sound logic and sensible opposition melting swiftly away.

Thus they set off to the search, two girlish white ladies under thirty and a boy of eleven traversing a forest that seemed to tremble with menace in every silent shadow.

* * *

Hobomok had trained John well, for he soon picked up his mentor's tracks. His mother and Priscilla seemed duly impressed. For John the feat meant nothing since his teacher had made no effort whatever to conceal his passage, making it easy to follow provided one knew how to track like an Indian. The boy suspected this negligence bespoke his friend's morose state of mind. Yet it also contained an element of comfort and reassurance. If grounds existed to fear attack from the Massachusett, they would hold Hobomok as responsible as any of the whites. He would have taken precautions of concealment no matter the depths of his personal agony.

John's certainty on this point rendered him considerably more confident regarding the safety of his charges. His father would certainly disapprove of this reckless jaunt in any case, but if John had refused, he believed his mother and Priscilla would have tried to follow Hobomok on their own.

The trek, not easy for one as comparatively experienced as he, proved immensely more difficult for the young women. The little group had to push through dense thickets and difficult paths, uncovering hidden trails almost any other white pursuer would have missed completely.

"Do you know where he is heading, John? His destination?"

"I think I do, Mother."

"What kind of place?"

"A place to be alone..." John glanced back at them.

The women looked intrigued.

"A secret place," Priscilla mused.

"That is something many of us like to have," Hester said, "those who take our praying seriously."

"Is it possible Hobomok is a Christian?" Priscilla said.

John hesitated. "No, I do not believe he is. Not yet. He asks many questions, though. He wants to know how and why our God is different from the gods of his people. But he does not want his questioning known."

"Why not?" Priscilla asked.

"The Massasoit would not approve."

"The great chief is faithful to his own gods?"

"Quite the opposite. He thinks all gods are nothing more than stories for women and children, the invention of strong minds to control the weak."

"And if Hobomok should become a Christian?"

"The Massasoit might well find himself another ambassador. So please, Priscilla, Mother, keep Hobomok's interest to yourselves."

"Does Francis know he asks Gospel questions?" Hester said.

"No, I do not think anyone does."

"Anyone except you. Monsieur Hobomok must consider you a trustworthy friend."

"I suppose." His mother squeezed his shoulder from behind.

* * *

However tormented by a troubled mind, Hobomok could not fail to hear the clumsy approach of the whites. Knowing this, John simply led Hester and Priscilla out into the small clearing and asked them to wait quietly for their quarry either to come out or run further off, in which case additional pursuit would be futile.

Fortunately, Hobomok emerged from hiding. John felt more than a little taken aback to see an arrow notched to his bow, but he returned it to his quiver as he crossed the clearing. Though he wore the customary mask of expressionless granite, John knew his man well enough to read the sadness in his eyes, the concern in his voice.

"What do you do here, John?" Hobomok demanded. "Why do you bring these women?"

John blushed at the unaccustomed rebuke.

His mother spoke up. "It is entirely our fault, Monsieur Hobomok. We asked John to bring us to you."

"We practically forced him," Priscilla added. The ladies wished no harm to John's friendship, and he thought the Indian sensed this.

"What do you want then?" Hobomok glared at them, but the women did not back down.

"We want to say to your people that we mean them no harm," Hester said.

"The blow that was struck fell only against certain troublemakers," Priscilla added, "and some of us had our doubts about the wisdom of that."

"Your people must be made to understand this," Hester said.

"How? The People run away from their villages, like frightened turkey birds."

"But, Hobomok," John said, "didn't anyone tell them they are in no danger from us?"

"Many tried. The wisest elders, the bravest braves, and Massasoit Ousamequin himself. But the People are in the fear of death. They run away, into the forest, into the swamp, no matter what anyone say."

"We must find them," Hester said, "we must tell them the truth."

"If the English approach, they will run all the more. They are afraid."

"Of the men! Of those who did the killing! We are the women of Plymouth. If we tell them our men will do no further harm, they will listen."

"Why would the People believe this? Women never know what men are going to do. Just as men never know what women are going to do."

"Monsieur Hobomok, we must try. You must help us to try. Otherwise we shall not be able to live with the burden."

The Indian spoke to John in Wampanoag. "These girls are very stubborn."

John answered in the same language. "You think?"

Hobomok laughed. He may not have fully comprehended Hester's explanation, but he stood considering, no matter how utterly useless the effort in prospect must seem. "Then, you want to seek out the People one at a time?"

"If that's what it takes, yes!"

Hobomok regarded them for a long time.

"Will you guide us then?" Hester finally said.

"We cannot find many."

"We shall not find any if you do not help us."

This led to further long moments of thought.

"Very well. I help, though I know not what good it can do, so few of us."

"Thank you, sir."

Suddenly another voice spoke up behind them.

"Be it all right if I come too, Missus?"

They all spun to look, the women almost screaming but too choked by terror to draw the necessary breath. Hobomok looked chagrined at not detecting the presence of another English blunderer.

John also felt a fool for not realizing they had been followed.

From under the rearmost trees young Edward Leister came out, barehanded and unarmed, without so much as the kitchen knife he had carried to the slaughter at Wessagusset.

CHAPTER 41

Seeking the Lost

"I saw ye tramping out and put my head to reckon why, Missus and Priscilla," was the best Leister could manage by way of explanation.

"You came for our protection?" Priscilla said.

"Don't know how much protecting I'm wont to do but calculated I'd better follow."

In other words he had reasons of his own. John knew Leister had remained uncharacteristically silent about the Wessagusset affair. Neither Edward Doty, the two boys' employer Mister Hopkins, nor the other young fellows in the village had been able to pry anything out of him. They only knew he came home covered in blood, pounding his drum and refusing to talk.

Hobomok looked him over—a large thick-necked boy, three or four years older than John, with muscular arms and shoulders—and bade him join the party. If the enterprise struck the Indian as quite mad, why not bring along another fool? Hobomok ordered Leister to relieve Priscilla of the water skin and take up the rear. Thus reinforced, they set out on their quest.

* * *

Eventually they came to the edge of a large swamp. Hobomok halted to look at them, gesturing at the black water ahead.

"I think many of the People hide in there. They do this when there is war and raiding."

"Very well," Hester said, sounding fully determined.

"You will make your clothing wet and dirty," Hobomok pointed out.

"Just tell us," Priscilla said, "if you know how to keep us from drowning."

Hobomok laughed, stern face crinkling into lines of kindness around the eyes. "Do not worry. I guide you."

They plunged forward, wading into the water. John wondered if anyone else shared his overpowering fear of snakes. Swarming insects formed the more immediate nuisance. He managed to settle down, planting one foot after the other in murky water a foot deep and sometimes higher.

They followed Hobomok in single file, obeying his instruction to step exactly where he did. The mud under the surface proved slick and grasping, and John had to concentrate mightily to keep from toppling over in the water. Priscilla was the first to do so, falling on her posterior with a great splash and grunt. Leister rushed forward to lend a hand, but Hobomok and Hester already had her by the arms pulling her up. Their guide seemed impressed when Priscilla shook them off and kept moving forward, however wet and muddy, without so much as a word of complaint. Edward dropped back to the rear guard position.

John knew their presence here was no laughing matter. The passing swamp shifted constantly and unrecognizably through a deceptive monotony of dark water and thick growth. As a man who had followed these invisible trails since childhood, Hobomok led them unerringly around the quicksand and bogs waiting to swallow up anyone foolish enough to attempt this trek without a reliable guide.

They moved through a lake of trees growing to a great height in spite of water that stood one to two feet deep at the base of their trunks. Their thick branches high above formed a canopy very little sunlight was able to penetrate. The little search party struggled on through this dim and receding light. John began to fear lest they be caught here after sundown. He shuddered to imagine the inky blackness of night in such a place.

Suddenly John thought he heard something. He lifted his eyes from the watery surfaces at his feet to look straight ahead. In the gloom he could make out small ridges of muddy terrain projecting a few feet upwards out of the swamp water, a series of little islands perhaps. Hobomok raised his hand to bring the procession to a halt.

John peered at the outcroppings of land. Hobomok lifted his head and shouted a greeting. Suddenly the little island directly ahead burst into life as a small group of Indian people came out from hiding in the bushes. John could make out three or four women plus two young men or boys.

Hobomok shouted his name and something else, which John could not catch, the words absorbed by the dripping leaves and seeping water. The Indians stepped forward toward the water's edge to peer back at them. John saw the change when they realized they were looking at a fellow Wampanoag accompanied by four white people. Instant panic ensued.

The Indians scattered, leaping off the island into the swamp and splashing off in all directions among the waterlogged trees, not bothering to remain together as a group.

Hobomok bellowed at them while he and the whites struggled toward the island as quickly as they could.

"Wait a moment! Listen!" John could understand what he was shouting now. "Don't be foolish! These women and boys want to help you!" The Indians persisted in their terrified retreat, which seemed to infuriate Hobomok. "You are in danger from your own stupidity, not from the English!"

The shadowy figures fled away, impervious to reason or insult. John knew Hobomok had lost his customary composure out of frustration. The vanishing Indians ran wildly, heedless of choosing a careful path. John feared they would perish in quicksand if they did not calm themselves immediately, which they gave no sign of doing. He and the three other whites would then be responsible for frightening them to their own deaths. He clambered up onto the muddy little island with the others.

Before he could recover his breath he saw movement in the little island's thick bushes. Investigating, they found a young Indian woman, not yet twenty, wrapped in a muddy wet blanket on the ground. Her eyes grew wide with terror at the sight of them, but her movements were feeble.

Weak she might be, but she began to scream in the Wampanoag language, "Please do not kill me! Please do not kill me! Help me! Help me!"

John knew his mother and Priscilla could not understand a word, but the poor young woman's desperation roused their deepest compassion. They knelt down on the muddy ground to take her in their arms. Too weak to offer much resistance, she sustained her cries.

"Please, no! Please do not kill me!"

"Be silent, girl," Hobomok ordered gruffly. "These English are here to help you."

"Hold still, dear, please." Priscilla placed a hand on her forehead, cast a swift look at Hester. "She's burning up with fever."

"Do you know her, Hobomok?" John said in Wampanoag.

The brave shook his head. "She is not from my village."

While the sick woman held their attention a sudden burst of noise erupted off to one side.

"Look out!" Leister shouted.

John spun to see a young brave running toward them with a raised tomahawk. John had no time to reach for his knife, but Hobomok interposed himself between the warrior and his mother.

"Do not kill her!" the young brave shouted. "I will take her away!"

"We only want to help her!" Unfortunately Hester cried out in French, which only John could understand and that barely.

Hobomok brandished his own stone hatchet. "Do not be a fool!" he shouted. "Do these women and children look like warriors? They are here to help you! Call the others back out of the swamp!"

The brave hesitated for a moment but then pulled back his tomahawk to strike. So did the older man.

"Lord Jesus, stop this!" Priscilla cried.

As the young man's arm was going back, his fingers somehow slipped on the wet handle and the weapon flew out of his grip, landing in the swamp water. Overwhelmed by fear, he whirled and ran off into the sodden wasteland, abandoning the young woman in spite of her desolate cries. All this took place in two heartbeats.

Hobomok lowered his own tomahawk and turned back toward the females. "I had to defend," he explained. "If I did not, he kill you."

"I know," Hester said, and the gentleness of her tone conveyed everything the Indian needed to hear.

"Hobomok," John said, waiting till the man looked at him, "thank you."

Hobomok nodded acknowledgement, then spoke to Leister in English. "Pick up that tomahawk, boy."

Edward dutifully waded into the swamp, found the weapon and tucked it in his belt.

Priscilla followed the young brave's flight with her eyes until he was out of sight. "Do you think that was her husband or brother?"

"Husband!" Hobomok snorted. "Brother would stay to fight."

For reasons obscure to John this made both women laugh despite the appalling circumstances.

"We need to take this girl back to Plymouth," Hester said. "Can you help us?"

They all stared at her.

"If we can only save one," she said, "it is better than nothing."

"She will probably die," Hobomok said.

"We must try."

John thought he could hear more splashing in the distance. There seemed to be shouting too. Perhaps the Indians frightened off this island had by their very panic flushed others out of their own hiding places. He had a sinking feeling all their good intentions were only making matters worse.

"Very well," Hobomok finally agreed. "We must make litter to carry her." He looked askance at his pool of prospective stretcher-bearers.

"Don't you worry, Mister 'obomok," Leister piped up, "you and me, we can carry the lass."

"We shall take our turn," Priscilla said.

"Not to worry, Missus, this big savage and me, we can do 'er."

John knew they would have to as he and the women were far too weak.

Hobomok set about cutting down stripling trees to form the frame. John had already learned the technique, so he began cutting vines with his hunting knife.

The feverish girl calmed down, her fear of instant death apparently assuaged. Priscilla searched among the bushes and came up with a few abandoned personal items including a small bowl and another blanket. Retrieving the water skin from Edward, she poured water into the bowl. Hester raised the Indian girl's head so she could drink, then wet her own handkerchief to wipe the patient's brow. All the others realized how thirsty they were.

"Don't drink from her bowl," Priscilla said. "Doctor Fuller says you should never eat or drink from the same implements as someone ill."

Everyone else took pulls directly from the water skin, keeping the bowl for the use of the girl.

John checked overhead, silently praying they would have the litter constructed and be out of the swamp before nightfall. He didn't mind blundering along a dry forest trail after dark. Such pathways were like a paved street in Leyden compared to this trackless marsh. Hobomok kept glancing upward as well. John knew he shared the same concerns.

* * *

Struggling through the remainder of the afternoon and a good part of the night, the self-appointed relief party made it back to the Cooke home before Francis could extract himself from the long, exhausting council deliberations to which he had been invited and felt obliged to return. In the end the participants found themselves mired in the same helpless state in which they began, unable to come up with any meaningful course of action. All suggestions for intervention, primarily from Winslow, had been debated to death, swept aside with great long-windedness as impractical and dangerous. The meeting broke up with a significant degree of bitterness and recrimination.

Francis arrived home at last to find a crowd gathered at his front door, mostly women and old folks, with a few children, attempting to listen or peep inside.

"Here, here! What's this?" Francis vented an exasperation already heated to a mighty boil. Guilty faces spun in his direction. "Don't you know how late it is? Go to your homes!"

The curious flock dispersed, running off as fast as they could scamper, trailed by one limping old saint leaning on his crutch. Francis surveyed their departure with an annoyance further inflamed by growing curiosity of his own. He pushed the door open and entered his house.

A pestilential stench made him recoil at once. He pulled back a step, sweeping the room with his eyes to identify the source of the odor.

He saw Philip Delano feeding logs onto the fire, many more than required for the faint chill of an early spring night. In front of the blaze lay a filthy young Indian woman on a pallet covered by one of the Cookes' best blankets. He noticed the Indian girl's face exuding a prodigious quantity of sweat, which began to break out on his own brow from the heat. Hester stepped out of the darkness with water bowl and towels. After wiping the girl's face, she dipped a smaller cloth in water and placed it on her forehead.

"What are you doing, Hester?"

His wife looked up matter-of-fact as you please. "Doctor Fuller says this is the best means to bring her fever down. Poor thing, she was so hot I feared it would burn the life out of her."

Philip flashed a grin at him. "What do you expect from such a woman, eh?"

Francis knew the Frenchman wasn't talking about the Indian patient. An oceanic wave of outrage broke over the weary rock of his astonishment. "But what is..."—Francis almost said "that savage" but restrained himself—"she doing here? In our house?"

"Where else was I to take her? We could not leave her out there to die," said Hester.

Her serene demeanor and the presumed self-evident logic of these expressions cried out for answers to many questions, but he began with, "Leave her out there *where* to die?"

"Ssh, Francis, do not disturb her. She needs her rest."

Though shimmering with agitation intensifying by the moment, he did manage to lower his voice. "Could we perhaps step outside for a moment, please, for a spot of conversation?"

Hester set the bowl down before the grinning Delano. "Philip, please make sure the cloth on her forehead does not dry out."

"Yes, Madame."

Francis took Hester's arm, led her outdoors and turned to face her.

She folded her arms, awaiting any comment from him with the benign majesty of the virtuous. Before any storm could rise to his lips Francis noticed people clustered in doorways all down Town Street, every eye fixed on the Cookes.

"Let's go where we can have some privacy." He grasped an arm once more to haul her back to their vegetable garden. Once out of sight and in darkness, he had to repress a sudden and most inexplicable urge to take her in his arms for a kiss. They needed to have this thing out, whatever it was.

"Now," he said. "Where, pray tell, did you acquire that filthy, stinking girl?"

"She can't help being filthy, Francis. We can wash her when she feels better. I am more than somewhat filthy myself, if you had taken time to see. One becomes dirty and muddy in the swamps, it is the natural course of things."

"*In the swamps*?" he bawled, then lowered his voice again. "What are you talking about?"

"What I talk about is the Indians believe we go to war against them. They think we make the plan to kill them all, and they have run away into the swamps, many, many of them. Did you not hear all this?"

"Of course I heard all this! What do you think I've been doing all day? Sitting in a meeting trying to find out if anything can be done! But what were *you* doing out in the swamps?"

"We go out to tell those poor people not to worry, they have nothing to fear from us."

"WHO did?!"

"Priscilla and John and Edward Leister and I, we ask Monsieur Hobomok to take us out there."

"You took our son?"

"It was more he took us, but do not worry, he is very tired but safely asleep in his bed."

"I am going to roust him out of that bed and beat him with a rod!"

"You shall do no such thing! He is good boy!"

"He must have taken leave of his senses! He knows the dangers of this land!"

"Take the rod and beat me. I am one who talk him into it."

"I'm not going to beat anyone," Francis admitted.

"Young Leister was great help to us with the Indian girl. Hobomok led us and helped carry."

"Are you all mad? You could have been killed, the whole barmy lot of you."

"God protected us," she said.

"Why did you attempt such a thing?"

"Someone had to."

"Why didn't you leave it to the council? Do you think we've been meeting all day for the sheer unmitigated pleasure of arguing ourselves blue in the face?"

"And what, in its so great wisdom, did the council decide to do?"

"Nothing. For there is nothing we *can* do!"

"Exactly. That is why *we* had to go."

"And what was the result, when you found some of these poor savages?"

Her voice grew husky at that. "They all run away at the sight of us. This young woman was too ill to crawl back into the bush."

"Exactly. And if these runaways fled at the sight of you, how do you think they would have reacted to a party of armed white men bringing these same tidings of reassurance?"

By starlight he watched her black silhouette visibly dwindle to a posture of defeat. Then it was he reached out at last and took her in his arms. Her tears flowed against his chest.

"Please, Hester," he said, "you must never do such a mad thing again, promise me."

"Very well." She wept softly against him. "We had to bring that young woman home. Hobomok says many, many will die of fever in the swamps. We had to try to save this girl."

"Of course you did, my love."

"Francis, we must tell those poor people we mean them no harm."

"They will eventually come round, when there are no more attacks."

"But how many will die first?" She pulled back slightly but not to escape his arms. He saw reflected stars as her eyes shown up at him. "And how they know we mean them no harm when we stick the head of a man on top of our fort?"

"I argued against that, but the captain won out. The display is intended as a warning. To any others who would plot against us."

"It is barbarous!"

"They do the same thing in London, you know. Expose the heads of criminals as a warning to others."

"That is why we cross the ocean, I think, to escape the tyranny of England."

"I wager they do the same thing in France! Stick the heads right up there on a pike!"

"I do not stay in France! I go to Holland in search of liberty and justice, and now I am here in America with you!"

Their voices were beginning to rise, and Francis strove to lower his own again.

"Now is not the time, nor do we have the power to settle these issues of governance. We haven't the votes, you saw that." He spoke scarcely above a whisper. "What we must do is concentrate on doing our own work. Cultivate our own fields and garden, see to the future of our own family."

"How can we?" she said in a low whisper of her own. "When so many are doomed to die? Do you not remember what you always say yourself? God loves the savages the same as he love us."

"Of course I remember."

"I am very glad to hear it."   Hester broke away from him and hurried back to the house.

CHAPTER 42

Thine Heaven which Is over Thine Head Shall Be Brass

The Indian girl lay feverish and out of her head for nearly a week. Hester brought John to her side more than once to translate the babbling, but he reported she made very little sense. When she called out in the night hours, she seemed to be calling sometimes for her mother, sometimes her husband. At such moments Hester's gentle touch brought a measure of comfort. The worst crisis passed on the fourth day, after which Dr. Fuller gave permission to stop burning the hot fire at night, much to the relief of everyone in the Cooke household. The fever broken at last, the patient began to take a little food.

Hester and Jane watched over her by day, with occasional help when possible from the overburdened but ever industrious Priscilla. Meanwhile, by a colossal experiment in bridling the usually ungovernable human tongue, those in the know somehow managed to shield the swampland escapade from public knowledge. Doctor Fuller held his breath lest some of the accomplices should develop fever themselves, but none ever did. Hester's absences from the fields, however, as well as Priscilla's distracted attendance to her own duties, all for the sake of some Indian girl, began to be noticed and commented upon. A few of the colonists openly celebrated this compassion toward the mysterious ailing savage. A substantial number did not. The disapproval diminished over time, especially as rumor of Hester's pregnancy swept the colony, no thanks to the Cookes and Philip who kept the matter to themselves.

One day Hester decided to walk down to the fields with a midday meal for the rest of the household. Anxious to enjoy such exercise while it was still possible, she left Jane, just turned ten, home alone with the convalescent. The rest of the Cookes and Philip had just broken to eat when everyone in the fields heard a high-pitched scream from the direction of the stockade. All turned with alarm in time to see the Indian girl come flying out the upper gate. Far behind ran Jane, source of the scream, pleading and crying for the fleeing patient to come back.

The Indian girl bounded along with an awkward but unwavering lope, looking apt to pitch over at any moment, but managed to stay on her feet across the long distance through the fields before anyone could shake off sufficient bewilderment to stop her. Poor Jane moved as though to pursue the girl right into the woods, but her father made a beeline to intercept the child, catching her up all unwilling into the strong grip of his arms.

Jane flailed against him. "I turned my back, and she was gone! I had no idea she could walk, Father, much less run!"

"Hush, Jane, it wasn't your fault."

With Francis comforting Jane, Hester plodded after the fugitive invalid as far as the tree line, where she found Hobomok sitting tranquilly against the trunk of an oak. It was said he enjoyed the strange spectacle of English men and women working side by side in the fields. He met her questioning gaze with gentleness.

"Why did she run, Hobomok?"

The Indian shrugged. "She looks for her family maybe."

"But she is not strong enough yet!"

"Strong enough to run."

"Did she not know we were trying to help her?"

"I think she know. But she must try...find her family."

Hester bent her head in defeat. "She never told us her name."

By the time she walked back to the Cooke acreage Francis had settled Jane down to work with her brothers and sister. He strode over and put an arm around his wife.

"Well, the poor girl. You did the best you could."

"I wonder."

"Of course you did. She'll be all right. You and Priscilla saved her life. You and the girls brought her strength back. Now we'll be free of the distraction. We can concentrate on what we're supposed to be doing."

"Oh, yes!" She shook him off. "The growing of the crops, that is the most important thing in this world!" She walked away muttering. "What must the Lord think of us?"

She left behind an exasperated husband who watched her go, mopped his heavily perspiring brow, then turned and saw that the children had been watching, their little faces troubled by the conflict between their parents, so unusual in the Cooke family.

"Get back to work!" he snapped.

At the sound of his voice Hester looked back and saw Francis immediately assume a posture of remorse for taking out their problems on the children. She stood watching for a moment as he glanced upward in the direction of the hot sun.

The day augured to be another scorcher.

* * *

The people of Plymouth worked on as day led unto day and days passed into weeks. The sun beat down relentlessly, unmitigated by the cooling showers of previous years.

The moment came one noonday when Francis knelt down in the dirt of the vegetable patch and examined some of the plants as Hester stood beside him, shading her eyes with her hand. The plants were stunted and dry, their growth level far short of this point last year, despite anything she could do. The vegetables, however, were not yet in as bad condition as the corn down in the fields.

He looked up at her, smacking the dust off his hands. "If we do not see rain soon, all the crops are going to die."

"Has it ever gone so long without raining?"

"Never."

"But this is only the third year our people are here. Perhaps there have been dry summers before we came."

Francis shook his head. "Not like this. I asked Hobomok, and so did John. The Indians are as worried as we are."

* * *

The beans and squash had been duly planted but came up slowly, their early development as stunted as began to be undeniable regarding the growth of the corn. By the middle of June the fearful word "drought" began to be heard, first in whispers and pillow talk, then openly. After years in the watery dominion of the Netherlands, drought was a new concept for most, though a few older saints remembered the occasional relatively dry summer in England as one of the most brutal misfortunes that ever befell a farmer.

One night Philip Delano dragged himself home in the darkness to find the entire Cooke family scattered in collapse around the central room, a group portrait of exhaustion and despair. He slid down to the hard-packed floor to join them.

"The plants are dying," Francis said.

"I know it." Philip joined the silence for a long time before speaking up again. "We have to irrigate them somehow."

"Bit difficult to make water run uphill."

"Then we have to carry water to the fields by hand."

"But where can we find it?" John said. "I was out with Hobomok. The brooks are drying up, and so are some of the springs."

"We have to try!" Philip said. "We cannot allow ourselves to sit here and perish without making every effort!"

"We've been fools not to be doing it already," Francis said. "Tomorrow we dig out every bucket and pot we can put our hands on. We're all about to become water bearers."

* * *

The idea caught on as soon as the first pail dipped in the first shallow stream. Within two days no one could remember who did it first. Every man, woman and child who could totter from creek to field spent long hours carrying vessels of precious water. The spring on Fort Hill and the entire length of its rivulet within Plymouth were quickly declared off limits for use outside the walls. As the level of the nearest outside streams grew progressively lower, Governor Bradford gave orders that water containers should not be filled to the brim, to prevent sloshing and waste on the walk to the crops, but this proved impossible to enforce. People watered their own corn, beans and squash to the fullest extent, and no one seemed particularly troubled that his neighbor might not have enough.

Encouraged by Hester, Francis brought an idea to Bradford that they organize a bucket brigade, but this sensible conception fell apart in squabbling over whose crop should be watered first. People feared their own plants would be neglected to the profit of some other's, and the whole cooperative notion died aborning in jealousy and strife. Schemes to irrigate the fields by constructing Dutch windmills ran aground on the same fatal shoal. The crisis worsened.

Water is heavy, and as July began the entire colony suffered the misery of aching backs and tortured hands. The strongest men and boys found they could no longer carry more than one bucket at a time, first shifting the weight from one hand to the other every few steps, then staggering with a two-handed grip an ever shorter distance from one brief resting place to the next.

No one could understand how in spite of all prohibitions and precautions the Fort Hill spring began running low, since its water bubbled up from deep within the earth, but run low it did. Some of the surrounding springs had dried up already, and so had a few streams. The disappearance of a running brook made a sad and depressing prospect. First the water level dropped and dropped until less than ankle deep, at which point it soon ceased to flow, evaporating into isolated pools that quickly stagnated, then dried up completely, leaving only a ghostly trail of parched and drying mud where a creek bed used to lie.

Most Plymouth folk had eyes only for the ongoing catastrophe in their fields, but the hunters such as Francis, Philip, other militiamen and a few of the more adventurous boys such as John knew what was happening out in the forests. The progress of drought made the game disappear from the region as desperate animals roamed far to quench their burning thirst. More and more the hunters came back empty-handed. They heard the same predicament had befallen the Indians, though they were better hunters and probably not quite as out of luck as the whites—at least not yet.

The inhabitants of Plymouth watched in horror as the wind began to carry off the parched topsoil, first as puffs of random dust, then as stinging clouds that blinded the eye and tormented the throat.

* * *

One day Big Hester found Little Hester out behind the house just as the child was pouring a tiny bit of water around the base of a garden herb. The little girl stared as the water vanished into the dust, barely leaving a trace, then burst into tears.

Hester rushed to embrace her.

"What is the matter, little one?"

"It is not enough, Mother. We can never carry enough water to keep anything alive."

"I know, my darling, I know."

The two Hesters held each other tightly.

CHAPTER 43

Hunger and Thirst

By mid July the shadow of death lay heavy upon the land. The crops barely clung to the last vestiges of life. The vegetable gardens had wilted almost as pitiably. Wild fruit trees and berry patches in the withering forests yielded no edible return. The bogs sank too low to sustain the growth of cranberries. All knew the doom of man and beast must shortly follow the inevitable demise of the grass and all remaining crops.

Game for the most part disappeared completely, deer and rabbits and wild turkeys alike either perishing or leaving the area in search of water. The woodlands grew ominous with the beating of Indian drums as the medicine men danced and beseeched their savage divinities for rain. Yet the heavens remained shut up.

The settlers at Plymouth held onto life by distributing the dwindling supplies from the fort. Dr. Fuller disbursed a meager ration for each household four days a week, soon to be cut to three. Otherwise the English harvested the provisions of the sea, which seemed to grow scarcer as multitudes of Indians did the same up and down the coastline. The Cooke household had to put out some of their number each day to fishing or to prizing clams, crabs and eels out of their hiding places along the shore. All the other families did likewise, which left fewer hands to the increasingly futile task of carrying water to the dying corn.

As seekers of food wandered further afield, they fell into occasional confrontation with hungry Indians. To this point the peace treaty held, and no bloodshed had broken out. Deeply worried, Bradford and Standish endeavored to quell the practice, sending out armed men on formal and necessarily communal search parties. Yet family members, anxiety-ridden over hungry loved ones, managed to slip out on their own in spite of the danger, which paled in most minds against the threat of starvation.

In spite of all efforts, whole days without food began to occur. Hester, as did most of the mothers, tried to put aside something against each morrow for the littlest ones, who did not fully understand why they had to go hungry. At those times when the fish weren't biting or the eels hid themselves too well, Francis insisted that she eat something too, along with Jacob and the girls. She complied, for they both worried terribly about the health of the child she carried in her womb, though so far her progress seemed normal in line with her previous pregnancies. How much longer this would hold true they could not say.

On the last, very hot Monday night in July, the twenty-eighth of the month as dated by the Julian calendar used in Plymouth, the exhausted Cookes gathered for another household conference. Francis sat at the rough table where they had meagerly dined, the children and Philip gathered round. Hester leaned against the wall clasping the family Bible in her arms. The only outsider present sat next to her, not some other white person but their staunch friend Hobomok. He had been spending a great deal more time in the company of the Cookes since her rescue attempt, behavior noted and much commented upon by others, who of course had no idea why the ever mystifying aborigine had adopted this practice, though most assumed it had something to do with her care for that ungrateful girl who ran off at the first opportunity.

"We have to do something, my friends," Philip said. "There is an answer to this, and we have to find it."

"But what, Philip?" John said.

The Frenchman could only shake his head with no trace of his usual insouciance.

"Hobomok," Francis said, "are you quite sure? Has there never been such a drought?"

"Never," the Indian said. "In all my life, in all the life of my father and of my father's fathers, the rain has never ceased for so many days together."

A long dismal silence ensued.

Hester spoke in a voice scarcely above a whisper. "Francis, I think I have found the answer. In scripture."

Every eye watched as she crossed the few feet to the table and laid the big black leather-bound volume open before her husband. She put her left hand on his shoulder and pointed with her right to a passage.

"Here, these two verses."

The others leaned forward curiously, but Francis did not read aloud.

For a long moment there was no reaction as he stared at the page by the flickering remnant of the nightly cooking fire, on which Hester had boiled a pair of good-sized crabs brought as a precious gift by their Indian friend, though the meal had not gone very far among so many.

Suddenly Francis flung himself up from the table in a fury, knocking over the bench, which spilled the two youngest children to the floor where they lay too astonished to cry.

"Woman, we need a practical answer!" he thundered.

He reached down, snatched up the Bible, and drew back to fling it across the room.

"Francis!" Hester screamed in horror.

The piercing agony in the precious voice arrested his arm. He lowered the Bible, which she snatched away and hugged to her breast as protectively as a mother with an infant.

"God forgive me," Francis said. "I must be going mad."

Jacob and Little Hester burst into tears, but Jane quickly shushed them. They obeyed with trembling. None of the Cooke children had ever witnessed such a parental display. Everyone stared at Francis with open mouth.

"Francis," Hester said, "I shall be as practical as any man could wish, for now. This family must have more food. So must everyone in Plymouth. No one can carry water without food. The mothers are beginning to starve themselves to feed the children, the same as happened to the *Mayflower* ladies. Once we exhaust the stores in the fort, the women will start dying again. You men must eat too, or you will not be strong for long."

It was Hobomok who spoke up then. "We go a-hunting, Mister Cooke. Maybe we bag a deer."

"All the deer are gone," Francis grumped, setting the bench upright and dropping down upon it. The girls and Jacob hovered near their mother.

"All the deer never go. We track one down."

"I cannot, Hobomok. We have to keep carrying the water. We have to keep the plants alive until the weather breaks."

"I'll go," John said. "If there be one deer out there, Hobomok and I shall find it."

"Well said, young brave," Hobomok said.

The boy saw his mother open her mouth, perhaps to protest, but instead she said, "Very well. But if you find a deer, we must share it with others."

"No!" Francis roared, striking the table with his fist. "You're out in those fields every day. You see how people won't help us when we need it. If the people of Plymouth want every man for himself, every man for himself it shall be."

"Perhaps we should be the family who take the stand against this every man for himself."

"No," Francis said. "If John bags a deer, it shall be *our* deer. The Cooke family deer!"

"Our friend might have something to say about that."

They all looked at Hobomok. "What Mister Cooke says, it makes good sense." He turned to John. "All right, boy, you and I... early in the morning, we go find the last deer in the forest!" He left at once to go down Town Street to his tiny sleeping lodge.

A remorseful Francis sought to reassure the three youngest as he put them to bed himself.

John lingered with his mother.

"Your father is beside himself," she said. "As soon as we start cooking meat, the aroma will draw everyone in Plymouth."

"He knows that. If we bag a deer, he'll turn it over to the council."

"Yes. He was only talking."

"Mother?"

"Yes?"

"Would you show me what you found in the Bible?"

She complied.

CHAPTER 44

The Last Deer in the Forest?

John arose before dawn to find his mother awake and waiting for him. She saw him to the door, where she laid hands on him and quietly prayed.

"Lord," she whispered, "please keep this my son safe under Thy mighty protection. Let this hunt be a success in Thine eyes and for the feeding of many hungry. In the name of our Lord and Savior Jesus Christ, amen."

She gave him a long embrace to send him out.

He found his father waiting at the spring inside the fort. Francis had brought along his musket, tinderbox and pouch. "You can take these, if you like."

As John knelt to fill a small Indian water skin from the nearly exhausted trickle, he regarded the weapon greedily. He had grown tall and strong enough over the last months to carry the heavy musket. Francis had given him lessons, and John was lately improving his aim.

"Father, I am not good enough yet. I had best stick with my bow and arrows. Besides, they're lighter to carry."

"Very well." As Francis gave a quick nod of his head, the flickering torchlight caught a glistening in his eyes. "You are growing up, my boy."

When John stood up Francis reached out to shake hands, a gentleman's timeless gesture for honoring a son on the threshold of becoming a man. John returned the powerful grip, but inside his heart broke for the strong comforting arms that used to enfold him when he was little. As if sensing this, Francis pulled him into the very hug he yearned for. John managed not to cry, as did his father.

* * *

With the first hints of dawn emerging in the east, John found Hobomok sniffing around for fresh sign at the edge of the forest. If anyone could locate game this was the man.

If Hobomok were not the most skilled hunter and scout among the Wampanoag, John dreaded to think what it would be like to go up against the best in friendly competition, much less a war. He could only hope as did his father that the Massasoit's people would ally with the English if the Massachusett tribe ever got round to seeking revenge. John found a degree of encouragement in Hobomok's hints that the troublemaker whose severed head now adorned the Plymouth ramparts had not exactly been mourned as the dearest and most loving heart that ever beat in the forest.

The long day's hunt manifested the skill and knowledge of Hobomok more fully than ever. He knew every stream and spring over a great expanse, every secret trail used by the wiliest animals. John had assumed they would head for the swamps, but Hobomok explained that as the bogs dried up the remaining water stank with poison. Healthy animals—if any such remained—no matter how thirsty, avoided the putrid swamp water as they did seawater. The hunters' best chance was to find a spring still flowing, and so they headed first north from Plymouth, then west.

By afternoon it became clear that the great dryness had penetrated deep into the surface of the earth for many miles around.

Spring after spring came up dry when they found it. Previously flowing streambeds taunted the weary and thirsty as cracked and dusty pathways leading only to death. The sight made John yearn to reach for the water skin, but he let Hobomok guide him as to when and how much to drink.

John often prayed as he walked, silently beseeching God not only for mercy, water and food, but for a display of His power that would somehow show His mighty hand to Hobomok, go far toward answering the man's questions, and bring him to saving faith in Jesus Christ.

Father, the young boy prayed in the silence of his mind, *you know my heart is as wicked and divided, and as doubting, as those who sought a sign from Christ, but I do care for this my friend, and I pray in Jesus' name that You would show Your mercy and power to him and to his people and to us all.*

At just that moment, quite abruptly, Hobomok stopped and held up his hand.

They paused in mid-stride, listening and watching. Hobomok pointed to the ground ahead, and John's heart leapt when he saw where the fresh tracks of a deer emerged from the trees and picked up the trail they were on, heading in the same direction. John knew they must be approaching one of Hobomok's secret springs, which John feared to find as dry as the others. But perhaps not. Perchance the deer scented water bubbling up from a greater depth under the ground than the drought had yet been able to breach.

The spring must lie close at hand, for Hobomok signaled the urgency to move downwind. Each drew an arrow from his quiver and notched it to his bow. John followed Hobomok off the deer path as carefully as he had ever stepped in his life. They crept around to approach the spring from the cover of sheltering trees. Moving soundlessly among the dried leaves and twigs proved agonizing.

John's legs, along with the muscles of his back and shoulders, tightened into cords of torment by the time they reached the edge of a tiny clearing. They leaned out for a furtive glance from behind separate trees.

Sure enough, a smallish young buck stood ankle deep in a small pool of reflecting water, busily lapping away without an evident care in the world.

John restrained the impulse to cry out with joy. They had to bag this fellow first, then transport as much of him as possible back to Plymouth.

He turned to Hobomok, who tipped his head in the buck's direction.

He wants me to take the first shot! With no time for argument or thought, John drew his bow back, comforted that Hobomok was doing the same. Concentrating every ounce of strength, applying every lesson his Indian friends had ever taught him, John steadied his aim and let fly.

The arrow struck exactly where he was aiming, exactly where it ought to reach the heart. Yet the buck sprang out of the water at full run.

Hobomok's arrow followed on the instant, striking an equally fatal target in the neck. The deer stumbled a few more steps, then collapsed with a loud thump that shook the ground.

"We have him!" John cheered, but Hobomok quickly hushed him, running forward with a knife. The deer turned out well and truly dead, but John saw his own arrow had not pierced as deeply as it should. Hobomok had buried his deep in the neck.

"It was your arrow killed him," John said.

"He would have died from yours."

"Perhaps. But only after we had to track him for miles and miles."

"We both killed him, little brave."

John was surprised to see Hobomok re-sheathe the knife and drop down on all fours to drink his fill of clear water from the spring.

John waited until he finished, then did the same before replenishing the water skin. He nodded in the direction of the deer.

"Aren't we going to butcher him?"

The usual procedure this far from home was to cut the animal up and carry only the best portions of the meat wrapped in the hide. Hobomok grunted no and handed his bow and quiver to John. Then he reached down and hefted the entire carcass up on his shoulders.

"Hobomok!" John was astounded at this feat of strength but had no time for more questions as the brave turned and staggered back in the direction they had come.

John struggled to keep up. "I could help, Hobomok," he said breathlessly. "We can string him from a long pole, and I can carry one end."

"Maybe later, near Plymouth. Now we move."

After a time they turned south on one of the main trails. John barely persevered as Hobomok's long legs ate up the distance. The Indian was only a man, though a powerful one, and eventually they had to pause for a rest. They moved off the trail. Hobomok carefully laid the carcass down, then took a long pull from the water skin. John followed suit.

"Why are you helping us, Hobomok?" John spoke in Wampanoag.

"Your mother, boy. I think she is what we call a Spirit Woman. A magical personage, greater than a shaman. A woman who knows the gods, who not only speaks to them but they answer her back."

"There is only one God," John said gently.

"She knows Him then. She loves my People, to the point of risking her own life to save theirs. You also did the same, as did

Missus Priscilla and the other boy. Thus I care for your people but especially for your mother and all who dwell in her lodge."

John was thinking this over when Hobomok suddenly came alert. His arm shot out for John and pushed him flat to the ground.

"Wha---?"

"Be quiet," Hobomok hissed, squatting at his side and attempting to make himself as small as possible behind a tree trunk.

John lifted his eyes from the dirt, Hobomok's hand pressing down on his back. Directly ahead John could see ghostly figures appearing out of the woodland shadows. These weren't ghosts, however, but Indians, who had now caught them with the deer in spite of all Hobomok's precautions. As the men approached, John saw with horror that they wore stripes of bright paint on their faces. To make matters worse, he knew enough of Indian dress to recognize that these were not Wampanoag.

This was a large war party of the Massachusett.

CHAPTER 45

The Heart of the Matter

Once bounced back from the initial surprise and his personal chagrin at being caught in such a manner, Hobomok more than recovered his boldness. He stood up. "This land is under the protection of Massasoit Ousamequin, who is at peace with you. Why are you painted for war?"

Hobomok used the Massachusett dialect, but John found he could understand it rather well. Edward Winslow had once told him Wampanoag and Massachusett came from the same family of languages, "related in the same way as Spanish and Portuguese, for example, though probably with far less difference between the two."

The eldest Massachusett brave answered. "We are not dressed for war, but for a spirit hunt."

This was a custom John had not heard of and did not understand, but anything sounded better than war, at least until Hobomok replied.

"The spirit hunt has led to war before this."

"Only when the spirits tell us to kill our enemies," the Massachusett said.

"If you are the ones guided by the spirits, why has a Wampanoag discovered and slain this deer and not you?"

Dearly wishing Hobomok would start behaving more along the lines of the diplomat Massasoit had appointed him to be, John took further fright when he noticed the Massachusett spokesman and his cohorts casting a bitter and unfriendly eye in his own direction.

"I do not think you take the deer for yourself nor for the People but to feed the worthless ones—the whites who came from the sea to trouble us."

"Whatever I do, I do by authority of Ousamequin."

The spokesman hesitated at this.

"We shall see."

* * *

Rough hands relieved John of quivers, bows and water skin. His dearly loved English hunting knife went to the headman. The deer carcass was bound at the feet and attached to a pole borne by two warriors. He and Hobomok were neither tied up nor beaten, merely taken under guard for a long trudge in another direction. After an initial period of confusion, John felt better when he realized they were headed southwest for the Massasoit's village rather than north toward the land of the Massachusett.

The war party, or whatever it was, had evidently decided to put Hobomok's claims to the test. To do otherwise would render insult or worse to the Wampanoag. Though the Massachusett, like all tribes, proclaimed their own superiority, the Wampanoag were a large people, and no one had any desire for needless strife, especially in the midst of catastrophic drought.

John knew it was not strictly true that the Massasoit had authorized Hobomok to help white people hunt, at least in so many words, but he had given his emissary wide latitude to do as he thought best. John felt fairly confident their quest for meat fell within Hobomok's power to decide on his own.

Still, he felt increasingly nervous as they approached the Wampanoag capital. News had traveled through the forest with its usual mysterious speed. When their captors brought Hobomok and John into the village, every inhabitant had already turned out to watch. They made quite an impressive throng despite all the known fever deaths and the otherwise missing who had never returned from their panic-stricken flight following the Wessagusset business.

As he was propelled through a growling and jostling crowd toward the central meeting lodge, John saw hatred written on every face, directed squarely at him. This terrified him profoundly, for the Wampanoag tended to value the young, red or white.

The Massachusetts came to a halt before the great lodge and shoved their captives forward for all to see. The crowd seethed with a fury worsening by the moment. John saw their implacable hostility now projected as much at Hobomok as toward himself—and not at all against the painted intruders. He wished he could seep down into the earth and be forgotten. He felt so frightened he could scarcely hold his mind together to pray, but pray he did, as desperately as ever in his life.

Finally the blanket covering the door of the great lodge was flipped aside, and the Massasoit came forth. Wearing the glorious red coat that had been his first gift from the new arrivals at Plymouth, he stood silent for a moment, effortlessly projecting a strength and dignity that slowly gained sway over all. John had seen the great chief before, but never this close at hand. He was astonished at how tall the man was, tall and very straight for his years. He recalled from some half-remembered Bible lesson that ancient peoples frequently chose the tallest and handsomest men as their leaders. Young Ousamequin must have been a match for the youthful King Saul.

Massasoit passed his stern gaze across every face. His perusal quieted the unruly to a stricter attention. Last of all his eyes fell upon Hobomok and John. Then he turned to the Massachusett spokesman.

"Why do you bring these before me?"

The Massachusett brave beckoned for the deer carcass, which the two carriers brought forward and cast on the ground. "The People are starving, and the English send out children to slay our game."

John shrank inside from the hateful scrutiny that blazed at him from all directions. Knowing full well the passion with which all the local tribes disrespected cowardice, he forced himself to keep his head up with as valiant an appearance as possible. He fixed his look on the chief, who had no more than a glance to spare for one so obviously inconsequential.

"I do not fear children," Massasoit said.

"A child must be dangerous indeed to turn a warrior of the People into a running dog for the whites."

Hobomok tried to leap at the man, but his own friends restrained him.

"Hobomok lives among the English only because I command him to do so. He is as much of the People as yourself or any brave."

The spokesman scowled, much displeased, but climbed down from the warlike posture plainly having no good effect upon the chief. "Very well, great Massasoit, shall I open my heart to you?"

"Speak."

"Will you send the child out of our hearing? He may be a spy to carry my words back to the Red Hair and the other murderers of my people."

"I shall not."

"Will you at least forbid the running dog from turning my thoughts into the English tongue that the child will understand?"

Hobomok spoke up at once. "I shall not translate a single word you speak into the English tongue."

"Very well." The spokesman spoke with an orator's flourish, clearly intended to sway the crowd while formally addressing their leader. "Wise Ousamequin, look about you. The soil of the earth is drying up into dust. The wind is hot and dry, and it carries the dust away. The corn has no water to grow. The streams have dried up. Now the springs are drying up, and the beasts of the forest go as thirsty as the corn. For many days the heavens have withheld their rain."

"You tell me nothing I do not know."

"In all my days I have never seen such a drought. The old ones from among the Massachusett have never beheld such a drought. Neither their fathers nor their fathers' fathers ever told them of such a drought."

"You speak truly," Massasoit conceded. "It is a great withholding of the rain, such as no man has ever seen."

"But do you not see, great chief, it is the fault of the English? They have slain four warriors of the Massachusett, and now the gods are angry."

"The gods are angry at the English, but they make the People suffer?"

"The gods are angry with us also, because we have allowed the murderers to go unpunished."

Massasoit remained impassive, but judging by the rising chorus of muttering and outcry, his people bought the argument whole. The Massachusett spokesman reached into his hunting pouch and drew out a rattlesnake skin, complete with rattles, which he shook before their faces. The deathly clicking noise sent chills running up and down John's spine. Then the spokesman threw the snakeskin down at Massasoit's feet. The crowd noise intensified.

"I have come, great chieftain, to ask the Wampanoag to join us on the path of war! Let us kill the English!"

The villagers roared their approval. John felt them surge around him. Hobomok moved closer, one solitary man determined to protect him. Blinking back tears in the determination not to show fear, John prayed.

"Let us kill the English," the spokesman howled, "and then the anger of the gods will be appeased! When the blood of the English flows, then will the rain come down from the gods!"

Massasoit stood imperturbable as the screaming and tumult multiplied into frightful culmination. John tugged on Hobomok's arm and shouted in his ear.

Massasoit raised his right hand. The frenzy began to die down at once.

When it had grown sufficiently quiet, Hobomok spoke up. "Great chief, the boy asks if he may answer."

This was an astonishing turn of events for the villagers and especially for the pompous and self-satisfied Massachusett spokesman.

Massasoit looked at John and nodded his approval. "The boy may speak."

Every enraged face glared at him. John swallowed hard, but he took a step forward. He thought he saw a hint of kindness in Massasoit's impassive face, so he kept his focus there. When John spoke, his boldness and the strength of his voice surprised everyone, including himself.

"Great Massasoit Ousamequin," John said, hearing loud gasps all around, stunned surprise at hearing him speak the Wampanoag language. "There are some of us among the English who also think Almighty God, Who is the true God and the only God, may indeed be angry at us for some of the things we have done."

These words created a sensation among the Indians—and within John also, for he'd honestly had no idea what he was going to say until he opened his mouth to say it. He thought he heard a stifled laugh from Hobomok's direction, but he kept looking at the great leader. Only then did he remember Massasoit's hard heart and resentful opposition to the slightest hint of Gospel truth.

Well, the die was certainly cast now, so John plunged ahead. "It is the custom from our sacred traditions, when we think we have done wrong, when God is displeased with us, to appoint a day for fasting and prayer." Since the Wampanoag had no word for book or writing, "sacred traditions" was the best he could do.

"What is fasting?" the Massasoit said, as well he should since John had used the English word, not knowing any Wampanoag equivalent.

"We go without food in order to devote ourselves fully to God. We spend the day making our prayers."

"What do you say in your prayers?"

"We confess our sins to God. We tell Him how we have done wrong and ask Him to show us anything we have not thought of. We ask Him for forgiveness. We ask Him to make our hearts clean before Him. Then, after all this is done, we shall ask Him for rain."

This was too much for the Massachusett mouthpiece. "Our rainmakers have been unable to make rain!" he bellowed. "Why should we allow the English to have a day with their God? We must take action while we have the strength!"

Massasoit pondered. John prayed silently, knowing his fate and perhaps all Plymouth's hung in the balance.

"Our gods have had their chance to make rain," Ousamequin finally said.

"Our gods are angry! Because of the English!"

Massasoit held up his hand again. "It is only right to allow the English time to pray to their God as well. After they have had their day, we shall see what will happen then." He turned to John. "You may go in peace. Let every man's hand be stayed from doing any harm against you and your people until we have seen the power of your God to make rain. I have spoken."

Massasoit turned and went back into his lodge, leaving the Massachusett contingent seething with wrath and frustration. As Hobomok placed a hand on his shoulder and walked him out through the sullen but obedient Wampanoag, who cleared a path before them, John marveled at the Solomonic fairness of Massasoit's decision. Though the great chieftain undoubtedly expected English prayers to prove no more efficacious than the rain dances of the Indians, he was willing to grant them a chance.

John was so relieved to escape with his life that he wasted no regret on the loss of the deer, which the Wampanoag took away for themselves, to the further vexation of the Massachusetts. But he did rather wish he'd asked for his knife back.

CHAPTER 46

Fasting and Prayer

"You have done bravely, my boy," William Bradford said.

John stood between his parents, his mother holding his hand while his father draped an arm around his shoulder. The governor and councilmen sat in grim array at their long table. Hobomok stood over to one side. Given the Indian brave's long and deep involvement, no one saw any reason to exclude him now.

"With the unanimous consent of the governing council," Bradford read from his brief proclamation, "I declare Thursday next the thirty-first of July a day of fasting, humiliation and prayer. We ask all the men, women and children in this colony to fast and humble themselves before God, examining our ways and confessing our sins personal and corporate, and giving thanks for His grace, that we might beseech Him with purified hearts for the mercy of rain and the end of this drought. In the name of our Lord and Savior Jesus Christ, amen. Given in Plymouth this twenty-ninth day of July, the year of Our Lord One Thousand Six Hundred and Twenty-Three." He signed the document.

"Thank you, Governor," Francis said.

"And we thank you, sir. Our thanks to your whole family, and especially to your fine son."

* * *

Hobomok betook himself out of Plymouth at once and spent most of that night and all of Wednesday traveling the forest, visiting all the nearby villages of the People, both to share and receive the latest tidings. The watch-and-see interval declared by the Massasoit held firm, he learned, among the Massachusett as much as the Wampanoag. The shamans of all the tribes afflicted by the drought, including Patuxet, Agawum, Nipmuc and others, suspended their own rainmaking activities, not wishing to produce any results whose thunder could be stolen by the God of the English. Most of the Wampanoag medicine men had already put a stop to dancing and ceremony the moment they heard of young John Cooke's words to Ousamequin.

Despite limited contact, most of the People in all tribes had heard rumors of the supposedly all-powerful God worshiped by the whites. The shamans saw this test as their great opportunity to kill and bury such idle chatter once and for all. Yet among those with no ax to grind, as his new Plymouth friends would put it, Hobomok discovered a surprising yearning, to whatever degree born out of desperation, that the unknown God might send forth this great power, might indeed turn out to be everything the English proclaimed.

The People struggled with hunger and thirst. They worried about the coming winter and the lives of their children. They longed for deliverance. They did not care from whence it came.

* * *

"I do not understand this God," the elder of the two young braves from Ousamequin's village said. "Is he the same as the Great Spirit? The God who is above all the other gods?"

"Yes, I think He is exactly the same as the Great Spirit," Hobomok said, "but the English say He is the only God. All the other gods are not true gods at all."

"Does their God live in trees and rocks and all the things we see around us then, like the Great Spirit?"

"No, they say He made the world and the sky and all they contain. He does not live in them, He rules over them."

"That is different," the second young brave said.

"I suppose it is."

"Where does he live then, their God?"

"Sometimes they say He lives in a beautiful place beyond the stars, called Heaven, where their dead go to be happy and live forever. Sometimes they act as though their God is standing right next to them but cannot be seen. At other times they say He lives in their hearts."

"Their God lives in three places at once?"

"More than that. They also say He is everywhere at the same time."

"How can all this be?"

"I do not know. But they say He knows what we are thinking, hears every word we speak, sees everything we do—good or bad—and remembers it all."

"All this sounds very confusing."

"To the English it seems to make sense."

The young man gestured at the night sky. "I only want to find out if He can make rain."

The first hints of dawn were just beginning to break on the day set aside by the English. Hobomok and his two inquisitive young companions had hidden themselves at the edge of the forest where they could observe Plymouth without being seen. They knew many others from among the People were doing the same, but isolated in twos and threes, unwilling to display their burning curiosity openly, thereby earning rebuke and enmity from the medicine men. The shamans, most of the village chieftains, and the Massasoit himself stayed home to scoff, waiting out a day they felt certain would prove as uneventful as any other.

Time enough later to plan for war.

At the moment no whites could be seen except four men with thundersticks walking back and forth on what they called the parapet. Ordinarily, Hobomok explained, men and women would be out in the fields at first light, frantically working to carry water to the dying corn. But not today.

"Will the English dance and beat the drum, as our rainmakers do?" the second brave asked.

"The English never dance, and they beat the drum only for war."

"What will they do then?"

"They will lie on the ground on their faces, and cry out to their God."

"The English are very strange."

"To us they seem strange, but what if their God *can* make rain? It will benefit the People, as well as the English."

"But how will we know it is truly their God who brings rain if it comes?"

Hobomok shrugged. "If He is powerful enough to bring it, He is powerful enough to let us know He did it."

"Bah," the first young brave said, "no one can make rain in this drought, not even a god."

* * *

Before the sun was well up, most of the people of Plymouth had gathered in the storage room of the fort, their customary Sunday meeting place. Hester noticed the prompt arrival of some with no particular reputation for religious devotion, doubtless drawn by the gravity of the situation. These few somewhat torpid worshipers included young Edward Leister and his longtime foe Edward Doty, who took seats side by side.

Miles Standish and his new wife were conspicuous by their absence, and Hester wondered if they had remained in the privacy of their home to count the rosary. The captain attended weekly services faithfully but never officially joined the church, thus feeding rumors of his Catholicism. He was both too beloved and too feared for anyone ever to confront him on the matter. Over recent weeks Hester had found a soft spot forming in her own heart for the gruff little man. Despite recurrent disagreement with his policies, especially the attack at Wessagusset, she had no doubt the Captain sought the best for the people of Plymouth—and for God.

The entire Warren family was in attendance. Hester noticed pretty little Sarah Warren casting furtive glances across the aisle at her son John. Ordinarily Hester would have found this amusing but today she wanted everyone to be serious. John himself already appeared deep in prayer, as grave as any of the men, including his father. Well, perhaps that was part of the attraction for young Sarah. Knowing this was not a day to sit in judgment of anyone but herself, Hester said a silent prayer for the Warren girl and for her son, for their lives, their hopes and their futures, whether together or no.

A stirring in the room drew general attention. Governor Bradford strode to the pulpit. Hester found it significant that on this one extraordinary day the leader of government would call them to their spiritual duty rather than Elder Brewster, their pastoral leader. Bradford looked around at their faces for a long moment, then began to speak.

"Brethren, we begin this day together, most of us, but do feel free to come and go from this place as led by the Holy Ghost. You know our purpose. The important matter is that every man and every woman among us, every boy and every girl, do business with God "

He looked down at the open Geneva Bible on the pulpit, then back up. "We all profess to be Christians here. We believe in Jesus Christ. We trust that His death upon the cross has paid the price for the guilt of all our sins. We celebrate the free gift of eternal life through faith in His sacrifice and resurrection. We are made the children of God not by any good works of our own, but through grace, the undeserved mercy of God."

Bradford paused again, meeting the eyes of everyone who gazed upon him.

"But sometimes, brethren, in the very safety and security of our trust in Christ, and our position through that faith and by God's enabling grace in the company of the redeemed, we begin to take our gifts for granted. We allow our hearts to grow cold toward God. The cares of this world and the deceitfulness of riches and the lusts of other things enter in, and choke the Word, and we become unfruitful. We forget that while eternal salvation is a free gift of God's love and mercy, through His faithfulness to His promises, our blessings in this life, as well as our future rewards, are contingent upon obedience, upon our own faithfulness. If we do not stay close to God, and obey Him, we walk in the greatest danger of losing our gracious fellowship with Christ. The fault is not on His side, I say, but on ours. Many of us believe our present difficulties have come upon us because in our selfishness we have neglected our divine duties, both toward God and toward one another. There is scriptural evidence for this, as has been pointed out to me by Brother Francis Cooke. I shall now ask Brother Cooke to share with us."

Hester looked on with emotion as Francis stood up in the men's section and opened their family Bible to the same Old Testament place she had drawn to his attention a scant three nights ago.

"This passage is from Second Chronicles, Chapter Seven, beginning at verse twelve," Francis said, "when King Solomon had dedicated the temple. 'And the Lord appeared to Solomon by night and said to him, I have heard thy prayer, and have chosen this place for myself to be an house of sacrifice.

" 'If I shut the heaven that there be no rain...' " Cries and gasps from the congregation made it difficult to hear the rest, so he waited for silence and read it again. " 'If I shut the heaven that there be no rain, or if I command the grasshopper to devour the land, or if I send pestilence among my people...' "

Knowing how profoundly the next verse had moved her, Hester prayed. Francis seemed to struggle quelling strong feelings of his own before he could read on.

" 'If my people, among whom my Name is called upon, do humble themselves, and pray, and seek my presence, and turn from their wicked ways, then will I hear in Heaven, and be merciful to their sin, and will heal their land.' "

CHAPTER 47

The Sound of Thunder, Over the Sea

The power of the verses Francis read struck deep. The overt reference to God shutting off rain hit with too much precision to be gainsaid or ignored. With all the staunch Bible readers in Plymouth, it seemed not only pathetic but downright Satanic that no one had made the connection before. People wandered out thunderstruck into the early morning sunlight. Some threw themselves to the ground and lay moaning in place.

The connection of the sin and disobedience of God's people to the withholding of blessing from the land could not have been more explicit. Though the prophecy had been spoken to God's chosen people Israel, who dwelt under the Law rather than Grace, the Plymouth believers had no hesitation appropriating its words for themselves, both as to the threat of discipline for disobedience and the inseparable and hope-inspiring promise of blessing and restitution after prayer and rectification. They considered themselves a chosen people after all, not in the same ancient sense as the Jews, but grafted into the living vine of Abraham's family through their faith in Christ. All mourned that they had briefly lost sight of having been called for a purpose other than their own gratification—called out from among the Gentiles, called out from the darkness of a lost world. And that holy purpose, in opening this new land to the west, was to set the light of Christ upon a hill for all that lost world to see.

* * *

Hester was among those, primarily ladies, who remained in the meeting room after her husband, elder son and houseguest Philip had left the fort to seek solitary refuge of their own. Though she had come across the verses and shown them to Francis, she did not exclude herself from their ramifications. She sat holding hands with Priscilla and her daughter Jane.

"I have failed you, Lord," she prayed aloud. "I have not put you first. I have not trusted you sufficiently. I have made my worries and fears an idol to rob Thee of my time and full devotion..."

Other women came and went from their circle and would continue to do so throughout the day. Their spoken sentiments echoed Hester's. This was a time to confess one's own sin and blame, not to indulge a judgmental tendency toward anyone else.

When time soon came for Priscilla to go mind the tiniest toddlers and youngest babes, she took her own opportunity to pray aloud.

"Dear Father," Priscilla spoke in her soft unassuming voice, "we have heard how the poor Indians have never seen or heard of such a drought as this. It strikes me that in all their years of darkness without Gospel light, Thou hast never sent upon them this manner of affliction. We ourselves are the only new factor here. Thus it is that the discipline of this thy people hath also fallen upon them, while the fault is ours, for we are the ones who have failed Thee, the people upon whom Thy name is called. Be merciful to us for our sins and failures, we beseech thee, and let that mercy redound also toward all those who suffer with us. Let there be an end to the loss of life among these dear people. Let them see the hand of Thy power and Thy great love and mercy, and let Thy good rain come down. Let all those who do not know thee be not only watered and fed by renewed rain, but let them behold by Thy gracious hand a harvest beyond anything that has ever been seen, that their lives may not only be saved in this world but that they might know Thee, and drink the Gospel water that satisfies all thirst, the faith in Jesus Christ that raises all of us poor sinners up into life everlasting."

Priscilla had to pause before she could go on. Around her all the other ladies quietly wept. "Dearest Father, make it possible for all of us, newly arrived and native alike, to sit down together once again to a great harvest supper of Thanksgiving. Not only this year, we pray, but down through the years, on and on, and let it be that we may all sit down together someday at the great marriage feast of the Lamb, when we are reunited forever in the Kingdom of God…"

* * *

A few miles to the west, the exasperated Massachusett braves languished in the uneasy embrace of the Massasoit's hospitality. Their spokesman approached the Massasoit as Ousamequin's family waited for the breakfast pot to boil, meager as it was. The war party could scarcely be denied a share of the precious venison since they had taken the kill from the white boy and his traitorous Wampanoag companion in the first place. At the moment, however, the spokesman had other concerns.

"Why do you allow your people to go watch the village of the English? So many of them?"

The great chief shrugged. "It does no harm to watch."

"Then why do you not go watch yourself?"

"Whatever happens, we will learn soon enough."

The spokesman lowered his voice. "When the God of the English fails, then will you take the warpath against them?"

Ousamequin shrugged again. "Let us wait and see what will happen."

"Do you worship the God of the English also?"

"I will never worship the God of the English, but let us wait and see what will happen."

* * *

After spending time walking and praying with John in the fields, Francis went on to pray with other men and boys, in small groups and singly, here and there throughout the plantation. Before long, however, he had to face what he had been avoiding, the necessity to be utterly alone before God. He drifted away from all others, found an isolated spot amid the Cooke family corn, and dropped down to the earth. All the plants, corn, beans and squash alike, were thin, parched and stunted, but the corn had still grown high enough to conceal a man lying flat on his face.

"O Lord, I do not know what to think or say," he prayed softly. "Most of our people are quite aware of the selfishness and greed in our lives. They mourn the way we have neglected our holy duties, as indeed we have. Yet we were selfish and greedy in different ways before the change in our system of property. The new way is more reflective of your rules of ownership and property in Thy laws, so holding property in common was certainly not the solution. The problem is in our hearts as it is in my own, dear Father, I do confess it and pray your help to think of others and their benefit whilst I rightfully pursue such blessings from my own hard work as are appropriate.

"It troubles me, though, that no one outside my own household seems the least troubled by the affair at Wessagusset. I can only come before you in regard to my own participation. There is no point making excuses that I saw it as my duty as a soldier and defender of my own people, for I do not know how these principles stand in the light of your holiness and love. Thou knowest how haunted I have been by the memory of that poor man I killed, though he was trying to kill me, though only because he and his companions had been lured into our trap. If not for profound weariness of body, O Lord, I suppose I should not have slept an hour in all these ensuing days.

"I am devastated to think I have sent a lost soul out of this world. I acknowledge before Thee my responsibility and guilt for this killing and my part in all the others. Forgive me, dear Father, for Jesus' sake, I beseech thee, and restore unto me the joy of my salvation…"

* * *

Hobomok and his two young companions witnessed fascinating behavior as soon the English began to drift out of the fortress meeting place. They watched men wander unsteadily, hands and faces lifted to the sky, hardly seeing where they walked.

Men—and before long some of the women as well—reached the cornfields, where they flung themselves down, clawing the dusty soil as they wept. Knowing how the undemonstrative English disdained the emotional display all too common among the People, Hobomok felt quite astonished at the storm of intense feelings playing out before them, as robust as the keening of mourners for a death.

"Have they been drinking strong water?" the first young brave asked.

Hobomok shook his head. "They like their beer, these English, but they do not drink enough to behave as these do."

"What is beer?" the second young man said, taking a stab at the unfamiliar English word.

"Strong water, but not as strong as the Wessagusset men drank."

"Ah."

* * *

The long hot morning hours passed. Throughout the village of Plymouth the colonists prayed and cried out to God as their governor had asked, usually alone, sometimes in small groups.

"Dear God," Philip Delano prayed aloud and alone, but also in French for utmost privacy, though well hidden among his own dying corn plants, "Forgive me my great guilt for raising my hand against the savages. It may be the objectors were right, that we should have waited longer for Thy guidance. Perhaps we should not have taken matters into our own hands. But most of all, forgive me for the pride I took in it. Now I feel nothing but shame…"

* * *

William Bradford sought the solitude of his own study. "Lord, I confess my pride. I have sought Thy leading, but forgive me the times I have hastened to make decisions out of my own intellect, not abiding long enough to hear the still, small voice of Thy Spirit... not poring over Thy precious Word sufficiently..."

* * *

The Warren family returned to their own house, where wife and daughters watched Richard pace up and down for a time. Then he stopped abruptly in place and dropped to his knees to lead their private prayers, something none of them had ever witnessed before. They joined him on their knees.

* * *

The day waxed long and hot as ever. All around the forest perimeter watching Indians grew weary and disappointed. By shortly after midday some began to drift away.

The first young brave with Hobomok peered at the harsh sky over the croplands. "Not a cloud anywhere."

"Let me look," Hobomok said. He rose and began to climb the high tree they sat under.

"Let me do that, Father."

"You boys think I'm too old to climb a tree?"

Hobomok's sons laughed but stood watching apprehensively as he climbed high into the tree, to a point where he could gaze far out toward the east. Legs and one arm wrapped around the trunk, he shaded his eyes and squinted into the distance.

"See anything?"

"A little cloud, far are out over the great water at the edge of the earth."

"That is all?"

"Yes. One little cloud, the size of a man's hand."

His younger son blew a cynical honk through pursed lips. "Bah! What good is that?"

* * *

The hours continued to crawl by. Hunger slowly lost its power to torment the flesh, so focused did the worshipers become on their prayers and lamentations. By mid-afternoon, after spending a long time walking and praying in their corn acreage, Francis, John and Philip went looking for Hester and the other Cooke youngsters, whom they found back at the meeting house, where Priscilla had brought the children after the other mothers picked up their little ones. Several clusters of men were scattered about as well, but the two men and boy from the Cooke household joined Hester and Priscilla at their women's group.

"Please, sisters," Francis said, "I trust you won't mind if we join you at your prayers." Jacob went into his father's arms, but otherwise no change was made.

Hester prayed. "Dear Father... Dear Father... Dear One... We know You are a loving God. We know You are the God of forgiveness. We know You have forgiven us in Christ for our many sins, those we have confessed throughout this day and those we do not remember to confess. Now we do most humbly pray in Jesus' precious name, please heal our land. Please pour out Your rain... from Heaven..."

So intense was the murmuring of agreement from the others that they almost missed the distant rumble.

Priscilla was the one who raised her head to listen.

"What was that?" some brother said on the other side of the room.

Hester raised her own eyes. She and Francis looked at each other.

The deep rolling noise came again, still very distant but unmistakable.

"The sound of thunder?" Philip said. "Over the sea?"

The other women looked up. All over the room heads rose from prayer, ears perked. The waiting faces wore the stunned expression of those almost too fearful to hope. John Alden rose and walked from across the room to put his arms around Priscilla. People held their breath, listening. The air itself seemed to quiver with anticipation.

The thunder rolled again, unmistakably. It seemed to be drawing closer.

* * *

In the Massasoit's village the Massachusett spokesman paced up and down outside the great chief's lodge, impatient for the remaining hours to pass until end of day. Would the old man not then agree that the God of the English had proved himself no more powerful than the gods of the People?

Hopefully the Massasoit would allow the entire village to listen to persuasion, and the spokesman's sound arguments for war would be carried far and wide to all the Wampanoag. He was already far along in planning his oration when he heard the thunder. He halted in place, his heart first leaping then freezing in his chest. Surely that could not… There it was again—a deep rolling rumble, followed by another—and then another, the loudest yet, loud enough to shake the ground.

The Wampanoag emerged from their lodges, mostly the young and the old or those too lazy and uncurious to spend the day watching the English village. Some moved slowly and deliberately, some excitedly, but they soon filled the open spaces between the lodges, their faces lifted expectantly and fearfully toward the darkening sky.

The Massachusett party gathered in a group, glancing at each other without a word, then turning their eyes upward with the others. The thunder rumbled louder and closer. They watched as an enormous black cloud drifted over the face of the afternoon sun, casting the village and surrounding forest into shadow.

The spokesman felt the cold grip of fear, but he struggled to find words of disparagement. "We have seen dark clouds before, but without rain."

The other Massachusett men nodded.

A drop of water struck the spokesman square in the middle of his forehead. He jumped in fright, but none of the other uplifted faces appeared to notice.

"The corn plants are thirsty and weak," he cried desperately. "A hard rain will kill them all!"

That was undoubtedly true, but no one paid him the slightest attention. His own braves, like many of the Wampanoag, began holding out their open palms, waiting to see if rain would truly come.

* * *

The whole Cooke family came out of the fort and stood waiting together with Philip, John and Priscilla Alden at the top of Town Street. The rain began with an almost imperceptible patter. It came down softly and tenderly, continued to come down without ever falling the slightest bit harder, almost as gently perhaps as the mists that watered the Garden of Eden and the whole earth in the days before the great flood. The entire population of Plymouth had come out of their homes by now, but for the moment no one bothered with head covering. Every man in sight had either left his hat indoors or stood holding it in his hands. The tender wash of mild rain concealed Hester's crying to some degree. She was far from the only Plymouth inhabitant thus affected.

Philip stuck out his palm. "The thunder was very loud, but the rain is so gentle."

"He announced its coming from afar," Francis said. Indeed the thunder seemed to be dying out.

"I've never seen anything like it," John said. "Have you?"

Philip shook his head.

"Praise God," Hester said through sniffles and streaming tears. "Praise God!"

Francis lifted both hands and gazed upward. "Who is like unto Thee, O Lord? From everlasting to everlasting, Thou art God."

Jane held the youngest girl and boy by the hand. Their parents hugged all the children in turn.

"I want to go look at the corn," Philip said.

"As do I," John and Francis said in unison.

Up and down the street many others had the same idea. People began making their way to the upper and lower gates, where they streamed out toward the fields.

Hester took charge of Little Hester and Jacob. "Perhaps you'd like to go too, Jane."

"Yes, ma'am!" Jane followed the others toward the upper gate.

"I want to go!" Jacob said.

"You're needed here, my son, you and Little Hester. We need to go look at our garden." After hurrying the few steps to their house,

Hester took them inside long enough to dry them off and make sure they were adequately covered.

* * *

By this time Hobomok and his two sons had fallen sound asleep under the tree. The last good rumble of departing thunder brought Hobomok awake in an instant. Blinking through momentary confusion, he pulled himself to his feet and lurched forward to the edge of the tree line.

A vast dark cloud covered the sky. He spun to look in all directions as his sons ran out to join him, rubbing sleep from their own astonished eyes. All around Plymouth they saw scattered inhabitants wandering through their cornfields, behaving less demonstrably but in some ways more strangely than in the morning. Now they walked with unbowed heads and occasionally uplifted hands. They spoke little but occasionally threw their arms around one another, including neighbors Hobomok knew had treated one another as enemies only days before. This remarkable conduct took place in a mood of fervor, exaltation and overwhelming relief.

A wet-looking mist seemed to obscure the view. Hobomok stepped forward a few paces, coming out from under the last sheltering branches overhead. His sons did the same.

In the open they discovered it was no damp mist darkening their outlook. This was rain. Quiet, calm, steady, feathery to the touch, utterly unhurried—but rain nonetheless.

None of them could speak at first.

Hobomok was well known among the People as a courageous man, but what he saw shook him more than anything else in all his days.

He trembled.

* * *

The moment she spotted John out in the cornfields, Sarah raced out of her family's acres and right up to him. "O John, isn't it wonderful?"

John was terrified Sarah was going to throw her arms around him, but she thankfully refrained. "Yes," the boy managed to croak out.

Francis, Jane and Philip turned away to hide irrepressible smiles. Sarah's obvious devotion and John's intense discomfort seemed to unlock some measure of the joy bursting to break out from within them all. Jane giggled. The men chuckled. John turned bright scarlet. Sarah, unabashed, gushed out an unremitting flow of pure delight.

Richard Warren arrived a few steps behind his daughter.

"It's wonderful, gentlemen, but we're going to need more rain than this."

"We shall have it," Francis said happily. "All that we need."

Warren studied the assorted plants. They already looked more green and vigorous to most eyes, but the former London merchant could only perceive his usual half-empty cup. "These plants are weak, barely clinging to life. This misty rain is fine, but if it starts coming down too hard, it'll kill the whole crop."

"It won't, my friend," Philip said. "The Lord God knows more about growing crops than we do."

"Yes, yes," Richard said, sounding ashamed of himself. "You're quite right of course."

* * *

The soft rain had brought a cooling chill to the summer air, and the Massasoit kept a blanket wrapped around his shoulders as he sat staring into the little cooking fire

One of his wives came to the door of the lodge. "Do you not wish to see the rain, Ousamequin?"

"I have seen rain before," he said sourly.

His wife nodded. "The Massachusett are returning to their own village."

"Fine. It will be good to see them go."

"They have already departed. Without saying farewell."

"Better yet."

* * *

By this time in fact, the Massachusett party was already some distance north, anxious to reach their own territory and homes. The spokesman and his party had breached etiquette quite intentionally in not saying farewell to the Massasoit. If the stubborn old man took this as a deliberate insult, fine—that was exactly as intended.

"Do you think the God of the English did this?" one of the braves said.

"No!" the spokesman said angrily. "Our Massachusett medicine men have been dancing the rain dance for many days. Who can say why it came? This rain will benefit the People, not just the whites!"

Suddenly a thunderous outbreak of rustling noises came at them from the front. The war party halted in place. The crackle and rattle of leaves and brush resolved into the loud thumping of small swift feet. The men scarcely had time to react as a swarm of small animals appeared and sped past them. They barely glimpsed frantic rabbits, squirrels and other creatures, all running full out in the direction from which the braves had come. All heads spun round to watch them disappear into shadows and thickets. Larger animals, deer perhaps, crashed by some distance away, heading the same direction. Though astonished, none of these hungry men and experienced hunters was in the mood to pursue.

"They've scented the water," the oldest brave said. "The rainfall."

Just as the words came out, both he and the spokesman suddenly became aware that no rain was falling on them—and had not been for some time. This recognition quickly dawned on the rest. The trail beneath their feet lay as dry and dusty as ever. The burning sun beat down through the dying leaves overhead as hot and pitiless as ever. The entire party had been completely intent upon rushing home to share renewed hope with relatives and friends. Not a man among them had noticed how or when they had passed out of the misty rain and back into a nightmarish region of drought. Fearfully, without speaking a word, they began to search for an open prospect looking back toward the Wampanoag land.

The crest of the third hill they climbed offered a spacious view toward the south. They stood looking in silence. Far away, beyond the tops of the most distant trees, they could see the dark wall of rain continuing to fall.

The spokesman flung himself to the ground, screaming in frustration as he clawed the dry and thirsty earth.

From this perspective all could see that the great dark rain cloud was not the monster they had thought, covering the whole land from horizon to horizon. It was in fact a rainstorm of limited size, hovering over the land of the Wampanoag—and not over all the territory of the Wampanoag either. The dark cloud formation stood centered—and apparently stalled in place without moving at all—over the spot where the hated whites had built their odd wooden village known by the strange-sounding English name of Plymouth.

* * *

Hobomok and his sons remained standing in the rain looking out over Plymouth and the surrounding farmland.

"What good will one rain do anyone?" the younger boy asked.

"This will not be the last," his father said. He held the palms of his hands out into the cooling flow, then used them to wash his face.

"Do you believe in the God of the English then?" the elder son said.

Hobomok stood looking up into the sky.

"He is not the God of the English. He is the God of all People."

CHAPTER 48

The Second Thanksgiving

A day with no work to do left the men and boys of Plymouth at a complete loss, like liberated dungeon slaves blinking painfully in the unfamiliar light of freedom. They drifted into groups as far from the stockade as possible so as not to be put to shame by all the hardworking women and girls laboring diligently at their cooking and other preparations for the first day of feasting.

The late November day glowed with unseasonable warmth to the point that the men had set up the tables and benches outdoors, though within the town walls for the sake of reasonable precaution. Once the harvest had been gathered and the hunting for game accomplished, all the new furniture hewn and assembled by John Alden and his woodworking apprentices, men's work for the celebration had come to an end. Women's tasks went on as usual, however, and for this first festival day they had begun with the lighting of fires before dawn. Now mouthwatering aromas drifted down from Fort Hill and from every house along Town Street.

This was the first weekday most men's work had been put aside since the day of fasting and prayer, but a far more pleasant occasion by every measure. That crucial event, filled with tension and wearisome spiritual effort, had nothing of holiday or festival about it. At least, that is, until God began to pour out His mighty power.

Beginning that memorable day, a misty and gentle rain had fallen almost daily for weeks, sometimes for only one or two hours per day, sometimes much longer, without inferring in the slightest with the necessary tasks of farming. This phase had continued until a few days before harvest time, when all precipitation abruptly ceased until after the crops were brought in.

The native shamans, rather than acknowledge the power of Him they called the Englishmen's God, intensified their rainmaking ceremonies, imploring intervention by their own divinities. In a few cases rain had indeed followed these rituals, but it invariably came with so great a violence of wind and downpour that the dried-out corn and fragile vegetable crops were utterly destroyed. The contrast with circumstances at Plymouth could not have been more obvious to any observer, red or white.

Vaguely dissatisfied to stand around joking with all the other useless fellows, John Cooke drifted off by himself and took up a post sitting on the same log at the edge of the woods where he had once shared a memorable noontime meal with Sarah Warren. Here he could keep watch for the Massasoit, his villagers and any other Wampanoag who chose to join the fun for the next three days. John sat quietly, enjoying the breeze and basking in the fading glory of autumn. He thought back over all that had happened over the course of the year.

A noise from behind caught his ear, and he turned as Edward Leister shambled up, nodded a greeting and sat down beside him.

"Ye think many will come?"

John nodded. "Methinks there may be more of them than there are of us."

"Surprising. All things considered."

"You mean after what we did?"

"*WE* nothing," Leister said.

"My father was there."

"Aye, your da' was there but not yourself. I was in the thick of it. 'ad blood on me 'ands, I did." Leister had never spoken of Wessagusset until this moment, staring down at his hands as if they still bore the stain.

"You mustn't forget, it was Massasoit who proposed the course of action you took."

"Faint comfort, me lad... Still lie in bed of a night, wishing I could take it back somehow. And to think I begged to go!" He let loose a bitter little laugh. "Ah, well... Reckon them Massachusetts won't be in attendance."

"They would not have come, though the troublemakers had lived. This is Wampanoag territory. From what I hear the tribes north and west of here have nothing to celebrate in any case."

"Suppose you're right. Still, when you've 'ad blood on your 'ands... When you've done murder..."

"Edward, the blood of Christ washes away all our sins, no matter how great."

Leister sat brooding, a troubled look on his face.

"Would you explain that to me, John? I've never quite understood."

For a long time they sat quietly talking, and John had reason to be thankful for parents who encouraged their children to memorize scripture. Finally they bowed their heads together, and John led the older boy in prayer.

"Amen." Almost as soon as Edward said it, they heard a large group approaching along the nearby trail in a mood of laughter and frivolity, with no attempt at concealment.

When the Indians came into sight the boys saw the Massasoit striding along in front, leading what appeared to be the entire population of his village, old and young, male and female. Just behind walked a number of young braves bearing game to contribute to the feast. John counted three deer, and behind these other hunters carried wild turkeys and rabbits beyond numbering. This opulence made plain how the continuing presence of rain had drawn abundant game to the area.

The Wampanoag women carried jars and bundles with prepared victuals of what appeared to be an astonishing variety. John could picture his mother delightedly tasting each food and boring in on the cooks to find out everything about the preparation. No doubt he would be the one called upon to translate. John did not mind in the least as long as he got his fair chance to compete in the games.

The English boys popped up from the log as a gesture of respect.

The great chief raised his right hand. "Greetings, young brave."

"Greetings, Great Chief. This is my friend Edward Leister."

Massasoit gave the taller boy an appraising look.

"I hope he is ready to run and wrestle. I have brought boys of all ages to compete."

When John translated Leister appeared touched by this kind acceptance. "Tell 'im the boys of Plymouth will take everything 'is lot can throw at us, and throw it right back."

Massasoit laughed when he heard this and laid a friendly hand on John's shoulder as they walked out into the sunlight that led to Plymouth.

* * *

A surprisingly large number of the Wampanoag, who were used to eating while sitting or reclining on the ground, "like Romans," as Winslow put it to discourage any feelings of European superiority, quickly took to the English custom of sitting at table and seemed highly amused and delighted to do so. The Plymouth families insisted on seating visitors at all their tables, thus making sure both groups were well interspersed. More bashful guests reluctant to sit at table were cheerfully served on the ground, where they felt more at ease.

Pewter plates and goblets intrigued the Indians as well, though the usage of forks—still rare in England but acquired by the Leyden pilgrims from the more cosmopolitan Dutch—would remain untested or awkward at best for their be-feathered guests. Appetite abounded on all sides, especially as the meal came after the first hours of play and competition.

At the initial sitting down to feast that afternoon, ladies came forth from the cooking areas to set the first course on every plate. Priscilla placed it before John, and he smiled at what he saw, knowing the puzzlement that had to afflict both Indians and white newcomers alike. Each plate soon contained nothing except five lonely kernels of yellow corn.

Governor Bradford rose to offer both welcome and explanation. "Friends and brethren, there was a time during our first winter on this shore when our food supply was so reduced that each inhabitant could only be permitted five kernels of corn per day, drawn from the planting supply preserved by our dear friend Squanto's unfortunate villagers. If God had not seen fit to provide deliverance, none of us would have survived to enjoy the present happy occasion. It seemed fit to us, the elected elders of this plantation, that we should begin our thanksgiving by this remembrance of those bitter days."

Bradford soon called upon William Brewster, who stood, bowed his head and led in prayer.

John kept looking as the rest of the English bowed their heads over the nearly empty plates. Whispers passed among the Wampanoag, and though few could comprehend the English words, all seemed to understand that the elder was speaking to the same God who brought the life-giving rain to this tiny region where the Plymouth English and their most fortunate Wampanoag neighbors lived, while rain had been withheld everywhere else for many miles around.

Given so majestic a display of God's power, no wonder the savages felt such awe and genuine fear. Truth be told, the inhabitants of Plymouth had themselves rediscovered the fear of the Lord to a vastly greater measure than once seemed possible. Almighty God was the God of Love, and plenteous in mercy for those who called upon Him, but He was also just and unspeakably holy. John hoped none of these events would ever be forgotten.

Reflecting on all this—and in the warm glow of having been used to comfort Edward Leister, who joined the Cooke family at their table, to the surprise of many—it came upon John what the purpose of his life must be. He wanted nothing so much as to share the Word of this true and living God who made Heaven and Earth, to be His instrument in helping many others by proclaiming the good news of Jesus Christ and guiding the faithful to glorify Him in their lives. In future years, John would look back upon this moment as the time he first felt the divine call to the ministry.

Almost at the same time, with his eyes still open, he caught Sarah Warren staring intently in his direction, as usual, but the expression on her face—a most remarkably beautiful face, it suddenly came to him—indicated she somehow understood that serious spiritual business was afoot, perhaps for them both. He nodded at her. She nodded back. Then they both bowed their heads and closed their eyes.

"Dear Heavenly Father," Brewster brought his prayer to a close, "We thank Thee for all the blessings Thou hast brought upon us, for our lives, our liberties, our land, and the privilege to enjoy them. We thank Thee for these our guests and for the grace Thou hast bestowed upon us all. We thank Thee for this time to play and enjoy and to become acquainted in the harmony of friendship. We thank Thee for this food and ask Thee to bless it to our bodies. Mayest Thou bless this land, O Lord, and establish the power and truth of Thy Word to all who come after us, to the furthest generation. May they and we never forget that Thy blessing upon this our common nation is incumbent upon our obedience to Thy leading and Thy commandments. We pray this with all thanksgiving in the name of our Lord and Savior Jesus Christ. Amen."

At the conclusion of the prayer, every English man, woman, and child reached forth and began to chew the kernels of corn as the wonderful aromas of the cooking drifted over them all.

After a moment's hesitation, the Wampanoag ate their kernels as well.

CHAPTER 49

That Men Might Live

The snow lay deep upon the land.

After the long drought of last summer, the unending snowfall bore down upon the parched and vulnerable forests with fearful and deadly effect. The single file of plodding Englishmen struggled on and on in their snowshoes, traded for from the Indians or homemade in Plymouth, the latter variety carefully modeled on the Indian patterns. The company pushed ahead relentlessly, over and sometimes through snow that came to a man's waist or much higher.

Francis and other experienced hunters alternated which one of them would walk the point. Since these happened to be taller, their leading position allowed Captain Standish a somewhat easier trek following the tracks and snow paths they created. No one alluded to this practice in jest or otherwise.

Standish insisted on bearing one of the heavy bags strapped to his back along with his musket and sword, a load no lighter than burdened the others. As often before Francis felt nothing but admiration for their captain's fortitude.

The unarmed Edward Winslow carried a heavy pack on his back as well, marching steadily as a trooper behind the captain.

They came upon a small treeless field, the sort of place the Indians might have cleared years ago to create a corn patch. Francis hoped it indicated the nearness of the Massachusett village they sought. He longed for warmth as they slogged forward, even the smoky stench of the worst Indian hovel. Yet he knew the militiamen might have to gather wood to build the warming fires themselves. Some of these people were too weak from starvation to accomplish that most basic life-preserving task.

"There it is," Philip said.

The waddle-and-daub huts loomed up out of the biting wind, distinctive shapes in a world of white. As they moved closer the Plymouth men saw innumerable snow-weighted branches of surrounding trees that seemed to grip the village in sinister embrace, like clawing talons of death.

Francis prayed they had arrived in time. Distrust of white men ran rampant through the Massachusett people, not without reason to be sure, and the precise location of their villages was hard to come by. This one had been learned of earlier in the week on a similar expedition. Despite the great distance from Plymouth, Standish had insisted with the governor's concurrence upon mounting another rescue mission immediately. Weary as they were, every volunteer understood how delay by a single day could mean death, especially for the old, the young, and the ill among the Massachusett—the most vulnerable.

As they walked in among the huts, the signs were not hopeful. The latest snowfall lay unmarked by human footprints, but at least the wolves had not come.

By established practice, the men hung back as the kindly Winslow handed over his burden to another and then moved from door to door, announcing their presence in the tribe's own language and quickly making clear the nature of the white men's mission. Winslow would be the one to negotiate the trade. Early on the English had learned by trial and error that the highly self-reliant Indians resented charity from the white newcomers even in the midst of starvation, so now the delivery of precious food was always couched as a matter of trade. Winslow and the others tried to accept as little payment as possible. A nominal trade would be quite sufficient, but some villages insisted on loading them down with furs, moccasin boots, extra snowshoes and other practical wares. Whatever a particular village wished to trade, the Plymouth party always accepted, then left the full complement of food, enough to see them through until spring.

Hope proved to have its usual rejuvenating power, and gaunt faces soon filled every door. Standish's men gently entered the lodges to deposit sacks of food while Winslow bartered with the village chieftain.

Some of the fires had indeed burned quite low or gone out. All the huts were running low on fuel. Soon most of the whites were out in the woods, either chopping firewood or breaking up the ice in the frozen creek to resupply the village water jars more expeditiously than could be done by melting snow.

Francis and the captain entered a hut crowded with the old and the ill huddling together for warmth. Young women appeared to be caring for these as best they could in spite of not looking all that fit themselves. Standish set a bag of corn meal and a bundle of frozen venison down near the fire. As he rose, an old woman reached out and gripped his ankle. The captain and Francis looked down at her as she spoke with great intensity. Though neither man understood a word, they knew she was thanking them from the depths of her soul.

Standish looked at Francis, who saw tears streaming down into the tough little man's beard.

"Poor people," Standish said.

"Thank God we can help them," Francis managed to reply, shrugging off the straps of his own heavy load.

"Yes." The captain struggled for self-control. "Thank God."

* * *

As the birth of her new baby drew closer, Hester found herself more easily tired out and drained of energy in all the work of maintaining a large household, and she felt deeply grateful to her daughter Jane for taking up the slack. The ten-year-old found excuses to hover around, always ready to help or replace her mother at any particular task. Hester realized what Jane was doing but could feel only gratitude as her own stamina flagged.

"Why don't you sit down, Mother?" Jane said for the thousandth time, "Let me handle this."

Murmuring her usual embarrassed appreciation, Hester drew back and lowered her weight onto a rough-hewn chair that made up in strength for what it lacked in European polish.

"I pray your father will be safe."

"Oh, he will be." Jane put in full duty at comfort and exhortation in addition to her volunteer service in cooking and housework.

"It's a Massachusett village they've gone to." Hester always worried when that was the case, but so far there had been no trouble, despite the slaughter of last summer. In fact Winslow, who had been anything but acquiescent at the time, recounted that Massachusett men had on more than one occasion expressed acceptance and understanding as to why the English had taken the ferocious step they had. Hester suspected thankfulness for the food saving their lives in the present might engender a more tolerant view of the past—for now. Once the critical hour passed, she feared long memories of the deed would feed enmity between red man and white for years to come. She believed Winslow secretly felt the same.

"They'll make better time once they're rid of the meat and corn," Jane was saying. "They'll spend tonight in the village they're helping, tomorrow night in Cummaquid, and make it home the day after."

"Unless they are loaded down with trade goods."

"Mister Winslow will contrive not to accept too much. They'll be here in time for supper the day after tomorrow."

The baby chose that moment to do a little kicking. Hester placed her hands on her midriff and closed her eyes for a moment.

She felt an urgent longing for Francis to be with her when the baby came. He had promised this would be his last expedition until after the birth. Hester had not demanded this and felt a little guilty about it, but Francis assured her there was plenty for a militiaman to do in Plymouth while the others were out distributing the lifesaving food from what had turned out to be a harvest bountiful beyond the remotest imagining.

"It's marvelous, isn't it, Mother," Jane said, "how God gave us enough beyond our own needs to help the poor Indians?"

Hester snapped her eyes open and gazed at the little mind reader, who often demonstrated this proclivity for seeming to know exactly what her mother and others were thinking. Fortunately, Hester and the rest attributed the gift to wisdom and instinct—and possibly the work of the Holy Ghost. Back in Europe the little girl might be brought up on charges of witchcraft.

"God blessed our land," Hester said, "and it is incumbent upon us to bless others."

"Amen." Jane turned back to her pots and pans.

Hester thought back on her futile efforts to rescue terrified Indians from the swamps in the wake of the murders. No one would ever know how many perished from fever and other perils at that time. Yet unquestionably many, many more would have died this winter if the people of Plymouth had not been enabled to help. This enabling certainly came by way of that miraculously enormous harvest from such limited acreage. More than one Plymouth resident had compared it to the miracle of the loaves and fishes. Perhaps more importantly, at least to Hester's way of thinking, every single family and individual agreed to donate supply to the fullest extent possible, though at the cost of limiting their own consumption—as well as the potential for personal profits on native merchandise that could be exported to Europe. All that would come in due time. For now the saving of human lives took priority.

She knew all this went back to the day of fasting and prayer, which led directly to the miracle of the rain. The Indians knew this as well as the whites, and most of them apparently saw the Plymouth settlement's present generosity as strength rather than weakness, not always the case in such matters. Probably the "trading" aspect had a great deal to do with this perception. Though most of the white women had initially objected, it seemed allowing the Indians to pay for the food, however nominally, somehow preserved the dignity of both parties to the transaction. She knew Francis feared that in future this process would in all probability come to be looked upon as mere ruthless exploitation by the white interlopers, but for the present no one had any better ideas since the tribes were so averse to out-and-out charity.

Many more such lessons would have to be learned in years to come.

Hester knew this land would pass on, beyond her earthly life, beyond Jane's, beyond her new baby's, as a vast legacy to future generations. The great continent that lay out there beyond the forests, extending nobody knew how far toward the west, was meant for more than the native tribes constantly at war with one another, for more than a few European colonists clinging precariously to the Atlantic shore. It was meant for a nation, and not just any nation, but a nation composed of those from every tribe of earth who loved liberty and sought freedom to worship the true and living God as they saw fit.

Perils would come upon that nation, Hester knew, and she prayed that the generations to come would learn the lesson that the God of mercy was also holy, ready to curse the land based on disobedience to His Word, and the behavior He was concerned about was not that of the unbelievers, but of the people who were called by His Name. Yet He always stood ready to heal the land completely if His people humbled themselves, and prayed, and turned from their wicked ways.

Feeling the new baby, anticipating the joy of another young life to nurture and cherish, Hester prayed for her own descendents, that they would be given wisdom and courage to choose aright.

Hester had no way of knowing, as she prayed, that the great land between the oceans would become the United States of America. She had no way of knowing, nor had Abraham Lincoln as he shared a brief narrative of this true story in the White House two hundred and forty years later, that some of her descendants would reside for an appointed time in that same White House. They would be very different men, these descendants, with divergent political philosophies, but each had to take a stand on difficult and disputed ground, both as professing Christians and as patriots who loved their country in all its seething division. All would be called upon to lead the United States of America during time of war, to advance the cause of human freedom, and to make difficult and controversial decisions in the loneliness of power, at hours of maximum peril to the nation and the world.

The names of those descendants are Franklin D. Roosevelt, George H.W. Bush and George W. Bush.

EPILOGUE

Wade Jordan in the Colorado Mountains, October 1896

Wade Jordan had been dreaming about Lincoln every night, sleeping out on the trail under the cold stars of impending winter. He had seen the President only that once, when he signed the national Thanksgiving proclamation thirty-three years ago. Obviously he had made a vivid impression. Wade could recall the lean lined face, the sad troubled eyes, and the high Midwestern voice as clearly as if he had seen and heard him only the day before.

Memory certainly played tricks on a man. Wade sometimes had to concentrate to call back memories of his first wife, Betsy Conrad Jordan, who had followed Wade for love from her native Vermont, much to the disapproval of her family, after finding a tall, hard-looking westerner, cowboy hat in hand, standing in the little Warwick Village cemetery paying his respects at the grave of her older brother, a boy she only dimly remembered, who had once saved Wade's life at the cost of his own. Her beautiful face and her dear voice sometimes eluded him now, covered over these many years in a dusty grave down in Apache country. He knew that grave did not contain her spirit, though, for she awaited him in Glory, where she would shine as the stars, forever and ever. In his preaching Bible he carried an old albumen photograph of Betsy in their first year of marriage. He believed his current young and pregnant wife Nancy, only a couple of years older than Betsy had been in the picture, would not be upset if she ever happened to find it. He had always been lucky or, to put it more properly, blessed in the women he fell in love with, except for that first one, back during the war. Nancy had married him with eyes wide open, knowing the basic facts of his past and fully cognizant of the age difference between them. Still, he kept the picture squirreled away and never looked at it when Nancy was anywhere around, fearing she might be hurt if she caught him. God knew he loved both women just as much.

Yet despite any failings of memory, he could summon Lincoln up in a moment, and his sleeping mind often did, though intermittently. Although Wade had often been accused of superstition over the years, mostly for believing the Bible and everything it said, he had a very practical turn of mind. To a certain extent he did believe in signs and portents, in circumstances as a means of guidance, but only when they lined up with scripture, fortified with prayer. However down to earth he tried to be, nonetheless, he had noticed that whenever he dreamed about Lincoln, it seemed to come as a warning, "Watch out." Something was about to happen, and chances were it involved danger, to others and for himself. Maybe he had that mindset because of personal history.

After seeing Lincoln that time, Wade had returned to the violent war in the west, a succession of exhausting marches and horrifying battles leading to the hard fought culmination of eventual victory. He missed out, however, on serving under Uncle Billy Sherman in the long march to the sea. Shortly before leaving Washington in November, 1863, Wade had suddenly been promoted to captain and immediately received orders transferring him as a replacement officer, much against his wishes, to the command of General George H. Thomas, already world famous as the Rock of Chickamauga, who had himself just been promoted to commander of the Army of the Cumberland. Over time, despite his initial disappointment at this reassignment, Wade developed even greater feelings of hero worship for the unassuming but utterly brilliant Thomas than he felt for Grant and Sherman. All the battles were terrible, even under a general determined to win them at the least cost in the lives of his own soldiers—there had been no Cold Harbor to tarnish the record of General Thomas. At any rate, perhaps Wade connected meeting President Lincoln to the storms that followed. Still, that didn't explain why violence seemed to break out whenever he started dreaming about poor Mr. Lincoln.

After all, God used dreams to warn people back in the Bible days, and unlike certain other and fancier preachers, Wade didn't put it past the Lord to use some of the same old miraculous methods today. As he rode the mountain trail he consequently kept a sharper eye out than usual—and he was extremely vigilant anyway, a habit from his many years of riding as a lawman.

In truth it was largely because of Lincoln that Wade had ultimately wound up a preacher—or a Christian—at all. This was odd, since some folks back in Illinois claimed Lincoln as a young man had incurred a reputation as a bit of a doubter, even a mocker and a skeptic. All that could have been the murmurings of his political enemies, of course, or the tall tales of Lincoln's envious and in many ways despicable former law partner, but somehow Wade thought it fit.

Not all people of great faith start out that way. Young men tend toward rebellion and questioning. Wade started out along those lines himself, in spite of Godly grandparents and other strong Gospel influences. There was no good reason Lincoln could not have done likewise, though some people didn't want to admit it, especially since the president had never publicly affiliated with any church, as far as anybody knew.

Wade once met a former Roman Catholic priest turned Gospel minister who declared Lincoln had not trusted Christ as his Savior until after the Battle of Gettysburg. This fellow, at one time successfully defended by Lincoln in a law suit brought by officials of his former denomination, claimed he had heard this from the president himself during a White House visit, the last time the former client saw the man alive. Wade knew Lincoln had certainly told the Pilgrim story sounding like a believer.

In spite of everything his grandmother had told him and read to him out of the Bible, it was Lincoln's little story about the Pilgrim fathers, briefly told, that really started Wade thinking maybe God did have His hand on this fallen world after all, indeed that God really existed. The good and compassionate Lord preserved Wade's life through a lot of tough and violent years before he finally came around. It terrified him to remember how many times he had come close to getting killed, to going out into eternity without Christ, before he finally got it through his thick skull and hard heart to believe the Truth.

He shook his head, thinking about his early years fighting in the war, working as a troubleshooter for the Union Pacific railroad, fighting Indians, and then the beginning of his years as a deputy United States Marshal, witnessing miracle after miracle of grace and protection, all the while stubbornly refusing to yield, to recognize he needed forgiveness, and to accept God's mercy. Truly, as his grandmother had prayed, the Lord had protected him with a mighty hand, working on his heart the whole time. That belated realization explained why, on a rare railroad journey back east to Washington and then Boston on U.S. Marshal business, he made that little side trip to Warwick Village, Vermont, so many years after the war, paying his respects to the boy who died to give Wade a future and a hope.

After the signing and the storytelling at the White House, Wade remembered, he stood in line to shake hands with the president, and when he got to the head of the file that burdened and melancholy man seemed almost delighted to meet someone taller than he was, if only by a couple of inches. Lincoln had to look up into the eyes of the young lieutenant, something that didn't happen too often to the president.

For a moment the proverbial cat kept a firm grip on Wade's tongue as he shook the presidential hand. Then instead of saying anything about how Mr. Lincoln needed more guards, as planned, he blurted out, "What happened to the boy, sir?"

The president looked puzzled.

"John Cooke," Wade explained, "in your story."

"Ah. Well, first of all, he married the Warren girl, Sarah."

"Figured that much." They both grinned.

"He went on to become an ordained Baptist preacher, which would have been quite a revolutionary step for that bunch."

"Reckon so, sir." In retrospect Wade, who eventually became an ordained Baptist preacher himself, realized this little comment signified Lincoln's awareness of how doctrinal issues kept Christians split up into camps, frequently quite hostile to one another over disputes both great and trivial. Perhaps there were reasons the president had never affiliated with a denomination.

"Tell you one thing," Lincoln went on, "John Cooke always insisted that Indians could come right into his church anytime they wanted and be completely equal with everybody else."

Wade nodded. "Makes sense, sir."

"To us, son. People gave him a lot of grief over it, just as a lot of folks would now, but John Cooke never wavered to his dying day. An American native or any man of different colored skin was just as good in God's eyes as any white, so John Cooke thought and so he practiced."

"I'll keep that in mind, Mister President."

"God bless you, son, and protect you."

Wade staggered away from the encounter with the last words ringing in his ears. They matched word for word the last thing his beloved grandmother had said when she saw him off to war, which turned out to be the last time he ever saw her.

Another irony of the situation and Lincoln's comments was that years later it was a courageous Indian Christian, a tragic peacemaker and outcast from his own tribe, in part for his supposedly traitorous religious compromise with the world of the white man, who finally led Wade Jordan to trust in Christ. Eventually Wade came to understand that every believer had by the very fact of becoming a Christian committed a traitorous betrayal of the entire world system, thereby opening the door to unrelenting hostility and in some cases outright persecution by people still blinded to the Truth.

Fortunately for Wade, his own conversion happened before he met Betsy, who never liked the violent side of his work and would never have left Vermont as his newly married bride if he had not been a believer. How sad that she had never lived to see him make the transition from marshal to preacher, though in the lawless circuits he had to ride, in his years as a widower, he had to use his guns and fists almost as often as when he wore a badge.

In truth he shouldn't be on the trail now, with a young wife at home and a new baby on the way, a child who would be younger than Wade's own grandchildren, at least the ones already born. He should never have agreed to this assignment, but Doctor Baxter, whom the Baptist circuit riders all jokingly called "the bishop," practically got down on his knees and begged, promising that Wade would be able to make it home before the snows fell, though how any man could know such a thing without the gift of prophecy he couldn't say.

Wade was riding for a town named Caldwell, nestled at the foot of a steep valley high in the Colorado country, an isolated basin where rich lodes of gold and silver had recently been discovered. A little gold rush was now underway, comparable on a smaller scale to the big ones Wade had witnessed in the Dakotas and Nevada over the years. The major circumstance Doctor Baxter pled was that Caldwell was a town full of sinners, without a church or an open witness of any kind, and someone needed to bring them the good news of Jesus Christ. The good doctor wasn't asking for a permanent mission or founding of a church, just a week of Gospel meetings. Wade figured he could handle that. He and Nancy had prayed about it, and here he was. But every mile he rode he felt that much more anxious to have the meetings over with and get started back.

He felt relieved when he topped a high ridge at long last and caught first sight of Caldwell sitting in the valley far below. It took him another hour to ride close enough to take a really good look. When he did, all thought of Nancy or Betsy or anything else personal went right out of his mind.

With his experienced lawman's eyes, Wade instantly knew the town was in trouble. He reigned in Black Tempest next to a Quaking Aspen grove a considerable distance above Caldwell, gave the reins a couple of turns around the saddle horn, and sat pondering.

"Doesn't look good, does it, girl?"

The mare whinnied with what sounded like genuine concern, and he gently patted her flank. She was the great-great-granddaughter of Ranger, the big black who got Wade through the Civil War, the building of the Union Pacific, and his early learning years as a deputy marshal, and she had a lot of that old boy's intelligence, as well as the same speed, stamina, and strength.

Wade reached into a saddlebag and took out his excellent old pair of Swiss-manufactured field glasses. Black Tempest held still as he studied the main street of Caldwell in the distance. The evidence that chilled him at first observation held true.

The main street stood completely deserted, empty of human foot traffic and with only three horses tethered to the hitching rail in front of one building. An empty street was the last imaginable circumstance one expected to find in a town newly aflame with the first wave of gold fever. No miners just off shift looking for a glass of whiskey. No carpenters running around building new structures as fast as they could throw them up—he could see some wooden frameworks, but nobody was working. Middle of the day, and not a soul in sight. People ought to be out trading at a store or business, but they weren't. No women gossiping, no hawkers out drumming up customers for fleecing in the gambling halls, no old men sitting around on a porch, yapping and spitting tobacco juice. Wade could not see a single dog, and if the dogs were hiding... Well, that was a bad sign, really bad.

Wade's long years wearing a tin star had taught him the signs of a town in trouble, and he knew exactly what kind of trouble to expect. Cholera or some other contagion could clean out the streets of a town, leaving people huddling and afraid if they weren't already hightailing it for an uninfected region, but that kind of trouble had a different look. There would be angels of mercy moving around, brave ordinary citizens who had appointed themselves nurses, or at least gravediggers bringing out the dead.

This town looked like gun trouble. Or to put it more exactly, outlaw or drunken bully trouble. The kind of trouble sprouting from guns in the hands of the wrong kind of men.

Wade sighed. He sat in the saddle and prayed for quite a stretch, keeping his eyes wide open and his senses fully alert.

A part of him wanted to turn Black Tempest around and go riding back. Back to the little ranch he had finally been able to afford. Back to his beautiful young wife and the baby she was carrying. Back to a world of relatively settled law and order, where he could go visit his and Betsy's children and their own kids, his beloved grandchildren.

But he knew he couldn't just hightail it out of here. He was a man sent from God, and while he hoped preaching the Gospel would be enough, he knew he had to do whatever it took. He remembered what his grandmother called him years ago, out of her reading of the Old Testament—a mighty man of valor.

He wasn't so sure about the mighty part anymore, or the valor ever. He had always been just a man doing his job, whether as a soldier, a lawman, or a preacher. Now he felt more like an *old* man every day. But he also knew, though he was ordained a man of peace and without the official power of the law anymore, he was not the sort who could ride away and leave a lot of innocent people at the mercy of evildoers.

Years after hearing Lincoln's little talk about the Pilgrim fathers, Wade had taken a visit to a big city as an opportunity to go to a public library and read up on them. It was probably true the Plymouth Pilgrims had gotten ahead of themselves by eliminating those Indian troublemakers as they had. It was certainly not something to be proud of, especially considering the innumerable deaths that resulted when so many terrified Indians fled into the swamps. The Pilgrims received a scathing letter of rebuke to that very effect from their pastor John Robinson back in Holland.

But he wondered if kindhearted Christians like Hester Cooke ever realized that sometimes it was simply necessary for good men to resort to force in order to restrain evil. The Apostle Paul certainly talked about this when he said those who bore the sword did not do so in vain. It was strange, after hearing Lincoln's little story, how often he wondered if a woman who lived almost three centuries earlier would approve of Wade's own actions. Down through the years he had only used his weapons to defend either himself or others. He always tried to defuse dangerous situations without violence if at all possible. His sheer physical size often helped in this regard, and he planned to try his best to be a peacemaker again today.

Still, one had to be prudent. He dismounted and led Black Tempest into the Aspen grove until they were hidden from sight. He checked his Winchester from the saddle scabbard and the Colt peacemaker he wore in a holster, tied down gunfighter-style on his right leg. He had two more Colts in a double-holstered gun belt in one of his saddlebags, and he checked them too. By long habit he kept all his firearms clean and well oiled. He retrieved his nice little .32 and stuck it down in his left boot, his throwing knife in the other. He clipped the scabbard with his Bowie knife onto his belt at the small of his back, under his coat. Over many years he had gotten used to being a very large target for a great many very dangerous men. Whenever he might be walking into a fight, he preferred to have as many weapons about his person as possible. Though he saw nothing wrong or spiritually inappropriate about this, he grinned to imagine what a lot of nice churchgoing folks would think about a preacher packing this much artillery. But those people had no idea how dangerous a wild western mining town could be. He did.

Before closing the saddlebags he patted the most important weapon of all, his trusty old black leather preaching Bible, the same one his grandmother gave him when he left for the army. The Word of the Lord was sharper than any two-edged sword, even to the splitting asunder of spirit and flesh.

Wade led the mare back onto the trail and mounted up. He looked around, praising God for the beauty of all he saw and for all the good he had been able to do in his life. He prayed once more for his family, for the people of Caldwell and for his own protection.

Then he nudged his horse forward and rode down the long hill toward the town.

HISTORICAL NOTE

The Second Thanksgiving is a work of historical fiction, yet almost every character named in the body of the 1623 narrative actually existed except for a tiny number of composite characters, such as the bad-tempered Mrs. Taylor. Every major incident in the Plymouth story and most minor ones are either documented or strongly implied by the historical record, with one exception. (That one purely imaginary exception, though perhaps not completely impossible given the situation and the personalities of those involved, is the account of Hester and Priscilla's trek through the swamp.) Details of personal behavior, interpersonal conflict and actual conversation, of course, are obviously the product of the author's hopefully sanctified imagination.

Beyond the above, the only intentional tampering with the known facts has been to change the order and timing of certain events for dramatic purposes and to attribute the actions of one actual person to a different one, again for purposes of drama, story structure and compression.

In terms of historical scholarship the matter most in dispute today is the precise nature of events surrounding the killing of the four Indian braves at Wessagusset (present day Weymouth Massachusetts). Nearly all accounts agree that the four Indian victims were alone in the hut with Plymouth forces when Miles Standish began the slaughter by killing either Wituwamat or Pecksuot with his own knife. Some more recent writers, apparently beginning in the so called progressive era from the late 1890s through the early 1900s maintain that a larger body of Indians waited outside and that a battle then erupted in which as many as five Englishmen were also killed and possibly additional Native Americans as well. Some of these writers also maintain that Pecksuot was a chieftain rather than a mere brave. Both these assertions may be in part the product of liberal white guilt and politically correct wishful thinking, neither of which is by any means a purely recent phenomenon. On the other hand, they could be right. For now the evidence appears inconclusive, at least for a non-scholar with no dog in the fight.

If a large Indian force held its own in a pitched battle, however, it would seem more difficult to explain the subsequent panic that drove so many to flee into the swamps, as well as the failure to follow up with additional attacks on the whites. It's also difficult to understand how the narrative of events sent to Pastor John Robinson in Leyden (sometimes spelled Leiden), thereby earning his stinging rebuke, could have been quite so triumphant in tone if there had been any loss of English life, to which he made no reference in his letter or subsequent writings.

Pecksuot, whatever his tribal position, certainly participated in attempting to raise all the local tribes against the English. Reasonable arguments are made to this day both that the Massachusett braves' fears of displacement were correct on the one hand and that Standish's preemptive strike was fully justified on the other. Understanding and sympathizing at least to some degree with each perspective, the present novelist has attempted to present both sides in a fair and convincing manner. As to the attack itself, I chose to go with the early version I strongly suspect is the most accurate, the account that happens to be the most limited in scale as well as the clumsiest and most grotesque. This intuitive and ultimately artistic decision could well be wrong, but if a more spectacular version of the murders proves to be correct, it really doesn't change very much. All the versions reflect rather poorly on the Pilgrims, though surely more so for those with the majestic gift of 20/20 hindsight than for people under threat at the time, concerned about saving their own lives and those of their families, in the same way that their Massachusett enemies were concerned about their own lives and families.

In any case, though some details are disputed or lost to history, the most important incidents dramatized in *The Second Thanksgiving* are firmly established. These include but are not limited to the confrontation with the Wessagusset traders, the wreck of the shallop in the storm, the rainy night in Cummaquid, the arrival of the *Anne*, the decision to abandon what we would now call socialism in favor of private property and free enterprise, the subsequent squabbling, Ousamequin's timely deliverance from death by constipation, his grateful warning and murderous advice about possible attack, the preemptive killing of at least four Massachusett braves, the disastrous aftermath that cost many Native American lives, the prolonged and terrible drought, the day of fasting and prayer, the coming of the rain—which through some strange convergence of meteorological factors fell and saved the crops and game *only* in the immediate area of Plymouth, the gentle rain continuing on a nearly daily basis for *months*, from the day of fasting and prayer in late July until just before the harvest in November—and the generosity of the Pilgrims in preventing local Native American groups, including the Massachusett tribe, from starving the following winter. All this is true. (One of the best and earliest sources for most of these facts is Governor William Bradford's straightforward and utterly unemotional account in his memoir, *History of Plymouth Plantation*. If memory serves, the present author first encountered the amazing story of Plymouth in 1623 through Peter Marshall and David Manuel's *The Light and the Glory* with more details in Marshall's additional popular works about America's providential history.)

Our American nation thus did begin with a miracle, an ongoing miracle of human survival certainly but specifically the answer to the prayer for rain in the great drought of 1623. This astonishing event not only recalled the Pilgrims themselves to their spiritual priorities but led to a number of Christian conversions among the Indians, though no one can now say how many. The fact that Native American attendance at English churches became an issue for the next generation would seem to suggest the numbers were not small. We do know that within fifty years virtually the entire Wampanoag tribe had converted to Christianity, building their own Congregationalist and Baptist churches, cooperating with Puritan and Separatist scholars to translate the Holy Bible into their own beautiful and eloquent Massachusett dialect—the first complete Bible printed in America—and sending young Wampanoag seminarians off to Harvard for training in the reformed faith.

The original inspiration for striving to write Native American dialogue so eloquently came from a short story by William Faulkner, but the capacity of the Massachusett language group to handle complex Biblical ideas so proficiently certainly demonstrates the correctness of this approach. On another point of dialogue, the few surviving records, lessons and letters of homeschooled Separatist and Puritan children reflect an astounding intellectual maturity. The brightest pre-teens among them easily read, wrote and spoke at a higher level than most modern American tenth graders. To a modern reader this may seem strange, but children have always had to grow up fast on the frontier.

These Plymouth folk in our story are real people with real descendants, including eight American presidents with proven ancestors aboard the *Mayflower*: John Adams, John Quincy Adams, Zachary Taylor, U.S. Grant, James A. Garfield, Franklin D. Roosevelt, George H.W. Bush and George W. Bush.

It should be obvious that Philip Delano is a direct ancestor of Franklin Delano Roosevelt, who takes the presidential cake with eight lineal forebears who sailed aboard the *Mayflower* (not including Philip, who arrived on the second Pilgrim ship, the *Fortune*). One of FDR's lines of descent goes through John Cooke and his wife Sarah Warren, the girl who set her cap for John as soon as she laid eyes on him—if not before. Recent scholarship seems to have created some dispute as to John's precise age in 1623. I chose the traditional attribution of 11, rather than 14 or 15, partly because I felt a younger boy's encounter with the Massasoit (a title, by the way, though the Pilgrims mostly used it as a name) would be more dramatic, but also because I believe it likelier that Sarah would be flirting with a boy near her own age rather than an older teenager.

Francis and Hester Cooke are direct ancestors not only of Roosevelt but also of George H. W. Bush and George W. Bush through their daughter Jane. In addition to Francis, the Bushes had four other ancestors aboard the *Mayflower*: John Howland, Elizabeth and John Tilley, and Henry Sampson, for a total of five.

The highly practical Richard and Elizabeth Warren include among their descendants President Ulysses S. Grant, known to the Union armies of the west by 1863 and to most other Americans not long afterward simply as The General. Only in recent years have historians finally begun to look past scandals Grant had nothing to do with, beyond trusting a few men he shouldn't have, in order to appreciate his good qualities and genuine achievements in the presidency. To cite only one train of reconsideration, President Grant fought harder and took more direct action to secure the full rights of citizenship for African Americans than any other president until the modern Civil Rights era began in the 1950s.

As to Grant's abilities as a military commander, we might do well to consider the opinion of his chief adversary Robert E. Lee:

"We all thought Richmond, protected as it was by our splendid fortifications and defended by our army of veterans, could not be taken. Yet Grant turned his face to our Capital, and never turned it away until we had surrendered. I have carefully searched the military records of both ancient and modern history, and have never found Grant's superior as a general. I doubt that his superior can be found in all history." Interested readers would do well to consult the extremely fair and balanced source of this quotation, *Grant as Military Commander*, by the late British army officer, World War II spymaster, linguist and military historian General Sir James Handyside Marshall-Cornwall.

After nearly four hundred years of enthusiastic procreation, untold thousands of Americans other than presidents and military heroes stand in a line of descent from the Mayflower Pilgrims. Many of these progeny have no clue they possess this remarkable and inspiring link to national beginnings. To cite only one, the beautiful and talented actress Ashley Judd learned by way of the television series *Who Do You Think You Are* that she is directly descended from Elder William Brewster, the devout layman who served as the first Plymouth pastor. Such discoveries no doubt await many other Americans who don't happen to be celebrities, just "ordinary" citizens living their lives and making valuable contributions on a daily basis. Modern Americans without Mayflower DNA can still look back at these spiritual and political forerunners with gratitude and authentic connection. In the words of Ben Franklin, "All blood is alike ancient."

As Elder Brewster would say to us today, in the eyes of God no human life is "ordinary" or without value, for He loves us every one, not only sending His rain to fall on the just and the unjust, but calling forth a People for Himself from all nations, beginning at Jerusalem and going out to the ends of the earth.

Though the first President of the United States George Washington made a practice of issuing a Thanksgiving Day proclamation, subsequent presidents neglected to do so, leaving the holiday to be celebrated inconsistently on a regional or state-by-state basis, which is where matters stood when Mrs. Sarah Josepha Hale began her four decades-long campaign of editorializing, letter writing and lobbying. The success of this extraordinary Christian lady, in this and many other endeavors, is all the more amazing in light of the appalling legal status of women at the time. No nation will ever be perfect under the present dispensation, but Mrs. Hale both comprehended and felt overwhelming gratitude for her country's unique blessings. She knew from Whom all blessings flow.

Thanksgiving has been celebrated as a national holiday in the United States of America every November since President Abraham Lincoln issued his wartime proclamation on October 3, 1863.

ABOUT THE AUTHOR

Born in South Charleston, West Virginia, Douglas Lloyd McIntosh is a filmmaker and professional screenwriter. His Master of Fine Arts thesis production for the Graduate Institute of Film and Television, New York University, is a 53-minute drama, *The Girl Who Ran Out of Night*, about a teenage runaway. This film has been used all over the world to lead thousands of people to trust in Jesus Christ as personal Savior. As a screenwriter Doug has written many scripts and teleplays for Hollywood production companies, national television networks, Christian organizations including Focus on the Family and Chuck Colson's Prison Fellowship, and influential filmmakers including Francis Ford Coppola, Steven Spielberg, and Michael Mann. In 1997 TV Guide named his *Miami Vice* episode for Mr. Mann, "Out Where the Buses Don't Run," one of The 100 Best Television Episodes of All Time. His half-hour television drama written for the Missouri Synod Lutheran Church, *Waiting for the Wind* starring Robert Mitchum, Rhonda Fleming, and Jameson Parker, has been widely used for Christian grief counseling. More recently, Doug adapted the Janette Oke novels *Love's Long Journey* and *Love's Abiding Joy* for the Hallmark Channel. All of the latter are widely available in DVD and for online video download and streaming from Amazon.com.

P.S. Worried about Wade at the end? Don't be. It's the rampaging outlaws in Caldwell who are in trouble now.

For publication alerts on upcoming books by Douglas Lloyd McIntosh, please send your email address. Questions or comments from readers always welcome.

AUTHOR CONTACT

doug@douglaslloydmcintosh.com

Made in the USA
Monee, IL
27 November 2020

49843671R00256